PURGATORY
BAY

PRAISE FOR *BLEAK HARBOR*

"Bryan Gruley's *Bleak Harbor* is an electric bolt of suspense, packed with twists and surprises. Gruley's plot races along, powered by characters—big and small—who truly crackle. A masterful follow-up to his Starvation Lake trilogy."

—Gillian Flynn, #1 *New York Times* bestselling author of *Gone Girl*

"The best book Gruley has ever written and unlike any other crime book I've ever read."

—Steve Hamilton, two-time Edgar Award–winning author of *Exit Strategy*

"Bryan Gruley creates a fascinating calamity of flawed characters, each hiding secrets in the haunting town of Bleak Harbor. His portrayal of an autistic boy's kidnapping, and the subsequent efforts to find and rescue him, gradually and brilliantly exposes the decidedly dark underbelly of both the town and all those living in it. I dare you to put the book down. I couldn't."

—Robert Dugoni, #1 *Wall Street Journal* bestselling author

"The myth of the happy family! Bryan Gruley dives deep into twisted psyches, well-hidden secrets, and dark, explosive desires. Welcome to Bleak Harbor. Be afraid."

—Tess Gerritsen, *New York Times* bestselling author

"Vivid, spellbinding, and laced with tension, *Bleak Harbor*'s labyrinthine mystery is packed with characters so real you want to buy them a beer—or hide under your bed to pray they don't come for you. If you're not reading Bryan Gruley, you're missing out."

—Marcus Sakey, bestselling author of *AFTERLIFE* and the Brilliance trilogy

"A deep dive into the deepest secrets of a one-family town and its leading family that sometimes gets murky, even exhausting, but is never less than enthralling. And you'll finish it with a wonderful sense that you've finally come up for air."

—*Kirkus Reviews*

"Gruley brilliantly defies convention. He performs a dazzling magic routine worthy of Houdini, each trick dependent upon the next, growing in complexity and intensity until the finale. Think *Rashomon* as told in alternating chapters by Elmore Leonard and George V. Higgins."

—*The Arizona Republic*

"Gruley is a talented storyteller at the top of his game, and this might just be his best effort so far. Taut, smart, entertaining, and packed with a variety of types of tension, *Bleak Harbor* is one of those books that make readers keep flipping pages until everything has been said and done. Luckily for them, the author has something up his sleeve."

—Criminal Element

"Bryan Gruley is not afraid to go dark, so prepare yourself for a twisted domestic noir plot. Gruley also knows how to craft vivid characters that readers truly care about, so do not be surprised when he manages to tug on those heartstrings as well."

—BOLO Books

"Bryan Gruley knows how to surprise readers and keep them on the edge of their seats."

—The Real Book Spy

PURGATORY BAY

BRYAN GRULEY

THOMAS & MERCER

Published by Thomas & Mercer, Seattle
www.apub.com

Amazon, the Amazon logo, and Thomas & Mercer are trademarks of Amazon.com, Inc., or its affiliates.

ISBN-13: 9781542016544 (hardcover)
ISBN-10: 1542016541 (hardcover)

ISBN-13: 9781542092883 (paperback)
ISBN-10: 1542092884 (paperback)

Cover design by Shasti O'Leary Soudant

Printed in the United States of America

First edition

For the Polley sisters,
Jo and Kathy,
my first fans

Blessed are those who hunger and thirst for
righteousness,
for they shall be satisfied.

—Matthew 5:6

PROLOGUE

March 18, 2007

"Miss? Your license again, please? Just to reconfirm."

The Michigan state trooper standing over Jubilee was a rucksack of a man with jowls as pale and greasy as diner pork chops, his eyes tiny bullets buried in his cheekbones. The smudged nameplate on his left breast pocket read *Christian*.

Jubilee, hungover, throat parched, head pounding, sat in an angle iron chair with too-high arms in the state police post at Lapeer, an hour north of Detroit. She had driven past the post a hundred times, tapping her brakes at the sight of the blue-and-gold cruisers parked outside the low brick building. She had never been inside until one hour and fourteen minutes before.

"Reconfirming what, Officer Christian?" she said.

Christian straightened, looking offended. *Who's he to be offended?* Jubilee thought. She had assumed that *she* was the victim there, although she didn't know of what because the cops wouldn't tell her anything.

"Reconfirming your particulars, miss." His voice was a high-pitched rasp, like when her late grandfather had spoken to her after coming off his ventilator. "I need your driver's license. We didn't get a good copy of it the first time. It's routine procedure."

They had rousted her from Tessa's house just after six a.m. All they would say was that she had to get her wallet and come with them immediately. "What is going on? Is something wrong?" Mrs. Fluegel had asked repeatedly, to no avail.

Jubilee had sat uncuffed in the back of the state police cruiser, siren blaring as it raced up M-24, the speedometer creeping toward a hundred miles per hour. She'd felt afraid, not because of the speed but because the air inside the car seemed to have been drained of oxygen, the officers silently, implausibly angry, though they wouldn't answer her questions, wouldn't even look at her.

At the post they'd stuck her in a chair with a seat that made her have to keep scooching back and told her to stay put, as if she were still a child, not seventeen years old and a high school senior recruited to play soccer goaltender at Princeton in the fall.

"Why am I here, Officer?" she asked.

"Miss, I'm only going to ask for the license one more time."

Jubilee felt the cold damp beading on the back of her neck, the nausea spreading in her gut. She wondered if the cops had called her parents, who were at the family cottage up north, a three-hour drive away. Jubilee had stayed home in Clarkston for the weekend. Her mother had warned her not to go to any parties, and of course Jubilee had ignored her.

She started humming, softly so the officer wouldn't hear. Humming the song that had been playing in her head when Mrs. Fluegel had woken her from drunken sleep, the uniformed officer standing incongruously in the door of Tessa's bedroom.

All Jubilee could think was, *Oh shit, my dad is gonna be pissed. Oh shit. They can't arrest me for drinking a few Corona Lights—hell, Tessa was doing frigging Jäger bombs with Bobby. Shit, Mom will not be happy . . .*

"Miss Rathman," Christian said. "I need your license, please."

Jubilee kept humming as she dug in a pocket for the license. She had read that humming could keep you from puking. It seemed to have worked the night before, when she had thought she might barf in Bobby's half bath off the kitchen—she might have sneaked a couple of Jäger shots herself—and had started humming along with the song blaring outside the bathroom door. She didn't know the name of the song or the lyrics, but it had a bouncy chorus that was easy enough to hum. And she had not puked.

"Here," she said, handing Christian her license. "Please don't lose it."

He took the license and started to walk away.

"Hey," Jubilee said. "Could I at least call my parents?"

Christian turned halfway back and hesitated before answering. "As we said, there's been a situation."

"You didn't say anything about any situation."

"We'll let you know when we know."

The cops had taken her cell phone. She remembered one nonsensical text she'd gotten when the party at Bobby's parents' house had just begun to rock, a little after midnight. It was from her younger sister, Kara: 2Ju xkYaf .. 8983a. Jubilee figured she had raided their parents' liquor cabinet again. Kara never learned.

"Can I just call my parents? They'll worry."

The eyelids surrounding Christian's bullets narrowed. He canted his head, studying her anew. "Tell me, Miss Rathman." Christian held the license up in front of his face. "Jubilee Magdalena Rathman." He dropped the hand holding the license. "Magdalena? Is that some sort of Italian thing? *Rathman* doesn't sound Italian."

"Excuse me?"

"You haven't yet blown into the Breathalyzer this morning, have you, Jubilee Magdalena?"

"I wasn't driving, Officer."

"Trooper," he said, before he walked away.

The room smelled faintly of garlic. Christian crossed the tile floor to an office about twenty feet away. Jubilee felt an urge to walk over and open the door and scream, *Tell me what happened, dammit*. But she refused to be one of those girls who used hysteria as a crowbar.

She watched the cops in the office: Christian, another man, and a uniformed woman who appeared to be in charge. The door was closed, but Jubilee could see through a window.

Every few minutes another cop would walk past, ignoring her or giving her a sideways glance without really looking at her. She wondered if they'd been ordered not to engage her.

A clock on the wall above the office said it was 7:38. Jubilee's parents would be awake by now, her mother putting the coffee on. Jubilee wished she had her phone, wondered if they knew where she was, if they had called, why the cops wouldn't put them through.

In the office, the woman leaned her rump against a desk, hands on her hips, her face a mask of too much makeup glowing in the fluorescent light. A ring as big as a walnut engulfed her wedding finger. Next to her on the desk was a beer mug filled with pencils and pens, a stapler, and a small brass trophy in the shape of a star.

Christian stood at a fax machine a few feet away, pages spewing into his open palms. The other male trooper stood with his back to the window, arms folded, nodding as the woman spoke. Every few seconds, the woman would glance at Jubilee through the window. She looked concerned, though whether the concern was for Jubilee or something else Jubilee couldn't tell.

The pages kept churning out of the fax—she could just hear the dull click and whir—and Christian scooped them off one at a time, giving each a cursory look before placing them facedown on a stack next to the machine. Then a page appeared to catch his attention. He stopped stacking, his eyebrows edging upward as he studied it. He touched a button on the machine, turned, and walked the page over to the woman.

Jubilee leaned forward in the chair and saw the woman's eyes widen ever so slightly. She lifted her eyes toward Jubilee.

Jubilee rose from the chair.

The woman dropped the page and came off the desk, barking something at the cop who wasn't Christian. He spun toward Jubilee as she shoved the office door open and saw the woman's nameplate: *Sgt. White*.

"Miss Rathman," he said, "you need to go back to your seat."

"What's going on?" Jubilee addressed herself to White while pointing at the fax. "Show me."

Christian reached across the desk for the page he'd given the woman. "Here," he said.

"Christian, no," the woman said, stretching to grab his arm. She was too late. Christian dangled the black-and-white photograph for Jubilee to see. The picture showed a boy, almost entirely naked, splayed unnaturally on the edge of a pond. Jubilee knew the pond.

"This your brother?" Christian said. "Joshua, right?"

Jubilee felt the burble in her gut again, willed it back down, and without thinking snatched the brass star off the woman's desk. It was heavy, and one point of the star bored into Jubilee's palm, though she wouldn't notice until she was in the ambulance covered in blood, her own and Christian's.

She lunged at him and snapped the trophy at his face, flinging her forearm out like she would to stop a soccer ball flying at her in the net.

She was going for his nose, but the other male cop deflected her arm as he grabbed her. One of the star's points spiked Christian's right eye. He fell back against the fax machine, screaming as Jubilee crashed to the floor beneath the other cop, smelling his breath and sweat and the starch on his uniform, hearing him spit into her ear, "Get down, you little bitch. You're under arrest."

1

Twelve years later
Thursday, 9:15 p.m.

Ophelia is not answering.

Mikey Deming ends the call, tucks her phone into a cupholder, decides she'll go to her sister's apartment. The lights of downtown Bleak Harbor beckon as Mikey drives the shore road, the familiar bay dark and silent on her right. She checks the dashboard trip meter. She's made good time.

Maybe Ophelia went to bed and turned her phone off, although she rarely does the latter. Maybe she's staying with Gary tonight. But Ophelia knows her sister and niece are on their way from Ann Arbor. Why wouldn't she expect a call?

Mikey hears the voice of her husband, Craig, in her head: *Why don't you be Michaela and let Ophelia be Ophelia?* She glances at Bridget. Their fifteen-year-old is asleep in a jumble of pillow and black fleece, her face hidden while waves of her red hair spill out from under the fleece stitched with a gold *W* on the shoulder, white earbud wires striping her hair. Silent and peaceful, even though she has such a big weekend ahead.

"Go Washtenaw Pride," Mikey whispers, smiling.

With a finger she swabs a tear from an eye. She pictures her father in the bleachers, screaming, *GOOOOO PRIIIIIIDE!* again and again, regardless of whether Bridget's team was ahead or behind. How happy it would have made him to be in the stands this weekend, narrating the game like a play-by-play announcer for Ophelia, who is blind. "G-Pa will be rooting for you from heaven," Mikey told Bridget as they packed her sticks and hockey bag into the car.

The weekend will be good. Mikey is sure of that. Whatever happens on the rink, win or lose, skate well or not, will happen. There will be time with Ophelia, time with Ophelia's boyfriend, the smell of the house on Bleak Harbor Bay that will bring Bob Wright back to life, if only in their minds. And there will be time with Bridget, often so hard to snatch at home between school and work and practice and games.

Mikey's phone buzzes. Craig calling.

"Hey," she whispers.

"Everything OK?"

"Heading to Pheels's place. Bridget's out."

"Good. She'll need her energy."

"When are you leaving?"

"Right after this breakfast with the deans. Of course they had to schedule it for this Friday."

"Be safe. I love you."

"Me too."

Mikey had an easier time getting Friday off from her job as associate director of the Richard T. Willing Literacy Center in Ann Arbor. She knows Craig would be with them if he could. Bridget's hockey means more to him than to Mikey, maybe even more, Mikey suspects, than it does to Bridget. This weekend looms large for their daughter's future: five games, the best girls' teams in North America, college scouts watching. Bridget has heard already from Wisconsin, Colgate, and Darwyn Tech. She's holding out for Harvard. Her father's hoping for Wisconsin. Mikey just wants her daughter to be happy. She doesn't care what makes Bridget happy—hockey or microbiology or accounting or geography— so long as it's something that wakes her up each day with purpose and meaning, something that won't scare her so badly that she'll come to the conclusion that she has to walk away. Like Mikey did.

She's glad for a few days away from her job. She likes it, mostly, especially the one-to-ones with the kids and adults who come to learn to read. It reminds her a bit of what she loved most about being a newspaper reporter: interacting with opaque strangers who gradually become real people, almost familiar. But since her promotion to associate director, Mikey has been spending less time with people and more with grant applications and other paperwork. Financially, the literacy center is scraping by about as badly as the *Detroit Times* was when she left nearly twelve years ago.

The bay road becomes Blossom Street and curves into the heart of Bleak Harbor. Lights are on at Nucci's Nice Guy Tavern. Otherwise the street is dark but for the furry glow of faux gas lamps. In three months, it will be crowded and blazing light with vacationers from Chicago and Detroit and Indianapolis. This is March, chilly and damp with winter's last wheezing breaths.

Mikey passes Kate's Kakes, Strawman Drug, the pizza joint that changes names every year or two, Casurella Fudge. At the intersection of Blossom and Lily, the clock tower on the Bleak Harbor Bank & Trust building says 9:17 p.m. Mikey turns right onto Lily, which slopes downward toward the vacant harbor docks. She's about to take a left onto Jeremiah when an SUV lurches out from a driveway on her right into the middle of the street and stops. She slams on the brakes, stopping just short of the SUV's rear bumper, one arm instinctively reaching out to keep Bridget from pitching forward. "What the hell, idiot?" she says. She looks at Bridget, who merely shifts her head from one side of the seat to the other, still asleep.

The SUV looks similar to the black Volvo that Ophelia keeps, but the license plate is from Ohio. *Of course,* Mikey thinks, because everyone in Michigan knows Ohioans can't drive for shit. Maybe it's carrying a girl playing in the tournament. Maybe the driver saw the Washtenaw Pride sticker on Mikey's windshield and decided to have some fun with her.

Mikey doesn't really care; she just wants to get to Ophelia's. But the Ohio Volvo doesn't move. Mikey doesn't want to honk and wake Bridget, so she puts her car in reverse, backs up a few feet, and starts to maneuver around the Volvo on the left. Then Ohio veers in front of her and brakes again.

"Come on, jerk," Mikey says under her breath. She backs up again, again starts to move around the SUV, and again Ohio eases forward to obstruct her. She squints to read the license plate, commits it to memory, then backs up again, faster now, and tries to squeeze past along the curb. This time Ohio doesn't move. She looks at the car as she's creeping past. Through the tinted side window, she sees the shadowy outline of a head turning toward her.

The window begins to slide down. Mikey looks over, expecting a middle finger. Instead she sees a man's face—at least she thinks it's a face, not a mask. She gasps as she swerves left and bumps up onto the curb. "Oh my God," she says as he stares across at her. She thinks the face might be grinning, but it's so grotesquely deformed she can't be sure.

Bridget bolts up, the fleece falling away.

"Don't," Mikey says. "Don't look."

Ohio speeds away.

"Mom," Bridget says, "you scared me." She twists to look out the passenger window. "What happened? Who was that?"

"Just some jerk, probably drunk," Mikey says. In her head she repeats what she saw on the license plate: *W19BB6*. "Everything's fine."

"You always say that."

"Look, we're almost to Ophelia's. Get ready."

Mikey takes a breath and swallows hard, hoping Bridget doesn't notice her unease, then turns onto Jeremiah. The street is lined with Victorians built in the late nineteenth century, after Joseph Estes Bleak came from New England and transformed a swamp along Lake

Michigan into a small but thriving timber-and-shipping hub. She parks in front of a gray two-story trimmed in forest green and drab white.

Ophelia rents the first floor. The house is dark but for a finger of light in the bay window facing the street. Mikey doesn't see Ophelia's Volvo by the curb. Maybe it's in the garage. Ophelia can't drive it, of course, but she insists on having it because she's Ophelia. Her business partner borrows it on occasion.

In the front yard stands a sculpture Ophelia fashioned from scrap metal and aluminum wire. A boy on a skateboard balances on one bent leg, arms flung triumphantly out to his sides, head thrown back, presumably shrieking with laughter. A word is inscribed on the top surface of the skateboard: *Lucky*. Seeing it makes Mikey's throat catch, as always, and she thinks, *Zeke. You can't get lucky if you don't try.* A larger version of the statue towers over Blue Star Highway north of Bleak Harbor, one of seven sculptures Ophelia has constructed along the road.

Bridget is shaking out her hair. "Want me to go up to the door?"

"Wait one second." Mikey dials her sister again. Again it goes to voice mail. Ophelia is a sound sleeper. And stubborn when she wants to be left alone. "Let's let her sleep. We'll see her in the morning."

As they circle back through the lifeless downtown, Mikey keeps a lookout for Ohio. Did the face in the window actually have only one eye? She makes a note to look for him at the rink tomorrow.

"Look at the bay," she tells Bridget. "Isn't it beautiful?"

The water is a black mirror, stars reflected as pinprick glimmers on the glass, stretching from the beaches along the bay road to the far shore, where the old Bleak Mansion squats atop a sandy slope peering down on the city. Seeing the house with its peaked roof and pink turrets as a young girl always gave Mikey a little thrill, like she was glimpsing one of the castles she'd read about in picture books. One day, she used to think, she'd write about her own castles.

"Does anyone live there anymore?" Bridget says.

"I don't think so. The old lady died a while back. The property's all tangled up in lawsuits."

"That's sad."

"Who's this?" Mikey's Bluetooth is ringing. "Gary?"

"Hey there," Ophelia's boyfriend says. "Welcome back."

"Thanks."

"Hi, Gary," Bridget chimes in.

"Hello, hockey goddess. Can't wait to meet you."

"Is Ophelia with you?" Mikey says.

"Nope. I tried to get her out for dinner, but she begged off, said she had work to do and wanted to get some sleep before the big weekend."

Mikey encountered Gary Langreth once years before, when she was a night-police reporter in Detroit. He was in a briefing with the department's communications officer after a triple shooting on the East Side, sulking about having to deal with a reporter and giving her just about nothing. He somehow remembered it years later when they met in Bleak Harbor, maybe because Mikey was the rare woman covering night cops. "Props to you for handling assholes like me," he told her. After Ophelia started dating him, Mikey googled him and saw that he'd left the force a few years ago and come to Bleak Harbor to work as an investigator for the county prosecutor. What had prompted his departure from Detroit was unclear; veteran detectives didn't often abandon their pensions.

"She's not answering her phone."

"Yeah, well, you know what she thinks of phones."

"The phone is a privilege," Ophelia liked to say. "You have to ignore it sometimes to keep its specialness in perspective."

"You're staying at Bob's?" Gary asks.

"Yeah, more room there, and there's still some of his stuff to go through." Her father kept the house on Bleak Harbor Bay after he went into assisted living two years ago. She and Ophelia have been trying half-heartedly to sell it ever since. "Bridget likes to sleep in G-Pa's bed."

"I wouldn't worry about Ophelia. She probably conked out. She's very excited about the tournament. And of course it's her birthday."

Zeke's birthday too, Mikey thinks. "Of course," she says. "So we're having breakfast at Bella's? Eight?"

"Eight? Ugh," Bridget says.

"When's the first game?" Gary says.

"Eleven forty-five."

"See you at Bella's."

Mikey brakes and flicks her left-turn blinker. "Here we are."

She pulls into a gravel horseshoe drive in front of a one-story clapboard house with an attached garage. There must be ten thousand cottages like this one on lakeshores all over Michigan. That's why her father loved it so much. Before he moved the family there, when they were just weekending, Bob Wright would roll up to the house, toss his bag on the kitchen table, pop a cold can of Stroh's, and go directly out to the water, the screen door banging behind him as he took his first guzzle. He called it prioritizing.

Now a For Sale sign juts from a row of scraggly evergreen shrubs beneath the kitchen window. The sign is listing a little, as if it doesn't want to be there any more than Mikey wants it there. "Hmm," she says. "Ophelia was supposed to stop by and put a light on. So the furnace probably isn't on either."

"That's sad too," Bridget says.

"It'll heat up quickly enough."

"No, I meant the For Sale sign."

Neither Mikey nor her sister wants to sell it. But their father, in his late-life state, neglected to pay property taxes on the house for almost two years. Keeping it would be a costly hassle. "Yeah. We haven't had any bites, so maybe we'll hang on to it for the summer at least."

"I wish G-Pa was here."

Bridget opens her door, but Mikey stops her with a hand on her knee. "Everything is going to be great this weekend, Bridge."

"Stop saying that."

She tries to get out, but Mikey squeezes her knee harder and says, "I want you to have fun. Have fun."

Bridget stares at the glove box. "I can't get a scholarship having fun."

Hearing that breaks Mikey's heart a little. She wants to ask Bridget, *Aren't you having fun? It isn't fun to be out there on the ice with your friends?* But Mikey is afraid to hear the answer. Instead she says, "You'll feel better when all this college stuff is over, honey. Promise."

"What was that in that car?"

I don't know, Mikey thinks, struck by Bridget's choice of pronouns. *What* describes that face better than *who.*

"Just some Ohio jerk," Mikey says. "Oh, wait, that's redundant."

Bridget smiles a little. Mikey, feeling glad, releases her daughter's knee and says, "Let's get you to bed."

2

Katya Malone stuffs the papers into her backpack and drops it on the kitchen table so it's ready for the morning.

Malone has come to loathe budgets, learned to despise emergency reserves and parking ticket–revenue projections and having to stand before the hooples on the Bleak Harbor city council to defend her spending decisions. It's the worst part of being chief of the Bleak Harbor Police Department. Except, maybe, for dealing with the mayor.

She hasn't finished what she was doing, but she can't work any more tonight. She goes to the fridge and opens it, even though she isn't really hungry. There's pizza from Marino's left over from two nights ago, half a carton of cottage cheese, an apple, two oranges, a Kit Kat bar. Her phone begins to ring in the bedroom. She ignores it while debating whether it's too late to eat. She grabs the Kit Kat, shuts the fridge, and walks into her bedroom as the phone goes silent.

She sits on the bed and begins to unwrap the candy bar while gazing at the framed photograph on the dresser: a girl in a soccer uniform, scarlet and gold, the colors of the Bleak Harbor Blaze. Louisa loved Kit Kats. Malone gets up and walks to the dresser. She places the half-peeled Kit Kat in front of the picture. She smiles. "Good night, baby," she says.

She picks up her phone. The missed call was from her dispatcher. She wishes he had left a message. She'd really rather get under the covers than call him back. She stares at the phone for a few seconds, gives in, hits the button.

"Sorry to bother, Chief," the dispatcher says.

"What's up?"

"You wanted me to remind you about the hockey thing. You're supposed to be there at seven fifteen."

Great, she thinks. She's supposed to do something at the local rink for some girls' tournament this weekend. She looks at the clock on her nightstand. She'll have to set the alarm back an hour. "Tell me again why I agreed to this?"

"Deeth," he says. "Like teeth."

Deeth is the tournament official who has been hounding her to do a ceremonial puck drop to start the tournament. Malone doesn't know much about hockey, didn't even know Bleak Harbor had a hockey team. Before the day of the accident, Louisa played soccer and viola.

The mayor was originally supposed to do the puck drop, whatever that was, but he backed out, probably because he thought it beneath him, then sicced Deeth on Malone.

"Deeth, like teeth," Deeth literally said, with an exaggerated toothy smile from the chair opposite her desk at the station.

"Do we have a team in the tournament?" Malone asked him.

"We do," Deeth said. "We are the host team. We probably won't get far, but the girls will have fun."

"How did Bleak Harbor get this tournament in the first place? It sounds like a pretty big deal."

"It's a very big deal. Most years it's in Detroit or Chicago or Boston or some other hockey town. But some anonymous donor who apparently has a soft spot for the Harbor threw a boatload of money at our national hockey office."

Malone wishes the anonymous donor would throw her department a boatload of money so she could tell the mayor and the council to go pound sand. She can't keep up this pace, this seven-day-a-week cycle of work at the station, grab some fast food, work at home, and collapse, hoping she doesn't have that recurring nightmare again.

She loves being a cop, is proud to be a chief. But neither is enough. She needs something more, something other than the heat in her cruiser to make her warm, something other than the haul of late-night drunks to make her laugh, something more than the occasional fling to make her feel desired, someone who calls her Katya instead of Chief or Malone or Officer.

It might help a little if the damn council would fill the damn deputy chief slot that has remained vacant, at the mayor's insistence, for almost a year. But Malone also knows her frustrations aren't only their fault. She's trying to take things a day at a time, but that only goes so far when each day is haunted by the same memory again and again.

"All right," she tells the dispatcher. "I'll be there."

"Also, you have that press conference up on Purgatory Bay."

"Right." Malone is actually looking forward to that, out of curiosity about the property's owner, if nothing else. Her name is Jubilee, of all things, and her family was murdered years ago in a mob hit that, if Malone remembers correctly, was never solved. She and Jubilee have loss in common, if not the uncertainty about who was responsible. Malone wants to see how Jubilee handles carrying the burden, knowing how sloppily she herself has borne it.

"Eleven, right?"

"Yep. And since I have you, FYI, some woman called in a complaint about a driver in town. Ohio plate, probably somebody here for the tournament. She gave me the license number."

"Put a trace on it."

"Really?"

"No. Good night."

She shuts her phone off, drops it on her dresser, and strips down to her underwear, hanging her uniform on a bedpost. She looks at the bed, then over at the armchair in the corner of the room, debating, as she does each night, where she'll sleep, or try to. Lately she's been choosing the bed over the chair, and so far, the nightmare has not returned.

She kills the light, slips into the bed, and leans over to set the alarm. She taps in *6:15*, then reconsiders and backs it up to five forty-five, figuring she'll stop by Louisa's grave before going to the hockey rink.

3

The iridescent green triangle slides along a thin digital line on the flat-screen monitor, right to left along Blossom Street in downtown Bleak Harbor. As the green triangle turns on Lily, toward the bay, a second triangle, bloodred, shoots out from an alley and stops, blocking the green triangle and bringing its movement to a halt.

Jubilee taps a button. The graphic on the monitor is replaced by a video feed from a car interior. She leans forward in her chair, watches the driver's head turn to his left, the window open.

"Dammit, Caleb," she says. His self-indulgences have become more frequent, disturbingly so. She bats a few keys, shifting the view back to the graphic, sees the red triangle hurrying away as the green one turns onto Jeremiah. "Stick to the mission."

A damp breeze sluices through a vent that brings the outside air into the subbasement of the fortress on Purgatory Bay. The chill on Jubilee's forehead and cheeks tends to calm her. The room is dark but for the monitor's glow and the reddish flickers on her control board.

She glances at another monitor, with a camera's view through a window on one of the upper floors. Stars glitter over the tree-filled bluffs across the lake. The rest is blackness, with no other houses or buildings to light it. A clear night that she hopes bodes a clear morning.

Jubilee swivels right to another rectangular bank of four monitors. She reaches for a mouse and clicks it, and views appear on two. On one she sees two jowly men sitting at a bar, gripping half-full pint glasses, jabbering at each other; behind them, a wall is covered with framed photographs of hockey teams. An adjacent screen offers a wide-angle view of a hockey rink, players in dark and light uniforms moving in seemingly random directions after a puck Jubilee cannot make out. The devices Caleb planted inside the rink earlier this week are operational.

"Speed parameters could soon be violated."

The digitized female voice issues from a speaker in the ceiling high above Jubilee. "I can see that for myself," she replies without looking up.

"I detect annoyance."

"I'm not annoyed, Frances."

"I am doing my job, Jubilee."

Shut up, Frances, Jubilee thinks.

A digital gauge tells Jubilee how fast Caleb is moving: twenty-eight miles per hour, thirty, thirty-three. At thirty-four, she takes a joystick in hand and eases it back half an inch. The gauge rolls back to twenty-seven. At two miles over the limit but not below it, the cops won't care. Below it, they might suspect a drunk on his way home from Nucci's. Caleb cannot afford to get pulled over with the cargo he's carrying. He needs to get back to Purgatory Bay, where he's safe.

"Thank you, Frances," Jubilee says. She wonders again why she has spent so much Bitcoin on the dark-web coders who build virtual assistants for her. From Abigail to Belinda, from Carmen to Desiree to Ella, each one seems to get bitchier as she gets smarter.

The red triangle, Caleb at the wheel, snakes along Bleak Harbor side streets, avoiding the bay-shore road until it's a mile west of town, where it veers north along the Bleak River toward Purgatory Bay.

While she waits for Caleb to arrive home, Jubilee turns to a laptop on the desk beneath the flat-screen, clicks her mouse on an icon labeled *DuneWKZO*. A video opens. In the upper-right corner a signature reads

14july94. Jubilee manipulates her touch pad so that the view zooms in on a girl being interviewed by a television reporter. Jubilee has watched this video many times over the past year. It reminds her why she has set out to do what she's about to do, the mission to which she has committed herself. And Caleb.

The zooming pushes the chyron displaying the reporter's and girl's names out of the frame. The girl is talking, but Jubilee has muted the sound. She committed the girl's words to memory many viewings ago. Jubilee is more interested in how she says it, how her face and eyes can reveal whether she is telling the truth. How her ever-so-slight overbite pinches her lower lip when she lies.

Michaela, Jubilee thinks, *you are a liar*.

The girl is standing on a beach, skinny in a one-piece bathing suit swirled with yellow and purple. Though it's not visible in the telescoped frame, Jubilee knows a dune of creamy-golden sand rises behind her. The girl is pale except for a blotch of crimson on her left arm, where she must have failed to smear enough sunscreen.

Her eyes are puffed and reddish, apparently from crying, her nose also sunburned. She keeps swiping a wayward strand of hair from her face. She's fourteen years old. She clearly knows how to lie. She might not know it yet, might never admit it, but she's good at it.

Jubilee wasn't so good at lying at that age, but she's gotten better at it—a necessity.

"Nearing the tunnel entrance," Frances says.

Caleb's red triangle exits the river road, swerves onto a dirt two-track that isn't marked on the screen. The shape moves along through a void before it disappears, gone underground.

Jubilee switches to yet another view transmitted by a camera the size of a pencil inserted in the grille of the car Caleb is driving. She sees a black oval sliced by two cones of light emanating from the car's headlights and a line of small red lamps blinking in the road's centerline.

Jubilee glances back at the laptop. The television camera has panned away from the girl. Paramedics are lifting a gurney into an ambulance. Jubilee zooms the view back out, revealing the legend at the bottom of the screen: *BOY FEARED DEAD IN DUNE ACCIDENT.*

She has seen enough for now. She shuts the laptop. On the flat-screen monitor, the red triangle reappears and slows to a stop. Caleb is home.

Jubilee stands and exits the room into a corridor that leads to a locked steel door. She shows her palm to a keypad next to the door, hears a click, pulls the door open, and steps into a dimly lit cavern of concrete reinforced with columns of steel running up and down the walls.

The Volvo SUV with the Ohio plates is parked there, its innards still snicking after being shut down seconds ago. Caleb is on the floor next to the car doing one-armed push-ups, two with his left arm, then two with his right, back and forth, effortless. His training has paid off, at least physically.

"Had a little fun tonight, did we?" Jubilee says.

"Twenty-six."

Caleb counts the push-ups aloud, not even close to out of breath.

"Only the mission," he says.

"She saw your face, Caleb."

"Twenty-nine."

"Do not remove the mask. Never. You jeopardized the mission."

He stops, perches on one arm, his back as straight as a carpenter's level. "I wanted to see—thirty-one—if the GPS thing I placed on her car worked."

"It works. I can track her from here. Just as I can track you."

"It won't happen again."

Jubilee watches the muscles in his upper arms flex. He's gotten much stronger just in the last two months. She crouches next to him, starts to reach a hand out to touch him, draws it back.

"The cargo is in the car?" she says.

"Thirty-six," Caleb says. "Asleep on the passenger seat. I will put her in her room when I finish."

"Good. Then switch the Ohio plates for Wisconsin."

Now Jubilee lets her hand come to rest on his hip as it rises and falls. "We have worked so hard for this, Caleb, both of us. You have worked so hard. In twenty-four hours—less than that—we will have—"

"Righteousness. Yes. Thirty-nine. Is the Ho Ho ready?"

"Next to your bed, as always."

"Forty-two. Only one?"

"One will be plenty. You need to get up early and prepare the drones before you leave for Detroit. You have your first task to complete at dawn; then the funeral begins at nine a.m. I will be at the press conference at eleven, but Frances will be monitoring."

"I am ready. Forty-four."

Jubilee removes her hand, rises from her crouch. She looks at the Volvo, imagines the blind woman unconscious inside. "Please put her in the room and get to the roof."

"Forty-eight." He switches arms. "Forty-nine."

———

The clock on Jubilee's nightstand says 12:11 a.m. Two minutes till bedtime. She opens the nightstand drawer, lifts out the Bible. A felt pen marks a spot near the back of the Bible. She uses the pen to flip it open to the marked page, at Matthew, chapter five.

Halfway down the page on the right are the Beatitudes. *Blessed are the poor in spirit,* reads the first, *for theirs is the kingdom of heaven.* A piece of paper torn from a steno pad is scotch-taped to the page on the left. Jubilee looks at the list of names she has scratched there, pronouncing them one by one in her head. Then she replaces the pen, closes the Bible, returns it to the drawer, and slides under her blanket, closes her eyes.

"Righteousness," she whispers once, then again and again, as she does every night, until she falls asleep.

The alarm will wake her, as always, at 2:42 a.m.

4

Caleb steps back from the drones, lifts his gaze to peer across the mansion roof to Purgatory Bay. A half moon hovers in a dishrag of cloud, splaying a haze of yellow across the water on the opposite shore.

The day will be clear, Caleb decides. Good for what he has to do.

He left his bed, looked longingly at the drained syringe on the nightstand, thinking, *No Ho Hos for a while now.* Then he dressed, ate a bowl of microwaved farro with kale, and climbed the stairs in the northeast tower to the roof.

The drones shine dully in a chiaroscuro of moonlight and shadow, arranged in a semicircle, perched on a ring of concrete slabs of varying heights. Each drone is equipped with a different weapon. Jubilee wanted each to have its own way of killing so that the satisfaction of the strike would not become repetitive, would remain fresh and invigorating whether the victim died of a bullet or an arrow or a poison dart.

Caleb has his own way of seeing the drones with which he's spent so much time. He has given them names—Simon, Ralphie, Percival, Piggy, Roger—after the characters in the shaggy paperback he found one late, dark evening as he jogged through the forest nestling the bay.

He likes these moments on the roof with the drones. This is where he trained himself and each of them to behave. He's sorry that, as Jubilee has cautioned, he might not have any more nights like this on the roof.

Once, she explained the meaning of Purgatory Bay to him. She said purgatory was a place where troubled souls traveled to cleanse themselves before they ascended to heaven. Sometimes, Jubilee said, these souls had a selfless obligation to cleanse other troubled souls as well.

"No one goes straight to heaven," she told him. "Nobody is that good and pure. The only path is through purgatory."

Caleb assured her that he understood. He wasn't sure that he did, or that Jubilee believed him. What Caleb believes is that once he has completed the mission, he will be freed from purgatory, freed from this fortress, and allowed to walk freely in what Jubilee calls the "outer world."

He needs three drones for the day's missions. For the first and probably most dangerous, he selects Roger. Roger is fitted with a gun barrel that fires a .22 caliber bullet, relatively light so that Roger's computer can more easily hold a focus on the target and the recoil won't throw Roger into a spin.

Caleb walks to where Roger rests, bends down, runs a forefinger along one of the four propellers that make the drone fly.

"Roger," Caleb says. "Just a few hours."

"You are the drone, Caleb."

The voice startles him. He turns to see Jubilee, standing at the southwest of the brick towers positioned at each corner of the roof. She's glowering in the dim yellow glow, hands on her hips, wide awake after her two hours and twenty-nine minutes of nightly sleep.

Caleb hopes she didn't hear him speak to Roger. He hasn't told her about the names. She would probably consider it a distraction from the mission.

"Jubilee," Caleb says. "I am preparing."

"You are the drone," she repeats. "What the drone does is what you would do. The drone is an extension not just of your eyes and your hands but of your heart and your soul. It enables you to free not just us but others from purgatory."

"I am the drone."

Jubilee lifts an arm, points at Roger, says, "Not that one for the first target. Too much like them."

Them, Caleb thinks. The family of the target.

"I think he would be best," Caleb says.

"An 'it,' Caleb, not a 'he.' You are the 'he'; that is the drone."

"I understand."

She points at the slab two over from Roger. "That one," she says. "With the crossbow."

That one, Simon, is Caleb's favorite. He's always been harder to control than the others. He might dip down farther than Caleb intends or lurch out of a maneuver in the wrong direction while Caleb fumbles with the controller, watching Simon resist him on a tiny video screen. Caleb thinks Simon might be that way because of the miniature crossbow he carries. Jubilee had trouble figuring that modification out. Or maybe, Caleb likes to think, Simon simply has a mind of his own.

Caleb doesn't know precisely why, but he feels some admiration for Simon, for that particular quality he seems to have.

"No," Caleb says. "He's—that one's better for later in the day."

He hoped he wouldn't have to deploy Simon at all, but two of the drones have encountered technical problems. So Caleb planned to have Roger, Percival, and Simon complete the day's tasks, in that order.

"You heard me," Jubilee says. "The crossbow first. That one is important."

"Yes."

"Now let me hear your stutter."

Caleb looks at Simon. "I r-really w-w-wish we w-would—"

"Fine. Don't overdo it. Just enough to keep people off-balance." Jubilee looks at her watch. "Almost time for you to go. Focus, Caleb. No hesitation."

"No hesitation."

5

"Mom. Where's my other white sock?"

Bridget shouts it from the bedroom. Mikey's in the kitchen, making her daughter a cup of tea with brown sugar, herself a coffee, black. A printout of the day's tournament schedule is spread on the kitchen island. Mikey looks forward to watching the games, less so to the parents who'll be watching with her, dropping the names of college coaches recruiting their perfect daughters.

Please, Mikey thinks, *don't make me one of them.*

She turns away from the counter toward the bedroom. "A hockey sock? How would I know, Bridge?"

"You washed it."

"My job is to wash things; your job is to keep track of them."

"It's probably stuck in that stupid thing in the dryer. Coach is going to kill—" Bridget goes quiet, then says, "Oh, got it, never mind."

"Your tea is ready, honey."

No answer now. Mikey's used to it. Sometimes they still talk with the closeness they had when Bridget was ten. Sometimes not. Mikey tries to remember what her father told her about having teenagers: Keep listening. When the inevitable strain seeps into the conversations, shut up and listen harder.

Mikey walks out of the kitchen with her coffee and Bridget's tea. She stops at the doorway of the room where she and Ophelia and

Zeke slept when they were kids. Zeke in the single bed, Ophelia and Mikey in bunks on the opposite wall. One of Zeke's hockey sticks, black tape fraying from the blade, still stands in a corner beneath a Beastie Boys poster. Ophelia hated the Beasties. "I can't believe I'm even related to you," she would say to her twin, and Zeke would loose his high-pitched chicken cackle and say, "*Hello Nasty*. You just nasty, that's all."

Mikey smiles then, remembering what day it is, thinking, *Happy birthday, Zeke and Pheels.*

She sets Bridget's cup on an old phone stand in the family room—"Tea's out here, Bridge"—and continues onto the screened porch, out the porch door, and down the outer steps to the beach.

Clouds are moving in. Sky like porridge hovers over the empty Bleak Mansion across the bay. She steps up onto the boat dock, walks out to the end. The morning is quiet, the water so still she thinks again, as she did when she was little, that she could walk across it to the shore where downtown Bleak Harbor sits to her left.

She tried to call Ophelia earlier, without luck, then sent a text—pheels u there?—to which her sister has yet to respond. Mikey wonders if it has something to do with the date. Ophelia hasn't liked her birthday much since Zeke died on the dune north of Bleak Harbor. One year, maybe a decade after he suffocated, she took a banana cake that Mikey had made her, jammed three firecrackers into the pan, and blew it up—her favorite cake—on a picnic table in her backyard, while Mikey watched in horror from the kitchen window. It ruined Mikey's pan, as well as the day.

Mikey looks to her right, toward the channel that winds from the bay through those dunes out to Lake Michigan. She sips her coffee, steam warming her neck and cheeks. She could stand here all morning. Sometimes she did, as a child, counting the boats as they puttered past. Dad bought the cottage and moved the family here from suburban

Detroit almost twenty-six years ago, after Superior Motors terminated him and a few dozen other white-collar engineers.

Bob Wright had rented a number of different cottages for family vacations in Bleak Harbor. The one he wound up buying was his favorite because of its bayside vantage and breathing distance from the traffic drunkenness of downtown. He had a pension and a part-time job at Crova Hardware, while Mom worked as an emergency room nurse at Bleak County Medical Center.

Her coffee tepid now in the March chill, Mikey turns to go inside. She sees Bridget through a gap in her bedroom curtains, pushing one arm through a sleeve of her gray-and-gold Washtenaw Pride hoodie, talking on her phone with the other. Mikey knows she should keep moving into the cottage, let her daughter have her privacy, but she stands there anyway, less to spy on Bridget than to savor an unguarded moment in her girl's life.

Bridget gets her other arm through the other sleeve, then scoops her wavy tresses up and over the hood, reminding Mikey, with a spike of love mixed with apprehension, that her only child will soon be an adult. Mikey can't see her face, but now Bridget is turning her head back and forth in an exaggerated way, as if she's not only refusing the person on the other end of her call but persuading herself to refuse. She could be debating a teammate about how to line up for a face-off. Or she could be talking with Quinn, who is her boyfriend. Or was. Or will be again. It depends upon the day and Bridget's mood.

Like so many mothers, Mikey knows the feeling. But she refuses to take it or anything about her daughter for granted. Mikey's own mother never recovered from the afternoon when she was on duty at the ER and the paramedics brought Zeke in after the dune smothered him to death. Mikey didn't help much, shunning her mother for the suffocating pity of her friends.

Eventually, her mother drifted out of Mikey's and Ophelia's lives on a cloud of antidepressants and vodka. She and Bob Wright divorced, and she wound up, the last Mikey heard, somewhere in the Southwest. For a while, there were at least birthday cards, until there weren't. Mikey hasn't heard from her in years.

Mikey cannot bear the thought that she and Bridget might ever be so separate, or so separated. She has vowed to herself that she will never lose Bridget, and she will never let Bridget lose her. So her daughter's diffidence and distance silently weigh on Mikey. She hangs on to a time two years ago when she thinks she broke through to her daughter, if only for a precious moment. She hopes Bridget hangs on to it as hard as she does.

———

Bridget was thirteen, playing for a team sponsored by a chain of Detroit-area oil-change shops. She started the season well, scoring a goal or an assist in each of the first eight games.

She wasn't a timid player, never shy about jostling in front of the net or fighting for pucks in corners. But suddenly she became more aggressive than Mikey had ever seen her, running into opposing players who didn't have the puck, slashing them on the arms with her stick, taking needless penalties, even telling a referee to go to hell, which earned her an early exit from that game. Craig was weirdly thrilled to see their daughter playing "with an edge." "You can't teach that," he would say. "College coaches will be all over it."

Mikey was not all over it, because it wasn't the Bridget she knew—hardly sweet but no foulmouthed bully. Once, driving home after practice, Craig not in the car, Mikey asked Bridget if things were all right. "Everything's fine," Bridget said.

But when Mikey asked a second time, Bridget answered only after looking away, out the passenger window. From the reflection of her face in the glass, the unfamiliar clench in her jaw, Mikey knew everything was not fine. "Mom," Bridget said one evening a week later. Mikey was rushing out to a fund-raiser for her literacy program. "Can we talk a minute?"

Mikey had her jacket on and car keys in hand, already running late. But the pleading lilt in Bridget's voice stopped Mikey cold. She dropped her keys in her purse and said, "Let's sit down, honey."

"But you have to go."

"No. Sit."

Mikey made cocoa. They sat at the kitchen counter. "You can't tell anyone this, Mom," Bridget said.

Mikey hesitated. What was her duty here? How could she tell anyone anything if she didn't *know*? Her daughter wanted to confide in her, and she wanted to listen. "All right," she said.

"Not even Dad."

"I said all right."

A girl on Bridget's team—she refused to name her—had sidled up to Bridget on the locker room bench one afternoon after practice. They had both been half-undressed, in underwear and sports bras damp with sweat, shin guards and skates on the floor at their feet. At this particular moment, the other girls had all been in the showers or already dressed and gone.

The girl had put her hand flat on Bridget's back. Bridget had thought nothing of it at first. She and her teammates touched and hugged all the time. It was part of the natural bonding that made a team a team. Boys did it; girls did it. But this girl had slid her hand slowly downward, playing her fingers along Bridget's spine, then sliding her hand under the elastic band of Bridget's underwear and taking hold of one of her butt cheeks, smoothing it first, then squeezing it.

Mikey stiffened, as she imagined Bridget had, at the thought of the girl's fingers crawling over Bridget's spine like a cockroach. She leaned into her daughter and said, "Did she say something, honey?"

"I'm not done."

Bridget continued. She said she'd told the girl to stop. The girl had yanked her hand out from Bridget's underpants and moved away. The next time they'd happened to wind up alone, in a hallway waiting for the Zamboni to finish resurfacing the ice, there had been the girl's hand again, this time slinking up Bridget's back and around to her left breast. Again, Bridget had pulled away, told the girl no.

"OK," Mikey said, choosing her words carefully. "Then—"

"She told me I was a little slut," Bridget said.

"A 'little slut'?"

Bridget began to cry then, which made her angry, which made her cry even harder. Mikey came out of her chair and put her arms around her daughter.

"She lied," Bridget said.

"Of course she lied."

"No, Mom." Bridget choked back a sob. "That's not what I—she lied. I never did anything with that girl. She lied to everyone."

Tears welled in Mikey's eyes. She understood.

Bridget never brought it up again. Mikey asked about it later in the season, and Bridget insisted the girl had stopped and it was over. And what about the rumors the girl had spread? What about the texts she had blasted to Bridget and her friends? "It's fine," Bridget told Mikey. "Nobody believes her. I'm ignoring her now."

Which Mikey desperately wanted to feel better about but could not. It was all she could do to keep her promise and not call the coach. Without knowing the name of the girl, she sat in the stands watching the remaining games of the season and looking for the tiniest sign—a too-long hug after a goal, a misplaced pat on the rump—that might identify the culprit and supply Mikey with a focus for her anger. She sat in the stands wondering which other parents might know, wondering what the girl might have told her own parents. Mikey would have sworn off hockey altogether if she could have. But she could not, because it was Bridget's life, not hers.

The next season, Bridget left the oil-change team and joined the Pride.

———

Mikey is watching her daughter through the window, mesmerized, when Bridget swings around to face her, and Mikey, startled, stares down at the beach and walks toward the cottage. Her phone starts to go off in the back pocket of her jeans. She takes it out.

"Gary," she says. "Good morning. Find Pheels yet?"

"Uh . . . no, actually. Hold on."

Bridget loves the spinach-and-feta croissants at Bella's. And she worships her aunt. But Mikey knows Bridget nevertheless won't be totally present. She'll be thinking of the eleven forty-five game against Edina—"Mom, they haven't lost to anyone outside Minnesota in like a hundred years"—followed by a four fifteen matchup against a team from Boston's South Shore—"Who calls a hockey team the Baked Beans? Seriously?"

"Gary, where are you?"

He doesn't answer. Mikey waits just outside the cottage. She hears creaking, the soft thud of footfalls. "Hey," she says, "are you at Ophelia's house?"

"One second."

She pictures Gary standing on the planked porch at Ophelia's back door. The porch is at once rickety and quaint, freshly painted each spring at Ophelia's insistence, a concrete planter in one corner, a rusting charcoal grill in another. She hears a series of short, sharp noises, apparently Gary rapping his knuckles on the door.

"Ophelia?" he says.

"She's not there?" Mikey says. He must not have the phone at his ear. *Come on, Pheels,* she thinks. *Your niece is here.*

"Ophelia," he says again.

And I'm here, dammit.

He gets back on with Mikey. "I don't know what to think," he says. "I checked with her business partner, by the way. He saw her yesterday afternoon at the boutique, said she seemed fine, was excited about you guys coming to town. He wasn't expecting her today."

· "Good, I guess," Mikey says.

She can hear Gary moving around, imagines him leaning down to peer into the kitchen window facing the porch. "I really don't want to wake the people upstairs," he says. "They might still be asleep."

"What about her car?" Mikey says. She decides not to go inside the cottage, where Bridget could hear. "Is the car there?"

"What is it with your sister, Mikey?" She hears the crunch of him walking across gravel. "Why does she do this?"

"Do what?"

"You know, just—shit. It's locked."

"The garage?"

"Who locks their garage in Bleak Harbor?"

"You don't think somebody stole it?" Mikey says.

"Two things: this is not Detroit, and nobody steals Volvos. Hang on, might be able to see in over here."

Bridget appears in the cottage screen door. "You know I have to eat soon," she says. "Who are you talking to?"

"Drink your tea. We're leaving in a minute."

"Were you spying on me?"

Mikey ignores Bridget's question, takes a few steps toward the water. A gull hunting breakfast skims past just above the surface of the bay.

"Where are you looking?" she asks Gary.

"Side of the garage has winter shutters, but one's splintered. Looking—ah, there it is. The Volvo's here."

"So," Mikey says, "her car's there but . . . dammit, Ophelia. Is the house locked too?"

"Don't know." Gary's crossing gravel again. "I didn't actually check. I walked in once through an unlocked door, and Ophelia about took my head off. Privacy violation. You know."

"You have my permission," Mikey says.

"She might be in there."

"I'll take the hit."

"If you say so. Going around to the front."

Mikey waits, watching a pair of gulls fly past toward Lake Michigan.

"Well, heck," Gary says, "the garage is locked, but the front door is not. Should I go in?"

Sometimes Gary is just too damn nice. "Just go in."

"Mom. Are we going?"

Mikey spins to face Bridget, who's standing outside wearing her Pride jacket and wool cap. Mikey wants to hug her.

"One minute, sweetie."

"That's what you said before. I have to eat, Mom."

"There's a note here," Gary says.

"You'll have to wait, Bridge."

"Why were you spying on me?"

Mikey shakes her head, holds up a hand for quiet. Bridget goes back inside, the door slapping behind her.

"What note?" Mikey asks.

"It might be Ophelia's handwriting, so to speak."

Mikey's sister has been legally blind since she was sixteen, the victim of a degenerative ocular disease. Ophelia has never been totally accepting of her condition. That's why she tries to write even though she can't see what she's writing, why she has a car she can't drive.

"Is it on the door?" Mikey says.

"The kitchen table. On a sheet of paper that looks like it was torn out of one of those fancy writing books."

Maybe one of Ophelia's journals. She uses them to sketch rough designs of her sculptures. Her drawings aren't perfect, but she's good at making them come to life as giant roadside statues.

"What does it say?"

"It's a little hard to read. Kinda looks like one of those things you have to copy to get into certain websites."

"A captcha."

"Yeah. I think it says, 'Can't believe' . . . then I'm not sure what it says . . . 'Ends'? 'Ending'? I think?"

"I'll be able to read it. And she's not there?"

"It's all quiet, but I'll look around."

None of this is good. Ophelia goes dark from time to time—that's who she is—but Mikey has trouble believing she'd do it to her niece. She pictures Ophelia lying hurt or ill somewhere Gary hasn't looked yet.

"Just wait," she tells him. "I'll be there in five minutes." She ends the call and goes back inside the cottage. "OK, Bridge, get your gear. Let's go."

6

Twelve years earlier

The three caskets were closed, of course. The dead—Edward Rathman, wife Heather, and daughter Kara—had been shredded by shotgun blasts at close range, then left to burn in the fire that had reduced most of their Northern Michigan cottage to ash and stone rubble in barely an hour.

Jubilee stood unmoving by her younger sister's coffin, her two closest friends, Sam and Tessa, at her elbows. Sam was stoic, a hand light on Jubilee's back, and Tessa was sobbing intermittently into a wad of tissue. Jubilee was so numb she might as well have been encased in ice. She had yet to cry for the loss of most of her family.

Father Eustace had spoken briefly to the mourners crowded into the funeral parlor about healing and forgiveness. Jubilee thought he'd intended those words in particular for her—she had rebuffed his pleas for a Catholic burial mass—but they'd floated past her like soap bubbles, empty and weightless. The people who had brought about this terrible day had rejected healing and forgiveness. Those notions were as alien to them as mercy to a scorpion.

Jubilee had taken special care in choosing Kara's casket, making sure the hardware was in silver, which her sister preferred to gold. The funeral director, canting his sweat-beaded head to one side, had told her it was her decision, of course, but having one casket in silver and two in gold could bring about a "distracting clash" for mourners.

"I see," Jubilee had told him. "I haven't checked the price of gold lately. Is it higher than silver?"

The funeral director had righted his head then and leaned back ever so slightly from Jubilee. "One silver and two gold, then," he'd said. "Of course. And again, we are so sorry for your loss."

There was plenty of money for the arrangements. Jubilee's father, Edward Rathman, had been a fastidiously careful man, the kind who'd still balanced his checkbook with a highlighter, a red pen, and a five-dollar calculator. He had presciently secured more than a dozen life insurance policies over the years and stowed ample savings in bank accounts spread from the US to Switzerland to the Cayman Islands. The FBI eventually would freeze any accounts it could while the investigation into the Rathman murders proceeded. And Jubilee would learn some wrenching lessons about her father's business and the threadbare line between honor and betrayal.

Father Eustace caught Jubilee's eye from across the room, gave her a barely discernible nod. She looked away. He stepped out in front of the trio of caskets among the clusters of red, white, and yellow roses. Clasping his hands together at his chest, he made a perfunctory sign of the cross before asking for quiet.

Jubilee noticed Phillie standing at the back of the room. Phillie was one of her father's oldest friends and general counsel for KopyKwik, the small chain of copy shops her father had owned. He had finally rescued her from the state police post the morning of the murders and had stayed close since, advising her on what to say or not, what to sign or not. Phillie caught her gaze now and closed his eyes once, a blink he intended as a comforting nod.

Jubilee tried to give him a smile, probably fell short.

"Let us pray," the priest said. Jubilee stared at the floor, her head hollowed of words, as the priest recited an Our Father, Hail Mary, and Glory Be. She heard Tessa's sniffling, Sam's mouthing of the verses. She felt her body wanting to float up and above the room, through the ceiling, into the sky, the stratosphere, the deep inviting blackness beyond. But Jubilee refused to go, even in her mind.

Unbidden, she imagined the odor of formaldehyde. She made herself recall the morgue, Sunday afternoon, how she should have turned her cell phone off. It had buzzed with texts and emails and alerts as the assistant coroner had slid the drawers out one by one, drawn the sheets back a few inches. Phillie had stood behind her, one hand on her shoulder, urging her with whispers to not punish herself so, whispers Jubilee had not heeded. "Pull it back a little more, please," she'd said with each body, letting the images sear themselves onto the surface of her brain.

Then there was Joshua.

———

The Rathman vacation cottage had only two bedrooms. The three children crowded into the one with a trundle bed against one wall and a single on the other, barely two feet between them.

Jubilee's seven-year-old brother recoiled at sleeping alongside his pubescent sisters. This was a savage delight to Jubilee and Kara, who flaunted their unstrapped bras and slid-down panties while Joshua jammed his head beneath pillows and yelled, "You're so ugly, stop."

Their father hired a contractor from Alba to expand a pantry off the kitchen into an even smaller bedroom, adding a narrow bathroom with a sink, a toilet, a door with a bolt, and a window facing a stand of evergreens fringing a frog pond. "Why is he so special?" Jubilee asked her father one day over the scream of the contractor's table saw. Edward Rathman pretended at first that he hadn't heard. When Jubilee asked again, he responded with one of his patented glares, this one saying, *You asked for it.*

She glared back, thinking, *No, Dad, Joshua asked for it.* It must have worked because he said, "Don't you dare, little girl."

She and Kara left Joshua alone the first weekend he slept there. "Let him get comfortable first," Jubilee told her younger sister. "Then we'll scare the shit out of him."

Their next weekend at the cottage, the girls sneaked outside after making sure their parents and Joshua had fallen asleep. They slid around the side of the house along the river, moving slowly through the dark, feeling their way between the birch and pine to the edge of a trapezoid of dispersed light thrown by a security lamp on the cottage roof.

In their hands they each clutched two eggs. Jubilee also had a canister of coffee grounds she'd collected without her mother noticing. She made Kara lug a cinder block from the garage.

They stopped at Joshua's window. Kara dropped the cinder block, jumping back before it landed on her bare foot. "Quiet, idiot," Jubilee hissed. "You want to wake him up before we do it?"

"It's heavy," Kara whispered. "You carry it."

"Shut up. Prop it up against the wall." Jubilee handed Kara the canister. "Hold this and give me those eggs."

"Here."

"I said shut up, OK?"

Kara shrank back a step while Jubilee climbed onto the cinder block, steadying herself with a hand against the cottage wall. The shade on Joshua's bedroom window was still down from when Jubilee had tugged it there that afternoon. She had also knotted the drawstring just enough to make it difficult for Joshua to undo so she and Kara would have time to make their escape.

Bracing her knees against the wall, Jubilee took an egg in one hand and tapped it lightly against the window glass. She checked it, saw the hairline crack, then pulled her hand back and flattened the egg on the glass in a splat of yellowish goo. She took a second egg, cracked it lightly, then crushed it on the glass six inches to the right of the first egg, at exactly the same level. Then she took the last two eggs and smashed

41

them together between and six inches below the first two. With her two forefingers she smeared the yolks and whites together in a semicircle pointing downward.

Two eyes and a frown.

Jubilee turned to Kara. "The coffee."

Kara handed up the canister of grounds. Jubilee scooped out a handful and squeezed them into a wad in her palm. By now, Joshua was probably awake, wondering at the sounds outside his window, feeling the stirrings of fright in his belly. She pasted the wad of grounds into the middle of the first egg splat, then made another wad and stuck that into the middle of the second.

The shade inside the glass fluttered. Joshua was up, all right. Jubilee jumped off the cinder block, adrenaline giggles rising in her throat, and grabbed Kara's arm. "Over here. We have to watch."

Crouching, the sisters scrambled into the darkness. "Ouch ouch ouch," Kara said as she stepped barefoot across a scatter of acorns, Jubilee telling her to shut up while trying not to laugh out loud.

They hid in a cluster of pines as the window shade shook this way and that before it finally began to jerk upward. By now the eggs and grounds were running down the glass like teary mascara, but Jubilee thought the menacing face she had tried to draw was still visible enough to give her brother an extra scare.

The shade snapped up. Joshua's face, round and pale as the moon, flashed in the wash of light, his eyes and mouth agape, his hands plastered against the glass. His sisters couldn't hear him, but Jubilee imagined him yelping with fright like he did the time she'd tossed a wriggling live crawfish at him in the rowboat. Both Jubilee and Kara were laughing now, clapping hands over their mouths to keep from being heard.

Kara gave them away. She used her cell phone to take a photo, forgetting to disable the flash. Joshua, blinking, stopped trying to jimmy the window and squinted through the dark. He pointed and shouted something, then disappeared, no doubt gone to tattle.

"Way to go, squirt," Jubilee said.

"What do we do?" Kara said, not laughing anymore.

Jubilee shrugged. "Nothing to do. Enjoy it while it lasts."

"Mom's gonna be mad. We're gonna get grounded."

"Whatever."

Naturally, Edward and Heather Rathman went harder on their oldest. "Juju, you know you should know better," Jubilee's mother told her. They sentenced Jubilee to a weekend in, Kara a Saturday. Jubilee assured her sister that they were not done.

Their next time up north, they waited until Joshua was asleep. Jubilee knew he'd be restless with his unrepentant sisters in the house, but she had made sure to guzzle two Red Bulls around nine o'clock so she could outwait him. It was after one a.m. when she roused Kara—"Up, Kara-Bear. Don't forget the towel"—and they slipped outside the room. In the hallway by the kitchen, Jubilee told her sister, "Wait while I get the stuff."

She returned with a fat plastic cheese-puffs jar held to her chest. She nodded at Kara, and they slid through the kitchen to their brother's bedroom. They knelt at the door. The finger on Jubilee's lips was meant not for Kara but for what was in the cheese-puffs jar with the holes poked into the lid. She unscrewed the lid, leaned the jar down toward the crack beneath the door, and started shoveling the insects out. "Shush, little babies," she said under her breath. She looked at Kara squatting beside her. She was banging her knuckles together, excited now as the 113 crickets they'd caught that afternoon scuttled into Joshua's room.

"Towel," Jubilee said.

Kara snugged the towel against the door crack so no crickets could escape. The chirping hadn't yet reached a pitch as they scrambled back to their room. They left their door open until they heard Joshua scream.

That time it cost Jubilee a month of weekends, her sister a pair. Jubilee had to skip her best friend's sixteenth birthday party downstate to go up north. The day of the party, she was eating breakfast when Joshua said, between spoonfuls of Honey Nut Cheerios, "I'm sorry you have to miss Cali Jo's birthday."

Jubilee looked at him. He wasn't being a smart-ass. He really was sorry. "You're a little shit," she said. "But it's OK."

"I liked the eggs thing," he said. "It was scary, but it was"—he reached for a word he might not have used before—"creative."

He was wearing a Red Wings T-shirt and had just enough freckles on his cheeks that Jubilee knew girls were going to like him.

"Big word there, little guy," she said.

"How did you get all those crickets?"

"I broke a nail, that's how. Actually, two nails."

"You didn't use duct tape?"

Jubilee raised an eyebrow. "Duct tape?"

"You can use duct tape to get them. It's easy. Newspapers work too. My friend Dickie showed me."

Jubilee recalled the feel of the cold mud through the knees of her jeans as she and Kara had dug for crickets in the woods near the swamp.

"Whatever. It kinda sucked."

"Thank you for going to so much trouble for me. Isn't that what big sisters are for?"

Jubilee realized at that moment that her brother might actually be OK someday. "Shut up and eat," she said.

———

She could only imagine what had happened in his bedroom up north on the night of the murders, the inscrutable blasts from elsewhere in the house, the reek of kerosene as it spread across Joshua's floor before flashing into raw flame. The first responders had found him unconscious, near death, in the muck of the frog pond's shore, legs splayed into the water, T-shirt shorn off in places, seared into his skin in others, weeds and lily pads striping his seven-year-old back.

He was doomed to survive.

———

"That fat guy is FBI," Sam whispered into Jubilee's ear.

The man with the unruly shirttails and gray suit stood against the wall across the funeral parlor. Sam was obsessed with the articles about the murders in the *Detroit Times* and the *Free Press* and the local crime blogs. "There are more frigging reporters and cops here than people who give a shit," he said.

"You're a jerk, Sam," Tessa said.

"He's fine," Jubilee said. "It doesn't matter."

Jubilee had noticed the federal agent. Every now and then he would lean his shiny comb-over head down and say something, as if to himself, though he must have had a microphone hidden somewhere. Not exactly undercover. Jubilee had caught him looking at her earlier. She'd sought and held his gaze until he'd looked away, pretending to reach for something inside his jacket.

Pussy, she had thought. *What do you want from me?*

Father Eustace finally finished his benediction and nodded toward Jubilee. The funeral directors, three skeletal white guys who looked as if they had been cloned at twenty-year intervals—father, son, grandson—stepped behind each of the caskets.

Jubilee thought of Joshua then, wondering if there would have been a fourth white guy to stand behind her brother's casket if he hadn't been—how had her aunt Loretta put it?—blessedly spared by God's loving hand.

"I'm sorry, Auntie L," Jubilee had replied, "but Dad and Mom and Kara were the ones who were spared."

The caskets began to roll down the aisle between the rows of chairs. Jubilee felt one of the skeletons beckoning her. She started to move toward him, glancing sideways at Tessa, her eyes saying, *What do you have?* Meaning alcohol.

Tessa mouthed the words, *In the car.*

Jubilee slid behind the last casket, followed by her two friends. An electric organ began to drone in the background. Jubilee had told Aunt Loretta she preferred no music, but there it was anyway. "For the other people who came to support you," her aunt would later insist, as if those people would have said, if asked, "Yes, please play something suicidal on a Hammond organ."

Jubilee dropped her eyes and focused on a fingerprint marring the silver handle of Kara's casket. She didn't care about the fingerprint; she just focused on it so she wouldn't see the pitying looks of her uncles and aunts and cousins and neighbors, or hear the whispers of her classmates gathered in the back of the room, the sympathy laced with vile gossip, as if this were not a triple funeral but a pep rally for the blessedly spared, *hang in there* and *have faith* and *your brother needs you* and the other drivel people said when they were actually wondering whether a hot lunch might be served.

She stepped out into the chilly sunlight. The caskets ahead of her moved through a bristle of people lining both sides of the concrete walk. They were leaning in, pointing at Jubilee with pens and notebooks, boom mikes and tape recorders. Cameras whirred and clicked as the reporters shouted questions Jubilee had no interest in answering. She tried to block them out, but snippets made their way to her ears: . . . *you think that* Times *coverage led to the . . . Jubilee, do you know if your father's shops were laundering money for . . . what about the Petruglias and their connections to your father's business?*

She noticed the comb-over agent again. He was standing alongside the walk in a topcoat that looked older than Jubilee, his arms out from his sides as if to warn the reporters back from the sidewalk. As she caught his eye, she spied a young reporter ducking under his left arm to step onto the walk in front of Kara's casket. She was wearing a green wool winter cap stitched on one side with a white Michigan State Spartans logo. She held a pen in one hand and a recorder taped to a notebook in the other, but she kept both at her sides as she spoke.

"Miss Rathman," she said. "I'm sorry."

For a second, it stopped Jubilee. Because, although so many people had told her they were sorry, it sounded as if this woman, who was older but not that much older than Jubilee, actually meant it, actually felt some inexplicable remorse, actually wasn't just using *sorry* as a polite opener to ask a question, as if she actually was standing inside Jubilee's horror, not outside looking in.

"I see," Jubilee said.

"Could I ask you—?"

"Stand back, miss."

Comb-over swept the woman out of the way before Jubilee could hear the rest of what she was saying. Jubilee glanced back once before she ducked into the limo behind Tessa. She didn't see the woman in the cap again, but she told herself as Tessa dug into her handbag for the flask that she would not forget her.

7

Mikey pulls to the curb in front of Bella's in downtown Bleak Harbor, looking past Bridget through the café's picture windows. She doesn't see Ophelia at any of the half dozen tables.

Mikey hands Bridget a credit card. "Take this, get us a table, order whatever you want. I'll go get Aunt Ophelia."

Bridget takes the card and looks Mikey up and down, considering. She's not as curious as she is hungry. "OK."

Mikey finds Gary Langreth standing in Ophelia's kitchen. He's wearing jeans and a black down vest jacket over a gray T-shirt bearing a Bleak County Prosecutor logo. She spent a bit of time with him and Ophelia on a previous weekend visit. Then his shirt was streaked with white plaster of paris dust and gooey smears of paint after helping Ophelia build a miniature version of one of her creations. He didn't seem to mind, which Mikey liked. Ophelia has had plenty of other boyfriends Mikey didn't like much. She's impressed that Gary has lasted five months with her.

"Mikey," he says, leaning into her with a hug. "Good to see you."

"You too. She's not here?"

"Not that I can see," he says. "Here." He hands her a sheet of paper. "I don't get it. Maybe you will."

"You looked in the bedroom?"

"I looked everywhere. Sorry."

"Let me look at this."

The handwriting does resemble a captcha, something Ophelia herself has never seen. Wavy lettering, just legible enough, a child's scrawl.

"Is it Ophelia's?" Gary says.

Mikey turns the page sideways and back again. "It's been a while since she handwrote me something," she says. She thinks she can make it out but doesn't much like what she thinks it says. "It looks like she could have written it," Mikey says. "'Can't believe' . . . looks like 'ending.' What do you think?"

"I'll go with that," Gary says.

"Come on, Ophelia. Not today. Not on your birthday, not on Zeke's birthday. Where the hell are you?"

Gary starts to answer, but Mikey doesn't hear because she's firing out of the kitchen into the front room, as if she'll find Ophelia sitting there with a cup of tea on the orange corduroy sofa. But all she sees is the hideous couch and a phony fireplace and a coffee table that looks like someone in baseball spikes danced on it.

"Shit," Mikey says. She turns and pushes past Gary, back toward the kitchen. She takes her phone out, sees she had the sound off, switches it back on. Still no calls, no audio texts from Ophelia. A text from Bridget: where r u?? She goes out on the back porch to get some oxygen, the air like a damp washcloth on her face. *Can't believe it's ending?* she thinks. *What is she talking about?*

"Mikey," Gary says. "I found this, too, on the seat of the chair near where the note was."

He hands her a plastic baggie that contains a beige rectangular sliver of plastic. It's blank on one side. Mikey turns it over, sees a faded orange logo, *8*, on the back. Super 8.

"Why would Ophelia have a motel key?" she says. "She doesn't like to sleep anywhere but her own bed. And why is it in a baggie?"

"I put it there in case, you know, the police. No idea on the motel key. We never stayed in a motel."

"Do you think it matters?" she says.

"No idea. Maybe."

"Are there any Super 8s near here?"

Gary thinks for a moment. "I know there's one in Coloma. There was a meth bust there last year. Bunch of boneheads up from Hammond."

Mikey sets the key on the table. "Jesus, Pheels," she says. "The bedroom."

Mikey hasn't been in Ophelia's room more than once or twice. It looks as she thinks she remembers it. The bed is made, three pillows fluffed against the headboard, a wool throw their mother made, gray striped with pink, stretched across the bedspread. Ophelia's fuzzy blue slippers are on the floor beneath a five-drawer bureau.

On the nightstand, a frayed shoelace marks Ophelia's place in *All the Light We Cannot See*, in braille. Mikey allows herself a small smile. Next to the novel rests a Bible in braille. Ophelia doesn't believe in God or anything like it, but she loves many of the Old Testament stories, especially the book of Tobit, about the pious old guy who turns blind after sparrows crap in his eyes but later has his sight restored with a smear of fish gall. Ophelia likes to paraphrase his first words in the tale: "I, Ophelia, have walked all the days of my life on paths of fidelity and righteousness—except that time I got shit-faced on Fireball with Kenny and let him bang me in his sister's bed . . ."

The white cane, striped with bright-red electrical tape, leans in a corner next to the bureau beside the bed. Ophelia has never used the cane, except at costume parties. Two framed photographs stand on the bureau. One is of their parents, Bob and Eleanor Wright; the other is of Mikey and Ophelia and Zeke, kids on a beach, skinny and tan. Ophelia is asleep on the sand while Zeke mugs, about to pour a plastic bucket of water over her head. Mikey looks on in a mixture of hilarity and horror, hands clapped to her mouth lest she wake her unsuspecting sister.

Mikey has always loved—or maybe *admired* is the better word, although Ophelia would disapprove—how her sister keeps photographs on her walls, on fridge magnets, on shelves, on her bureau, even though she cannot see them. As if the two-dimensional images come alive in some third dimension that exists in Ophelia's head or heart.

The far wall in her bedroom is covered with the colored-pencil sketches of what eventually become Ophelia's roadside sculptures. Ophelia uses a penknife to notch the pencils along their barrels to identify each as ochre or scarlet or royal blue. She uses these varied colors she cannot see for the benefit of the volunteers and friends who help her erect the sculptures.

The drawings are fixed to the wall with pushpins. Mikey has warned Ophelia that if she ever wants to leave this place without forfeiting her security deposit, she will have to spackle all those pinholes. Ophelia invariably puts a finger to one of the punctures in the plaster and tells her sister it doesn't matter: nobody can see those holes anyway. "I can't even see them," Ophelia said once, and they both laughed.

"You've seen these before, I assume," Gary says.

"Yeah," Mikey says. "She sketches better than she writes."

"I guess so."

"There seem to be more up than before."

"Sometimes she takes some down and replaces them," Gary says. "Depends on her mood." He steps to a wall and gestures toward a sketch of some type of fish that appears to be leaping out of water. "This is one of the ones that was vandalized."

"Vandalized? What are you talking about?"

A shadow of regretful surprise crosses Gary's face. "She didn't tell you?"

Of course not, Mikey thinks. As close as they are, Ophelia insists that they remain so by being careful about what they tell each other, what might make one or the other worry without need, what might make one feel the urge to *do something* that needn't be done.

She shakes her head, says, "*One* of the ones that was vandalized?"

"Some smart-asses have been defacing her sculptures."

"Like how?"

Langreth zips his vest down, then up again. "It's probably just kids," he finally says. "The police are looking into it."

"How were they vandalized, Gary? And there was more than one?"

"Yes, more than one." He scans the wall. "That one too," he says, pointing at a tern standing on one leg in a pond. "And this," he says, brushing his hand across a rendering of the skateboarding boy sculpture that's standing out by the curb.

Zeke, Mikey thinks, and again her throat constricts, this time squeezed with anger. "They messed up the one in the front yard? I didn't see anything that—"

"No. The bigger version out on Blue Star."

"How exactly?"

As Gary tells her, Mikey looks past him to the sketches, her gaze crisscrossing the wall. The sheets on which Ophelia drew are everything from the pages of her journals to yellow legal pad tear outs to art-shop paper to the grease-stained backs of restaurant menus.

"Besides the paint, they cut one of the legs off the boy."

"A leg? What for?"

"A souvenir? For the hell of it is all I can figure," Gary says. "It didn't knock the sculpture down because it's not really held up by the legs; they're held up by rebar stanchions."

"One leg?"

"Yep."

"Nice. No legs on the fish, I guess, but still they blacked out the face?"

"That was the first one vandalized. It sits off the highway a bit and has more cover than some of the others. And there's that dirt road that runs into the picnic area along the beach, so they could've parked without being seen as easily."

Mikey imagines the fish—a smallmouth bass, she believes, from their childhood fishing excursions with their father—towering over the west side of Blue Star Highway, two picnic tables and a cast-iron charcoal grill standing behind it.

"Little bastards," she says. "Why the faces?"

"All I can figure is that's the paint they happened to have, so they put it where it would be most noticeable. Funny thing is, Ophelia kinda liked the black face on the fish."

"It's not some racial thing, is it?"

"The last I looked, Ophelia was white."

"Well, she is blind; maybe that's what the black is about. So when did all of this stuff happen? And why didn't you, or somebody, tell me?"

"I assumed Ophelia would have said something."

"She didn't. When was this happening?"

"Just the last few weeks. Sorry."

Mikey turns away. "Hey," Gary says. She feels his hand on her shoulder. "Everything's going to be OK." She turns to face him. He's holding up the Super 8 key. "Tell you what: I'm going to give this motel key to the police. The note too. They might find something."

He's trying to help. Instead he's scaring her. "Let's just"—she can feel herself stammering, the catch of her tongue—"let's wait awhile here."

"Whatever you want. She's your sister."

"I mean, she's going to just show up." Mikey wants to believe it.

"Right," Gary says. He doesn't sound like he believes it either. "But it wouldn't hurt to let the police know. Better safe than sorry, right?"

The police. Evidence in baggies. This can't be happening. Mikey and Ophelia and Gary are supposed to be sitting at Bella's with Bridget, talking about the hockey tournament and Ophelia's birthday. Now they're going to the police?

She feels the familiar tightening in her throat, as if she tried to swallow a stone the size of her fist. For an instant she returns to that day on the dune, the cops scrambling around, the ambulance, the TV lights grotesque in the July sun.

"Do what you think is right," she says.

"Look, Mikey," Gary says. "There are no obvious signs that any-thing"—he hesitates, the cop turned prosecutor choosing his words carefully—"untoward happened here."

"No obvious signs? Wait."

She goes to the bedroom closet. One of the twin doors is open. A handful of dresses hangs inside. Two pairs of sneakers and a few dressier shoes lie in a jumble on the floor alongside two rolled-up yoga mats. Mikey leans into the closet, shoves the dresses aside, looks both ways.

"Her bag's not here," she says.

Gary comes up behind her. "Which?"

"The only one she ever uses, a big floppy over-the-shoulder thing she got in Windsor. She doesn't leave Bleak Harbor without that."

"Well then, that's good, right? It means she left on her own."

"But for where? With who? Why would she leave with her niece coming to town?" The note from the table flashes again in Mikey's head, the crooked writing, the stilted, loaded words: *Can't believe . . . ending.*

She pushes the thought away.

"I don't know, Mikey. We don't know. But look, it's going to be OK. She's probably just fooling with us. I'll bet she's waiting for us at Bella's. With that bag."

No, Mikey thinks. Bridget would have let her know by now. Or it's possible that Ophelia told Bridget, *No, don't tell your mom; we'll surprise her.* Maybe it's all a big joke. Mikey imagines Ophelia sitting at a table with Bridget, showing Mikey a middle finger as she walks into Bella's. She looks around the room again, decides she's had enough for now.

"Bridge must be getting antsy," she says. "Let's go."

"I'll meet you later. Gotta make a stop first."

8

"Katya."

Gary Langreth waits in the doorway to the Bleak Harbor police chief's office. He knows not to simply walk in on Malone. She's approachable. On her terms.

She's standing at the window behind her desk, her back to Langreth. The sill is filled with framed photographs of a pretty young girl, Malone's late daughter.

"We haven't found your sculpture vandal yet," Malone says, still staring out the window. "Is there something else?"

"There might be. Do you mind turning around?"

She lifts a picture from the sill. It shows the girl in a frilly white dress with an emerald ribbon entwined in her blonde hair. Malone sets it back down, then turns to face Langreth. The strands of premature gray pulled back behind her ears do nothing to diminish her natural beauty.

"It's nuts up at the rink," she says.

"Why were you there?"

"Had to do this ceremonial first-puck thing," she says. "Barely dawn, and the stands are packed with people from all over the place. How can I help you, Mr. Investigator?"

Malone loves to remind Langreth of his made-up role as an "investigator" for the county prosecutor. He wants to think she does it because she wishes he worked for her.

"Ophelia Wright," he says. "She's missing."

"She didn't leave you a note on the pillow?"

Langreth isn't surprised that Malone knows he's been dating Ophelia, nor that she'd make a crack about it.

"Nope," he says. "Did you?"

Malone shakes her head, smiling. Eight or nine months ago, they had that one night together—actually, closer to morning. He'd told Malone before that about his rule that he didn't sleep with cops. But then, he'd made that rule when he was a cop himself, and he wasn't a cop anymore, at least not officially.

"All right, enough," Malone says. "What's going on?"

He tells her what he knows, how it wouldn't be like Ophelia to up and leave with her sister and niece arriving. Malone listens, then says, "You think this has something to do with the sculptures?"

"Possibly." His phone plays two electronic bars of "I Fought the Law." He looks down at the text alert: not Ophelia but Mikey. "Somebody's been messing with her."

"How long has she been gone? Assuming she's really gone."

"I last spoke with her around seven last night. I didn't hear anything that made me think she was going somewhere or she was in any sort of trouble. In fact, now that I think of it"—he looks past Malone at the windowsill, recalling—"she said she'd gotten some good news."

"From?"

"I don't know. She went right from that to how she wanted to get back to her book, and then she was off the phone. Your guys have nothing on the sculptures?" Langreth says. "No leads?"

"Nothing concrete."

He waits a beat, then asks, "What about the mayor?"

"What about him?"

"He can be a vindictive jerk, as you probably know. Did you check him out?"

"That your temper I'm seeing, Gary?"

"Come on, Chief."

When he was still a cop, he beat a guy damn near to death one night—which was bad, but maybe not as bad as him not being able to remember one second of it later. Not to mention that the guy in question, who was not even close to a good guy, was nevertheless the wrong guy to nearly beat to death.

Which is why Langreth is in Bleak Harbor, working on bumbled break-ins and bar fights for the prosecutor, instead of home in Detroit being a real cop.

"I know what you're thinking, Gary," Malone says. "I'm aware that Mayor Fisher used to date that woman and maybe he wasn't happy about the breakup. Don't go anywhere near him yourself, understood?"

"I wasn't thinking about it."

"You're not a cop anymore."

"Thanks for reminding me. You got some kind of thing for Fisher or what?"

Malone gives him a look that tells him Malone is not Fisher's biggest fan. "I work for him," she says. "He tells me whether I can get the oil changed in the squad cars or not. What was this Ophelia doing with him anyway?"

Langreth has wondered the same. He shrugs and says, "She has a mind of her own." He fishes in his jacket pocket, feeling the two baggies, one with the note Ophelia left, the other holding the Super 8 key. He takes out the one containing the note, leaves the other in his pocket. "We found this on the kitchen table at Ophelia's place," he says.

He hands the baggie to Malone. She spreads it on her desk blotter and reads it through the clear plastic. "Do we know this is the woman's handwriting?"

"You know she's blind, right?"

"I've heard. How do we know she wrote this?"

"Mikey, her sister, thinks she probably did."

"*Thinks* she *probably* did," Malone says, shaking her head. "And it says, 'Can't believe' . . . what is that? 'Ending'? Is this—sorry."

Malone doesn't want to say *suicide note* because Ophelia is Langreth's girlfriend, but she might as well have.

"I don't think so," he says. "I doubt it means anything, but maybe you can get a print from it?"

"We can try. That all? I gotta get to Purgatory Bay."

"What's going on?"

"The woman who lives by herself there is having a press conference for a teenage-suicide group she started. I'm the official prop."

"Do you get a per diem?"

"She didn't mention that."

"She doesn't get out much, does she?"

"Nope. But she reached out to me, and it's a good cause."

"Yep. OK, I gotta get somewhere too."

"Not Fisher's, got it?"

Langreth suppresses a grin. "Got it."

Walking to his car, he reaches into his pocket and fingers an edge of the Super 8 key inside the baggie. He's decided not to give it to Malone just yet. Otherwise, he won't be able to go show it to her boss.

9

9:39 a.m.

Vance Robillard rolls over, feels the asphalt dryness in his throat, the familiar ache behind his left eye, like someone is trying to yank it through the back of his head with a claw hammer.

The phone on the floor is ringing. Robillard edges toward that side of the bed, realizes he's still wearing his pants from last night.

"I'll be fucked," he says.

He stares over the edge of the bed at the phone, a black, clunky relic that he has carried with him for more than thirty years as he moved from Downriver to Palmer Park, before the first divorce, to Corktown to Delray, before the second one, and finally to his current residence, a brick bungalow on Hubbell Avenue, northwest Detroit.

He takes pride in having one of the last landline phones in the city. He's an old-school kind of guy. And you can actually hear people on the other end.

He does wish the aged phone, like the one on his newsroom desk, could tell him who's calling so early—9:40, early for Robillard anyway—on a Friday morning. He has an arraignment to babysit in Dearborn, but that's not till two, so he's worried the city desk is calling to send him somewhere else first.

The answering machine finally clicks on. "Hey, Robo," the woman's voice croaks. Robillard hears the clacking of keyboards, the background score to his thirty-nine years at the *Detroit Times*, and pictures the editor sitting on her double-wide ass at the city desk, headphones glued to her head. "Listen," Shannon Martelle says, "forget the arraignment. Something crazy's going on in Bloomfield Hills. Some idiot flew a drone into a funeral procession, almost killed a kid. Thing is, it's the Petruglias. Guaranteed something effed up's going on. Ourlian's on his way, but well, you know, he might need adult supervision. Call me. You'll love this."

The machine clicks. The clacking stops.

Robillard swings his legs over the edge of the bed, slowly sits up, his knees stiff with arthritis, undoes his belt, and dips a hand into his boxers to scratch his graying nuts.

Don't tell me what I love, he thinks. *I know what I fucking love.* Which isn't much besides Tanqueray and the onion rings at Vivio's. Even the Tigers have been shifted to Robillard's shit list—actually, more like a book than a list—after they let Scherzer and Verlander and Martinez go.

"No calls at home before noon, God dammit," he scolds the machine. He starts to lean over to give the thing a little whack, but a twinge in his lower back pulls him up short. "God dammit."

He's annoyed at Martelle, no news there. But he also knows his irritation has less to do with the wake-up call than her knowing precisely how to push his buttons.

The Petruglias.

The blessed, brilliant, perverse, endlessly evil, endlessly inventive, and amoral Petruglias. Detroit's premier mob family, the one that keeps all the other families in line, the one that decided when fentanyl trumped meth and then when hacking Bitcoin lockers was better than fentanyl, the one that emerged as a Mafia force the year Robillard was born, 1957, and has consumed virtually all of his newspaper career, or at least the best parts of it.

He once calculated that stories involving the Petruglias make up as much as 40 percent of the thousands he's written for the *Times*. That probably jumps to 50 percent if you count the stories he chased and wrote that never saw print because of the pussies on the desk or the lawyers shitting their pants. But for sheer ball-busting, colleagues-in-awe, cute-interns-wanting-to-screw-him, tell-me-how-the-hell-you-got-that-story quality, the Petruglia stories might as well be the only ones he's ever written.

Especially the killer series he did some years back with the help of that youngish reporter chick with the boy's name.

If someone were to press him when he was righteously oiled, Robillard might actually admit that he can, in a way, count the Petruglias on the short list of things he loves. Even though he hates them. Or thinks he hates them. Or hated them once, long ago, before they became the thing he thought about most of his waking hours. Sometimes he considers what the Petruglias think of him. He wants to think that, at the very least, they respect him. Family members from the don himself, Vincent, down to an eleven-year-old kid named Donny have told him he's a piece of shit. Which is, to a crime reporter, a peculiar term of endearment, like a hug from the kids, if Robillard had any.

Still, after all the years and stories, he sometimes wonders if any of the Petruglias give him a first thought, let alone a second. After all the times he's exposed their soulless brutality, he has to wonder why none of them have ever made an attempt to get him out of the way for good.

Wouldn't that be the ultimate compliment? He likes to dream sometimes about how they might do it. A bullet or three to the head? A knife through the jugular? A wire digging into his neck?

He reaches to his nightstand for a Marlboro. The pack crumples in his hand. He notices the soggy butt of his last smoke in the melted ice at the bottom of his three a.m. glass of Tanqueray.

Against his knees' will, he raises himself off the bed and creaks his way over to his dresser. Stacks of old *Times* issues stand on each side of it. The top of the dresser is a litter of coins, an old rosary he can't throw away because his long-dead mother gave it to him, soiled boxers he has been meaning to take to the laundry. He opens the top drawer and rummages through the white socks and handkerchiefs, guessing he's out of cigarettes. He shuts the drawer and goes to the closet. Sometimes he tosses a couple of cartons on the top shelf. None there today.

But there are four fresh bottles of Tanqueray. Robillard takes one down, spins off the top, and lifts it to his mouth. He holds the gin in his mouth for a few seconds, swishing, and swallows. "Yessir," he says, then takes another gulp, caps the bottle, and sets it on his nightstand.

He closes his eyes and stands there, willing himself to recall when he last bought cigarettes. Slowly it comes to him. The party store on Livernois. He can't remember whether he went there before or after the drinking at Abick's, but he believes he bought a carton of Marlboros. It's in his car, in the driveway next to his house.

"Shit," he says.

Luckily, he already has pants on. He leaves the belt undone, snatches the Detroit against Everybody sweatshirt off his bedpost, pulls it on, descends the stairs barefoot to the ground floor.

He undoes four dead bolts and steps outside. The concrete is cold on the bottoms of his feet, the sky a leaden ceiling over the decades-old redbrick bungalows up and down Hubbell.

He sees an orange flyer stuck under the driver's side windshield wiper of his Crown Vic. *FEEL LUCKY*, shout the white block letters at the top of the paper. "Oh, I do, baby, every damn day," Robillard tells it. He glances at the street to see if flyers adorn other windshields. He doesn't see any. Maybe their owners have removed them.

Robillard leaves the flyer under the wiper and slides behind the steering wheel, shutting the door behind him. The stale reek of cigarettes would choke almost anyone else, but he breathes it in like the fragrance of a daffodil. He snaps the glove box open and pries out the mangled carton of Marlboros he jammed in there yesterday. Tearing off one end of the box, he dumps a cigarette pack onto the seat, unpeels the pack, slides out a smoke, pops it into his mouth.

A book of matches from Honest John's is lying on the floor mat between his feet. He reaches down, picks it up, sees it's empty. He should've grabbed matches from the kitchen. The dashboard lighter won't work unless the car is started, but his keys are back in the—no, wait, they're in the pocket of the pants he slept in.

"Yessir," he says, pulling the keys out.

It takes Robillard three tries to start the car, and then a sports jock's voice with a rasp of absolute certainty blares from the dashboard: ". . . how this management continues to tolerate a coach this uninspiring, this, frankly, disrespected by his own players, the guys who are supposed—"

Robillard pushes a radio button, then thumbs the lighter in. It's chilly in the car, so he cranks up the heat too.

Another voice, more measured, female, comes over the speakers: ". . . tragedy averted at the funeral of Regina Salve Corelli, sister of the late Detroit mob boss Vincent Petruglia."

The lighter pops out. Robillard lights his cigarette and takes a long suck while listening to the news report. "Police say a drone zoomed through the air aimed directly at Petruglia's teenage granddaughter as she emerged from the church on . . ."

Robillard switches it off. He trusts the newscaster, but he doesn't want to know too much, or it could distort his own reporting on the incident. He takes another hard drag, thinking, *Jesus, who's stupid enough to go after a Petruglia kid? In front of the whole damn family?*

He shakes his head, takes another drag, blows the smoke out in a cloud that billows against the inside of the windshield. "Good morning, sunshine," he says.

———

A woman walking a pit bull finds him an hour later. He's slumped against the driver's side window, unmoving, his left eye mashed shut, a tiny gash along the brow and a smear of blood on the glass, as if he might have been butting his head against the window. His right eye and his mouth are open wide. One of his hands is curled at his throat, the other limp on the inside door handle.

"Oh, dear Lord," the woman says, stumbling backward. Her dog edges away from the car, growling. The woman takes a cell phone from her coat pocket. The dog starts barking. "Jesus, Lord help us all."

10

10:55 a.m.

The reporters assemble in a ragged two-deep semicircle at the top of Jubilee's horseshoe drive, twenty feet from her front door.

Jubilee watches them in her kitchen on a flat-screen mounted on the wall. They seem to her either very young, in their twenties, or at least twenty years older. Naive hopefuls and stubborn holdouts, working for blogs and free websites, a campus newspaper, two local TV affiliates, two radio stations. She figures today is more likely to appeal to the Fox outlet than ABC, but she's hoping both pick it up. It is, after all, a good cause.

She had to take a pill last night. She doesn't like taking pills, but she needed to sleep, even if only for the two hours and twenty-nine minutes she usually does. Today is a big day. She might not sleep again at all until tomorrow or Sunday. Or maybe ever.

"Frances," Jubilee says. "Are we ready?"

"We are ready," comes the automated voice. Jubilee asked the anonymous programmer to supply a voice that most people would consider soothing, so Frances speaks in a soothing contralto that makes her seem less like an automaton, a bit more like a friend.

Jubilee can't remember when she last thought about a friend. Her best pals, Tessa and Sam, gave up years ago trying to get her to go out or just answer their calls and texts. After the funeral, Jubilee went into a sort of hiding from which she never emerged. After moving to

Purgatory Bay, she couldn't see what her friends could offer her. They were busy at college, playing beer pong and planning supposedly productive lives. While Jubilee was planning her mission.

"Good," Jubilee says. "Please let the reporters know the ground rules."

"I will do so."

Jubilee turns up the audio and zooms in on her visitors' faces. Police chief Katya Malone has come, at Jubilee's request, to represent Bleak Harbor, the closest town to the bay at four miles to the southwest. Jubilee thought it would give the event more legitimacy in the eyes of the reporters. Malone stands a few feet from the lectern in her royal-blue-and-navy uniform.

"My name is Frances," Jubilee hears. "I am Ms. Rathman's assistant."

The group as one looks for the source of the disembodied voice. "Ms. Rathman will be out momentarily," Frances says. "But first, a few ground rules. If you cannot abide by these rules, we will not be offended if you leave. We hope you will not be offended either."

Jubilee is aware that these reporters are hungry to know what lies within her house's three stories and how the tragic, tortured Jubilee Rathman survives alone in here. She knows they've come less for what she is about to tell them about the teenage-suicide-prevention program she leads than out of fascination—some might call it morbid curiosity; some might call it newspeople trying to sell their wares—with her and her reclusive existence in her walled-off mansion on privately owned Purgatory Bay. She's seen their eyes roaming over the parched-white concrete walls, the matte-black eaves and gutters, the tinted windows framed in black.

They cannot see the dozens of miniature video cameras and listening devices hidden in the walls and windows, through the gnarled forest surrounding the house, all along the twelve-foot-high, spike-topped walls that encase its yard, extending down to the bay. The more cynical among them probably suspect they're being watched, especially after they had to have their press credentials and thumbprints scanned to gain entry through the front gate.

In a moment they will see Jubilee in the flesh for the first time since—she tries to recall. Was it in Colorado? Or the airport upon her return to Michigan after the suicide? It doesn't matter.

Today is a big day.

Jubilee has been on television a few times before to promote the Joshua Project, albeit only remotely, from a makeshift studio inside her house. She has allowed only one journalist into the mansion, a just-out-of-college photographer from the *Kalamazoo Gazette*. Jubilee let her spend an hour shooting pictures and video of the kitchen, the sweeping balcony view of the lake, the rock climbing wall inside the gym. There was no interview to speak of, just Jubilee describing the rooms as blandly as she could and asking forgiveness for the absence of Joshua, who she said wasn't feeling well.

That was three years ago, before Joshua died in the Rockies and Caleb was born.

This morning marks the first time she will appear in person before such a media cluster since the days immediately after the murders at her family's cottage in Northern Michigan. She remembers how she blinked at the camera lights and shrank from the clamor of voices pressing upon her, the voices straining to sound sympathetic in their pathetic urgency. She remembers her dad's lawyer, Phillie, standing at her side, his hand on her back or her shoulder, moving along and away from the "barking hyenas," as he was inclined to call the journalist mobs.

She walks to the front door now, leaves it closed for the moment. She calls up the video stream she was watching in the kitchen, turning down the audio because she can hear Frances from where she's standing.

"The ground rules are thus," Frances intones, and Jubilee thinks, *"Thus"? Who the hell programmed that?*

"There will be no questions about Ms. Rathman's personal life. There will be no questions about her beloved brother Joshua's passing.

There will be no questions about rock climbing. Any violations of these rules will result in instant termination of the press conference. Thank you."

Jubilee glances at her phone. 10:58 a.m. She makes a half turn to her right and looks at herself in a mirror on the vestibule wall. Still slender, still postured—her mother used to say she was as composed as a Russian ballerina—still with the muscled calves from booming kicks halfway down the soccer field. She imagines herself, as she did every day as a little girl, in a red-white-and-blue jersey, running out on the field while the throngs in the stands chant, *USA! USA! USA!*

She is not that girl anymore.

———

Jubilee brought Joshua to Purgatory Bay four years after the murders. After the countless months in hospitals and burn centers and the predictable media barrage on the yearly anniversary of the massacre, Jubilee still did not feel safe at the family house in Clarkston, a Detroit suburb. She lay awake at night imagining a hired Petruglia hand appearing in her garage with a gun or a wire or a plastic bag, even though her attorney, E. Jonathan Phillips—Phillie, as she and Joshua called him—assured her that the Petruglias would leave her alone. Once she had secured legal guardianship of her brother, she decided to leave. She knew she'd never find a place out of the Petruglias' reach, but she couldn't stay where she was.

Phillie knew someone who knew a woman connected to Bleak Harbor's namesake family. The estate of the deceased matriarch was trying to unload a small lake and empty parcel of land four miles north of the city. The story went that Joseph Estes Bleak had been traveling from Massachusetts to the town that he would christen Bleak Harbor in the 1860s when a blizzard bogged him down for weeks on the shore of a desolate bay. He christened it Purgatory because it was his last waiting place before he claimed his heaven, Bleak Harbor.

The asking price for Purgatory Bay was $1 million, but Phillie told the estate lawyer to keep things private and Jubilee would pay $1.3 million cash, the money coming from her father's deep well of life insurance and savings. The locals knew almost nothing of the deal until a temporary fence plastered with No Trespassing signs appeared all along the rim of the property.

Bleak Harbor's city council initially rejected Jubilee's petitions to build on the bay. But Phillie hired a public relations firm that persuaded TV camera crews from Chicago and Detroit to shoot stories about how Bleak Harbor was abusing a young woman who had already suffered more than enough. It wasn't good for the tourist business that filled the city's coffers. The council relented.

Barely a legal adult, Jubilee was learning about quit deeds and title searches and construction liens and easements while her peers were doing beer bongs and skipping college sociology classes. She and Joshua kept to themselves, literally walling themselves off from the world and the threat of further punishment by the Petruglias. Jubilee rarely ventured into town. She had nothing against the townspeople of Bleak Harbor that she didn't have against almost any other human being. She just didn't belong with others anymore.

One night, she gathered up all of the soccer gear she had socked away in a closet in the house—jerseys, shorts, shoes, goalie gloves, team photos, newspaper clippings, medals, trophies, ribbons—and hauled it all down to the beach below the house. It took her three trips, mostly because of the trophies. She built a fire with kerosene, charcoal briquettes, and pine logs until the flames licked at her chin. She thought, for one second, of falling into it, letting it take her beyond her purgatory into whatever hell or heaven lay beyond. Instead she dropped each piece of her glorious soccer past onto the fire and watched each one flicker and crinkle and shrivel and disappear.

She never could have done what she did on Purgatory Bay without Phillie. He coached her through every step, told her what to sign or not, helped her find Western Michigan doctors for Joshua, sent cakes on birthdays for her, Joshua, and Kara, emailed her healthy recipes, and reminded her time and again that her father had been a good man who'd been put in a difficult position, and if his copy shops really had laundered money for the Petruglias—Phillie would never address that directly—Edward Rathman had done what he'd done because he'd thought it was best for his family.

If she had been capable of feeling love in any tangible way, she was sure she would have felt it for Phillie.

One evening she made a rare trip into Bleak Harbor for a city council meeting. She had filed for permission to formally rename her property Paradise Lake. She told the council the new name might prove a tonic to Joshua, who she said was struggling with depression. It wasn't exactly the truth; Joshua had had trouble weaning himself from the painkillers to which he'd grown addicted during his endless recuperation. Many days he did not get out of bed. Phillie had suggested that making his home a paradise might help, if only a little.

The council seemed amenable, but it didn't matter because the new mayor, one Harland Fisher Jr., was not. "Was the property not named Purgatory Bay when you were buying it?" he asked Jubilee as the council and the audience of a dozen or so citizens watched. A scarlet blotch on his forehead made him look as though a pagan had doused him with blood. "If my information is correct, you bought the property without notifying this council, and now you come here asking for our assistance," he said. "Whereas, in my opinion, the fortress you have built is a blight on the idyll of our community. And who knows whether your family has truly cut its ties to the Mafia? I'm sincerely curious as to why you have been spared, Miss Jubilee. Can you answer that for me?"

Phillie leaned into her ear then and whispered, "Enough."

At home that night, Jubilee eased Joshua's bedroom door open, leaving the light off. He was sleeping, uneasily as usual, his mouth and nose and sinuses still not what they should have been after all the skin grafts. She whispered, so as not to wake him, "The terrible people in the outer world want us to live in purgatory forever. We will. But you, Joshua, must change."

She closed his door.

In her own room, she lifted a Bible from the nightstand drawer. A pen marked the page in Matthew's Gospel where Jesus pronounces the Beatitudes. Jubilee had underlined the one about those who hunger and thirst for righteousness. On the opposite page was a sticky note bearing five names. She took the pen, added two:

fisher

harbor

———

Now Jubilee's phone buzzes with an alarm: eleven o'clock.

She opens the front door, hearing the cameras click and riffle. *Like crickets,* she thinks, falling back to that long-ago night with her sister, Kara, creeping along the floor to Joshua's bedroom. She forces a smile as she approaches the lectern. Camera lights flash on. She turns to the police chief, shakes her hand, thanks her for coming, steps to the lectern, blinks, tries on another smile, not too wide.

"Good morning," she says. "I'm Jubilee Rathman, and I am so grateful that you came today despite the weather."

She unfolds a sheet of paper and sets it on the lectern next to the timer she placed there earlier, before the journalists arrived. She's in black jeans, black mules, and a black down vest over a heather turtleneck, her chestnut hair streaked with premature gray in a ponytail secured with a black silk bow. "You folks like predicting things, so please tell me spring is coming. Eventually, yes?" She waits for the titter, it comes, and she says, "Thank you."

Microphones and tape recorders are arrayed around the lectern. The reporters stand only a few feet from Jubilee but keep the distance more respectful than they would for, say, a county commissioner or a police chief. After all, Jubilee Rathman is the bereaved young woman, perhaps the most bereaved in all of Michigan, as she is all too aware.

To her right stands a digital screen displaying a colored bar graph illustrating how the rate of teenage suicides in the United States has grown. "We are here today—I am here today—because of a serious and seriously underappreciated blight on our precious youth, as well as on the families who must come to grips not just with terrible loss but with the gnawing, numbing pain of guilt."

Jubilee stops again to gaze out past the cluster, nodding ever so slightly as the cameras snick and notebook scribbles quicken. She feels confident that she has struck the pose of poignancy and gravitas that the barking hyenas—which reminds her: she owes Phillie a call—crave for their readers and viewers.

She turns to Chief Malone. "I'm honored—as Joshua would be—to have the chief of police of Bleak Harbor support us today. I know that Chief Malone has to confront the tragedy of suicide in her work, and we hope to lighten her load with what we're doing today."

Malone, hands folded behind her back, nods and smiles.

Jubilee turns back to the reporters, scanning them left, then right, partly to make eye contact with each of them. It's harder with the younger ones gaping at their phones. She nods at the one from Fox with the frosted pageboy that always conjures the word *severe* when Jubilee sees her. Jubilee doesn't know the name of the ABC guy, but she recognizes him from Joshua's brief but well-covered memorial service at Saint Wenceslaus in Bleak Harbor. She doesn't recognize the others, probably because they work in print or online.

"My brother, Joshua," she says. The screen next to her segues to a photograph of her brother as a six-year-old, all Tigers hat and gap-toothed smile. "My brother would be just as pleased to see you all here helping to spread the word about the demons that bedevil not only those who succumb to them but those who are left behind."

She glances at the page on the lectern but doesn't read from it because, with Frances's help, she has memorized every word. "As you know, I'm referring to the core mission of the Joshua Project, which is to facilitate mental health services for family members who've lost a loved one to suicide. Unfortunately, mental health is not a high priority for our policy makers. Funding for mental health services in Bleak County . . ."

Jubilee continues. She glances twice at the timer on the lectern to make sure she finishes within four minutes. The news today is that the Joshua Project will donate $100,000 to three local charities. The organizations will expand their counseling of young people afflicted with depression and of families who've lived through suicides.

As Jubilee speaks, images appear and fade on the flat-screen in a languorous rotation: knitted-brow social workers listening to anonymous youths, craggy rock walls soaring against a blue sky, unsettling statistics (*32: Percentage Increase in Teen Suicide, Past Decade*), and Joshua himself—showing off a bluegill he caught, pedaling a bicycle down his childhood street in Clarkston, blowing out candles on a birthday cake—all taken before the murders at the cottage.

Jubilee makes no mention of that night and only one oblique reference to Joshua's death. At four minutes and eight seconds, she says, "I would be pleased to answer any questions you might have."

The Fox woman speaks up: Does Jubilee's donation suggest the private sector is better equipped to deal with people's "mental deficiencies" than public agencies? Jubilee decides not to challenge her phrasing but says as politely as she can, "I believe our public servants are doing what they can within their limited means. But I wouldn't be opposed to seeing, for instance, Whirlpool Corporation match my donation. They're not far from here, as you know."

"Jubilee," says the reporter in the wool cap. He writes in his notebook as he speaks, looking up and then down like a sketch artist working against a clock. "What would you tell parents who think their child might be, you know, at risk?"

"For suicide?" Jubilee finishes his sentence.

"Yes, of course, sorry." His pen goes still, suspended over his notebook. "Did your parents—I mean, oh my gosh, I'm sorry—I mean, did *you* see any signs that your brother was moving in that direction?"

"The question is off limits," Frances says.

"No, it's all right," Jubilee says. "I'll take it. Go ahead."

The reporter continues, "Have you . . . I mean . . . thought back and . . ."

"Have I second-guessed myself?" Jubilee says. "Have I blamed myself for missing whatever signs might have been there? Is that what you're asking?"

"Yes, please."

"Who are you with, please?"

"Me? The *Anchor* at Hope College."

"Let me answer your questions this way. I've given this a lot of thought, and I'm not one hundred percent sure Joshua really wanted to die."

"But—"

"Please let me finish. I don't believe we can know what's in that person's mind up to the very last second before she or he does what they've planned to do. As you know, there are many reports of people struggling to free themselves from a noose. Only Joshua would know whether he was at peace with his choice as he stepped off the edge of that crevasse."

"So you don't think Joshua wanted to do it?"

"I didn't say that. I said I wasn't sure. I'm still not sure. Which of course changes nothing. Even if at the last second, he wished he could have pulled himself back and lived another day, another hour, he still got to the point where he put himself in danger."

"But shortly after his death, you were insisting there was no way that he committed suicide, isn't that right?"

"Yes. I have a more, shall we say, nuanced view now."

"Ms. Rathman, could I ask a follow-up to that?" It's another of the young ones, a woman in a head-to-toe parka. "Do you think—and I'm not really trying to get supernatural here—do you think that Joshua's spirit lives on, for you at least, in some way?"

Jubilee gives the young woman a long look before answering. "I want to be perfectly clear about this," she says, the lie necessary to her mission. She sweeps her gaze across the entire group, then returns to the down parka. "Joshua's spirit does not live on. Joshua is dead. His spirit is gone. Forever. It does not continue to dwell in this house, or on this bay, or anywhere. Any other questions?"

An older reporter has edged her way to the front of the scrum. Jubilee sees she's not taking notes, so she probably didn't come here for the project announcement, probably could care less about the ground rules that Frances enumerated. As another reporter starts to ask something, the older one steps forward, interrupting.

"Ms. Rathman, forgive me but, you know, my job and all. Does it frustrate you at all that, twelve years later, the police have not solved the murder case?"

"Well, that's not precisely—"

Frances's voice booms over Jubilee: "The question is outside the bounds of the ground rules." The heads of the other journalists all turn to the woman posing the question. "If there are no more questions, we will ask you all to please move slowly—"

"No, no," Jubilee says, "it's all right, Frances. I will answer. But first would you mind telling me your name and affiliation?"

The woman tells her. Jubilee scans through the thousands of newspaper clips filed in the memory bank in her brain. She knows the byline.

A cop reporter for the Associated Press in Detroit. She came all this way. No amount of flattery or resistance is likely to dissuade her.

"Of course," Jubilee says. "What I would say is technically, the police did not arrest a suspect, but—"

"Right," the reporter interrupts. "The police couldn't—or wouldn't—find a suspect, so nothing happened."

"Something like that. And your question is?"

"Well, how do you feel about all that? Are you still in touch with the authorities? Are they still investigating? They won't talk to us."

"You're speaking entirely of what happened at our family cottage up north, yes? Not Joshua."

"The '07 murders."

"You should ask the authorities," Jubilee says. "I have not spoken with them in quite a while."

Now the woman is writing in her notebook. "Quite a while," she repeats. "Years? Has it been that long?"

"I really don't recall. I have tried to move on."

"You're such a young woman to be dealing with so much."

Twenty-nine, she thinks, *but I'm so much older.* "Many people deal with much more than I do," she says. She looks away to address the entire group. "Are there any more questions? If not, then—"

"I'm sorry," the same woman says, "but I wonder if you heard about the incident this morning in Detroit. The police say someone tried to kill a child at a Petruglia family funeral."

"Excuse me?" Jubilee says.

"There was an attempt made on a teenager's life. A Petruglia girl. She's OK, but would you have any comment?"

"Someone—I'm sorry," Jubilee says. She's trying to process what she just heard. *The child is not dead?* "Why would I—no," she says. "No."

"No comment? Or no, you haven't heard?"

Jubilee has to get inside the house. "No to both," she says. "I'm sorry, if you'll excuse me now. Thank you for coming and for your appreciation of the Joshua Project."

———

Jubilee closes the front door behind her and leans back against it, shuts her eyes.

"Jubilee," Frances says.

"Not now, Frances."

"The Detroit mission did not—"

"I said quiet, please."

"Yes."

Jubilee blows out a long breath and opens her eyes. She turns her head and leans into the peephole in the door. The TV people are packing equipment, the others filing out the front gate. The press conference was harder than she expected.

"Frances," she says. "You can make the bank transfers now."

"As specified last night, 33.3 percent to each of the charities?"

"As specified last night."

"I sent you a link to this morning's news from Detroit."

"Thank you. That's all for now."

Jubilee walks into the kitchen and steps out onto the house deck overlooking the bay. She wraps her arms around herself, hunches her shoulders against the cold. Glassine ripples slide past the old, barely used dive raft floating off the shoreline.

Jubilee chose this place for its quiet and solitude, for the high bluffs covered with thick forest, for the feel of dwelling within a sinecure against the outer world, however illusory that feeling might be. She imagines Caleb on the roof above her, so many nights leading up to this day, shrouded in darkness, working the drone controller with both hands. He would practice in the dark, only the dark, so he would not be detected.

Jubilee would watch from where she's standing now, barely able to make out the drones soaring and diving toward the water, then pulling up to skim like dragonflies at the luminescent orange targets Caleb had placed in trees, on the boatless boat dock, the dive raft. He crashed the first few but eventually became proficient enough that he could flick the edges of the flimsy plastic targets seemingly at will.

"Caleb," she says aloud. She looks down at her feet, shaking her head. She puts a hand in a pocket, grasps her cell phone. She wants to ask him what went wrong in Detroit, how it is that the Petruglia girl is not dead. But it would not be wise to contact him now, even on an encrypted channel. She leaves the phone in her pocket. She will have to wait.

11

The door to the dressing room behind the visitors' bench opens. Mikey perks up in her bleacher seat across the rink as the Washtenaw Pride goaltender, Henrietta—her teammates call her Hank—clumps into view in the doorframe in her bulky pads and her mask painted in swoops of gold and silver and black, the Pride logo emblazoned on the forehead.

"Come on, Pride," Mikey shouts, barely noticing that the rink's overhead lights blink once, twice, three times. Trudy Esper, mother of Pride defenseman Emma, reaches over and rubs Mikey's back, pumping her other hand into the air. "Let's go, Em," she yells. "Let's go, Bridge!"

Hank slaps her goalie stick against one leg pad, then the other, again and again, as the Zamboni finishes smoothing the ice for the game's third and final period. Hank is always first in line when the Pride emerges from their room, followed by the defensemen, the centers, and the wings, all in a specific order the girls adhere to each game. Bridget comes out eighth in her black-and-gold jersey, number twelve. She's too far back in the corridor to see now, but Mikey still gets out of her seat and stands on tiptoes to try.

The Pride is down three to one to Minnesota after two periods. As Bridget said, the Minnesota girls are good—quick on their feet, smart with their hands, happy to mix it up in the corners and the front of the net. But the Pride is hanging in. Bridget assisted on their lone goal, her wrist shot from the right circle deflecting off the heel of a teammate's stick and over the Minnesota goalie's shoulder.

The Zamboni exits. But a man in an orange jacket emblazoned with the word *STAFF* across the back steps between Hank and the ice, holding up a hand for her to wait. A woman in a matching jacket is doing the same at the Minnesota bench. Mikey sits. "What's going on?" she says.

Trudy shrugs. "Maybe just letting the ice set up?"

"Hope so."

Mikey glances over one shoulder, then the other, wanting to see Gary walking toward the bleachers with Ophelia on his arm. She checks her phone. There's a text from her husband. Craig just passed Battle Creek on his way to Bleak Harbor and wants an update on the score. But there's nothing from Gary. She and Bridget gave up waiting for him and Ophelia at Bella's. As they left the restaurant, Bridget asked, "What's up with Aunt Pheels?" and Mikey put her daughter off, saying, "Oh, you know her—she'll surprise us later."

But still Mikey hasn't heard a peep.

"Is everything OK?" Trudy says. "You seem a little preoccupied."

"It's just—nothing really." Mikey smiles. "Work stuff. I'm fine."

The truth is nothing has felt fine since she encountered that Ohio car last night. Normally she loses herself in Bridget's games, watching her daughter's every move, even when Bridget is sitting on the bench, her head swiveling back and forth with the flow of the game. But during the first two periods, Mikey's attention kept drifting elsewhere, to Ophelia and Gary. She actually missed Bridget's assist when it happened, saw only the video replay on the screens hanging over the bleachers.

"Oh no, look," Trudy says, "the girls are going back in the dressing room."

"That's not right."

"What is going on?"

Mikey catches a glimpse of Bridget's jersey as she and her team-mates walk back down the corridor to their dressing room. The organizers can't afford delays with so many games yet to play. They couldn't have called a halt without a reason. Mikey stands.

"I'm going to try to find out," she says. "Watch my purse?"

"Of course."

Mikey climbs out of the bleachers and down a flight of stairs to the main lobby. Players and coaches and parents dressed in team jackets and sweat suits mingle along the rink glass. The smells of cocoa and hot dogs grilling mix with the sour tang of sweaty hockey gear. A queue of girls in red-and-black jackets snakes through the crowd toward their locker room. It's the team sponsored by the Detroit oil-change shops that Bridget used to play for. Mikey wonders if Bridget's bully is still on the team.

She lets that go and surveys the crowd for a face. A team from Cleveland is scheduled to play after Bridget's game. Mikey thinks maybe she'll find the driver of that Volvo. But she sees nothing remotely like what she thought she had glimpsed through his open window.

Two women and a man, tournament officials Mikey does not recognize, sit at folding tables set up on the black rubber-mat floor. They're checking player IDs and selling World of Women Hockey Showcase T-shirts and pucks. Mikey waits behind a woman making a purchase, looks up at a TV suspended from the ceiling. The sound is on but barely audible against the lobby clamor. The weather forecast: high thirties, cloudy, occasional sleet.

"Can I help you out?"

The male official is speaking to her. He has white hair and an accent that sounds to Mikey, the onetime Detroiter, almost Canadian. Could be from Minnesota, too, or the UP.

"Yes, thank you," Mikey says. She gestures over a shoulder toward the rink. "Do you know what the problem is?"

"A problem? Minnesota's up, eh?" He grins. "No problem."

Mikey tries to smile along with him. "Your team is very good," she says, and as she says it, she overhears something on the TV that startles her. "But they just sent the girls"—she looks up at the TV, looking for the familiar word she thinks she just heard—"back into their dressing rooms."

"Ma'am?"

"I'm sorry. They've stopped the game. Do you happen to know what's going on? Or someone I could ask?"

The man turns to the woman next to him. She's fishing through a pile of T-shirts, looking for a size.

"They stopped the game?" the man says. "Did you hear that?"

"Um, no, ah, there it is, double XL." She turns to the man, then to Mikey. "Aren't they just between periods?"

Mikey looks over her shoulder at the rink, catching another glimpse of the TV. The news is back on. She addresses the T-shirt woman. "Both teams were about to step out onto the ice; then they told them to go back to their rooms."

"Who told them?"

This is going nowhere. "Some people in staff jackets."

"I have no idea, ma'am." She smiles, apologetic, beleaguered. "But you might check down at the tournament office"—she points to one end of the rink—"down in that corner."

Mikey backs away from the table, looking up at the TV. On the screen, a young woman is standing at a lectern, speaking into a cluster of microphones. Mikey immediately recognizes her: Jubilee Rathman. The chyron at the bottom of the screen says SISTER OF VICTIM ANNOUNCES GIFT TO LOCAL SUICIDE GROUPS.

Good, Mikey thinks, glad to see that the traumatized woman has recovered enough to turn her tragedy into a benefit for others.

Mikey weaves through a cluster of players from different teams giggling and trading team pins. She didn't hesitate when Bridget insisted the weekend before that Mikey buy two dozen Pride pins that Bridget could trade. Mikey loves to sneak into Bridget's bedroom after a tournament and check out the new pins that have joined the many others arrayed in a heart pattern on a bulletin board above Bridget's desk. Craig needles her about them, saying, "Do you have more friends on our hated and feared opponents' teams than on our beloved Pride?" To which Bridget replies, "Keep your enemies close, Dad."

Mikey squeezes past and, as she starts down the side of the rink toward the tournament office, hears a voice calling out.

"Michaela? Are you avoiding me?"

Maybe, she thinks. She knows the voice. Craig likes the sound of it more than she does. She spins around to face a towering man in a red pullover stitched over the left breast with the University of Wisconsin badger.

"Coach," Mikey says, extending a hand. "I told you, call me Mikey."

"Of course, Michaela," he says, taking her hand in both of his. "It's good to see you all the way from Ann Arbor."

"It's good—"

The coach leans in to interrupt her. That annoying habit is one more reason for Mikey to hope Bridget doesn't accept a Wisconsin scholarship. "You haven't been spending any time with my friends at Yost, have you?" he says.

Yost is the hockey arena at the University of Michigan. The Pride practices there on occasion. The UM coaches haven't expressed much interest in Bridget, but Wisconsin's coach is always asking when he's not asking about the other schools that have indicated they might like having Bridget on their rosters.

"Actually," Mikey says, smiling, "I have been avoiding you."

"I hope not," he says. His eyes are a shade of blue that reminds her of a city editor she had who abhorred the phrase *piercing blue eyes.*

"How's our girl?" he asks. "I liked her assist."

Not your girl, Mikey thinks, but she says, "So did I."

"She made a smart play—saw number seventeen's stick and just put it on the tape. You know, it's a simple game."

There's that phrase again. That inane, obvious, cloying mantra so many hockey coaches spout, though none as frequently as the Wisconsin guy. Mikey once calculated that she would hear that hockey is a simple game more than ten thousand times over four years at Wisconsin. She dreads it.

"Yep," she says. Her phone is vibrating with a text message.

"Have you seen the view of the bay from the parking lot?" the coach says. The Ice House, built by a late, wealthy Chicago grain trader who summered in Bleak Harbor, sits on a rise overlooking downtown and the bay. "It's so, you know, quaint. The place is darn lucky to get this tournament."

"I'm sure they're happy to have some people around," Mikey says. "It's usually dead this time of year."

Before she finishes the sentence, she sees the coach's eyes slide to his left. Mikey follows them and sees a goaltender from Erie, Pennsylvania, who's on the list of just about every college coach in the country. "Well," the Wisconsin guy says, "I hope we can keep in touch."

Seeing how badly he wants to chase the goalie and her parents, Mikey takes pleasure in keeping him there a little longer. "You don't know what happened with the game, do you?" she says, nodding toward the ice. "They kept the girls from coming out for the third period."

He glances across the rink at the empty benches, then sneaks a look behind him, where Mikey sees the goalie disappearing into the throng. "They had some sort of power problem," he says as he starts edging away. "Didn't want to chance the lights going out in the middle of the game. Looks handled." He takes her hand again, squeezes it. "I hope to see Mr. Deming this weekend."

Continuing toward the tournament office, she checks her phone. There are two texts from her boss at the literacy center and one from Gary:

sorry to miss u at bellas. be at rink soon

She stops walking and looks across the ice. The door behind the Pride bench is open now, and there again stands Hank, waggling her big paddle of a goalie stick, her teammates lining up behind her. Mikey recalls how the lights flickered earlier. She hadn't thought much of it then but supposes it wouldn't have been good if the rink went suddenly dark as a slap shot was flying toward a goalie.

No need to go to the tournament office now. She stays at the rink glass watching as both teams stream onto the ice. Bridget leaps out, legs and arms churning, hair flying behind her. She leans into a turn to Mikey's left, speeding toward her, and zips past, oblivious to her mother. Mikey smiles. She can't see her daughter's face behind the protective cage she wears, but she knows the look Bridget must be wearing, has seen it countless times over Ping-Pong tables and games of Yahtzee and made-up Olympic tubing contests on Halfmoon Lake. For Bridget at this moment, there is nothing but the ice, the puck, her teammates, the clock.

Mikey answers Gary's text as she starts back toward the bleachers:

Third period about to start. Nothing from Pheels here. You?

He responds almost immediately:

got a little busy. tell u when I get there

Got a little busy? Mikey thinks. *Meaning?* Another text buzzes in as she approaches the lobby swarm. It's not Gary but a Detroit number Mikey doesn't recognize. Normally, she'd ignore it, but maybe it has something to do with Ophelia. She opens it:

hope u're well. you hear robo bought it?

Robo? she thinks, then types, who's this?

The reply comes: your old pal Shannon

Mikey's old assignment editor at the *Times*. Mikey hasn't heard from her in years and hasn't minded a bit. She texts back:

What happened?

Robo, she thinks. Vance Robillard. The *Detroit Times*. A long time ago. A time she loved, a job she loved, until it turned into something else.

Shannon's next text pops up:

found dead in car at his house. cops not sure, maybe poisoned.

Mikey's knees go a little weak. She steadies herself, feeling suddenly alone amid all the bodies milling about. She starts to tap a response, then stops and looks up at the TV. The news has been replaced by video of one of the earlier tournament games. But Mikey remembers the word she thought she had heard a moment before, now certain of it:

Petruglia.

12

Gary Langreth parks his pickup on the gravel shoulder a few hundred yards short of the house on Blossom Hill. He doesn't want Bleak Harbor mayor Harland Fisher Jr. to know he's coming.

Avoiding the road, Langreth dips onto the incline through the forest and trudges upward. The sandy slope at the southern edge of Bleak Harbor was named for a Bleak daughter who had died of tuberculosis or typhoid or one of those horrible diseases people died from a hundred years ago. Langreth has forgotten which, if he ever even knew.

Everybody who actually lives in Bleak Harbor, as opposed to those who visit in the summer, knows Blossom Hill. It wasn't enough for the Bleaks to name most of the streets after their dead: Lily, Violet, Jeremiah. They tried to claim in some fashion, legal or not, every square inch of the geography.

But one cantankerous outsider sought to deny the Bleaks their claim on Blossom Hill. Langreth read with great amusement about Harland Fisher Sr. in a history book in his dentist's waiting room. Fisher Sr. moved his wife and four children from Niles in the late 1950s and plunked them at the top of the uninhabited hill, with a grand view of Lake Michigan and, on a clear night, a glimmer of light from the Chicago skyline. The Fishers squatted there for months, first in tents, then in a lean-to of two-by-fours and shingles, until Fisher Sr. succeeded in having an actual house built, all as he was being sued and threatened with eviction and arrest and worse by the Bleaks' bottomless supply of lawyers.

Fisher Sr., representing himself before a dozen or so judges over the decades, wielded a 1916 deed that purportedly granted his descendants title to 2.125 acres at the crown of Blossom Hill. With the long-distance help of a brother-in-law who had attended one year of law school, Fisher Sr. became adept at the sorts of procedural delays and paper dumps that would have made a corporate lawyer proud. Through it all, he maintained that the Bleaks wanted him off the hill merely because his house, thanks mostly to the hill, stood eleven and a half inches taller than the turrets of Bleak Mansion.

It was never clear where he got the money to keep fighting the Bleaks, but the townspeople found the drama entertaining. Somehow, he wore the Bleaks down. Or bored them into apathy. As the third- and fourth-generation Bleaks cashed out of Joseph Estes Bleak's industrial businesses in the 1970s and 1980s, they paid less and less attention to Bleak Harbor itself, let alone the scruffy Blossom Hill and the scruffy family that endured there. After Fisher Sr. and his wife died, their children scattered throughout the Midwest.

Except for the oldest, Harland Fisher Jr.

Langreth nears the last row of trees edging Fisher Jr.'s backyard. He turns his phone off, then squats and peers through the crotch of a double-trunk birch, sizing up the scene as he might have when he was a Detroit cop.

"Jesus, Harland," he says to himself. "What would your daddy say?"

The yard is a lumpy trample of browns and grays and dead dandelions smeared into slicks of mud. Langreth counts fourteen barbecue grills standing in a haphazard circle: Webers, Char-Broils, one of those egg-shaped contraptions, a squat black box he figures for a smoker. A mess of shovels and rakes juts from beneath an overturned wheelbarrow. Langreth has the feeling of being in the presence of someone who's constantly busy not finishing things. But he cautions himself not to underestimate a Fisher.

He steps out of the woods into the yard, scanning the windows on the rear of the two-story house. Plain white curtains are drawn in all of them. A roofed wooden porch stretches across the back of the house, its rain gutter drooping from the eaves like a broken arm. On the porch, three cast-iron chairs and a table, all painted black, stand next to an uneven pile of firewood. The table is stacked with cans of paint. Black, Langreth notes, like the stuff used to graffiti Ophelia's sculptures.

He walks toward the house, keeping his eye on the windows and the screen door that opens onto the porch. He probably shouldn't be here. He probably should have listened to Malone. But she didn't look eager to do anything, and really, Langreth doesn't give a rip. He's thinking he should have come here the day after the first of the sculptures was defaced. Because Harland Fisher Jr. was at one time sleeping with Ophelia until he wasn't anymore, and everyone knows he can be a vindictive prick. It's sort of his stock in trade.

"That's far enough, sir."

Langreth stops, looks up, sees Fisher's bald, bearded head in a second-story window. A scarlet blotch the shape of a five-legged beetle stains the peak of his forehead. The thing always gives Langreth the creeps.

"Mr. Mayor," he says. "Get down here. We need to talk."

Fisher adjusts himself in the window frame so Langreth can see the twin barrels of the shotgun he's holding.

"Haw," Fisher says, without smiling. "How's my girl?"

Langreth last encountered him at Wehling's Saloon two weeks ago. Langreth and Ophelia were at a table having olive burgers and beer. Fisher was sitting at the bar. He approached them, grinning. Langreth was about to get out of his chair, uncertain of what he might do, when Ophelia said, "Just go away, Harland."

"You can still feel me, can't you, baby?" Fisher said.

"I can smell you. Just go."

Fisher nodded at Langreth then, and said, "She's all yours."

Two nights later, the first of Ophelia's sculptures was vandalized.

"Somebody's been messing with her sculptures," Langreth says now. "I'm thinking you might possess motive."

"I thought you were under orders not to play Barney Fife anymore. Should I give the prosecutor a call?"

"Do you know anything about Ophelia's whereabouts?"

Fisher leans out over the windowsill. "Excuse me?"

"She's missing."

"What does that mean, 'missing'?"

"Missing, as in nobody knows where she is. Do you?"

Fisher shifts his weight in the window. "You mean *you* don't know where she is. Maybe she just doesn't want to see you anymore."

Langreth knows more than he cares to know about Ophelia and Fisher's tempestuous dalliance, because Ophelia told him all about it, sometimes in squirmingly graphic detail. It had involved a lot of screwing in places other than their bedrooms: in Fisher's office at city hall, in the shallows next to the boathouse at Bleak Mansion, atop the lifeguard tower at the foot of the Indiana Dunes. And maybe, less spectacularly, at a Super 8 motel. Langreth wouldn't put it past Fisher to have left the motel key in Ophelia's house for her next lover to find.

"You might be right about me," Langreth tells Fisher. "But I think she'd want to see her sister and niece. They're here for the hockey tournament." He reaches into a pocket and produces the plastic baggie he decided not to give to Chief Malone. He holds it up over his head so Fisher can see the Super 8 logo on the motel key. "Think the police might find your fingerprints on this, Harland?"

The beetle on Fisher's forehead crinkles smaller. "Can't tell what you got," he says. "But I doubt it has anything to do with me."

"It's the key to a motel room," Langreth says. "You and Ophelia have a getaway there? Maybe in Coloma? Or did you go all the way to Indiana?"

Fisher smirks, glances back over his shoulder, shakes his head. He's thinking, Langreth decides. He knows something.

"Wouldn't you like to know? You know, between you and me and Ophelia and the chief, you're in a kind of quadrangle, eh?"

How does he know about Malone? Langreth thinks, feeling his anger start to spike, imagining what he could do to that beetle splotch with a gun butt. He sucks in a breath, holds it, lets it out. Like his shrink taught him. Then he says, "We found the motel key in her kitchen this morning."

"Sure you didn't find it in her bedroom?"

Fisher's stringing him along, trying to distract him, Langreth figures. Because he knows something. "When's the last time you spoke with her?"

"Tell me, Langreth." Fisher squints into the distance, toward the lake. "Whatever happened with your partner in Detroit? I hear he got his full pension. You, on the other hand, did not get your full pension, did you? So you're stuck working in this little shit town."

How does he know this stuff? Langreth thinks. Still, he's not about to bite. "We're not here to talk about me. I need you to help me find Ophelia."

Fisher repositions the gun so the barrels aim toward Langreth. "And I need you to get off my property before I call the real police."

"You had nothing to do with what happened to her sculptures?"

"I'll admit I didn't mind hearing about it. But no. Not my style."

But still, Langreth thinks, *you know something.* "We'll be checking the Super 8s, Harland. I'll be back if I find your footprints anywhere."

"You won't." Fisher gestures toward the road with the shotgun. "Get going now. You don't want to lose another job."

Langreth makes his way back to his car, wondering how Fisher could possibly know about the Detroit cop who was with him the night he almost beat that guy to death. The settlements with the department were supposed to be confidential.

He turns his phone on. There's a text from Mikey; two from his boss, the Bleak County prosecutor; and one that just arrived from Ophelia Wright. He punches that one up, stops walking to read it:

is this our goodby?

He reads it again, then a third time and a fourth. He's relieved that Ophelia appears to be out there somewhere but a little surprised that she seems to be breaking up with him. Or maybe he's misinterpreting. Maybe she's just having a little fun with him.

He texts her back:

??? where are u? call plz

He starts walking, ignores his boss's texts, hits the one from Mikey:

Nothing from Pheels yet. You?

He gets into his car, bats out a reply:

got a little busy. tell u when I get there

13

Fisher watches Langreth disappear around the corner of his house, climbs down from the window, leans the shotgun against a wall, and moves to the computer at his stand-up desk.

He's glad he knew enough about Langreth's shitcanning in Detroit to yank his chain about it. The minute he heard that an ex-cop had signed on with the Bleak County prosecutor—the pay cut must've been a whopper—he suspected the guy had a mess in his past, and sure enough, some googling and a few phone calls later, Fisher knew about him and his partner pummeling some meth head into paralysis after stumbling over him in a crack house. The partner, who was sleeping with a deputy chief, got a six-month suspension. Langreth got an early career exit. Luckily, he had attended Wayne State University with the Bleak County prosecutor, who'd bailed him out with a $45,500-a-year gig.

As Fisher's daddy taught him, it's always good to have accurate information on adversaries, especially if you're likely to have a lot of them, as an elected official like Fisher is prone to. Gives you a bit of leverage, gets people guessing what you know or you don't. Fisher could tell from Langreth's face that he was guessing himself. And then Langreth pulled out that laughable bullshit about a motel key. Fisher's no fancy pants, but he'd sooner die than sleep in a Super 8.

After that encounter at Wehling's, Fisher expected to hear from Langreth again. But he never thought the guy would have the balls to confront him on Blossom Hill. Which makes him think Langreth was probably telling the truth about Ophelia being missing. Which is news to Fisher. Which pisses him off, because there's not much in Bleak Harbor that's news to him. If he worked at a newspaper—if those things even exist anymore—they'd probably call him a goddamn investigative reporter. He'd probably win a goddamn Pulitzer Prize.

But Fisher doesn't collect information only to dole it out for the so-called public good. Even though he's mayor of Bleak Harbor—hell, *especially* because he's mayor—he knows the public good is a fantasy, as everyone knows, even if they won't admit it. And information—who's humping whom, which city employee has her fingers in the till, the real reason why the county clerk suddenly resigned—is a marketable commodity that can be turned into cash or leverage or pure, sweet, delicious schadenfreude.

Harland Fisher Jr. is his father reincarnated. It's as if Harland Sr. never really died of prostate cancer—his body just succumbed, while his soul, if that was the word for it, passed into Junior.

In 1960, Senior was facing eviction from Blossom Hill when, in a Stevensville bar not far from the spot-welding plant where he worked the afternoon shift, he happened to meet Lucy Strathem.

Buxom, redheaded Lucy Strathem was drunk on Seagram's and rage at James Estes Bleak, grandson of the city founder and then-current resident of Bleak Mansion with his wife, Catherine. Lucy, twenty-seven years old, was James Bleak's secret lover. Along with, as Lucy had recently discovered, another woman, three years younger than Lucy.

When Harland Fisher Sr. happened upon her, Lucy was getting up the alcohol courage to tell James Bleak's wife about their yearlong affair: how they'd trysted at motels up and down the Lake Michigan shoreline and on the bridge of the Bleak yacht, *Promises, Promises*; how he'd given her strings of pearls and designer dresses and promised to divorce Catherine and move Lucy into the bedroom in the mansion's northeast turret.

Fisher Sr. ordered Lucy a hot tea and assured her, lying, that he knew the Bleaks well, especially Catherine, and that he could use Lucy's lasciviously detailed information as a lever to extract for her more tangible benefits than empty revenge. "Retribution alone," he told her, fabricating a biblical quote on the fly, "gains a man no roof nor table. In other words, Lucy, screwing up Bleak's marriage ain't gonna buy you any pretty necklaces."

One month and $25,000 later, Lucy quietly disappeared from James Bleak's life. Fisher Sr. didn't take a penny of that first payoff but used what he knew to extend the blackmail into a long and profitable relationship, if not friendship, with James and, later, his son, Jack Bleak. Fisher Sr.'s blunt but discreet handling of the Lucy Strathem matter ensconced him as the Bleak men's secret go-between for their extracurricular women.

So that James and later Jack left no fingerprints of their own, Fisher Sr. made all the arrangements for the Bleaks' rendezvous, instructed the women in how to navigate the serpentine mansion tunnels, procured the gifts the Bleaks would bestow on the women without leaving a money trail, and intervened with cash when the Bleaks inevitably tired of banging the same youngster.

The endless litigation between the Fishers and the Bleaks provided cover. As long as they were fighting in court, who would ever believe that the crazy guy on Blossom Hill was the Bleak men's beard?

All the while Fisher Sr. plowed the money the Bleaks secretly paid him into his growing business of digging up unflattering information on other people in Bleak Harbor. The second story of the house on the hill filled up with file cabinets, teetering stacks of documents, and boxes bulging with tape recordings and, later, cassettes. Fisher Sr. fancied himself a mirror image of the classic private investigator. Instead of waiting around for clients to hire him, Fisher Sr. got the investigating out of the way first, then persuaded the unsuspecting targets to employ him. It was just as interesting as being a PI, with a simpler business model.

Some called him a blackmailer even as they were signing checks to him. Fisher Sr. told himself that, as long as whatever he uncovered was rooted in fact, he was no different than journalists, prosecutors, or anybody else who portrayed themselves as upholding the beloved truth. "I am an entrepreneur in the purest American tradition," Fisher Sr. boasted to his namesake son. "If you pay attention, you will inherit a very fine business."

Fisher Jr. started working for his father the day he entered Bleak Harbor High School, a place teeming with adolescent gossips who reveled in shitting on their friends and exes and parents and parents' friends. Junior compiled notes and furtive recordings of conversations in locker rooms, hallways, buses, and restrooms. He and his father would discuss it on weekend afternoons as they fished on nearby Purgatory Bay, courtesy of the Bleaks, who owned it.

By the time Senior died, Junior had converted the piles of old paper on the second floor into digital records housed in triple-encrypted hard drives and servers. Two entire hard drives were devoted to the Bleak family, which Fisher Jr. used to extract a $5 million bounty when he and the Bleaks announced a settlement of the ancient dispute over Blossom Hill.

Fisher Jr. kept assisting Jack Bleak with his assignations while turning his spying skills on elected officials and the summer Chicagoans and Detroiters who deigned to tell Bleak Harbor how to improve itself. The trove was instrumental in Fisher's building a campaign war chest that helped him get elected mayor, a moment that he was certain had his father howling with laughter in his grave.

———

The ten monitors arranged on Fisher's standing desk flash on. He directs his mouse to the one framing a matrix of two dozen video screens, the feeds from cameras placed around town by the Bleak Harbor Police Department.

Or, as Fisher sees them, *his* cameras.

He ran for mayor promising to bring competence and security to Bleak Harbor after some zit-faced kid hacked the cops and the county and some banks and made off with a pile of cash he then started distributing to what seemed like every permanent resident of the city but Harland Fisher Jr. Once in office, Fisher fired the police chief and replaced him with the woman who had essentially let the zit-faced kid get away, expecting she'd then be beholden and compliant, which she was, most of the time. She didn't say a peep when he told the council they needed to take control of the police video system. Which meant Fisher took control of it. Sure, he lets the cops use it when they need to, but Fisher can access the cameras and their records anytime he likes.

He clicks his mouse to enlarge one of the boxes in the video matrix. It displays the view from a camera perched on a utility pole along Jeremiah Street. At the moment the black-and-white picture shows a placid boulevard lined on both sides by Victorians fronted by broad lawns, cars at the curbs, a youngster pedaling his bike down a sidewalk toward the bay. The bay is a sliver of pale gray at the far end of the street, six houses past Ophelia's first-floor rental.

Fisher clicks out of the live view. He wants to see what happened last night. He checked Ophelia's street around six then, when she usually walks home from her downtown shop with her business partner. He didn't see her, but she could have left early or gone to dinner with Langreth.

Which reminds him. He grabs his phone off the desk, pulls up his texts. One from Ophelia arrived the night before as he was watching the

Red Wings shut out the Blackhawks. Its appearance at 10:46 surprised him, partly because Ophelia hadn't texted him in weeks, partly because she isn't usually up past ten. "Sweet Ophelia," he said to himself, then, "What the hell?" as he read the text:

isths goodby?

Now he says aloud, "We said goodbye, girl. Least you did."

He sets the phone back down and hits a button that reels the videotape backward to the night before. Fisher stops it at 6:01, reverses it, and switches it into a choppy, frame-by-frame, fast-forward mode.

He finds it hard to imagine Ophelia actually "missing," in the sense that she was forcibly abducted. He doesn't know a soul, certainly not in Bleak Harbor, smart enough, or for that matter stupid enough, to abscond with Ophelia Wright against her will. Fisher can still feel the bolt of pain in his left nut from her abruptly lifted knee the night he tried—gently, he thought—to maneuver her into her bedroom. She wasn't yet ready to do it in her bedroom, apparently—and never was with Fisher—although she was happy to go after it almost anywhere else.

He wonders now if maybe he should have seen something coming, especially after that goofy text last night. And then there were the defacements of her precious roadside sculptures. He can understand why Langreth might think a prickly bastard like Fisher who'd been thrown over by Ophelia might seek revenge. But Fisher really didn't have a thing to do with painting black faces on Ophelia's imagined masterpieces. Although now, reconsidering, he wonders if Ophelia's text was an accusation.

Not guilty, he thinks.

At 8:27:05 on the video, a car pulls into the frame. It appears to slow in front of Ophelia's house. Fisher hits pause. He leans into the monitor. The car looks like Ophelia's Volvo SUV. He can't tell if it's black like Ophelia's because the video is black and white, but its color is dark, so it might be.

He hits the play button. The Volvo creeps past Ophelia's, then stops, sits still for a few seconds, then backs up, stops again, and turns up the driveway. Fisher loses sight of the car as it passes behind the house.

Gotta be Ophelia's car, he thinks. *But who's driving?*

He reverses the video. The Volvo backs up onto the street. Fisher slows it so he can watch frame by frame, trying to divine who's at the wheel. Of course it's not Ophelia, but it might be her business partner, who doesn't own a car and uses her Volvo sometimes to shop for supplies. Fisher sees a head in the driver's seat through the rear window, but only in silhouette because of the dusk. He doesn't think there's anyone else in the car, though Fisher can't be sure because his view is obscured somewhat by the camera angle.

He hits pause again and zooms in on the license plate. Ophelia, naturally, has a vanity plate on the car she cannot drive: *VISEE*, French for "sight." The up-close view of the plate on the Volvo in the video is too blurry to discern letters or numbers, but the plate appears to be white with a darker trim that could be blue, as on standard Michigan plates. Fisher shifts into a separate monitor and googles *state license plates*, bringing up a colorful five-by-ten grid. Arkansas, Virginia, Ohio, California, and others are white with blue trim, like Michigan. Not much help there.

Fisher runs the tape again, then stops it just as the car is about to vanish behind the house. He wants to see if anyone is watching from a window in the house. A light is on in the living room—Ophelia turns lights on even though she can't see them "so it doesn't look like a ghost lives here"—but nowhere else. Seeing no other signs of life, he sets the tape back on fast-forward mode and leans away, idly scratching his forehead beetle. This could take a while, but he has all night. And isn't it a mayor's civic duty to know everything happening in Bleak Harbor?

The video unspools—8:32, 8:44, 8:52—as visually static as a still painting of a still street in a small town on a cold, damp March night. Fisher tries to recall what Ophelia texted him to end their relationship. Something about wanting more than just sex, which made Fisher laugh, because at times it seemed that sex was all she ever wanted, at least from him.

He texted her back that he would be fine with a platonic something or other, but Ophelia already had blocked him, making Fisher laugh again. He didn't hit her up again, although he did have a few too many cocktails that one night when he sidled up to her and Langreth at Wehling's.

A blink of light on the video screen rouses him. "Whoa there," he says, stopping the tape, then reeling it back thirty seconds, a minute, two minutes. The scene is as it was: empty street, parked cars, bare oaks, house dark except for the light in the living room window.

Fisher clicks play.

Five and a half seconds pass on the meter at the bottom of the screen. A light comes on. Looks like the kitchen. But Ophelia only turns the kitchen light on when she has visitors. Fisher assumes that whoever was in that car must now be in her house.

Another minute passes. Another thirty seconds. Then the light in Ophelia's bedroom window flickers on. Fisher leans into the monitor, squinting. He sees exactly what he thought he saw.

There's a head in silhouette in Ophelia's window. The head is too high to be Ophelia. Fisher assumes it's the back of someone facing Ophelia. *Langreth? Nah,* Fisher thinks. He zooms in, tries to focus, but again it's too fuzzy to tell more. But it's not Ophelia, and he or she is in Ophelia's bedroom. Fisher can almost feel the pain in his left nut again.

The head moves away from the window. The light stays on. Another six minutes pass. Fisher sees nothing more in the window before the light goes off, the bedroom window now dark. He dollies the video view back again. He waits. Thirty-two seconds have gone by when he notices twin ovals of dull light pooling on the side driveway.

The Volvo's taillights. And then the Volvo.

As it backs onto Jeremiah Street and turns to face the camera at an oblique angle, Fisher can clearly see two people in the front seat. The Volvo proceeds toward the camera, toward Fisher. He waits until it's almost out of the frame, as close as it can get to the camera, and hits pause.

"Goddamn," he says. Ophelia is sitting in the front passenger seat. Fisher can't see all of her face, but a spray of light from a streetlamp illuminates the fluid curve of her nose. She liked Fisher to lick her between the eyebrows. She asked him once if he could see the yellow specks flickering at the backs of her afflicted eyes. He told her yes, he could, and she grabbed the skin at the back of his neck and squeezed it till it stung and said, "No, you can't."

Next to Ophelia sits a man shrouded in darkness, a hand gripping the top of the steering wheel—it has to be the man who was allowed into the bedroom. It can't be her business partner, who would be sitting lower in the seat. This guy takes up a lot of space.

Fisher squints at the screen. *Wait,* he thinks, *is that Ophelia's Volvo? Or this guy's?*

Fisher points his mouse at a different monitor, selects a directory called EmailFun, and clicks on Emails_Ophelia. He's no hacker, but he sneaked a look one evening at Ophelia logging into her email account. They were getting along fine then, and he promised himself that he would never use her emails for his own gain. Unless, of course, he absolutely had to.

He scans the saved sent and received emails. There are a bunch from Langreth, almost as many from Ophelia's sister, Mikey, some from suppliers who helped with Ophelia's sculptures, and several weeks ago, one from an address he hasn't focused on before, charl0tt7@bh.com. The subject line reads: Your sculptures. Fisher opens it. The body says: Your work is impressive. It is a shame that vandals would insult it. Might you have a more secure email address? Please email me from there and we will talk about future projects.

Probably some lesbian hitting on her, Fisher thinks. *Boo hoo, let's sleep together.* Ophelia whined a lot about what had happened to her sculptures. Fisher had a video camera near the one with the kid on the skateboard, but it had been on the blink for some reason. Obviously, somebody had been messing with her then. Maybe the same someone is now. Maybe this Charlotte whoever.

He maneuvers the mouse back to the paused image of the Volvo carrying Ophelia away. He right-clicks, sending the picture to a printer across the room. The printer hums.

Shit, Fisher thinks, *maybe she's legit missing after all.*

14

Ophelia counts her heartbeats against the ticking clock in her head, as she long ago trained herself to do. Sixty-nine beats per minute. Maybe seventy, seventy-one. Too high now. Earlier it was too low, in the midfifties, as it might be on a hungover morning.

She can't trust herself, though, because she's had to stop counting and start again twice, having trouble she doesn't normally have. She feels groggy and seminauseous, a knot of thistle pricking the edges of her brain, as if she'd had more than three glasses of red the night before. But not exactly that way. She doesn't recall a bit of drinking, only that she was in a car that brought her here.

Wherever here is.

She sits up as straight as she can, places her palms flat on her thighs, closes her sightless eyes, listens to herself breathe. *Even breaths,* she tells herself. *Slow, even breaths.* She knows she should feel afraid, but she refuses to succumb. *There must be a reason for this,* she keeps repeating in her head. *I will not panic. I will never panic. I will never panic again.*

She's trying not to think of Mikey and Bridget and Gary and anyone else who must be wondering where she is. She's focused for this moment instead on why someone would bring her here. She's trying to fathom what she could possibly have to offer someone who would steal her away.

She's sitting in an armchair. "Hello?" she said when she woke up on the bed next to the chair, wrapped in a silk sheet. When there was no answer, she said it again and could tell from the way her voice sounded that the room was not large. It feels like a room in a house rather than an office or some other place of business, but Ophelia can't be sure.

What time is it? she thinks, instinctively reaching again for her cell phone, as she did when she awoke, again patting each pocket in her jeans, again finding nothing. She already searched her bedclothes, the pillowcase, the hardwood floor beneath the bed, hoping she'd merely dropped the phone, knowing as she searched it was probably futile. Whoever had brought her here must have her phone. And her drawings and models. They were in her favorite bag in the car that brought her here. Where are they now?

There must be a reason for this. No panic. Never panic.

She stands and turns to her left, stretching an arm out, then a little farther, and finding a wall. She moves to face the wall, stepping gingerly with her bare feet—someone may have taken her shoes, too, because she couldn't find them by the bed—so she doesn't stub a toe. She moves slowly along the wall, sliding her hands ahead of her, stepping to her right, moving deliberately, hearing her breathing, feeling her heartbeat, encountering nothing until the wall ends in a corner.

Ophelia turns, following the wall. Three steps later, her right hand bumps into something slightly raised, and her fingertips slide along a smooth contour. A window frame, perhaps, or a doorjamb. She steps more quickly to her right, slides her fingers up and beyond the contour, detects with her forefinger a gap between the contour and another, flatter surface. She raps it with a knuckle, hears the hollow retort, then slides her hand across the door to the knob. Tries to turn it. It doesn't give. She twists it in the other direction and leans her body into the door. It's locked from the other side. She steps back, puts both hands atop her head.

No panic. Never again.

"Ophelia."

When she first hears the voice, Ophelia thinks of her phone, feels a swell of relief, and turns around toward the chair and the bed, thinking her phone is calling out to her.

"Everything is fine, Ophelia."

Ophelia looks up, imagining a face above her, a video camera, something watching. She feels her heartbeat starting to rat-a-tat, takes a big breath, says, "Who are you? Where am I?"

"I am Frances," the voice says. She sounds like a woman of about Ophelia's age, late thirties or early forties. There's something about her voice, though, that's unreal. Like the digitized voice on Ophelia's phone. "Please sit. The sedative should have worn off by now, but we don't want to take chances."

Ophelia spins slowly in place, trying to locate the woman, to sense what she cannot see, though she's beginning to suspect she wouldn't see anything even if she could see. "Who's 'we'?"

"I am Frances. Please sit."

"I am not going to sit."

Frances doesn't respond immediately. Ophelia reaches behind herself for the doorknob in case someone tries to enter the room. She waits, trying to quiet her heart. An image of Bridget pops into her head, the way Ophelia always pictures her, with her wide face encircling the high cheekbones and smooth forehead Ophelia loves to caress with her fingertips. *My favorite,* Ophelia thinks. It's what she always calls Bridget, because it's true. She has a laugh like Zeke's chicken cackle, and whenever Ophelia is feeling down, she will call Bridget, who always answers, and tell her a stupid joke—the stupider the better—so that Bridget will cackle and make Ophelia feel better.

Ophelia lets the image go. She can't afford it now. She moves back to the door and begins to follow the wall around again. Maybe there's a window, or a closet with a hatch leading to a cellar. She listened to an audiobook once where someone escaped a locked room through an air duct. She can't just sit here waiting for this Frances chick.

"Ophelia."

It makes Ophelia think of her friend Billy's kitchen. He's making salsa verde for chilaquiles and saying, *Alexa, how much garlic?*

"Go away, please," Ophelia says, "until you want to tell me where I am and why I'm here and when you'll be taking me home."

She moves past another corner and starts down a third wall as Frances replies, "There is no way out, Ophelia."

"Go away, Frances. You're not real anyway."

"Caleb will be in shortly with something for you to eat."

Caleb.

Ophelia stops and remembers. How strong he was, how easily and swiftly he detached her phone from her wrist, like she was an eight-year-old. How the feel of his skin, like dried mud on a riverbank, reminded her of the lizard Zeke had sneaked into her bed when they were still young enough to share a room. How she dreamed of that lizard crawling up and down her arms as she writhed in her sleep.

And how she was a fool to get in that car. A greedy, gullible, totally unlike herself fool.

———

She was surprised to hear the car pull all the way up the driveway. It seemed presumptuous, given that the young man picking her up was a stranger. Usually visitors parked on the street.

Ophelia opened the kitchen door for him. He remained outside, on the porch, awkward, as if he wasn't sure whether he should come in. She heard one of his heels tap-tap-tapping the porch boards.

"I'm here," he said, hesitating, "on behalf of M-Ms. White."

"Yes, I've been expecting you. I'm Ophelia." She reached through the doorway with her right hand. It hung there for a second before she felt the tips of three of his fingers touch hers and then let go, as if he was afraid to touch her. "What's your name?"

"I am Caleb."

"Caleb. Welcome, then. Are you going to come in? I could use your help with my things."

She heard him step inside, felt his presence, estimated that he was taller than her by at least a head, maybe as tall as Gary. "Would you like something to drink?" she said. "Some juice or a glass of water?"

"Yes, I w-would like some w-water, please."

From the timbre of his voice, Ophelia guessed his age at no more than twenty-three or twenty-four. She wondered if he stuttered because he was nervous about meeting someone new—especially an older woman, a blind older woman at that—or if he had a speech disorder. It didn't sound quite right, although, of course, an impediment wasn't supposed to sound right.

She took a bottle of water from the fridge and handed it to Caleb. "Here you go," she said. "My sketches are in the bedroom. Over here." She moved toward her bedroom, but he stayed where he was, drinking. She heard his gulps, imagined his Adam's apple bouncing. He set the bottle down on the kitchen counter. Ophelia could tell by the sound it made that it was empty.

"S-sorry," he said. "I was thirsty."

"This way."

She started toward the bedroom as a cell phone began to ring. Not hers. She had turned the ringer down because she knew Mikey might call. She'd see her sister and niece in the morning. She was happy about that, but now she had some important business to tend to, an opportunity.

"Do you have to get that?" she said. "It's OK."

"I do. One m-minute."

She could tell from his voice that he had turned away from her. She heard the rustle of clothing, pictured him fumbling his phone out of a hip pocket, heard something spilling onto the table, maybe coins or credit cards. He certainly seemed nervous. That was funny to Ophelia, because she considered herself about as harmless as someone could be. He stepped across the kitchen, farther from her. She could just make out what he said into the phone:

"Yes, I know . . . Everything is fine . . . I will." No stutter that she could discern. She felt him turn back toward her. "S-sorry again."

"That's all right."

She smiled as she led him into her bedroom. She almost never allowed men into that room. Ophelia was determined not to let those sounds and images—the strangled moans, the sweat beads along her hip bones—hover in that room, distracting her and hobbling her imagination, because that room was the sanctuary where she designed her sculptures. She liked to show lovers her work, but they didn't need to cross the threshold for that. She had made an exception, once, for Gary. She wasn't sure she would make it again.

But Caleb was there merely as a chauffeur, to deliver her to a secret patron who had expressed her appreciation for Ophelia's sculptures with two checks totaling $7,500 written from a Detroit bank account for Charlotte White LLC. Ophelia had happily endorsed the checks and deposited them in her bank account. Charlotte White had said she intended the money for repairs to the sculptures that had been defaced.

Now this mysterious benefactor had begun talking to Ophelia—strictly via an encrypted Mailfence account Ophelia had opened at Charlotte's request—about a more substantial donation in return for a more ambitious creative endeavor. Charlotte wanted to see first, in person, what Ophelia proposed to do with a gift of, say, $25,000 or even $50,000.

Charlotte had to be sure at the same time that nobody knew who or where she was. The woman had said she was "inordinately" wealthy, heiress to the estate of a semifamous entrepreneur she hadn't named, and her wealth sometimes attracted the wrong kinds of people, so her privacy was paramount. The alliteration had pushpinned the word *paramount* to Ophelia's brain. She hadn't told anyone about the chauffeur picking her up for a visit with Charlotte White.

Ophelia had done some internet searching, using a braille keyboard and a digital audio assistant. She'd found no heiresses who appeared to be her Charlotte but plenty of reassuring newspaper and television stories about anonymous donors appearing from nowhere to help the less fortunate. Whoever Charlotte White was, her $7,500 was absolutely real. Anyway, Ophelia would soon shake her hand.

"The newer drawings are on the wall next to the bureau," she told Caleb as he walked into her bedroom. She heard him stop near the dresser, which stood beneath a window facing the street. "And you can see some foam models I made over there." She pointed in the direction of the built-in shelves on the wall beyond her bed, a drawing table beneath them. "I've been working pretty much nonstop since Charlotte made her very sweet offer. I have a number of things to show her."

"That one," Caleb said, "is b-beautiful."

"Which?"

"The loon? It is a l-loon, y-yes?"

"Next to the dresser mirror? Yes, that is a loon."

"I l-like loons. Loons d-don't like to g-g-go on land."

Really? she thought. *A young male who appreciates loons, let alone a drawing of a loon.*

"That's right," Ophelia says. "They're excellent swimmers, but their feet aren't good for walking. That drawing is part of one of the sculptures I want to make. I have a model, too, that we'll take with us. There's a big handbag in my closet, over there, if you don't mind putting the things in there. Most of them are in a stack on the floor there."

"Y-yes. Some people ruined your sculptures."

"Yes, they did. Painted the faces."

"They t-took a leg too? That's t-too bad."

"That, too, for what ungodly reason I have no idea. But if they hadn't, well, maybe I never would have heard from Charlotte."

"We should go."

"You will bring me back tonight?" Ophelia said. "It's OK if it's late; I just need to be here in the morning. I have family coming."

"That will be fine."

They unpinned the drawings and gathered the scale models into Ophelia's big bag and put it in the car. Ophelia sat in the passenger seat. The seat and the door handle felt familiar.

"Is this by chance a Volvo?" she said.

"Y-yes," Caleb said.

"I have a Volvo."

"Please, ma'am, your seat belt."

Ma'am, she thought as she buckled in. "Do you mind telling me where we're going? At least the general vicinity?"

"As you know, p-p-privacy is paramount. So."

"Right. But you know, it's not like I could find it on my own."

Caleb didn't respond.

Ophelia took out her phone. "I just want to let my sister know where to meet in the morning," she said. "Then I'll turn it off."

"No," Caleb said. "Privacy is paramount."

"It's just a—wait, what are you doing?"

She yelped in pain as he grabbed and twisted her wrist, the phone falling from her hand. "Caleb, that hurt."

He didn't answer. She heard the console being flipped open. She reached for the door and said, "Let me out of this car now."

Then she felt a poke like the sting of a wasp in the meat of her upper arm. That was the last she would remember.

———

When Ophelia hears the door open, she bolts up from the bed and immediately starts to shake. *Quiet,* she tells herself. *Calm down.*

"Please stay where you are."

"Caleb," she says. She smells the aroma of food. Broccoli. Cheese. Tomato sauce of some sort. She holds up the wrist Caleb squeezed to take her phone. She can feel the bruise.

"You hurt me," she says.

"I brought you something to eat."

"Where is Charlotte, Caleb? Or does she even exist?"

Caleb doesn't answer. She hears him moving closer.

"Stay away from me."

He stops. He's standing near, about two feet away.

"You d-don't need to be afraid," he says. "Ch-Charlotte will be here in a while. I'm going to put this down over there."

Ophelia feels a flicker of relief at his acknowledgment of Charlotte. Though he could be lying.

"If I don't need to be afraid," she says, "then you should give me my phone so I can let my family know where I am."

"I c-can't do that now."

"Caleb, I guarantee you they're looking for me. My boyfriend works for the county prosecutor."

Saying it makes her feel even more helpless than she did a second ago. She realizes she has no idea how long she was in that car, how far she is from Bleak Harbor. She doesn't even know if it's still Thursday or Friday. She blurts, "What time is it?"

Caleb is over by the armchair now. She hears him setting something down. There must be a table next to the chair she didn't notice earlier. She imagines climbing on top of it, finding that air duct for her escape. He ignores her question about the time, saying, "I hope you like the f-food."

She can tell from his voice that he has turned his back to her. She calculates that he's six, maybe seven feet away. Two strides. She takes her injured wrist in her hand, pushes her thumb into the bruise, feels the pain.

"Just take me home, OK?" she says.

Before Caleb can reply, Ophelia leaps across the room, flailing with open hands at where she expects his face to be. She gets him good with the heel of her right hand across a cheekbone. It feels as rough and dry as the plaster of paris she uses on her sculpture models.

"No," he says, grabbing her with one hand beneath an armpit and lifting her off the floor.

"Bastard," she shouts, kicking at him with her dangling legs, slamming her left hand into his neck, clawing at the skin, which is like leather that's been slashed into jagged ridges with a serrated knife. Then she's swinging away from him as he looses a guttural roar and flings her backward onto the bed.

"No," he yells. "No. Never touch."

Ophelia scoots herself back against the wall, her left palm tingling with the recollection of Caleb's neck. She can hear him standing a few feet from her, breathing hard, smelling of sweat, when a voice booms over the room. A female voice that sounds like something that might issue from a laptop. "Caleb," it says. "Remove yourself."

"Caleb," Ophelia says, holding up her palm as if he might be able to see what she felt. "What happened to you?"

She hears his footsteps, the door opening and slamming shut. Then the woman's voice again:

"Ophelia. Do not touch Caleb. Ever."

15

Not again, Malone thinks.

The Bleak Harbor police chief has done the abduction thing before. That case was a wild-goose chase that almost got her killed. She learned that people don't know other people as well as they think they do.

Now she's reminding herself of that very thought as she sits at a table in the packed bar at the hockey rink. Across from her is Mikey Deming, sister of Ophelia Wright, who is co-owner of a boutique on Lily Street that Malone has never been in. Ophelia is missing. Supposedly.

Mikey called the station as Malone was driving back from the press conference she had attended at Purgatory Bay. She was feeling good at the time, glad to have met Jubilee Rathman. Malone thought her an impressive woman for all the tragedy she had endured.

The tavern is a tight triangle of wood paneling and tile floor sandwiched into a second-floor corner of the rink, thronged with people wearing jackets and hoodies blaring the logos of their teams, as if the tournament were being played as much off the ice as on. The floor is sticky, and the air smells of burnt pizza. A wall to Malone's right is covered with framed photographs of men mugging in hockey jerseys. Video screens behind the bar display a live feed of the game going on below and replays of earlier games.

"So, Ms. Deming," she says. "What can you tell me about your sister?"

"Please, call me Mikey. It's actually Michaela, but my father wanted a son."

Her smile is fleeting. Malone figures her to be in her early forties, a bit prematurely gray, meaning she might be a worrier. Worriers make Malone's job more difficult. She thinks of Jubilee and whether anything could possibly worry that woman anymore after losing her entire family.

"OK, Mikey."

"Ophelia is, well, Ophelia. Though not quite like her namesake."

"From Shakespeare?"

"Right. *Hamlet*. My mother played Ophelia in a high school play and fell in love with the drama of it all, Ophelia going insane for the sake of love. So: Ophelia. We call her Pheels."

"Your sister isn't quite so melodramatic?"

"Not so much about love. Her passions are reserved for art—"

"Her roadside sculptures."

"—yes, and doing everything she can to prove that her blindness cannot keep her from doing, well, everything she can, or wants."

Malone leans into the table, straining to hear Mikey over the click and slap of hockey sticks and some out-of-town blowhard bitching to the barmaid that the referees are "homers." She'd bet twenty bucks he'll be cut off before the day is out.

"I like those sculptures," Malone says. "Has Ophelia been blind her whole life?"

"No. She started losing her sight when she was"—Mikey thinks for a second—"eleven or twelve. At first, she just had cloudy vision in the center of her eyes, although none of us knew because of course she didn't tell anyone. It progressively got worse. You couldn't tell from looking at her that anything was wrong. Her eyes looked perfectly normal—well, gorgeous. She has gorgeous blue eyes. She's never had a problem with men. Or at least with attracting them."

"And now she can't see at all?"

"I don't think so, although to talk to her, you'd think she can see through brick walls. The truth is—"

They both jump at the crack of a puck whacking the plexiglass window at the end of the bar. "Jesus," Malone says, turning. No one else in the bar seems fazed. "I'm sorry. You were saying . . ."

"I was just going to say that Ophelia's blindness has probably been less of a disability to her than the memory of our brother's death."

"When was—I mean, what was his name?"

"Zeke. July 14, 1994. An accident on the dunes north of town."

Malone was in grade school then in Grand Haven, north of Bleak Harbor. "I'm sorry to hear that," she says. "Was he older or younger?"

"He was actually Ophelia's twin." Mikey smiles. "We like to say he was lucky not to be named Laertes."

Malone returns the smile, but she's recalling the note Gary gave her, the one Ophelia may or may not have written. "When did you last speak with your sister?"

"A couple of days ago on the phone," Mikey says. "She was very excited about seeing Bridget—that's my daughter, the one playing in the tournament, Ophelia's niece; they're close—and then we were texting Wednesday and yesterday morning, and then she just went dark."

Malone's phone buzzes on the table. "How so?"

"Well, I thought we were going to have dinner somewhere last night, but then Pheels texted that she had some business to take care of in the evening, so she'd see us Friday—this morning. That actually worked better for Bridget, because we didn't have to leave Ann Arbor— that's where we live—before school was out. So I said, *How about if we just stop at the house late when we get in, just say hi?* She never responded to that."

"And that was when?"

As Mikey picks up her phone, Malone sneaks a peek at her own, sees a recent text from Mayor Fisher:

Did you send langreth my way?

Malone is annoyed but not surprised.

"I sent that text at ten thirty-eight yesterday morning," Mikey says. "Then I sent two more while we were en route. Bridget texted too. No reply."

"Is it unusual for Ophelia to just leave you hanging?"

"Yes and no. Sometimes she gets, I don't know, preoccupied, and I don't hear from her. But this was odd, because we were in the middle of a conversation." Mikey's eyes go wide. She waves her hand over her head. Malone turns around to see Gary coming into the bar.

"Do you know Gary Langreth? Ophelia's boyfriend?"

A little better than you might guess, Malone thinks. "I do," she says.

She looks up at him towering over the table. When they first met, Gary Langreth reminded her of an early version of her former husband, before that loser had started sleeping with a local pharmacist. He'd been stealing away with their daughter, Louisa—or so Malone had convinced herself—when she'd chased him on the twisting roads outside Bleak Harbor and his car had slid off the road into an oak, killing Louisa on impact.

"Chief," Gary says.

"Langreth."

"What did you find out?" Mikey says.

He sits next to Mikey, says, "Have you heard from Ophelia?"

"No. Have you?"

He slides his phone faceup to Mikey. She reads the text once and looks at Gary, her face a question mark, then rereads the text. "What the hell is that?" she says. Squeezing back tears, she shoves the phone to Malone. "Dammit, Ophelia."

Malone reads the text aloud: "'Is this our goodby?'"

"It's like that note she left in the kitchen," Mikey says.

Malone addresses Gary. "She hasn't called you?"

"Not yet." He reaches into a pocket and shoves a plastic bag at Malone. Inside is a Super 8 key. "We found this in Ophelia's bedroom."

Malone picks it up, turns it over, sets it back down. "So you had this when you were in my office?"

"Sorry. I wanted to show it to somebody else first."

"You mean Fisher."

"Who's Fisher?" Mikey says.

"Longtime local, now our mayor," Gary says. "He dated your sister for a bit before me. They had kind of a messy breakup. You didn't know?"

"Ophelia doesn't tell me every single thing. As you can see."

Gary looks at Malone and says, "I think he knows something."

"About Ophelia?" Mikey says.

Fisher always knows something, Malone thinks. It was Fisher, in fact, who told her about Gary's Detroit career troubles. "I will check in with him," she says. "Meantime"—she picks up the baggie holding the Super 8 key—"what am I to do with this?"

"Get a print?"

"I'm sure I can get hundreds of prints, Langreth."

"Just trying to help, Chief."

"Mikey," Malone says. "I want to ask about the note you found in Ophelia's kitchen. Are you sure that's her handwriting?"

"Pretty sure. Plus"—she looks at Gary again—"it's like what she sent you."

"Yes," Malone says. "Do you have any idea why she would write that? Both notes?"

"You're asking me something else, aren't you, Chief?"

"I'm sorry. I don't know your sister."

"Ophelia has occasional bouts of depression. But she deals with it. I can't see her doing anything dire."

"Does she take medication?" Malone says.

"She—yes, she does. But let's just say she's not—oh, Bridget, Craig." Mikey gets out of her chair. "Can we drop this subject for now, please?" she asks Malone, then waves. "Bridge, honey, over here."

Malone turns to see Mikey's daughter weaving through the bar crowd, showered hair damp on her shoulders, a butterfly stitch stuck to her chin. Following her is a man in a black-and-gold Pride jacket and matching baseball cap. Mikey comes around the table to hug Bridget, and as she does, Bridget's gaze falls on Malone.

Shit, Malone thinks, *the uniform.*

"Why are the police here?" Bridget says. She looks from her mother to Gary and back again. "Where's Aunt Pheels?"

"What happened to your chin, baby?" Mikey says.

"Nothing. A stick. Why is this officer here?"

Craig Deming slides around to his wife. "Sorry I'm late," he says. "I caught Bridge coming out of the dressing room."

"I hate ties," Bridget says.

"That Minnesota team was good. Did anyone say anything about the lights going out in the middle of the game?"

Bridget ignores the question as she uses her hands to shake out her hair. "We should have won. What about Aunt Pheels? Is she coming later?"

Malone watches Bridget, thinking of her Louisa. Would she have been as pretty and as sulky at fifteen? "Bridget, Mr. Deming," Malone says, standing. "I'm Chief Katya Malone of the Bleak Harbor police. And maybe you already know Gary Langreth of the Bleak County Prosecutor's Office?"

"I've heard of him," Craig Deming says, shaking Gary's hand. "The entire police force of Bleak Harbor, eh? Who's minding the parking meters?"

"They're helping us, Craig," Mikey says. "Gary heard from Ophelia, so that's good."

"It's good if we know where she is."

"Not sure yet," Gary says. "But we'll get there."

"Ophelia," Craig says, shaking his head. "Right now we need to get Bridget some food. She has another tough game coming up."

Malone glances toward the bar. That out-of-town guy is blathering again about the refs.

"They have wings here," Mikey says.

"Hockey-rink chicken wings," her husband says, frowning. "Excellent."

"Just sit down, Craig."

He sits next to Malone. Bridget goes around the table to a chair next to her mother. Craig takes his hat off, sets it on the table. "We appreciate your help, Chief," he says. "Mikey has filled me in. I hope she told you this isn't the first time Ophelia has up and disappeared."

"Not in so many words."

Craig turns to his wife. "You didn't tell them about the wedding?"

Mikey's face goes slack, her eyes wide. "Craig," she says.

"We came here for a wedding for one of Ophelia's friends, I don't know, six or seven years ago. Her *best* friend, at the time."

"Craig."

"Ophelia was supposed to do one of the readings. She never showed."

"She had a good reason. And she was at the reception."

"I see," Malone says. Her phone is pulsing again. "Excuse me."

She turns away from the table. Fisher just texted her an image along with a message: I have more. let's talk, chief.

The black-and-white image on her phone looks to be from a city camera on Jeremiah Street. A car is passing. What appears to be a woman sits in the passenger seat. The driver appears to be a man. A large man.

The time stamp on the image is 9:16 last night.

Though she had little say in the matter, it still annoys Malone that the mayor, not her department, has domain over the city's security cameras. It's even more annoying that Fisher seems to think he, not Malone, is Bleak Harbor's top law enforcement official, a sort of shadow sheriff who uses the budget and the cameras to manipulate her.

She turns back to the table, phone in hand. If the bar—hell, the entire rink—weren't such a zoo, she would take Mikey and her husband aside. But there's no aside here.

"Mikey," she says, "where does your sister live?"

"On Jeremiah Street, off Lily."

"OK." Malone shows her the phone. "Something just came in that, I don't know, might be nothing." She sets the phone down in front of Mikey. Gary and Craig also lean in to look. "That wouldn't be your sister in the front seat, would it?"

Mikey pulls the phone close. "What is this? Who took it?"

"It's from a security camera on Jeremiah. Taken last night a little after nine."

"That's late for her to be leaving her house. But doesn't it look like she's leaving?"

Now Bridget leans in. "Oh my God, Mom," she says. "That's Aunt Pheels. That's how she sits, like"—Bridget leans her body the other way—"on that angle. And that's her car, isn't it?"

"Why the hell does she have a car anyway?" Craig says.

"Please, sir," Malone says. She can tell that Mikey isn't listening now. She's staring at the photo, her face gone pale. "Mikey?"

She looks up at Malone. "Is this the only shot you have?"

"For the moment, yes. Why?"

"I can't see the license plate." She's suddenly agitated; Malone can't tell why. "I need to see the license plate."

"Why? So you can see if it's Ophelia's?"

"It was Ohio." A tremor has crept into her voice. "He had an Ohio plate."

"Wait," Malone says. "Did you call the department last night?"

"Yes, yes, I—I'm sorry; I should have mentioned it."

"You left a plate number with the dispatcher."

"Yes, an Ohio plate."

"OK. We're running that." Malone points at the phone. "Do you think this is the same car?"

"Mom," Bridget says. "Are you talking about the guy who woke me up?"

"Yes, that man."

"Hey, you," Malone says, turning and directing her voice toward the loudmouth at the bar. "Pipe down, or that'll be your last beer of the weekend." The man throws his hands up as if to say, *Who, me?*

Asshole, Malone thinks.

"Mikey," Gary says, "that *is* Ophelia, isn't it?"

"That is Ophelia."

"What about the driver?"

Mikey is visibly shaking now, her eyes welling. "Mom," Bridget says, wrapping her mother's shoulders with an arm. "Are you OK?"

"It's a man. The driver is a man. See? It has to be that man. He was—he blocked us on Lily Street. He tried to scare us."

Malone reaches across the table for Mikey's hand, feels it trembling. She thought that the woman in the car might be Ophelia, might offer Mikey and her daughter some reassurance. She didn't expect this.

"Mikey, talk to me," she says. "What happened last night?"

"He had a face." She looks at her husband. "I told you. He put his window down. Just for a second." Bridget wraps an arm around her mother. "I couldn't tell if he was laughing at me or if his face was just like that."

"Like what?"

"It was dark," Craig says. "You were tired."

"He had a face?" Langreth says. "What kind of face?"

"He had—oh God, he has my sister." She pulls Bridget closer. "That man. That man with the face."

16

Twelve years earlier

"So he's going to get away with it?" Jubilee said. "This animal, whoever did this, is just going to go free? The Petruglias will just walk away?"

Pine County prosecutor Anthony Ralko didn't appear to hear her. He was peering through reading glasses at some papers on his desk.

"Mr. Ralko?"

"Yes, yes," he said. "We need a final decision. I'm afraid it might not be to your liking, Jubilee."

Ralko had been elected to six consecutive terms as prosecutor of Pine County, a rectangle of inland lakes and golf courses 220 miles north of Detroit. He had inhabited this first-floor office in the redbrick courthouse in the county seat, Starvation Lake, for twenty-two years, longer than Jubilee had been alive.

"Please," Jubilee told Ralko, "I don't need another lecture about the glories of the law."

"Child," he said. "There is no need—"

"I told you not to call me *child.*"

"I'm afraid you are a child, dear."

"You can stop with *dear* too. I'm eighteen, the guardian of my brother, and apparently the only one in this office seeking justice for my family."

Ralko stood, his brown leather chair swiveling away, his back to Jubilee. He went to his credenza, a mahogany beast devoid of anything but photographs of Ralko with his wife and two sons, his late parents, and his beloved younger sister, with whom he spoke each afternoon after he completed his work and she hers as a teacher of the deaf somewhere downstate. "This is Portia," he had told Jubilee one day, handing her the picture. "She helps the less fortunate. I'm so proud of her."

Now the prosecutor turned to face Jubilee again. "I worry about your anger, Jubilee," he said.

She looked at the third steno pad she had filled with notes about her conversations with Ralko, court hearings, lawyer conferences. "I don't want to get mad," she said. "I want to get even. I cannot get even if you don't conduct a proper investigation."

"Young lady, I—we—are doing our level best. But unfortunately, we have a paucity of evidence to provide a sufficient basis for a charge of manslaughter, let alone first-degree murder. Despite the inhumane nature of the alleged crimes."

"*Alleged?*" Jubilee said, feeling her butt coming off the chair. "Are my mother and father *allegedly* dead? Half of my sister's head *allegedly* blown away? Is that what you meant to imply, Mr. Prosecutor?"

Ralko hated when she called him that. She got a little thrill seeing his left cheek twitch. He peeled off his reading glasses and pointed them at her. "Forgive me," he said. "I am simply following the law."

"Why won't you let Oakland County help, Mr. Prosecutor?"

He started shaking his head. She wanted to slap his wrinkled face. "We take care of our own laundry here in Pine County—"

"No, you'd rather have an outlet mall than justice for a ruined family, isn't that right, Mr. Prosecutor?"

Ralko set his glasses down on a blotter. "Excuse me, young lady?"

"What happened to Oakland County?"

The prosecutor in Oakland County, a mostly well-to-do enclave north of Detroit, had desperately wanted to help with the case. She had argued that she could establish venue because most of the Petruglias lived in her county; indeed, it was the Michigan State Police, not the

Pine County sheriff, who had investigated on the night of the massacre, and Oakland County within hours had sent forensics experts to assist. All Oakland needed was Ralko's cursory courteous nod, and the Petruglias would have had to face the vastly greater prosecutorial resources of Oakland rather than Pine County.

It had almost happened, before it hadn't.

Now Jubilee slid a sheet of paper out from her steno pad and slapped it on Ralko's desk. The top of the page bore a Pine County Clerk's Office time stamp dated two days earlier. "Here," she said, out of her chair now, almost screaming. "Here's what happened to Oakland County."

———

One month before, Ralko had been emailing Jubilee's attorney, E. Jonathan Phillips, that Pine County would soon be turning the investigation over to Oakland County. Then Arvanites Brothers, a real estate development company in the Detroit suburb of Bloomfield Hills, filed documents with Pine County seeking zoning approval for an outlet mall on the outskirts of Starvation Lake.

The filing wasn't publicly disclosed.

Jubilee happened to hear some locals gossiping about it while she was having bacon and eggs one morning at a diner called Audrey's. She knew that name, Arvanites. The company had handled real estate for her father's business. But the main Arvanites client, everyone downstate knew, was the Petruglia family.

Jubilee had a hunch.

She might have let it go if Ralko hadn't canceled his appointment with her that morning after her breakfast at Audrey's, saying he had the flu, or if he hadn't then stopped answering Phillie's emails.

Her next time in Pine County, she visited the county clerk's office. The clerk was useless, but Jubilee figured out on her own—she was used to doing that by now—how to find what she was looking for.

The deed to the twenty-two acres where the Petruglia organization's favored real estate firm proposed to build was held by one Hubert Z. Stone of Ceresco, Michigan. It didn't take much googling for Jubilee to determine that Hubert Stone's wife was one Portia Maureen Ralko Stone, the portly woman with the uncertain smile in the photo on the Pine County prosecutor's credenza. Ralko's sister.

The clerk appeared to be annoyed when Jubilee offered a debit card to pay the four dollars for the single page she wanted.

"Quarters and dimes better?" Jubilee said.

She folded the page and slipped it inside her steno pad.

———

Now Ralko picked up the page Jubilee had laid on his desk, squinted at it, shrugged. "You understand nothing," he said. "Like a child."

Jubilee felt the jolt then, stabbing her first in the throat and tearing through to her jawbone and back teeth, the tendrils stretching to her collarbone and neck as she tightened them all against the sob she refused to let escape—not this time, not again—in front of Ralko.

She was so tired of crying. At the University of Michigan burn center. At the coffee shop up the street. On the living room sofa at the house in Clarkston.

"I'm sorry, Jubilee, but it's probably best if you go now. I will call your lawyer, Mr. Phillips, and tell him what we discussed."

Jubilee wasn't listening. Her eyes were closed, and she was humming a song, conjuring Joshua. She hadn't seen her brother since yesterday because she'd had to drive here to meet with this coward.

He needs to know, she thought. *He will know.*

She opened her eyes and looked at the phone squeezed in her left hand. She opened the email Tessa had sent that morning. She had attached a photo of herself with Joshua, Tessa smiling, Joshua's face wrapped in bandages: Hang in girl, Joshie LOVES U, we LOVE you. XXXOOO.

Still humming, Jubilee touched a fingertip to the picture of her brother's shrouded face. She looked up at Ralko. "Did you know, Mr. Prosecutor, that my brother was burned so badly that they had to take fingerprints to establish a record of his ID?"

"I'm very familiar with the case," Ralko said.

"Are you familiar with the term *debridement*?"

"What is your point, exactly?"

"Debridement—I'll oversimplify it so you can understand—is the process of removing dead, burned skin so that new skin can grow. It can be extremely painful."

Ralko hit a button on his phone and said, "Can you send in the deputy?"

"You know," Jubilee continued, "every day, about two hours from now, a doctor comes into my brother's room at the U of M burn center. Every day. For his debridement. Are you listening?"

"Listening to what?"

She hit a button on her phone and extended the phone toward the prosecutor.

"What is this?" he said.

The first sound out of Jubilee's phone was the voice of a woman. It was at a distance—Jubilee had been standing on the opposite side of Joshua's bed as she'd recorded—so the woman's words were too muffled to be intelligible. But her tone was audibly soothing.

Next came the voice of a boy. Pleading.

"No," he said, then louder: "Please, no. Just. Not today. Tomorrow morning. Please . . ."

Then Jubilee's voice: "It's OK, Joshie. It'll be over soon."

"Young lady," Ralko said. "That's quite enough."

The boy's begging grew louder. "No, leave me alone. Please, please."

"That's my brother, Mr. Ralko," Jubilee said.

"I know what—I understand. Enough, young lady."

She turned the phone volume as high as it would go. "Hear that? He's eight years old. He should be at Clarkston Elementary learning how to draw parallelograms. Instead he's being tortured."

The screaming started then. Ralko put his hands to his ears, punched the intercom button again on his phone.

"Deputy," he shouted.

Jubilee wanted to grab the letter opener out of the Cooley Law mug on Ralko's desk and plunge it into his neck. She wanted to collapse on the floor and vomit out sobs. She wanted to beg somebody, anybody, to do something, anything, to make the Petruglias pay for what they had done to her family, her brother, her life. Joshua was screaming, then catching his breath, screaming again.

Jubilee bit her lower lip until she felt the blood pool warm on her gums. She felt a hand on her shoulder. "I'm sorry, Ms. Rathman," she heard the deputy say. "Please."

As he ushered her out, Jubilee started making a list in her head. She wasn't certain yet what she would do with the list, but she knew there would be justice for her family. And she knew that she would never, ever cry again. She walked out of Ralko's office for the last time with the taste of blood in her mouth.

17

"I cannot believe you brought up Bonnie's wedding."

Mikey spits it at her husband when they're standing outside the rink entrance. She dragged him out here, momentarily leaving Bridget with two of her coaches. The wind has kicked up, a tinge of dampness on the air.

"I thought the chief should know who she's dealing with," Craig says. "We shouldn't be sending her on a wild-goose chase."

"Ophelia wanted to be there for Bonnie," Mikey says, almost shouting it, jabbing a finger into Craig's chest. "She thought she could do it. But she couldn't. And you know why."

Mikey recalls Ophelia's friend in her wedding dress beneath the arch of yellow flowers set up on Emerald Beach just south of Bleak Harbor, attendees waiting in white folding chairs. She pictures Ophelia listening from down the beach, unable to come closer to the stretch of dune where Zeke had died. She remembers how Ophelia reached across her kitchen table and grasped her hands as she explained to Mikey why she hadn't been able to come to the ceremony, how they both cried a little then, and laughed a little, thinking of their brother.

"OK," Craig says. "I'm sorry. Can we talk about something else? Like maybe our daughter?"

"Bridget's tough. She'll get through this."

"I know. You're right. Listen, I'm sorry about the wedding thing. It just came out. I wish it hadn't."

Mikey looks away from him, across the parking lot. She loves her husband even if sometimes he's a horse's ass.

They met as reporters at the *Detroit Times*, twenty-two-year-old Mikey a cop beat reporter, ten-years-older Craig Deming covering business. They worked together once on a big running story about the prosecution of a Superior Motors executive who'd been caught selling intellectual property to a Korean competitor.

Craig Deming was good with his auto-industry sources, but he could not make a deadline. It drove Mikey nuts. The first time he asked her out, she imagined herself waiting alone in a restaurant, irksome pity in the waitress's eyes, and told him no. After he left the *Times* to teach journalism at Michigan, he invited her to speak to a class.

It seemed innocent enough. Afterward they went for beers that stretched past midnight. She'd had too much to drink to drive back to Detroit from Ann Arbor, so she slept on Craig's couch. With him.

After they married and had Bridget, he gradually became the most punctual person Mikey knew, almost aggravatingly so, always on time, always cranky when Mikey or anybody else wasn't, especially after Bridget started playing hockey.

"Bridget played well this morning," Mikey says. "It's too bad you missed it. She made a really nice play on the tying goal."

"My dean was late, of course. As always."

"Your loss," she says, enjoying his discomfort after he brought up the Bonnie wedding.

"One of those Minnesota players is on Wisconsin's list too. That Weiss girl. She's no Bridget, but she can play."

"I don't like that Wisconsin coach."

"So you've said."

"There was a little delay between the second and third periods. Some problem with the lights."

"That's what happens when you have a really big hockey tournament in a really small town."

"I happen to love this place."

"I know, I know," Craig says. "I kind of love it too. More in summer than now, though. Should we go back inside?"

Bridget doesn't play again for more than an hour. Mikey has no desire to stand around in the lobby with all those parents. She was starting to feel claustrophobic in there earlier. Which reminds her.

"Did you see the news about Robillard?" she says.

"Who?"

"Vance Robillard. From the *Times*. He died."

"Oh, Robo. What a character. No, I did not hear. No surprise, though, right? The way that guy lived, it's hard to believe he made forty."

Mikey's phone starts ringing in her pocket. "Sounded like he might have been murdered," she says.

"Well, that sucks. Is that your phone?"

She takes it out. "Unknown number. No, thanks."

"It might be a coach. Maybe Wisconsin."

"I talked to him earlier. That was plenty."

"Mikey, this is our daughter's future."

She exhales, exasperated, answers the call.

"Hello?"

"Michaela Deming?"

The voice is female but sounds computerized. Mikey hangs up. "Frigging robocall," she tells Craig. "Let's go find Bridget."

They're barely back inside when her phone starts ringing again. She looks, and again, it's an unknown number. She ignores it. Bridget is at the other end of the lobby along the rink glass with three of her teammates. Mikey wonders if she has told them about her aunt Ophelia. Probably not, she decides. Bridget wouldn't want to distract them from the tournament. Later, maybe tomorrow, she'll tell them, after Ophelia is back home safe.

Mikey's phone vibrates in her hand. *Leave us alone,* she thinks, looking at it. A voice mail has come in. She starts to delete it, then remembers what her husband said. It really might be a coach. Or maybe Chief Malone, or Gary, or another someone looking for Ophelia.

She waits. The recording begins.

"Mrs. Deming," says the same electronic female. "Ophelia has not committed suicide."

Mikey turns around so Bridget can't see her. "Craig," she says.

He steps closer. "What? Ophelia?"

The voice continues. "My name is Charlotte White. I wrote the note you found in Ophelia's kitchen. I'm guessing that worried you. But I—"

"Where are you?" Mikey says, as if the voice were live and not a recording.

"—wanted to be sure to secure your undivided attention."

"Who is it?" Craig says.

"Ophelia is alive and well, for now."

The call ends. Without any demands, not even an acknowledgment that Mikey will hear from this Charlotte White again. Mikey feels the tears hot in her eyes as she hits replay and listens again.

This time she hears a song she doesn't recognize playing faintly in the background.

Ophelia is alive and well.

For now.

She hands the phone to Craig. "Listen," she gasps. "Someone named Charlotte White has Ophelia."

18

Xavier Christian hates to think it at a funeral luncheon, and he sure as hell won't say it aloud, but this has to be the best pastitsio he's ever eaten.

The lamb is tender, the noodles have a little bite, and there's just enough béchamel to make the dish tasty without being soggy. Who would have thought a chef—an Italian chef, at that—cooking for a couple of hundred people could get it so fricking perfect? Especially since the lunch was delayed after the incident at the church; the cops kept everyone from leaving right away.

He squints across the room at the buffet, hoping for seconds. The line of black dresses and dark suits is still long. Good thing he filled his plate so full the first trip. He wipes a chunk of bread through a puddle of sauce, pinches it around some ground lamb, stuffs it in his mouth. *Sweet Lord Jesus,* he thinks. *This is even better than—*

"You," comes the voice behind him. He knows the voice and the painful jab of her knuckle into the muscle between his neck and shoulder. He wants to say, *What the hell, woman?* but that wouldn't be good for his professional or personal future. Instead he turns and says, "Gemma. How are you holding up?"

"You should close your mouth when you're eating," she says. She's barely taller than him when he's sitting, and at least twenty years younger, but Gemma Petruglia is not to be trifled with. She used to be squat and a little wide beamed, but yoga and half marathons changed that. Her elevated role in the family business has made her even sexier, another thing he can't say aloud.

"Sorry," he says.

"We need to have a conversation. Come with me."

He gives his plate a baleful glance, decides it wouldn't be smart to take it with him, promises himself he'll come back to this joint some night for a peaceful dinner by himself. He pats his mouth with a napkin and stands. "Where to?"

She answers by striding away toward the back of the room. Christian gives his food one last look before following.

———

"Can you please tell me what happened this morning, Christian?"

Gemma's calm inflection has the unsubtle sharpness of an icicle point as she paces between the walls of the restaurant's supply room. Each time she moves from left to right and back again, she passes a chrome-colored door secured with a padlock. Christian guesses it leads to a meat freezer.

He doesn't know much more than what he heard in the buffet line, which is that somebody—maybe from another family, maybe a wacko—took a shot at seventeen-year-old Dora Petruglia as she was leaving the church. Christian didn't see it because he'd ducked out after skipping Communion. Now he's hoping nobody, especially Gemma Petruglia, noticed.

"I'm glad nobody got hurt," he says. "Especially Dora."

Gemma stops in front of the freezer door, turns to face Christian, folds her arms. "Let's review," she says. "We are attending the blessed funeral of my aunt Regina. We are at Saint Hugo of the Hills, where we always have family funerals and everyone loves our family."

"Yes, ma'am, I was—"

"Quiet, please."

"Yes, ma'am."

Christian is starting to get the idea that he is in a tough spot. He's been in them before, but most of those were in his former career as a Michigan state trooper. His work for the Petruglias has been lucrative but not all that dangerous, especially since Gemma has been gradually extracting the family from such risky businesses as opioid smuggling. She's taken heat from her uncles and aunts—including Aunt Regina before she died—for letting those profits go. But after watching a cousin overdose on Oxy two years ago—lips chalk blue, hands clutching his throat as he struggled for breath—she had decided that that particular money was no longer worth it.

The family has shown patience and given lip service to her humanitarianism, but unfortunately for Gemma, she has not found means of replacing that surrendered cash flow. Her plan to insert the family as a middleman in the Bitcoin business has so far been a bust, and Christian has heard rumblings, probably fomented by one of Gemma's younger brothers, that her job might be in trouble. Which doesn't bode well for her life either.

"So we're walking out of the church, an orderly, beautiful procession, and the next thing I know, everyone is screaming, and my beautiful niece, who's going to dance at Juilliard in the fall, is on the ground bawling her eyes out. And next to her, on the sidewalk, is this contraption, this flying thing."

"A drone?" Christian says.

"A drone that shot an arrow at my niece. Can you tell me what a drone is doing at my aunt's funeral?"

"I—"

"Understand, Christian, this was not some amateur fanatic who just screwed up and accidentally flew his drone into our funeral procession."

The room is beginning to feel cold, even though the freezer door is shut.

"I'm sorry, ma'am."

"Do not *ma'am* me."

She starts to pace again between the metal shelves stacked with fat cans of spaghetti sauce and boxes of napkins. "Do you happen to know, Christian, what else happened today?"

Jesus, he thinks, *what kind of goddamn quiz is this? Her grandfather Vincent would have just come right out and said what he had to say.* "I'm sorry—I don't know. But I'm so glad that Dora—"

"So," Gemma says, "you didn't hear about the newspaper reporter?"

Christian blinks. His right eye has begun to throb, as it often does when his stress level spikes. "No, m—Gemma."

"His name was Robillard. That name doesn't sound familiar?"

"Vaguely," Christian lies. "Should I—"

"I will ask the questions. And yes, you're damn right you should know it. His nickname is—or was—Robo."

"Again, my apologies—"

"What exactly is your job, Christian?"

"I work for the family business, Gemma. I'm loyal to the family. I hope there's no question about that."

"I'm not questioning your loyalty. I'm questioning your competence. What is your actual job, though? What is your number one priority?"

Christian blinks again, ponders. His responsibilities have changed over the past few years. Making pickups. Keeping in touch with certain law enforcement buddies. Manning the door at family events. Now and then, visiting people who haven't honored their business obligations, his least favorite part of the job—although he had to beat a guy up once, and that was nostalgically fun, like the old days slapping drunk drivers around on M-59. He even babysat Dora once, come to think of it, when she was only seven or eight. He doesn't think any of these are what Gemma wants to hear. But he has one other idea.

"The Rathman girl?" he says and immediately regrets making it sound more question than statement. But Gemma doesn't say anything right away; she just turns and faces the freezer door while Christian waits.

"The Rathman girl," she finally says. "What's her name again?"

"Jubilee," Christian says, exhaling, relieved. "Jubilee Rathman. I'm supposed to keep tabs on her. That's one of—that's my top priority."

He remembers Jubilee Rathman, all right. *That little bitch,* he thinks, feeling a warm seep of tears leaking onto his right cheek, his eye never the same since she shoved that damn trophy into it at the state police post when he was still a trooper. As far as Christian is concerned, she and her whole family deserved what they got. He remembers what Vincent Petruglia told him when he joined the crew: *Disloyalty is a cancer.* Jubilee's old man was a cancer that had to be—what was the word? *Erased?* No, *eradicated*—a cancer that had to be *eradicated*. The Rathmans had it coming.

"Let's go back to that reporter," Gemma says, her voice echoing faintly off the stainless-steel door, Christian wishing he could see her face. "Robo. Vance Robillard. The police this morning found Robillard dead in his own car in his own driveway." Gemma turns back around to face Christian. She has that look on her face, the lips pursed into an angry kiss, the dark eyes narrowed, a look that makes him want to bolt from the room and run for his life but that later, he has to admit, will make him want to jerk off.

"Suicide?" Christian says, hopefully.

"Not quite." She puts a forefinger to her lower lip, staring into Christian. Again, he waits. Finally she says, "Someone gassed him."

"Holy shit. How?"

"How? I don't care how, Christian. I want to know what Jubilee Rathman is doing these days."

He's having trouble keeping up with the whipsawing between Jubilee and the reporter. "I think—I mean, I know she's living in a mansion on the other side of the state. Pretty much keeps to herself. Her brother threw himself off a mountain in . . . I think Colorado, a couple years back."

"A couple years back? A couple years?" Gemma steps across the room until her face is inches from Christian's. "That's all you have? What was she doing a month ago? Or last week? Or yesterday? Isn't that your job? Aren't you supposed to be on her case every damn minute of her damn life?"

"I . . . I have a file at home, Gemma . . . Ms. Petruglia, if I can just—"

"Do you think it's merely a coincidence that on the same day that someone made an attempt on the life of my blessed niece, someone succeeded in killing that reporter? Do you?"

Her spittle sprays his chin and cheeks. He doesn't dare wipe it away, but it scares him because he can feel Gemma's own fear, can see the knowledge in her eyes that the attempt on Dora could be her downfall. Or worse. "Tell me what I can do," he says. "What can I do, Gemma?"

She takes her forefinger and places it on his right cheek, her fingernail pricking the skin below his eye. "What's with your eye?" she says.

It takes him back to that morning at the state police post. Jubilee came at him out of nowhere. The next thing he knew, his eye was on fire with pain, blood spurting through his fingers as he clutched his face and fell backward, hitting his head on the fax machine. He could hear his partner screaming at the kid, calling her a little bitch, which is exactly what Christian thought as he lay in the ambulance, what he thinks when he's putting drops in the eye every morning, what he's thinking now as Gemma's fingernail digs into his cheek.

"Just a condition," he tells her. "Getting old."

She removes her finger. "Where is this Rathman girl? Or woman?"

"About two hundred miles west of here. On a lake."

He really has kept up with Jubilee Rathman, dammit. She's a pathetic recluse living off her dead rat daddy's life insurance. No,

Christian doesn't know what she was doing yesterday or last week, but he knows where she is and can find her anytime he wants. Come to think of it, he got a cell phone alert this morning about some press conference she did, something about her dead brother and suicide prevention.

"What lake? Lake Michigan?"

"No, inland, way smaller." Christian knows the name, or knew it. He focuses on the freezer door, begging his memory for help. Something religious. Not hell. Not—wait, he's got it. "Purgatory Bay," he says. "Near this little city on Lake Michigan, Bleak Harbor."

"Bleak. Purgatory. Who would want to live there?"

Something comes to Christian then. "I know a guy there," he says.

"Go then. Now. And report back."

———

Christian waits until he's in his car to check his cell phone. He wants to see what that Jubilee press conference was about. Then he plans to check in with the guy he knows in Bleak Harbor.

When his phone comes on, it bleeps again and again with call and text alerts. His ex-wife has been trying to call him for the past forty-five minutes. *Probably needs a good lay,* he thinks. *Or just ran out of shitty vodka.* He calls up the first voice mail. The transcription is gibberish, and when he listens, all he hears is her sobbing.

"Christ, Sally, what the hell happened?" he says.

He goes to the next voice mail. The only words he can make out between his ex's choking are *little Lance.* Lance is his eleven-year-old grandson. Christian sees him mostly at Christmas, sometimes Thanksgiving when Lance's mother, Christian's daughter, isn't hosting. He doesn't go anywhere near his daughter if he can help it.

He calls up the third voice mail. His heart is thumping, his eye pulsing again. The transcription pops up before he can listen:

Transcription Beta (low confid . . .

"Why aren't you call _____ *little Lance* _____ *the hospi-*
tal _____ *critical condition uh* _____ *oh God* _____ *flying thing*
_____ *call me . . ."*

Christian opens a window so he can breathe, then hits the little play arrow on the phone screen and puts the phone to his ear. He shuts his eyes, listening. He drops the phone into his lap and lowers his forehead to the steering wheel. He takes deep sucks of air, lifts his head, picks up the phone, reads the transcription again.

"Sorry, Lance," Christian says. "Got a job to do."

He pulls the car squealing out of the restaurant lot, headed west, toward Bleak Harbor.

19

Caleb bites into the cheeseburger as the woman emerges from the double automatic doors of the Home Depot. She's pushing a shopping cart filled with trays of plants, bags of topsoil.

Preparing for a spring she will not see.

Caleb watches her through binoculars from the Volvo, parked in the Meijer Thrifty Acres lot across the street. He chews the burger slowly, savoring the unfamiliar tastes, the sweetness of the ketchup, the sour tang of the pickle. Grease dribbles from a corner of his mouth, oozing along his jawline. Jubilee wouldn't be happy. She has cautioned him against such "self-indulgences." They are for the weak, she tells him. She and Caleb cannot afford to be weak.

She would probably be even more upset that, to eat the cheeseburger, Caleb had to remove the customized synthetic mask that hides his scars and bloated tissue from judgmental eyes. She has warned him never to remove the mask on his rare ventures to the outer world. "People will not forgive you, Caleb," she always tells him. "Remember the festival?"

Caleb begged Jubilee to let him walk around at Bleak Harbor's annual Dragonfly Festival. She dropped him off on a sweltering Saturday afternoon. The downtown was thronged with out-of-towners drinking keg beer from Solo cups in their green-and-yellow Anisoptera Always T-shirts. Caleb wore a black hoodie with the hood tugged close around his head. He began to sweat, then to itch. He slipped into a portable toilet and peeled off the mask.

"Do you remember how those people looked at you and then looked away?" Jubilee has said. "How some of them couldn't *not* look? How they laughed? This is a cruel and cynical world, Caleb, and you need to accept that, as I have. You need to be ready to strike out at those who would harm you before they harm you first."

Now, though, he figures he's safe sitting in an isolated patch of the Meijer lot, watching the woman with the shopping cart through his tinted window. He has draped a napkin over the tiny camera mounted inside the dashboard so Jubilee cannot keep an eye on him. As long as he completes his tasks, he thinks, she won't punish him too severely, won't keep him from his necessary doses of Ho Hos.

———

Caleb left Purgatory Bay for the first piece of the mission the day before, Thursday morning, in the Volvo with the Ohio plate. Jubilee gave him a credit card, a cell phone, and a fabricated driver's license. The license was for a young man in Kentucky who had recently been killed in a hit-and-run. She told Caleb to stay off interstates where possible and gave him a map she'd made of state police posts between Detroit and Bleak Harbor so he could avoid those too.

He knew he was embarking on a harsh but necessary mission. He was doing it for Jubilee, his provider and protector, the one who had kept him sheltered and fed and had taught him the many things he now knew how to do, taught him how to survive in a world hostile to people like Caleb, people who weren't like those dwelling in the outer world. She had also kept him supplied with Ho Hos, something he had learned he could not go without. As long as he did what she asked, he would not go without, and what she had asked so far was not that difficult.

Still, Caleb had wondered about the outer world, where he had spent almost no time. He almost never left the compound on Purgatory Bay except to wander the forest ringing the water, which was encircled itself by a fence twice his height. Only in the past year had Jubilee taken him out driving, as one of the last pieces of his training.

The mission offered Caleb a chance to be on his own in the outer world. He would be without Jubilee and Frances nagging him about his push-ups and pull-ups, about eating every bit of his five daily meals of fruit and vegetables and dry grains and protein drinks, about lock-picking exercises, about his late-night drills with the drones, about practicing the stuttering that Jubilee thought would make him less threatening in public. It would give him a glimpse of what his life might be like once the mission was completed.

After leaving the compound Thursday, he drove first to a FedEx in Ypsilanti, just east of Ann Arbor, and dropped off a prepaid package addressed to the Bleak Harbor Police Department. The parcel held part of one of Ophelia's sculptures he had stolen a few weeks before.

He arrived at the Richard T. Willing Literacy Center in Ann Arbor a few minutes after noon. The center sat in the middle of a line of adjacent stores and offices wrapped in beige brick and kelly-green awnings. Caleb parked the Volvo facing the road, its rear to the literacy center, and watched in his mirrors for Michaela Deming's silver Prius to pull in.

She had an eleven forty-five appointment at the school superintendent's office in Saline, about twenty minutes away, per Jubilee's reconnaissance via the sieve of a computer Michaela used at the literacy center. Jubilee figured she would return around twelve thirty and do a few office chores. Then, later in the afternoon, she'd collect daughter Bridget from the Ice Cube rink and start out for Bleak Harbor, the hockey tournament, and her sister, Ophelia.

Caleb spied a doughnut shop in his side-view mirror. He remembered doughnuts, thought for a moment about getting one. But Jubilee would notice if he left the car for longer than it would take to implant the GPS device on Michaela's car. No doughnut, he decided. Immediately he felt an urge for a Ho Ho dose. He would have to wait until he was back on Purgatory Bay.

He let his thoughts drift to the loons at home. He imagined the male floating beyond the dive raft, then the female emerging from the water fifty yards away. They had left the bay in October. They would be back in a few weeks, if Caleb remembered correctly from last year. He'd always thought they were lucky to be able to come and go whenever they wanted. He assumed they considered the bay their home, though at moments when he was feeling lonely, he wondered whether they thought of home as somewhere else—Florida or Maryland or the Carolinas, places Caleb knew little about.

Michaela pulled into the lot at 12:27. Caleb watched her park in a space in front of the literacy center and exit her Prius as she was rummaging through her handbag, in a seeming hurry. *Take your time,* Caleb thought. He clicked the stopwatch on his phone—one of the five and only five apps Jubilee had installed on it—as Michaela unlocked the glass front door and went inside.

When the stopwatch hit 3:00, Caleb turned the app off and scanned the lot. It was a slow day at the doughnut shop, and other people were out at lunch, as Jubilee had hoped. Caleb opened the Volvo door and stepped out. He touched his mask to make sure it was secure and adjusted his hood and sunglasses so that his face could not be clearly seen. Then he lowered his head and walked toward the doughnut shop.

At the shop he turned a hard left and proceeded down past a pickup truck and three empty parking spaces to the Prius. As he walked, he slipped the GPS device from the pocket on his hoodie. He stole a quick glance through the door of the literacy center and, seeing nobody, turned another left as he passed Michaela's car.

It was fortunate that she hadn't backed in because Jubilee wanted the GPS under the rear bumper, where she was least likely to happen upon it. At the rear of the car, Caleb squatted and slapped the magnetized device onto the metal frame behind the bumper, making sure it stuck. He returned to the Volvo and drove 4.7 miles to a motel off I-94.

Jubilee had made a reservation so that he'd be off the road and out of public view for a few hours before he went to collect Ophelia, who wouldn't be home until after her store closed at seven p.m. "Ophelia will do what we want her to do," she had told Caleb. "She wants to believe that someone takes pity on her and wants to help her. Wanting to believe can be even more dangerous than believing."

Caleb sat in the car gathering the courage to go into the registration office, staring at the yellow-and-red sign towering at the edge of the lot. What was a Super 8 anyway? Were there only eight in the world? Were there a Super 1 and Super 2 and Super 3? This one didn't look nearly as super as Jubilee's compound on Purgatory Bay.

The bark of Jubilee's voice from a tiny speaker beneath the dashboard startled him. "Go in, Caleb."

The registration office was smaller than Caleb's bedroom. A television behind the counter showed two men sitting at a desk, talking and waving their arms as if they were angry about something. Beneath their images, words wrapped in red, white, and blue said the men were talking about something called the GOP.

A woman waddled up to the counter. "Can I help you?" she said. She wore a powder-blue polo shirt and thinning hair the color of one of Caleb's carrot shakes. A name tag pinned to her shirt said *Georgia*.

Georgia canted her head down as she approached, maybe trying to peer up under Caleb's hood. "Hello, M-Miss Georgia," he said, keeping his eyes lowered. "I have a r-r-reservation."

"Is that a mask?" Georgia said.

"N-no, m-ma'am. I'm on a program to treat a skin condition."

"Really? I wear masks, too, and they cost and arm and a leg, but I'll be damned if they do me the least bit of good."

Caleb didn't know exactly what she meant, but she didn't seem upset. He set the credit card and Kentucky license on the counter.

"Ellison, OK," Georgia said. She started tapping keys on a computer. "Just passing through?"

"Yes, m-ma'am," Caleb said.

"Excuse me?"

Jubilee had told him not to say anything more than absolutely necessary, as anything he said could be misheard or misinterpreted in his hood-and-mask-and-stutter mumble. She had warned him, too, against interacting too much with anyone whose irrational fright might make them suspicious.

"I said y-y-yes. P-passing through."

"Where are you headed?"

Jubilee had anticipated the question. "T-Traverse City."

"That is a very nice place. Going on business?"

Caleb kept his gaze on his shoes. Georgia was making him nervous. "I have f-f-family there."

"But you're from Kentucky?"

Caleb had memorized the details on the phony license. "Sh-Shelbyville," he said.

"Shelby or Simpson?"

The question confused him. He resorted to what he'd committed to memory. "I'm f-from Shelbyville. 1124 M-Main Street."

"Oh," Georgia said. She slid a slipcover containing a plastic key across the counter. "My great-grandpa came up here from Simpsonville in the forties, got a job at Ford's. You know Simpsonville?"

Caleb picked up the key. "Which r-room is it, please?"

"It's written on there." Georgia pointed. "You really don't want TV?"

He didn't understand the question, but he said, "That's f-fine. I've b-been on the road and n-need some sleep."

"Whoever made the reservation—maybe not you?—said the TV should be disabled. All I can do is shut the cable down. If you want to unplug the tube, too, go ahead."

At the room he followed instructions, hanging the Do Not Disturb sign, throwing the dead bolt, pulling the shades. Jubilee had told him she wouldn't call for a while so he could sleep.

The nightstand clock said 1:23.

His next Ho Ho dose wouldn't be for twelve hours. Caleb lay back on the stiff pillow, closed his eyes, imagined taking the dose, tapping the syringe, the familiar warmth washing through him.

He replayed in his mind what he had seen in his rear- and side-view mirrors as Michaela had parked her car. As in the videotapes Jubilee had shown him, Michaela had looked rushed. She'd gotten out of the car and slammed the door and taken two steps, then stopped, remembering something, yanked keys from her purse, unlocked the car, reached inside, leaned back out, and shut the door again before turning and bustling into her office, her purse and a backpack slung over a shoulder.

Throughout, her hair, shoulder length, sandy brown, had kept falling across her face, and each time she'd flipped it back out of the way, and then it had fallen again. Remembering this, Caleb thought, *Why didn't she tie it back somehow? Why did she put up with it?*

He tried but couldn't retrieve a clear, full glimpse of her face. She had turned so quickly away from the car, then ducked back inside without looking his way, so all he'd caught, for a split second, was her profile, the downy roundness of her left cheek, the gentle slope of her nose, the blink of an eye. He had seen her many times before in the videos and photographs Jubilee used in his training, but never like this, living and moving, unknowing and so vulnerable.

He shifted his head on the pillow. For the next four hours, he drowsed in snatches of ten or fifteen minutes. As always, his sleep was filled with dreams. Other people might have called them nightmares, but Caleb, as with so much else, had grown accustomed. In these he was lying on a concrete floor in a dark and silent room, naked. The pain started in his calves and slowly crept up his leg, through his knees and thighs and into his hips, until his twin pelvic bones felt like someone had driven a metal spike into each of them. The fever seized him then, the sweats, followed by the chills, the things that happened when he had misbehaved and Jubilee had refused him his Ho Hos. He swallowed, held a palm up in front of his face, could not see it. He stood, blind in the darkness, stepped slowly forward until he reached a wall. He ran his hand along the wall, concrete dust spackling his fingertips as he stepped sideways until he reached a corner, pivoted, moved down that wall into another corner, pivoted again, six more steps, another corner, and kept going until he heard the voice.

"Caleb."

He sat up in the motel bed, opened his eyes.

"I am Caleb," he said.

His phone was buzzing on the nightstand. He picked it up.

"Yes."

"It's time," Jubilee said.

She gave him the instructions for picking up Ophelia. "She will be ready," Jubilee said. "Do not stay there long. Get her out, get her cell phone, get her here. Do you understand?"

Caleb thought of the cars swishing past on the road, realized he liked the driving. "I understand," he said.

Two and a half hours later, standing in Ophelia's kitchen, watching her prepare herself, he took note of how excited she seemed and how ignorant of what was really happening. And how she looked at him without seeing what others saw. He had power. He left the note Jubilee had written on the table. He had no idea what it meant; he was simply following instructions, thinking of the Ho Ho dose awaiting him, not wanting to jeopardize that.

He did not notice that he dropped the motel key on the chair seat.

In the car with Ophelia, he did not hesitate to snatch her phone. He did exactly as Jubilee had told him, but he felt in that moment, hearing Ophelia's futile yelp of protest, as if he were the one making the decisions now, as if he were in charge, if only for a moment. And felt it again, a bit more strongly, as he put her to sleep with the syringe. With Jubilee, he had never had such power.

As he pulled from Jeremiah Street onto Lily, he checked the GPS finder on his phone. Michaela was just getting into Bleak Harbor, making her way down Blossom toward Lily. Caleb felt a swelling in his chest, something akin to pleasure that had nothing to do with Ho Hos. He pulled into an alley off Lily and waited.

"Caleb," came Jubilee's voice. "Proceed to the compound now."

He put the car in park, watching Michaela's car approach Lily. He wanted to see her face. And he wanted her to see his.

"Caleb. Now."

He thought of the dose waiting on his nightstand, decided Jubilee could not afford to punish him at this particular moment. The mission had begun and had to be completed the next day. Michaela made the turn at Lily. Caleb pulled into the street in front of her and pulled his mask off.

———

Now Caleb sits with his cheeseburger in the Meijer lot, watching the woman with the shopping cart. She will soon be in range.

He tells himself he will succeed where earlier he failed.

His first task that day, planting poison and a miniature camera in the reporter Robillard's car in the predawn dusk, went easily enough. But he faltered with the Dora girl. She was walking along the sidewalk outside the church, a woman at her side, maybe her mother, Dora clutching a purse. Caleb zoomed the drone's camera in on her face. He had memorized it from photographs, but Dora looked different at this particular moment. She was as pretty as Caleb remembered, but her face was contorted a little, as though she was crying. He zoomed the camera out then, feeling suddenly nervous. He had had a premonition of his drone, Simon, going down. Then, in an instant, Dora was invisible beneath a pile of people.

And Simon was gone, blown out of the sky by a flurry of bullets.

Caleb will miss Simon.

He wasn't as nervous with the Lance boy, maybe because he didn't look directly at his face while making the shot. Caleb collected the drone and packed it into the trunk tire well and proceeded to the next step of his mission, here with the woman coming out of the Home Depot.

As she turns up the parking lot aisle where her Chevy Suburban waits, Caleb sets the cheeseburger and the binoculars aside. He slides his mask back on, pulling it over the back of his head, smoothing it along his cheeks and jawbone, then removes the napkin from the camera inside the car. He picks up his phone, chooses an app Jubilee created, and aims the phone. It zooms in on the woman's face.

The app sings softly with a positive recognition of the woman as Portia Ralko Stone, sixty-four years old, of Ceresco, not far from here. Caleb likes the little tune the app plays; Jubilee programmed it to sound like the mockingbirds that sang to him as he flew his drones at night on Purgatory Bay, sometimes mimicking the whir of the flying machines.

The drone, Roger now, waits in a copse of pines behind the store on a makeshift launchpad Caleb fashioned from discarded wooden crates. Caleb bends to the floor for the remote controller, sets it in his lap, gazes across the street again at Portia Stone. Her sugary hair wisps around her head. She walks with a hitch in her gait, as if her left leg were three inches shorter than her right.

Caleb fits the GoPro mount to his head and flicks the camera switch on. As the woman points her keys at her Suburban, he takes the drone activator from the console and sets it in his lap. Portia Stone, he thinks.

Her husband's name is Hubert. She has an older brother somewhere in Northern Michigan. That's about all Caleb knows.

He hits two buttons in succession on the controller. "There, Jubilee," he says and just then feels a blot of nausea in his upper belly. He tells himself it's the cheeseburger, not what he's about to do.

The drone swoops into view above the Home Depot, a sliver of black menace, like a cockroach on the drab mattress of clouds behind it. It hovers momentarily before plunging downward into the parking lot. Caleb closes his eyes while trying to hold his head steady, then forces them open and watches as her forehead explodes and she collapses on the asphalt, her shopping cart rolling slowly away.

"Yes," Caleb says. "Yes."

20

Gary Langreth peers at a photograph just inside the front door of Ophelia's Lily Street boutique, Pheelin' Groovy.

The picture of her roadside sculpture of the skateboarding boy was snapped at night, the boy glowing in the exaggerated lighting. He figures the kid is Ophelia's late brother, Zeke, but he doesn't know for sure because she doesn't talk about him much.

"Ophelia wasn't lying about you being tall."

Langreth turns to the voice.

"Kiernan Poulin," Ophelia's partner says, extending a hand. "I'm sorry we haven't met before and that it's under these circumstances."

"For sure. Thanks for agreeing to talk."

"I don't know what I can tell you. Ophelia never fails to entertain, but this is totally unexpected. All she talked about all week was the tournament. Her niece was going to be lighting up the ice, and she was going to be there screaming her butt off."

"That was the plan," Langreth says.

He looks around, pretending to survey the walls of Bleak Harbor T-shirts and sundresses, the shelves of beach towels and swimsuits, conch shells you'd never find in Lake Michigan, pastel in every direction. But he's really deciding how much more he should tell this guy. Poulin knows only that Ophelia is not around. He's a short, muscled twentysomething—Ophelia said he's a powerlifter, constantly sipping at protein shakes—who carries himself with the easy manner of a born salesman. Which means he's also a gossip.

"Forgive me—could I offer you fruit juice or black tea?" Poulin says. "I'm not a coffee guy myself."

"I'm fine," Langreth says. "Listen." He reaches out and grips Poulin's shoulder just firmly enough to remind him that he's an officer of the law. At least sort of. "I need your help."

Poulin nods. "Whatever I can do."

"Do you have an office we could talk in?"

Poulin glances toward the back of the store. "We do, but I'm the only one here."

"Of course," Langreth says, feigning a smile. "Maybe you could lock the entrance for just a little bit?"

"Jeez. I'd hate to lock out customers at this time of year, when we get so little traffic anyway."

"Right, all those out-of-town hockey fans might want a Bleak Harbor something or other."

"I wish," Poulin says. "Can I just ask, if you don't mind, what capacity you're here in? As Ophelia's boyfriend or . . . you are a prosecutor, correct?"

"I don't mind. I'm not a prosecutor, per se, but I do some investigating for the prosecutor. And I'm here, actually, in both capacities."

That would be news to Langreth's boss, but Langreth doesn't care.

Poulin looks at the front door. "I suppose. Let me ask: Have you spoken with Ophelia's sister, Mikey?"

"I have."

"I guess it won't hurt if we use the office for a couple of minutes. But I'll leave the door open for customers. If I hear it chime, I might have to excuse myself."

That would be perfect, Langreth thinks. As he follows Poulin through the store to the office, he taps out a text to Mikey:

get over to the store. need a distraction

———

"Have you ever heard of a Charlotte White?"

Poulin sits in a swivel chair at a desk shoved up against a cinder block wall. A computer rests atop the desk, as Langreth hoped.

He's leaning against a stepladder propped against some shelving stacked with cardboard boxes. The wall behind the desk is covered with sketches in colored pencil, apparent rough starts on future Ophelia sculptures. Just to the left of Poulin's head is one that looks like a girl dressed in bulky garb, raising a stick of some sort over her head. *Bridget,* Langreth thinks.

"Don't you love her sketches?" Poulin says. "She is so talented, especially for someone who is sightless."

Ophelia wouldn't appreciate Poulin's phrasing, but Langreth just says, "Agreed."

"Charlotte White," Poulin repeats. "Isn't that—oh, no, E. B. White wrote *Charlotte's Web*. I can't say that I know the name Charlotte White. Should I?"

Mikey told Langreth about the call from "Charlotte White" when she phoned as he was parking in front of Pheelin' Groovy. The name rang no bells with him, but he can't see why it would.

Ophelia is generally guarded about her personal life, even when she's supposedly sharing it. To a degree, her caginess is one of the things that attracts Langreth, perhaps *because* he's an ex-cop and current prosecutor, a guy always looking for ways to exercise his curiosity muscle. And of course, there are her blue eyes.

"She said she's a friend and that Ophelia is with her."

"You don't really think she's been kidnapped?"

That seems quite possible now, Langreth thinks. But it's not a certainty yet, and he doesn't want to tell Poulin directly, because then everyone in Bleak Harbor will know, and that could spook this Charlotte character or whoever it was who ferried Ophelia away from her house last night. "I think it's more likely a misunderstanding."

"Are the police involved?"

"Yes, but not in any big way." Which is technically true, for now. He watches Poulin's face to see if he buys this.

"I'm glad it's not that serious," Poulin says. "Can you tell me a little more about this Charlotte person?" He gestures toward the computer. "Could she be one of our vendors? Or customers?"

"I was thinking that myself. But since you mentioned it, can I ask how Pheelin' Groovy is doing, business wise? You're a smart enough guy to know this isn't the only store like this in Bleak Harbor."

"Well," Poulin says, "we think our customer service sets us apart."

"Of course. Ophelia has said as much to me." It's a fib. Ophelia doesn't talk about her business any more than her distant past. Langreth isn't sure she even likes the business, except maybe for the name, Pheelin' Groovy, and that it supplies a bit of cash for her sculptures.

"But you know," Poulin says, "it's really not for me to say how we're doing. You should ask Ophelia."

"I would," Langreth says, grinning, "but."

"You don't think the store has anything to do with this?"

"No. I doubt it."

Langreth waits then. Interrogating suspects taught him to just shut up once in a while and wait for the other person to succumb to the natural urge to fill the silence—especially with a gossip.

Poulin spins his chair halfway toward the computer. "Let me just confirm something," he says. He slides a tray holding a keyboard out from under the desk and rolls himself closer. "It hasn't been our best few years."

"No?"

"Since old lady Bleak died, and the mansion fell into disrepair, and the estate's been trying to block public access to the beach, well, we've been getting fewer tourists, and fewer tourists means fewer dollars walking through our door. Everyone's door."

He bats a few keys, and an automated voice blurts, "Financials. First quarter."

Poulin says, "Oops, that's Ophelia's voice-over thing. I'll shut it off for now."

Langreth wants to look over Poulin's shoulder but figures it would be counterproductive. From his vantage he can see a white square bordered in gray and green pop up on the computer screen. It's filled with columns of what Langreth assumes are numbers.

Poulin shakes his head. "Yeah," he says. "Not good." The square disappears. "Let me search our vendor list for this Charlotte person. Do you know how to spell the name?"

"I don't, but I'd just try the obvious."

"OK, hang on." While Poulin types, Langreth squints at the text he sent Mikey. It says she read it. *So where the hell are you?* he thinks.

"No Charlotte White there," Poulin says. "Let me try one other place. If she's not there, I'm not sure I can help you."

Langreth is starting another text to Mikey when he hears the front door chime echo from a speaker next to the computer. Poulin jumps up. "A customer," he says. "I have to . . . I'm sorry."

"Not at all. Go ahead."

"Let me just close out of this. OK. Back in a few."

Langreth waits till Poulin is out the door, counts to ten, then moves to the computer. He clicks on the email icon; it wants a password he doesn't know or have time to guess. Instead he switches to the web browser and clicks on the pull-down that shows recent Google searches, hoping to get lucky.

His phone starts ringing. He pulls it out, just in case it's Ophelia, but it's a 734 number from the Detroit area that he doesn't recognize. He puts the phone away and refocuses on the search list:

fear of swimming
pistons fire Gm
how to scallop potatos
weather 10day tampa-stpete

He clicks into the day before, sees more unhelpful items, then goes back another day, and another, and then:

Ophelia Wright
American roadside sculptures
national Geographic
TheoStepovich

Langreth stops there. "Yep," he says. He looks over his shoulder at the office door, checks the time. Poulin should still be busy. *Stepovich,* he thinks. *Ambulance chaser. Bankruptcy lawyer.*

And then, farther down the list:

doyrself bankruptcy

Pheelin' Groovy is not having its best year, all right. Langreth wonders if Ophelia owes somebody money. If so, is it enough that somebody would grab her? He doubts it. But money problems usually lead to other problems. *Man,* he thinks, *Ophelia would kill me if she knew what I was doing.*

He's running out of time. He wishes another customer would come in and set off that door chime again. He tries going back another day, then one more, and then there it is:

charlott white

Langreth leans back, feeling clever. He'd say *bingo* if he hadn't known a cop who said it all the time and wound up with half his head blown off by a gangbanger tripping on crystal meth. He's about to follow the search prompt and find out who Charlotte is when he hears Poulin's voice a bit too near the office door for comfort.

He closes the Google window, steps away from the desk, and leaves the office. Poulin now is at the cashier desk, ringing up a man wearing Washtenaw Pride garb—Craig Deming, Mikey's husband. *Thank you, Mikey,* Langreth thinks. Craig and Poulin are making small talk when Langreth approaches. Seeing Langreth, Poulin says, "You guys know each other? This is Ophelia's brother-in-law."

"Ah," Langreth says, pretending he's never met Craig before. "Gary Langreth. I've dated Ophelia a bit."

"So I've heard," Craig says. "Nice to meet you."

Langreth turns to Poulin, shakes his hand. "Listen, I've gotta get to the courthouse. Thanks for the assistance."

Back in his car, Langreth checks his phone. There's a two-hour-old voice mail from his boss and one from the caller who tried him when he was snooping on Poulin's computer. He ignores his boss's message and hits the play prompt for the other one, puts the phone to his ear.

Jesus, he thinks, *that voice.*

"Hey there, shooter, how's by you?"

Who is this? Langreth thinks. *That voice.* Not like nails on a blackboard. That would be welcome. This is more like—what did that smartass detective call it?—the shrieking of ants being scorched with sunlight through a magnifying glass. Then the name pops into his head:

Christian, state trooper.

"You hear about your old pal from the pressroom?" comes Christian's recorded rasp. "Robo? Remember we had the dead pool on whether he'd last longer than Keith Richards? If you had Robo, you lose."

Langreth hears a car honk in the background. "Give me a shout, eh?" the voice mail continues. "I actually need a little travel advice. Seven three four, triple six, one two three four."

Langreth tosses the phone on the seat and pulls out onto Lily Street. *Christian and Robo,* he thinks. *One live slimeball, one dead one.*

21

The wind has kicked up, fanning ripples that scud on perfectly spaced diagonals past the sole house rising from the bluffs ringing Purgatory Bay.

Jubilee is wrapped in her arms on her third-floor deck, ignoring the March chill, taking a break. She woke today, as she does each day, at 2:42 a.m., the precise moment the fire trucks arrived at her engulfed family cottage on the night of the murders.

Jubilee saw Caleb off at five o'clock, watching the Volvo on video cameras as it wound through the forest surrounding the bay. She spent some time preparing for the Joshua Project press conference. Since then she has been hunched before a bank of monitors inside, observing, directing, cajoling. And she has reviewed, over and over, in slow and superslow motion, three separate videos of attempts on people's lives.

Now, watching the gentle waves of green tinged with purple churn from one end of the bay to the other, living their brief lives before they splash up against the dead winter shore, helps her find her inner peace, helps remind her that nothing lasts. Which to Jubilee is all right: the natural, irrevocable way of the world.

It's happening now, she thinks, dropping her arms to her sides, letting the March breeze blow cold around her. After all the long nights and early mornings studying drone manuals, taking online classes, teaching herself to code, scouring the dark web, practicing her shooting on an indoor range. *It's really happening.*

She wondered if, when the appointed time came, she would waver. She wondered if she would hesitate to say yes to the decisions she would have to make, decisions she knew almost no one else alive could make, justifiably or not.

Even last night, after she'd made sure that Caleb was asleep and the alarms were set for his early awakening, she asked herself if she might hesitate when she had to tell him to execute her plan in all its perfectly necessary and necessarily hideous glory. She said a quiet prayer then—to whom, she couldn't be certain—that her resolve would be strong. She knew the prayer had been answered, that in fact she had answered it herself, when the Associated Press news alert flashed on her phone at 10:57 that morning:

Legendary Detroit Reporter Found Dead in Possible Homicide.

Jubilee had wondered, even worried a little, whether she might falter in that instant of realizing the finality of her deeds, of knowing that there now could be no return. Instead she felt her heart swell with certainty that what she had set out to do would be done. Whether it was right or wrong, good or bad, no longer mattered to Jubilee. It would be.

Then again, she reminded herself in that moment that Vance Robillard of the *Detroit Times* was the easiest of her targets, perhaps because he was, in the desiccated void of his soul, the most despicable of them. Robillard had no one he loved or who loved him, just a scant few who in their own howling tunnels of loneliness might tolerate getting plastered with him at some Detroit hovel.

Caleb had planted a tiny video camera inside Robillard's car along with the poison stuffed into the heat vents, where it would become a weapon when Robillard turned on the car. When she watched the video earlier, Jubilee paused it at the moment it appeared that Robillard realized he was going to die. He was saying something, or trying to, his eyes bulging, foamy spittle flying from his mouth. The video was soundless, but his lips seemed to form the word *Petruglia*. His contortions made her wonder if he was relieved or even happy, or if the poison was simply doing its work. Before the feed went dark, Robillard lay still against the driver's side window.

Jubilee saved the video to a computer drive. Later she will attach it to an untraceable email account she created and send it to the ABC affiliate in Detroit so the whole country can watch Robillard die.

The names of the others she has singled out for retribution are printed on the short list she keeps in her nightstand Bible. Each morning before this one, she turned to the page of Matthew's Gospel where the list is pasted, reminding herself that their time was coming. Some of those who would die, of course, were innocents—no more deserving of the fates she had determined for them than Saint Michael the Archangel—just as Kara and Joshua had been wholly undeserving of the fates delivered upon them. These innocents, her victims, would not suffer. They would die without knowing they were dying. But their families would suffer for the rest of their lives. As Jubilee had.

"Your targets will not suffer," Jubilee told Caleb. "That is a promise."

Caleb nodded at that, repeated her words. Jubilee couldn't be certain whether he believed it enough to do what needed to be done.

The breeze goes damp. Jubilee feels a needle of rain or maybe sleet on her cheek. She turns away from the bay and goes back inside the house. She takes the elevator down to the second floor, the first, the basement, then gazes into a tiny window that recognizes the iris of her left eye and prompts the elevator to take her to the subbasement.

She had trouble finding a contractor willing to build so deep. One after another said it risked leaks and flooding that would compromise the house's foundation. She was willing to take the chance; they were not willing to take on the liability. Finally Phillie located a guy from the

UP who'd dug plenty around Superior, the nastiest of the Great Lakes. He was willing to come downstate for the few months it would take to build what Jubilee wanted. She paid him twice what he asked to assure that he would not speak of the project with anyone but her and Phillie.

The contractor wound up staying longer as she thought of other things she wanted—a state-of-the-art gymnasium with a climbing wall, a shooting range, a vast underground garage for the classic automobiles she told him she wanted to collect—"I'm still a girl from Detroit, you know," she said—and a clean, bright room for computers and other electronics where she would do her learning.

There would be no classic automobiles.

Jubilee had little desire, she told the contractor, to live in the outer world. She told the same to her aunts and uncles and to her friends from long ago, and finally they all stopped emailing and texting, as she'd expected they would. Only Phillie did she keep close because he had been so close to her father. The first time he heard her utter that phrase, *the outer world*, she could hear his concern in the pause that followed over the phone.

"What do you mean by that, the 'outer world,' Juju?" he said.

"Exactly what it means: everywhere but here."

"Here being Purgatory Bay."

"Yes."

"Forgive me, but that is so—"

"So sad," Jubilee finished. "To anyone from the outer world, of course it would be sad. Anything that isn't their experience is sad or tragic or regretful. But it's their existence that is sad."

"My existence," Phillie said.

E. Jonathan Phillips is a good man and resourceful attorney who had known Jubilee's father since they were frat brothers at Western Michigan University. Phillie tried for years to wean Edward Rathman and his modest collection of copy shops off their lucrative and ultimately perilous relationship with the Petruglia family. Rathman kept swearing to Phillie that he was done laundering money for the Petruglias, but at some point, it didn't matter what Rathman vowed because whether he was done with it or not was no longer up to him.

Despite his misgivings, Phillie remained a loyal counselor. Twice divorced and childless, he doted on Jubilee, Joshua, and Kara. Every year, he sat at the Rathmans' Thanksgiving and Christmas tables, and Heather Rathman declared when the children were all still in grade school that Uncle Phillie would preside at each of their weddings. Jubilee knows Phillie loves her. Sometimes she wishes he didn't because it makes the things she must do more difficult.

"You are an exception, Phillie," Jubilee told him then. "At least to me."

"When can I come for a visit? I want a personal tour of this amazing manse I've only heard about and seen drawings of."

She could not have that. She could not have Phillie in any way connected to her plans. He had to have complete deniability. Visiting her would complicate that.

"Now is not a good time," she told him.

"When will there be a good time?"

"I'll let you know, Phillie."

"Promise?"

"Of course."

The subbasement lights click on as Jubilee steps out of the elevator. She crosses to a locked door, where she gazes into another iris scanner that admits her into the computer room. She takes a seat at a bank of monitors set up on one of two triangular white desks. She puts on a headset with a microphone and clicks a mouse, and the screen facing her blinks to life.

"Caleb is nearing the fourth assignment," comes the voice from overhead.

"I can see that, Frances," Jubilee says. The bright-red triangle tracking Caleb is sliding slowly from east to west on I-94. "What went wrong with the Petruglia girl?"

"Caleb said there was a software malfunction."

"No. What do you say?"

"I am not confident that you want to hear what I say."

This is one of Frances's stock answers. Jubilee has wondered more than once what her anonymous creator was thinking when he programmed it. Now she thinks, *Geralyn. After I dispense with Frances, I'll name my next virtual assistant Geralyn.*

"I think I can handle it, Frances. What do you say?"

"His pulse spiked when he was about to shoot."

"So he got scared? Lost his nerve?"

"It was his first kill."

No, Jubilee thinks, *Robillard was the first.* Though Caleb hadn't witnessed that—he had just planted the device. Dora was a challenging first victim because she had plenty of help. Jubilee wishes she could have scheduled her later, but the funeral was the opportunity. The Petruglias are careful people.

"He didn't want to use that drone for that assignment," Frances says.

"I'm aware of that. What are you saying?"

"Analysis of video of Caleb practicing suggests that he liked a different drone."

"He *liked* it? The drone is a soulless assembly of plastic and software, Frances. How could someone like it? That's just stupid. You aren't programmed for stupid."

"There is also the possibility that Caleb was not yet ready."

For a second, Jubilee considers shutting Frances down entirely, but she realizes she's just venting her frustration at the failure to kill Dora—on an inanimate being. "He was as ready as he would ever be," she says.

In the video feed of the attempt on Dora, Jubilee saw the drone whoosh down upon the funeral procession and then veer off and circle back before going in a second time. By then the girl's protectors were alert to the threat. A man the size of a refrigerator wrapped Dora in his arms while another swung a hand holding a pistol into the air. Jubilee heard four sharp retorts.

Someone had shot the drone out of the air. Jubilee had prepared herself for possible failure. She wishes it hadn't happened with Dora, the young treasure of the extended Petruglia clan, salutatorian at Marian High School, champion debater, fluent French speaker, owner of a 4.6 grade point average, headed for Juilliard, far from the family business.

Before Jubilee willed herself to sleep each night at thirteen minutes after midnight—the very moment twelve years before that she had received Kara's garbled text about something happening at the cottage up north—Jubilee fantasized about the drone's hissing arrow splitting Dora's vanilla forehead into a splatter of blood.

But even more than Dora dying, Jubilee pictured, with near rapture, Dora's wake and funeral, how the Petruglias would wail and weep and vow their hollow revenge, their faces creased with anger at the news cameras prying into their personal horror. She imagined how she might infiltrate their grieving, in disguise or via surrogate or via, yet again, a drone, armed with miniature cameras. So she could watch again and again and again.

But there will be no funeral for Dora, no visible Petruglia agony. That is a grave disappointment, but Jubilee takes solace in the thought that there will be other opportunities for justice.

One hour ago, Lance Guilders, eleven years old, was running out onto the asphalt playground of a middle school not far from Ann Arbor. He was wearing a green winter vest over a black sweatshirt and bouncing a soccer ball.

The poison dart, fired from a drone hovering in a birch stand one hundred yards away, must have missed Lance's heart, or he would have perished on the spot. It isn't clear whether Caleb or the drone itself misfired. Caleb, apparently unnerved, flew the drone out of the birches. The drone's video feed shows children pointing and racing toward the drone before it spun and fled.

"What's the boy's status?" Jubilee asks Frances.

"Critical but stable condition at Saint Joseph Mercy Hospital. Local news has people on saying a drone was involved."

Jubilee knows that eventually somebody will start making connections. But by then she and Caleb will have completed their mission, with the final and most decisive steps just down the road in Bleak Harbor.

"I can't control that," Jubilee says. "Let's see what happens with Portia Stone."

"Yes," Frances says. "Ms. Stone is inside the Home Depot. Caleb is parked in the Meijer lot across the road."

"Thank you."

It's happening now, Jubilee thinks again. She activates another monitor. A camera feed shows Ophelia Wright sitting on the bed in her basement room, eyes closed and legs crossed in the lotus position. How eagerly she signed the checks from Charlotte White LLC, handwriting that Jubilee used to fashion the note Caleb left on her kitchen table to put a little scare into her lying sister, Michaela.

Seeing Ophelia look so placid startles Jubilee a little. She honestly expected something different from someone in her current circumstance. Anger. Frustration. Fear. Ophelia did take a swipe at Caleb. Now she meditates. It will make no difference. Jubilee isn't doing this to torture Ophelia but her sister.

Ophelia's cell phone yielded some unexpected gifts, including some old email exchanges with Harland Fisher, the mayor of Bleak Harbor who had stopped Jubilee from changing the name of her property from Purgatory to Paradise. Discovering his texts and emails in Ophelia's phone last night, she gleefully shot him a text from the phone about saying goodbye, knowing there was worse to come for Fisher. And then another, similar text to Ophelia's boyfriend Gary Langreth, for the fun of it. Let them all be as confused and frightened as she was that morning at the state police post with Trooper Christian.

Jubilee starts to cue her microphone to talk with Caleb, then decides against it. She already told him to hold his head steady with the GoPro, which she figured would help him keep his hands steady. She'll have to trust him now. She chooses her regular cell phone from the three on the desk before her and hits speed dial letter *P*. While the call goes through, Jubilee says, "Frances. Not a word while I'm on this call."

"Hello, honey," Phillie answers. "I watched the press conference. You were terrific. Tamed those barking hyenas. Joshua would be proud of you."

"Thank you. I've been meaning to call and say hi."

"You're brave, Juju. Was it hard?"

"The press conference?" *Yes, it was hard,* she thinks. Though not for reasons that would occur to Phillie. "Not too. You know, I was doing the do-gooder thing, and reporters are pretty predictable creatures."

"There was that one question, and . . . I don't know, the look on your face. The one about what happened this morning at the Petruglia funeral."

She wonders exactly what he imagined he saw. Chagrin, perhaps? Did she give anything away? "I hadn't heard that, but of course, it's terrible, whatever happened. Though, you know, they're in a dangerous business."

Phillie pauses before saying, "I know. I'm sorry you had to deal with it. I see the checks went out to the charities."

"Yep. All set. They do good work."

"Even though they're in the outer world."

"As I've said, there are exceptions."

The press conference was difficult mostly because she was distracted by matters at hand that Phillie knows nothing about. Yet the gathering was a necessary distraction in itself, a bit of misdirection for the media and for those who might try to discern her objectives before they come to fruition.

"Again, you're brave," he says. "But are you brave enough to join me in training for my next triathlon?"

"How many times do I have to tell you?" she says. "I don't do triathlons."

She glances at a third monitor, displaying the view from Caleb's GoPro. She sees an older woman, lumpy as a bag of onions, pushing a shopping cart. She's still unmistakably the woman Jubilee saw in photographs.

"They keep you young," Phillie says. He's a freakishly fit specimen for a man of sixty, a college cross-country star who never stops pushing himself, even as his knees and other joints rebel. Jubilee modeled some of Caleb's training on Phillie's workouts. "I worry that you're getting too old too fast, Juju."

Jubilee has considered that herself, though it doesn't really matter anymore. "You're nice," she says. "But now I have to go."

"Why? What are you doing? What's so important?"

Something in his voice says he isn't just joshing her; he really wants to know. "Oh, you know, teaching myself the viola," Jubilee says.

"Uh-huh," Phillie says. "Well, I'm going to show up on your doorstep one of these days, unannounced, and you'll just have to deal with it."

"And I will." As she says it, she wonders if she will ever speak to Phillie again. "I love you."

"And I love you, honey."

"Thanks for everything you've done for me."

"Don't get all mushy on me now. I'll see you soon."

Jubilee sets the phone down and leans into the monitor. A blur of gray slides into the upper right corner of the screen. She imagines the metallic purr of its vibrations high above Portia Stone's head.

Caleb and Jubilee modified this drone and others at a worktable across the room from where Jubilee now sits. The one designated for Portia Stone will take aim with its weaponry—the crude but effective equivalent of a high-powered rifle wielded by an expert marksman—and fire a skull-shattering bullet from a distance of precisely fifty yards. It will then fly one and a half miles from the Home Depot, where Caleb will collect it and move on.

The hatchback on Portia Stone's SUV pops open. She's starting to take the tray of plants out of the cart when the top of her head explodes like an overripe tomato. Her body falls across the cart, and the cart rolls away as she flops lifeless to the ground, blackness pooling around what remains of her head. Jubilee stops the video, spools it back, and replays it. Then replays it again. And then once more. Before she plays it a fifth time, she stops to recall the corrupt bastard Ralko showing Jubilee a picture of his sister, Portia, and telling her how proud she made him.

"Well done, Caleb," she says into her microphone.

When he doesn't respond right away, she says, "Caleb? You need to get to the rendezvous."

"I think I need a Ho Ho."

"Get to the rendezvous. You'll get what you need later."

"I understand."

"Be sure to remove the GoPro before you get on the road."

She watches him for another minute as he takes off the GoPro and puts the Volvo in gear. Then she saves the video feed of Portia Stone's demise and attaches the file to an email.

The email will originate from a server in the Bleak Harbor Police Department. The *From* field reads *deputychief@police.bh.gov*. On the *To* line Jubilee types *tawnyjane@tcnews.com*, a television reporter in Traverse City, and she cc's aralko@pinecounty.mi.gov. Her subject line reads, Prosecutor's Sister Dies in Bizarre Downstate Accident.

She hits send, closes her eyes. In her head she plays again the recording of Joshua screaming at having his dressings changed.

Jubilee opens her eyes, picks up the phone on which she's registered a number with the 315 area code, for upstate New York. She taps in a text to Bridget Deming's cell phone. Jubilee got the girl's number from a website called heretheyare.com for $39.50, a bargain. The text reads:

what's wrong w u? is it the stick? or yr skates? Something not right

Jubilee smiles as she hits send, then clicks on a monitor. A paused video appears, a stilled tableau of five girls in hockey gear, three in dark jerseys, two in light, hair straggling out from their helmets. Jubilee recalls herself at the same age, a high school sophomore and one of the best soccer goalies in the Midwest, the college coaches bantering with her parents on the sidelines, the emails from the recruiters, the scholarship offers. And how it all swirled away in pools of blood over one March night, as if none of her previous life had ever happened.

She hits the play button.

The view narrows as the camera slowly zooms in on the players converging on the puck. Jubilee feels the prickles of heat beneath the skin on the undersides of her breasts, hears herself begin to breathe a little harder.

She swallows.

The camera zeroes in on the player who reaches the puck before the others. The player gathers it onto her stick, flips it back and forth, then yanks it to her right with the toe of her stick as she loops around a girl in white, churning toward the goal, her ponytail hopping across the gold numeral 12 on her black jersey.

"There you are, Bridget," Jubilee says.

22

3:33 p.m.

The road along Bleak Harbor Bay is empty. That's good. Malone parks on the shoulder. She can just barely see Mayor Harland Fisher's bald head about a hundred yards away. He's waiting on a bench where they meet occasionally to discuss city business he prefers to keep quiet.

He hasn't seen her. She decides to just sit here awhile. She's tired. She didn't sleep well last night. She had the nightmare again. A naked man was tied to the oak on the winding road where Louisa died. As Malone approached, she saw that the man's bindings were actually snakes, yellow green and writhing. He was facing away from her, but she knew he was her ex-husband. She stood behind him, focused on the muscles tensing in his shoulders and back, imagining all the ways she could torture him. With razor blades. With fire. With a pistol jammed into his ear. With a cauldron of scalding water. She was choosing which she would use, growing excited, breathing harder, when the snakes disappeared and he turned to her, suspended on the tree in midair, and said, "I loved her too."

Malone woke up then, got out of her bed and into the armchair, where she dozed in fitful snatches until the alarm went off. As she dressed and made coffee, she felt the guilt creeping back in. Which made her angry, both at herself and at her ex, which made her feel guilty again. The cycle exhausts her. But there's no time or space in her life to confront it, with or without professional help. She works; she eats; she visits Louisa's grave; she does her laundry; she tries to sleep. She'd love to kick the car seat back and take a nap. But she can't. Not now. She can't be tired, can't look tired, can't act tired.

She opens the door and steps out. Fisher turns his head, nods in her direction. He supposedly has some information concerning where Ophelia may have gone in that Volvo that isn't hers. Malone assumes he'll want something in return. That's how it works with Fisher.

Malone has something else to ask him too. She just heard from Mikey. Mikey was upset, not entirely coherent, but Malone gathered that she'd received a disturbing voice mail. Mikey said the voice sounded automated, like a robocall, something out of a computer. Which made no sense to Malone—although it reminded her a little of the voice directing the reporters at that morning's press conference on Purgatory Bay.

———

Fisher checks the time on his phone. Chief Malone is usually a few minutes late.

Meeting here, on twin benches overlooking the channel that winds from the bay at downtown Bleak Harbor out to Lake Michigan, is part of their special relationship, as Fisher likes to call it. As mayor, of course, he holds sway over Malone's budget. At times, he knows, that drives her crazy, and he doesn't mind that one bit. But even more valuable to her, as Fisher sees it, are the city surveillance operations he oversees.

Those little video cameras planted around town have helped Malone do her job more than a few times. Like when she busted the Chicago punks who were posting Instagram photos of half-undressed girls in the beach restrooms. Fisher let her be the hero on that one, let her do the press conference to announce the arrests, even though he was the one who showed her the clips she used to nail those dumb shits.

Fisher prides himself on letting the chief have the spotlight even when he's the guy making things happen. In return, or so he imagines, she pretends she doesn't know—or maybe she really doesn't—about his other intelligence-gathering ploys, like the audio recorder he had installed on a lamp outside Nucci's downtown. Those are for his personal business, not Bleak Harbor's.

Now Fisher thinks he can help her with her latest little crisis, the disappearance of poor, pathetic Ophelia Wright. And he knows what he wants in return. The chief might balk, but he doubts she'll deny him. Something messed up is going on in Bleak Harbor. Fisher isn't sure what, but he assumes Malone doesn't want to be held responsible. And he's the one with the most power to hold her responsible.

He hears a vehicle door open on the bay road, turns to see Malone walking toward him. A breeze prickly with damp blows across his forehead, sleet probably on the way. Forty feet below him, the channel swirls violet and green. No fishing boats, which is good. And downtown Bleak Harbor is too far away for anyone to see them without binoculars or a telescope.

"Good afternoon, Katya," Fisher says.

Malone normally takes the other bench, farther from the lake, but now she comes around and stands facing Fisher. "Who the fuck is Charlotte White?" she says.

Charlotte *White*? Fisher thinks. He was going to offer Malone the email he'd found in Ophelia's inbox from charl0tt7@bh.com, no surname. How could Malone know about Charlotte, let alone Charlotte *White*?

"Whoa, what's with the potty mouth?" he asks, thinking, *Another sign something's not right around here. She never talks to the mayor that way.*

"I don't have time for games, Fisher," Malone says. "What do you know? Especially about your ex-girlfriend, or whatever she was."

Luckily, Fisher has more than that one email. He's spent the last few hours on his second floor, plumbing those video cameras. He's eager to show Malone what he uncovered, but she'll have to pony up first.

"I honestly don't know," Fisher says, trying to play it cool. "Why don't *you* tell me who Charlotte White is?"

"Fisher—"

"Mayor Fisher."

"Fisher," she repeats, "you're smart and certainly paranoid enough to know that kidnapping is a federal offense. If I happen to have the slightest suspicion that you are involved in one, I won't hesitate to call my friends at the FBI."

"Chill out." He stands. "I am not—"

"Sit back down."

"Can we just—?"

"I said sit and look the other way, or we can go talk at the station."

Fisher sits. This isn't going as he expected. Malone does occasionally feel the need to play hard-ass, probably because she's uncomfortable relying on a politician for her best detective work.

"Look, Chief, I did not kidnap Ophelia," he says. "Do you know the woman? You'd have to be insane to kidnap her. Can you—do you mind sitting down, please?"

Malone waits a beat, then sits next to him. "I think I can help," he says. He sets his shoulder bag on the bench between them. "What do you got for me?"

"Sorry, Mr. Mayor. We're not dealing today."

"Excuse me? Then why am I here?"

"Because you told an officer of the law you might have information material to an ongoing investigation. Failing to provide it is a felony."

Christ, she's serious, Fisher thinks. "Katya," he says. "Is everything OK? You all right?"

Malone stares out at the bay. "I really don't like kidnappings," she says. "And this one's weirder than the last one."

"How so?"

"I have a woman nearly in hysterics about her sister, who is blind and has been taken or is being kept by somebody or something that calls itself Charlotte White. This alleged person left a voice mail on the woman's phone that she says sounds more like a computer than a person."

"Siri abducted her?"

"And of course," Malone continues, "the blind woman and her family have a past in Bleak Harbor."

"Yes," Fisher says. "The brother. Sad story."

Fisher reaches into his bag and removes a file folder holding a single sheet of paper. He hands it to Malone. She reads the email charl0tt7@bh.com sent to Ophelia.

"So Ophelia was in touch with a Charlotte," Fisher says. "Maybe your Charlotte White? The Charlotte in the email was dangling a carrot that Ophelia might have found hard to resist, don't you think?"

"She wants to talk about 'future projects,'" Malone says, quoting the email. "It's like the proverbial old guy in a car, offering candy."

"Ophelia is a headstrong woman who could be blind in more ways than one. Did you learn anything from Langreth's motel key?"

"We might have a print, or maybe not. DNA, doubtful." Malone shakes her head. "We're searching for Charlotte White, with nothing to show for it yet. It could be an alias, could be the person doesn't even exist. No ransom demand, no demand of any kind, no threats, no deadlines, just this electronic voice: *Hey, Ophelia's here; we'll get back to you.*"

"What does the sister say?"

"So far, she's pretty useless. All she knows is Ophelia was supposed to be here and she's not."

Fisher waits. Maybe Malone will deal now.

"You have anything else?" she finally says.

"I might."

"All right. What do you want?"

"You know. Wehling's."

Fisher wants to plant a listening device in the private back room at Wehling's. The Bleak County commissioners huddle there after their weekly public meetings to hash out what they're really going to do. The city and the county have been in litigation for years over a matter of tens of millions of dollars that Fisher wants for the city.

"If I could hear what those guys are planning," Fisher says, "you could wind up with a hell of a bump in your budget, Chief. Maybe even fill that deputy spot you've been bugging me about."

"Why don't you just ask old man Wehling?"

"Wehling and I don't get along so well."

"So?"

"So maybe you tell him you're working a sting and you need to put some ears in there. Put a couple in the main bar and sneak one into the back room."

"You can't be serious."

"Or even, you know, get a warrant."

Something buzzes. Fisher reaches for his pocket, but it's not him. Malone looks at her phone, sets it aside. "What else do you have?" she says.

Malone's working him more than she usually does. "I think I have a better idea where that Volvo went."

"The one in the picture you sent me that picked up Ophelia?"

"That one."

"Where did it go?"

"Do we have a deal?"

"Where did it go, Harland?"

Fisher looks at the ground, then up and across the water toward Bleak Harbor, the buildings shrouded in late-winter mist, the barren docks and silent marina. He contemplates what his father would think if he gave Malone what she wants without getting what he wants. That's not how Fishers do business.

He looks at Malone, who appears to be looking down the channel in the direction of the lake. He wonders what is motivating her at this moment, decides he has absolutely no idea. He nods over his right shoulder. "Up that way."

"On Haroldson Road?"

"Past there. Then, you know where the road jogs left and then right, and there's a road hardly anyone uses that hooks off?"

"Toward Purgatory Bay?"

"Right. That's where the Volvo ended up."

"It could've gone past the bay and kept going."

"That's beyond the city line. I—we don't have any cameras that far."

"I was there this morning," Malone says.

"On Purgatory Bay? For what?"

"The woman who owns the place—I guess the whole lake?—had a press conference for this nonprofit she runs."

Fisher looks into the channel water. "Jubilee Rathman," he says. "I think she's a witch."

"What are you talking about?"

"You probably don't know this: she bought that property right out from under our town while our forefathers weren't looking."

"And?"

"And if I had been mayor then . . . well, it doesn't matter now. That's where the car turned off. Maybe the witch saw something. God knows she's got enough security up there. Razor wire, walls. Tighter than Gitmo."

Malone is looking at her phone. "I gotta call this guy." She gets off the bench and walks a few steps away. Fisher edges down the bench to hear.

"The what?" Malone is saying. "From where?" She's quiet for a moment. "Yes, of course it's her. All right, find Mikey. I'll be there shortly."

"What's up?" Fisher says.

"It's not good," Malone says. "I gotta go."

"What about our deal?"

"Like I said, check with old man Wehling."

"You don't want a deputy chief, then?" he says, but Malone is already trotting toward her car, phone on one ear. Fisher waits till she pulls away. He starts to walk toward his pickup, then breaks into a run, imagining his father chasing him, demanding that he get from Malone what he came for. He can't just let her get away with this. "Son of a bitch," he says, thinking he'll figure out who this Charlotte White is before Malone does, and why that Volvo went up toward the witch on Purgatory Bay, and what he might have stupidly missed in his surveillance the night before, and then Malone can decide whether she wants to ignore a perfectly reasonable request from the mayor of Bleak Harbor.

23

Cold sweat beads on Mikey's neck when she hears the question. She's sitting in a steel stall in an empty rink locker room. "Say that again?" she says.

"I need your sister's blood type."

Mikey, the onetime police beat reporter, has heard such unsettling questions before—asked some, too—but always as a disinterested observer watching other people digest the implications of what they've just been asked. *When did you last see your son? Do you keep any guns in your house? Would you like to speak with a lawyer?* She imagines within a second everything bad that the question could insinuate. She leans forward and says, "And you need it exactly why?"

"I can explain," Will Northwood says. The Bleak Harbor Police Department's tech assistant is sitting on a bench facing Mikey in a vacant rink locker room. "But I need to get the information first so we can find out what's what. I hope you understand."

"Yes, unfortunately, I do," Mikey says. Northwood is trying to be gentle, which unnerves Mikey as much as the question itself because she knows from her days at the *Times* that cops or their surrogates being gentle means bad news is coming. "Ophelia's blood type is A-positive," she says and then thinks, *Just like Zeke.*

"Thank you," he says, tapping on his cell phone.

Northwood found her and Craig in the bleachers watching Bridget and the Pride warm up before their game against Boston. He said he needed to talk to one or both of them immediately, out of the earshot of the other parents. Craig stayed so Bridget wouldn't worry any more than she already was worrying.

The locker room reeks of sweat laced with fruity body wash, the floor littered with balled-up wads of discarded tape. Northwood is a chunky man, probably in his early thirties, wearing saggy jeans and a polo that looks like he wears it five days a week.

He has explained to Mikey that he's not actually a police officer but is on the department payroll to assist with, as he put it, "geek forensics." Mikey never heard that phrase when she was covering the Detroit police.

Northwood is done typing but keeps staring at his phone. Finally he looks up, says, "Chief Malone is on the way."

"Fine," Mikey says. "Why do you need my sister's blood type?"

"It's not what you're thinking."

"Jesus, Bill—"

"Will."

"Will. Just say it. Did you find her?"

"No, it's not—" he stammers. "It's nothing like that, really." Mikey can almost hear him praying Malone will walk into the room and relieve him of saying whatever he has to say. "It's pretty weird, OK?"

"The last twenty-four hours have been weird."

"OK, so we—the department—received a package today via FedEx," he says. "It came in about half an hour ago, in a big, long box, wrapped in plastic."

"And?"

"It appears to be part of a leg that was stolen from one of your sister's sculptures."

The door swings open. Malone walks in.

"And," Mikey says, "it was shipped to the department by—don't tell me—Charlotte White."

"Thanks, Will," Malone says as she throws the dead bolt on the door. "I'll take it from here."

"Chief," Northwood says. He gets off the bench and moves to a locker across the room. "I sent the blood information in."

"What about the blood, please?" Mikey says.

Malone looks at Northwood. "You didn't tell her?"

"I was just about to."

"Christ," Malone says, lowering herself to the bench where Northwood was sitting. "We got a FedEx—"

"I know. A leg from one of Ophelia's sculptures. What about it?"

"It appeared to be covered in a sticky substance."

"There was a message too," Northwood says.

"Blood, then?" Mikey says. "My sister's blood?"

"Please," Malone says, "we're a long way from any conclusions. We suspect it's blood—it could be anybody's; it might not even be human blood—but we don't know for certain. We are checking. That's why we needed Ophelia's type."

Mikey closes her eyes, lowers her head to a hand propped on her knee. She can't escape the feeling that she's living one of the terrible stories she used to write for the *Times*, stories that made her think she had one of the most interesting jobs in the world. She finds herself staring at Northwood's shoes a few feet away. Wallabees. Laces undone. She looks up, expecting nothing. "Did you say there was a message?"

"I did," Northwood says. "It's just a sentence."

"And?" Malone says.

Northwood looks at her, then back at Mikey and recites, "Criminals are made, not born."

"Criminals are—what? What the hell does that mean?" Mikey says. She looks to both of them, can see they have no idea. She has no idea. She wishes, for a brief second, that she were a reporter again so she might know what to ask that would get her an answer that actually told her something. "Was there a return address on this package?"

"I think you said it as I was walking in," Malone says.

"It is from a Charlotte White."

"The address," Mikey says. "Where is this woman? Or where did she send this from?"

"A FedEx in Ypsilanti," Northwood says.

Ypsi, Mikey thinks. A shithole west of Detroit. She had to slog out there one Saturday night because a US marshal based in Detroit had shot his ex-wife and himself at the ex's boyfriend's apartment. A blizzard descended as she was driving home in the dark, and she wound up stuck for hours on the shoulder of I-94, waiting for snowplows and wondering why the dead cop hadn't bothered to shoot the boyfriend too. She never did find out.

"Ypsilanti sucks," Mikey says.

"Do you know anyone there?" Malone says.

"I'm sure we do because it's not far from Ann Arbor, but not any Charlotte Whites."

"Have you checked with—?"

"Craig and I have called or messaged every White we know. Which isn't many. No hits so far."

"And your sister never mentioned a Charlotte?"

"Not that I can recall. I think she had a high school girlfriend named Charlotte, but she was a Kleczynski or some other Polish name."

"Will?"

Northwood is preoccupied with his phone. A thin black wire dangles from his left ear. "Um, yeah, sorry," he says. "As you can imagine, we've found a number of Charlotte Whites in Michigan and adjoining states. There's a high school cheerleader in Brighton, a woman who runs a pizza place in Trenary, a retired state police officer in Swartz Creek, a horse trainer in—"

"And we have every one of our officers running those down," Malone says.

"Actually," Northwood says, "we have one officer stationed here at the rink, doing security."

Malone gives Northwood a look, then says, "I'll pull him—"

"Her."

"—her off that. The rink's fine. Check with the FedEx in Ypsilanti. They might have video."

"OK."

"What about the motel key? Do we have a print yet?"

"Not yet. You'll be—"

"How about DNA? That possible?"

Will shrugs. He has a finger on his ear, listening. "Long shot. Let's see what the fingerprint says."

Mikey gets to her feet. She'd like to slap Northwood in his earbud. "Do you people even give a damn about my sister? Do I need to call the state police or somebody?"

"The state police have been alerted," Malone says, and Mikey thinks, *I don't need attitude from you.* "Look," the chief continues, "you're anxious; that's perfectly understandable. But we're doing everything we can. We've also alerted our county sheriff and others nearby."

"Great," Mikey says. "Where is my sister?"

"This song," Northwood says.

"Are you kidding me?" Mikey shouts it at Northwood. "You're listening to a goddamn song? What the hell is going on here?"

Northwood pulls his earbud out and steps over the bench toward Mikey. "The song on the Charlotte White voice mail."

"So what?" Mikey says. *Where the hell is Gary?* she thinks. *Is anybody going to actually help?* "It's a radio or something."

"No," Northwood says, shaking his head. "No, ma'am. That's somebody humming. A person. Somebody in the background." He holds his earbud out for Mikey. "Here. Listen."

Mikey hesitates for a second, then takes the earbud and stuffs it into her right ear. "It might not mean anything, but"—Northwood looks at Malone—"it seems like someone's trying to send a message, and it's possible the song is part of it."

"We need to pay attention to every little thing," Malone says.

Northwood nods. "So we've learned."

Mikey listens to the voice mail again. It's hard to do without focusing solely on Charlotte White's voice. It's hard not to hear "Ophelia is alive and well for now." *For now,* Mikey thinks.

"Play it again, please," she tells Northwood. The tune in the background does sound as if a person is humming it, without any words. Mikey can't tell if it's a man's voice or a woman's, but it goes a little flat every few notes. She gives Northwood his earbud back. "I know I've heard that song," she says. "But it's one of those—"

"Right, you know it, but you can't place it," Northwood says. "I have an app that should be able to identify it, but it's on my personal phone back at the station. Again, it might be nothing."

Probably nothing, Mikey thinks, feeling a wash of anger not at this Charlotte person but at Ophelia, for not telling her so much about her life, then a stab of guilt for feeling angry. "The talking voice sounds like our Alexa at home," she says. "But maybe the humming is that man?"

"The man with the face?" Malone says. "Oh, hold on. I skipped right over a text while I was . . . hang on." She scrolls on her phone. "The Ohio plate. W19BB6."

"Don't tell me it's Charlotte White," Mikey says.

"No. It's registered to one Robert A. Kehoe. In Bath, Ohio."

"Which is where?"

Northwood is peering into his phone. "Kinda between Cleveland and Akron," he says. "A ways away."

"There's a Cleveland team in the tournament," Mikey says, feeling the tiniest scrap of hope amid her fear. "I watched them play a little this morning. I don't remember any—what, Kehoes?—on the ice."

"But you weren't looking for it," Malone says. "And it could be an in-law or a friend or a neighbor."

"We've checked the lot too," Northwood says, "but no Ohio Volvo."

"They could've been at their hotel or in town eating," Mikey says. She looks at Malone, pleading. "I'm sorry for getting upset."

"It's all right," Malone says. She turns to Northwood. "Will."

"Chief."

"I want you to find this Robert Kehoe; I want you to interview him about his car; I want you to ask him about any Charlotte Whites he might know, or any Whites he might know, or anything he might know about Ophelia, where he was yesterday and last night, and what he's doing at this very moment."

"On it."

"Bring him here if you have to."

The image of the Ohio man's grotesque face flashes again in Mikey's mind. Was that Robert Kehoe? "Thank you," she tells Malone. "I know you're doing your best. Is there anything else you're looking at?"

Malone looks away, at her phone, for a second. She's deciding something. "I do have a source, a local someone, confidential, who pointed me somewhere," she says. "When I know more, I'll let you know."

Mikey wishes that made her feel better. Instead, she's transported back twelve years to the *Detroit Times* newsroom. She's the wife of a college instructor, mother of a three-year-old girl, an ambitious young reporter who believes she's about to produce her best work ever and has no idea how short her future in journalism will be. She's standing at Vance Robillard's shoulder. They're editing a three-thousand-word story that's been months in the making. She can smell the lick of booze in Robillard's sweat, the cigarette smoke embedded in his wrinkled wrinkle-free button-down from Kohl's. He's lecturing her about confidential sources for the fiftieth time. "They're like Bigfoot," he says. "No such thing exists in this world."

She pushes herself out of the memory as the lights in the room flicker: off, then back on again. Northwood says, "I'm going to the station."

The room goes fully dark. "Now what?" Mikey says. "Come on."

"They had a problem earlier. I guess they didn't fix it."

"Look, Mikey," Malone says. Mikey feels her step toward her, a hand squeezing her shoulder. "Hang in there."

Malone leaves. Mikey stays, standing in the darkness, wondering if Ophelia is afraid, if she's resisting, if she's wishing she hadn't gone wherever she may have chosen to go last night.

"Pheels," Mikey tells the dark. "Come back to us."

As she exits the locker room into the dark corridor, someone bumps into her going in the opposite direction. "Hey," Mikey says, turning, her eyes adjusting to see a man with a broad back, head shrouded in a hoodie. "Careful there." He keeps going without acknowledging her.

Some rink-rat kid, she thinks.

24

Christian would love nothing better than to run the jag-off in the Mazda off the road and smack him shitless, but he has more important things to do. He has the prick's license plate; maybe he'll call the state police post at Battle Creek and get one of those boys to mess with the guy. Or not. For now, he just lowers the passenger window and shouts, "Fuck you," as he speeds past.

He slides into the right lane, checking the Mazda in his rearview. His bad eye doesn't like sideways movements. Usually it feels like a mild muscle pull; other times it's like someone jabbed a pair of tweezers into the eye and left them there. All these years, and he's still not used to it.

Christian didn't hesitate blowing past the exit to Chelsea, where his eleven-year-old grandson, Lance, lies in a hospital bed, victim of—*Are you freaking kidding me?*—a drone attack. He hardly knows the kid. He spent exactly one afternoon of so-called quality time with him, on a miniature golf course where the little shit, with a zit like a caterpillar egg bulging at the base of his nose, took like fifteen putts a hole, whacking the ball past the cup again and again, refusing help, finally telling his grandfather, "Stop talking; your voice sucks."

His daughter and wife will be ticked that he's not at the hospital, of course. But Christian and his daughter aren't too friendly anymore, not that they were ever all that cuddly. He'll call his wife later and make something up. He's way more afraid of Gemma Petruglia than his wife and daughter.

He can't figure out why anyone would try to hurt Lance unless they're trying to get to him. If somebody thinks they're going to hurt Christian this way, well, he knows he's an asshole to admit it, but they're mistaken.

He taps some numbers on his phone and puts it on speaker. He called the number earlier and left a voice mail. He'd gotten the number from a dispatcher at Detroit PD. Christian had met her years ago at some law enforcement convention, lots of panels about kissing criminals' asses so you didn't get sued. The dispatcher had been at the registration table handing out credential badges, and they'd had some fun with floaties in the hotel hot tub after everyone else had sacked out.

"Christian?" Gary Langreth says.

"Well, if it isn't Scary Gary. Yeah, man, it's your old pool-shooting partner. How's by you?"

Christian grins at the thought of Langreth grimacing at his voice. "Jesus," Langreth says. "How'd you get my number?"

Scary Gary, Christian thinks. They were stuck together in some cop pool league when Christian was working at the state post in Romulus. Langreth was a fine partner, good at spinning the cue ball like it was a yo-yo. And a decent enough guy, quiet most of the time, until he had too many Jack Blacks and started lecturing Christian on how to play. Christian let it ride. Then one night they were playing for the league championship, with $250 each in cash on the line, and things—actually, Langreth—blew up. Christian wasn't surprised later when he read about Langreth's ugly exit from the Detroit Police Department for a different blowup. He's hoping their own history won't get in the way of a friendly chat.

"Got it off the interwebs," Christian says.

"No, you didn't. You still with the state police?"

"Nope. Bagged that a few years back. Found better things to do than sit on my ass with a speed gun all day. This consulting stuff has gotten pretty lucrative with everyone freaking out about Muslims and Mexicans, you know?"

"I'll bet. Still shooting stick?"

"Every now and then. I'm still no Scary Gary. You?"

"Not for a while. Listen, I'm due back in court here. What's up? Something about that reporter?"

"Yeah, well, I thought you might like to know about that."

Christian's trying to sound sympathetic. He has to be careful. He can't afford to let Langreth know where he's actually going. But he wants a little help with the lay of the land. "Old Robo choked to death on some sort of poison gas in his own damn car in his own damn driveway. I bet you're loving that, eh?"

The *Times* reporter wrote a lot of stories about Langreth's expulsion from DPD, fed by department sources who needed a scapegoat. And he dubbed Langreth Scary Gary, a phrase that seemed to make every headline on the stories.

"You think the Petruglias took him out?" Langreth says. "I can't believe he lasted this long."

"Doesn't sound like their style," Christian says. "My department sources say whoever did it left some kind of smart-ass note on the windshield." A news bulletin interrupts the Rush song playing low on Christian's car radio. ". . . moments ago, reports of another drone attack in Michigan, and this one appears—"

"Holy—" Christian starts to say as he punches the radio off.

"What was that?" Langreth says.

"Nothing. Wasn't you who offed Robo, was it?"

"I doubt that's why you called."

"Ha. Yeah. I was hoping for a little friendly advice."

"I have about two minutes."

"OK. Me and the old lady are thinking of getting a place on a lake somewhere, maybe even retire there. We're looking up north, of course, but I've heard good things about your neck of the woods. What's Bleak Harbor like anyway?"

"I wouldn't move to Bleak Harbor."

Christian guffaws. "But you *did* move to Bleak Harbor."

"Needed a job. I mean, I haven't been here that long. It's basically dead nine months of the year; then all the assholes from Chicago and Indy and Detroit pile in. Not that you're an asshole."

Christian remembers Langreth flinging the pool stick across the table at him like a javelin. Just missed his bad eye. "Not that you are either," he says. "So we're thinking we might buy a little cottage, maybe even just a plot we can stick a double-wide on. But we want to be on water."

"Plenty of that on Lake Michigan."

"A little over our budget," Christian says. "Lemme run a few names by you. How about Long Lake?"

"One of the sixty-three Long Lakes in Michigan. This one's not very long. But it's pretty. I don't think you can have a boat wake."

"Good to know. Magician Lake?"

"Can't say I know it."

"Something called the Heavenly River?"

"A tributary off the Kalamazoo. I heard people used to fish there until an oil spill a while back. Had a drowning there last year, drunk teenager."

"Ah. And that runs up to Purgatory Bay. What's that like?"

Christian turns the radio back on as low as it will go, hoping to hear something about that new drone attack.

"The owner owns the whole shebang," Langreth says. "So probably nothing to buy there."

"Oh, the *owner* owns it, eh?"

"Still a smart-ass, eh, Christian?"

"I guess she must be rich as hell, eh?"

"Guess so."

"All alone on a lake in the middle of nowhere. She must have some kick-ass security."

There's a pause before Langreth says, "I've heard that. She keeps to herself."

"OK. Maybe I'll check out those other lakes. Appreciate the help."

"Can I ask you something?" Langreth says.

Christian hesitates, maybe a little too long, then says, "Shoot."

"The note on Robillard's car. What did it say?"

"Still a cop at heart, eh, Gary?"

"Just curious."

"Lemme think," Christian says. He glances at the odometer. Still a hundred miles to Bleak Harbor. "Something about feeling lucky."

"Doesn't sound like Robo was too lucky."

"Nope."

"Gotta go."

Christian stuffs the phone in the console, turns the radio up, and says, "Good talking to you too, Gary."

25

4:34 p.m.

"Gary."

Langreth looks up from his phone. His boss is standing in front of him, lips pursed, arms folded, not looking happy. Bleak County prosecutor Adelaide Cooper rarely looks happy of late, at least with Langreth. They were drinking buddies in law school. She has since gone sober and seems to have aged faster. Langreth has been wondering what they have in common besides some boozy late nights in the distant past.

"Did Van Zoeren bind the kid over for trial?" he asks.

They're standing outside the courtroom of Bleak County district judge R. T. Van Zoeren. Langreth wants to go back to what he was reading on his phone but knows that wouldn't be wise.

"Yes, he's going to trial," Cooper says. "I'm sorry you were indisposed. The judge had a question."

He drops his phone to his side. He knows he made a mistake stranding Cooper. She's a politician, not a litigator, loves the stage, hates the courtroom.

"Had to take this call, sorry," Langreth says. "I thought he'd wait for another—"

"Judges don't wait, Gary, especially Van Zoeren and especially for prosecutors. But we got lucky."

Lucky, Langreth thinks. The word from the note on Robillard's windshield resonates because it's part of something Ophelia likes to say:

"You can't get lucky if you don't try." And the word, *Lucky*, is inscribed on her sculptures of the boy, her brother, with the skateboard.

"You know," he tells Cooper, "I hope that young man's lawyer gets him to plead. I'd hope we could make a deal if the kid's willing to get some real help."

Cooper gives him a look. He can almost hear the reelection wheels grinding inside the salt-and-pepper curls wrapping her head. She's no fan of illegal dealers, especially now that two legal pot shops in Bleak Harbor are angling for the business. But Langreth saw plenty of kids in Detroit like the one who was just arraigned, decent dumb shits who got busted for selling a scrawny bag of weed and never found their way back out of the criminal maw.

"We will let the suspect's attorney approach us about any such arrangement before we go making one on our own," Cooper says. "Clear?"

"Crystal."

"See you at the office?"

"Gotta hit the restroom first."

Langreth goes into the men's room, safe from his boss. It's a classic old courthouse lavatory, built when Bleak Harbor's year-round population was three times what it is now, with a checkered tile floor and porcelain urinals stretching from your shoes up to your belly button.

He leans against a wall, takes his phone out, sees a text from Malone: call me plz. He goes back to the Google search he was looking at when Cooper interrupted: *drone attack mich*.

The headline at the top of the queue is from the *Washington Post*: Drone Warfare: Terrorism by Joystick. The next is a Wikipedia article on drones deployed as weapons in Pakistan. The third is from Reuters: Michigan Police Baffled by Drone Attacks; One Dead, One in Critical Condition.

"Holy shit" is right, Langreth thinks, repeating what Christian started to say before he abruptly silenced that radio. Langreth had a

hunch that Christian was driving and figured by the relative quiet, punctuated once by the blurt of a horn, that he was on a highway.

He calls up the AP story. Police have no suspects yet in three apparent drone strikes: one in the past two hours that killed a woman in Marshall; one earlier that struck an eleven-year-old boy in Chelsea; and a failed attack that morning in suburban Detroit on a seventeen-year-old girl at a funeral for a member of the "notorious" Petruglia family.

"Drones," Langreth says, shaking his head. He thinks of his buddy Shep using a drone to record his eight-year-old son getting up on water skis for the first time. It hovered like a dragonfly twenty feet above the boy as he wobbled and lurched before righting himself to cheers from Langreth, Shep, and Shep's wife in the boat. Ten minutes later they were watching it on Shep's phone, the boy all grins and shivers on the lakeshore.

Now drones are killers, Langreth thinks. *Ain't that the way of the world.* The Petruglias being targeted by a drone is almost funny. In Langreth's Detroit days, the Petruglias were known as supreme innovators in the art of killing, the first to freeze dead victims so the cops couldn't determine the time of the death, pioneers of using drugged and starving pit bulls as instruments of torture.

He calls up his contacts, scrolls to *D*, finds the name, hits the call button, hoping his old cop pal DeSimone hasn't changed her cell number again. He listens. Three rings. Four. She's making him wait.

"What are you thinking?" she says when she answers.

"I'm thinking how the hell did you get to be a Detroit police captain."

"Sheer, unassailable ability. And sleeping with the right people."

"Congrats, D."

"Here's what I was thinking," DeSimone says. "I was thinking I could get you to come home, rejoin the department."

Langreth looks up at a flickering ceiling lamp. "And I'm thinking the deputy chief might have something to say about that."

The deputy chief was boinking Langreth's partner when the two of them whaled on that meth head, who was, unfortunately, the nephew of a city councilwoman.

"Deputy chief is outa here," DeSimone says. "Taking early retirement, spending more time with the family."

Langreth knows he's not going back to Detroit. The city councilwoman is still there; her nephew is still in a wheelchair; the crack house where Langreth beat him up has probably toppled over.

"Thanks, but I gotta ask you something," Langreth says.

"Where are you?" she says. "There's an echo."

"Restroom at the courthouse. Did you hear about Robillard?"

"Oh yeah. I wondered if that's why you were calling. A shame, huh?"

"What the hell happened?"

"Forensics is still working on it. But it looks like he was gassed somehow, right in his own car."

In his own damn driveway, Langreth recalls Christian saying in his grating rasp. "I heard someone might have left something on Robillard's windshield."

"Yeah. And there was a video camera."

"Huh?"

"Whoever planted the poison also apparently installed a tiny camera inside the car. It was attached to the A-pillar on the passenger side, pointed at the driver's seat."

"So they could watch the guy die?"

"Looks like."

"Jesus," Langreth says. "What about the windshield?"

"There was something. At first we thought it was some neighborhood flyer. But it's too weird for that."

"How so?"

"For one thing, it's orange, so it looks kind of like a traffic ticket, at least from a distance. It's like the killer wanted to make sure the cops saw it, and of course that Robillard saw it."

"Handwritten?"

"No. Printed. Like from a Kinko's."

"What'd it say?"

"It said—get this—'Feel Lucky.'"

"'Feel Lucky'?"

Ophelia, Langreth thinks again.

"As if it was directed at Robillard," DeSimone says. "Though this obviously wasn't his lucky day."

"That's it?"

"No. So the 'Feel Lucky' is printed in white at the top of this flyer-like thing. Beneath it—we almost missed this—are some bumps—"

"Not braille," Langreth interrupts. "Tell me it's not braille."

DeSimone pauses briefly. "Why? How did you know?"

Langreth is trying to unscramble the thoughts tumbling over each other in his head. "I—you said bumps. So it is braille?"

"Yes," she says. "Maybe you should come and help us out with this."

"You looking at the Petruglias?"

Langreth says this despite himself. The Petruglias wouldn't have taken Robillard out. He wasn't worth the trouble.

"Of course we have to, if only to shut the media motormouths," DeSimone says. "But I don't know. Doesn't feel right."

"Agreed. So what does the braille say?"

"Why are you so interested, Gary?"

Langreth would love to tell her the truth, if he knew what it was. "Why do you think?" he says. "That guy helped screw my life up."

"True that. Hang on. Got the translation in a text."

A young man in a suit, carrying a burgundy-colored briefcase, comes in and goes to a urinal. Langreth feels odd just standing there, so he moves out to the hallway. The courthouse is pretty much empty.

DeSimone comes back on. "OK, your man Taylor says hello."

"Hello, Steve-O."

"His mom's blind, so he knows some braille. He says it says, 'Too bad you won't suffer like the others.'"

"The others?" Langreth says. "What others?"

The only "others" that pop to mind at the moment are the people targeted by those killer drones.

"No idea. Why are you so interested, bud?"

"Hang on." Langreth presses the phone to his chest, thinking. *Lucky* has to be a coincidence. But the braille too? He tries to remember if he ever told Ophelia about Robillard. He can't imagine why he would have. The situation is so screwy that he figures, *What the hell, why not ask a couple more screwy questions?* He gets back on the phone.

"D, you ever hear of a state cop named Christian?"

DeSimone is quiet for a few seconds. "Christian? No. Can't say as I have. Should I?"

"He was the guy I got in that pool hall thing with."

DeSimone laughs. "Forgot about that. What happened again?"

He and Christian were playing as a team for a nice pot against two guys who weren't close to their match. Christian kept missing shots he should have made, then pointing out how he'd left the cue ball in a great spot for the next shot he wasn't allowed to try. "You can't steal first, dumb shit," Langreth finally told him. By then, they'd both had too much to drink. Christian picked up a pool ball and fired it at Langreth, who ducked, then reared back and threw his stick, scoring a blue chalk streak along Christian's neck. The rest was a blur.

"I might have lost my temper," Langreth tells DeSimone.

"No chance."

"I don't think he's a cop anymore. Reminds me: he's rumored to be doing some freelancing for the Petruglias."

"Small world."

"How about this one," Langreth says. "Charlotte White?"

"Wright? Like *fight*?"

"White, like the absence of color."

"Charlotte White. Why? Does she have something to do with Robillard?"

"Maybe," Langreth says, though he doubts it. "I will let you know. Ever hear of her?"

"Let me think," DeSimone says.

As Langreth waits, he googles Charlotte White, wondering why he hasn't already. The queue unfolds: A soap opera actress. Some kind of health center. A half-dressed chick on Instagram. At the bottom is a link to a LinkedIn profile that includes the words *law enforcement*. He thumbs it.

"Damn," DeSimone says. "Why does that ring a bell?"

"Charlotte White," Langreth says. "Michigan State Police. Retired. Her last assignment was in Lapeer. Post commander."

"Oh shit," DeSimone says, laughing again. "Chucky."

"Chucky?"

"You know, Charlotte, Charles, Chuck, Chucky."

"And?"

"But actually, that's not why we called her Chucky. It was her makeup. It made her look like that serial-killer doll in the Stephen King movie."

As she's speaking, Langreth is typing Christian's name into LinkedIn. The state cop connection is probably just another coincidence, but what the hell? There can't be too many Xavier Christians—in fact, there are none, at least in LinkedIn. Nothing in Google, either, except another actor. Christian worked at the Romulus post when they played in the pool league. Did he ever work at Lapeer? Langreth can't recall.

"How do you know her?" he says. His phone starts vibrating. Malone calling.

"She and I and a bunch of other woman cops were at some conference on Mackinac Island. We had a ball. Took a bike ride around the island, and Chucky had a thermos of V and Ts. We tried a similar thing a couple years later, but you know, it wasn't the same."

Langreth makes a mental note to track Chucky down as a text beeps into his phone: Cooper. He has to get to the office. And check in on Mikey. And call Malone.

"Understood," he says.

"Why do you care about Chucky?" DeSimone says. "This is a weird conversation, even for you."

"We're looking for a Charlotte White. Could be an alias."

"I thought cops did the looking."

"Always a pleasure, D," Langreth says, meaning it. "By the way, that Chucky movie? I don't think that was Stephen King. Stay in touch, eh?"

"And you, my friend."

His office is in the basement. He should go directly there but instead takes a back exit to the parking lot and stands just outside the door, out of view of any basement windows. The sky looks as if he could reach up and touch the charcoal and gray.

He has a voice mail from Malone. He listens to her tell him about a package from Charlotte White, a broken-off sculpture leg covered in what looks like blood, the "Criminals are made, not born" message, the ID of a license plate from Ohio.

He pictures Ophelia's eyes, the wandering blue, how she seemed to search his face with them as if she could see, how that made him feel as if he mattered to someone again, as if he wasn't just a hot-tempered thug who'd thrown away his career. It made him want to wrap her in his arms and hold her. Ophelia would not have that, of course. She'd wriggle free and tell him what was next on their agenda for the evening, where they would have dinner, what she'd order, how they could go back to his house afterward and plan a summer trip up north. And he'd love it.

Now, wondering where she is, whether someone might be hurting her, a knot tightens beneath his rib cage, the knot he usually feels before he goes off on someone. He sucks in a breath as his phone starts ringing. Malone again.

"What the hell is going on?" he says.

"You got my voice mail?"

"Only listened to part of it before you called again."

"Never mind. I sent one of my guys up to Purgatory Bay. Your buddy Fisher said his cameras tracked the Volvo going up that way. Maybe the woman who lives up there saw something. She's got a bunch of cameras too. It's worth a check."

"Fisher has cameras?"

"He's a pain in the ass," Malone says. "But he's my pain in the ass."

"Am I officially on this case now?" Langreth says.

"Like you're gonna do what I tell you?"

She hangs up.

Langreth walks back inside, thinking, *Ophelia, what the hell did you get yourself into?*

As he starts down the stairway to his office, he realizes he just heard about Purgatory Bay twice in under an hour. *Christian,* he thinks. *Dumber than a nine-ball rack.* He and his wife want to retire to a small town? What about Long Lake, Magician Lake, Purgatory Bay? *What about it?* Langreth thinks. A trailer on Purgatory Bay? Not with—
Wait.

He remembers what he told Christian about Purgatory Bay: *The owner owns the whole shebang.* Redundant, he thought then, hearing his boss, Cooper, lecturing him about repetitiveness in his written reports. Then Christian responded, "She must be rich as hell, eh?" *Lake house, my ass,* Langreth thinks now. *How does Christian know the owner of Purgatory Bay is a she?*

He stops halfway down the stairs, turns, and goes back up the stairs and out to the parking lot. He slides into his car, starts it, and is about to put it in gear when he reaches across the seat, opens the glove box, and grasps the butt of his .40 caliber Glock 22. He takes it out, gives it a once-over. It feels fine, solid, light in his hand, ready. He puts it back and pulls the car out of the parking lot toward Purgatory Bay, promising himself he'll call Cooper later.

26

The quiet.

Ophelia knows quiet like a sibling, embraces it, revels in it, seeks it everywhere she goes. People seem to think that truly empty, unremitting quiet is easier for the sightless to find, as if they live in a vacuum not just of light but of sound and smell and even touch. Then there are the ignoramuses who actually believe that the lack of one sense somehow heightens the others, as if being unable to see bestows some secret, enviable advantage.

But here, where she's sitting, legs crossed on her bed, back straight against the wall, palms open on her knees, the quiet is nothing like any quiet she has experienced before. It's not an outer thing like it is everywhere else, in the office at her store, on a bayfront stroll, in her kitchen sketching sculptures, but an absence of that thing, an absence of anything. She's been sitting like this for at least an hour, she guesses, maybe longer, maybe two or even three hours, and she has not heard one sound.

Nothing.

She thinks of her twin, Zeke, as she often does in her quietest moments. Could he have heard them all shouting as he lay trapped in that suffocating cocoon of sand? Or was he enveloped in the pure, inevitable silence of death, alone in his desperate last struggle for breath?

———

They were standing on Jeremiah Jump, a tall stretch of dunes along Lake Michigan north of Bleak Harbor—Zeke, Ophelia, Mikey. It was ninety-six degrees on July 14, 1994.

Zeke had three shovels, a canvas bag of assorted other stuff, and a plan, of sorts. "I don't know," Mikey said. She had that older-sister look she'd been wearing since her fifteenth birthday, as if that new candle on the cake had bestowed on her some mystical measure of maturity when really she was just chickenshit. Mikey was a lot like Mom. Looked like her, behaved like her, was cautious like her, shrank from confrontation like her. Mikey was easily Mom's favorite, to the point that Ophelia sometimes called her Eleanor, after Mom. Of the twins, Zeke was the favored one, maybe because he was a boy, or maybe because Ophelia had a smart mouth she wasn't afraid to use. Mom was never shy about confronting Ophelia.

"You could get stuck," Mikey said.

"That's why you're here," Zeke said. "So you can pull me out. But it ain't gonna happen anyway. I got it all figured out."

"Like muskellunge?" Ophelia said.

"Are you kidding me?" Zeke said, feigning indignation. "Muskellunge was brilliant. We had bad luck."

"Uh-huh," Mikey said.

"But you know—"

"Yes, we know."

"—you can't get lucky if you don't try."

Muskellunge had been Zeke's attempt to re-create the ending of *Jaws 2*, when the shark gets fried by an underwater power line. He'd made a papier-mâché shark head and mounted it on an inflatable raft loaded with M-80s on long fuses. He'd been going to blow it up in front of the drunk adults at the bayside bars on a Sunday afternoon. Instead an unexpected breeze had separated the raft from the head, which had sunk while the adults had hooted and Ophelia, hooting herself, had recorded the debacle on a video camera.

Today's adventure was a scene from a Star Wars movie involving something that looked like an enormous mouth embedded in an enormous dune that devoured anything that fell in. Zeke called it "Return of Sarlacc," whatever that meant. Ophelia and Mikey had agreed to help in return for Zeke weeding the flower beds at the cottage.

Now Zeke thrust a shovel down into the dune sand and said, "Here." At his feet lay two more shovels, a video camera, a roll of metal screen their mother used to protect her tomatoes, some strips of plywood, and a sandwich bag of triangular pieces of beige-colored plastic.

"Wait," Ophelia said. She pointed at the plastic things in the cellophane. "Aren't those pointy things from one of Mom's necklaces?"

"Teeth," Zeke said. "For the sarlacc. When's the last time you saw her wear that thing anyway?"

"I don't like this," Mikey said.

"Stop being such a wuss," Ophelia said.

"Just dig," Zeke said. "Come on."

They knelt and dug. Ophelia looked out at the lake stretching to the horizon, Chicago, Milwaukee. Something was floating a hundred yards or so from shore. A boat? A buoy? She couldn't tell.

Sweat rivered down the sides of Zeke's face as he chopped into the dune. He looked happy. He always looked happy when he was working on one of his fantasies. Sometimes it ticked Ophelia off that he could be so happy about such silliness. She had to remind herself that he was just a kid like her, in fact eighty-three seconds younger.

At Zeke's direction, they dug a perpendicular tunnel that jutted out on one side and up on the other. Zeke propped up the sides with the plywood, then the tomato cages. "Now, the teeth," he said.

The idea was for Zeke to emerge from the hole through the teeth, screaming, then get eaten up again, descending back into the hole, while Ophelia shot video. He decided he'd go in through the side cavity to insert the teeth so he didn't disturb the top hole.

"This is a bad idea," Mikey said. "Mom's gonna kill us."

"No," Ophelia said. "She'll kill me. She'll give you a Twinkie."

Zeke ignored his sisters. He got down on his hands and knees and stuck his head into the sideways hole. The bag of necklace teeth protruded from his back pocket. "Pheels has to handle the camera," he said. "So, Mikey"—he twisted around and pointed behind him—"why don't you just hang back here while I go in? Will that make you feel better?"

Mikey said, "You think you're so goddamn smart."

"Because I am. Lucky too. Because I try. Pheels—ready?"

"Ready."

"Action," he said.

———-

What joy is left for me? Ophelia thinks.

The biblical citation appears in her head—Tobit 5:10—then dissolves as she recalls again that day on the dune.

Here I am, a blind man who cannot see the light of heaven . . .

Mikey would tell Ophelia later how her fingertips had brushed the bottoms of Zeke's sneakers, inches from where she could grab his feet or his ankles and heave him out.

Ophelia would remember, again and again, Mikey screaming "No" as Ophelia, panicked, gripped her sister's ankles and pulled her from the collapsed tunnel to safety, the sand covering the hole as Mikey emerged, coughing and spitting. "I had him. Why did you . . . I had him."

. . . but must remain in darkness, like the dead who no longer see the light!

The ambulance lights blinked in the afternoon heat, the beachgoers gawking in their bathing suits, the lake washing itself up as if nothing in the world had changed, the TV camera van, Mikey speaking blankly into the microphone, an officer sweeping her away from the reporter, beckoning Ophelia, Ophelia unable to pick up her feet.

Though alive—Ophelia chanting now, in a whisper, leaning her head back, slowly raising her arms—*I am among the dead.*

Zeke lying on the stretcher, his eyes vacant and bloodshot, the paramedic digging the sand out of his mouth with latex fingers.

And then comes Raphael, the angel of God: *Take courage! God's healing is near; so take courage!*

Ophelia opens her eyes, coming back to wakefulness, remembering where she is, that someone is probably watching, listening. Can that someone read her dreams? Can she or he fathom the guilty memory she has borne alone for so long? Is she here to be punished once and for all?

Earlier she let her fear, so useless, get the best of her. She reaches one arm behind her back and feels the scrape along the shoulder blade she suffered when the powerful young man—Caleb—tossed her against the wall. She feels the sting and smiles.

"Ophelia," comes the voice again, the woman's voice that warned her earlier never to touch Caleb. Ophelia doesn't sense anyone in the room. The voice seems to be coming from the wall in front of her or the ceiling. She decides not to answer, waits to hear the voice again.

Raphael, she thinks, *where are you when I need you?*

"Ophelia."

Ophelia undoes her legs, gets to her feet. "I guess I'm not going to be getting any help with my sculptures; is that correct?"

"It is almost time."

"Frances again? Not Charlotte?"

"You will find your shoes under the bed. Please put them on. You will be leaving shortly."

"To go home?" She feels a sudden lump in her throat, wills it down, steps in the direction of the voice. "Take me home, please."

"Caleb is coming."

"Just let me go home."

"Put your shoes on. The time is near."

27

The man on the video screen is maybe thirty, maybe a tad older, plump, the tails of his shirt sticking out from under his jacket and rumpled on his rear end. He's standing at the front entrance to the compound on Purgatory Bay.

Another view on an adjacent screen shows his SUV parked on the shoulder across the road, faced southward, toward Bleak Harbor. It bears the seal of the Bleak Harbor Police Department. The man at the gate does not strike Jubilee as a police officer or even a plainclothes detective. He looks more like a guy come to fix her furnace.

But then, she reminds herself, this is Bleak Harbor.

With the intercom phone on one ear, the man presses his pudgy face against the twin twelve-foot-tall iron doors, trying to see inside. The doors are pinched on either side by reinforced concrete pillars and walls topped with spikes laced with nearly invisible electrified wires. The wires aren't quite fatal but discouraging.

"Frances," Jubilee says. "Acknowledge him, please."

While she waits, Jubilee checks another screen framing a checkerboard of views from security cameras located in and around her property. The visual that catches her eye shows another car moving slowly up the road from the south. Two cars passing in one day, within minutes of each other, is unusual on a road that goes essentially nowhere but here.

And more unusual when the second car pulls over to the shoulder and parks, waiting, undoubtedly watching.

But for what?

She takes a mouse in hand, zooms the view closer. She can't yet make out the license plate or the driver's face, partly because the camera lens is blurred with droplets of sleet. Given the obvious curiosity, whoever it is will eventually come closer. Then she will act.

Jubilee hears Frances talking with the man at the gate. She blocks it out for now and turns to a separate bank of monitors. Soundless videos run in continuous loops on three of the stacked screens.

One shows a man sitting in the front seat of a car, smoking a cigarette. A second shows a crowd of people dressed in black moving down a sidewalk alongside a coffin. The third shows a clip from a TV station, a man being interviewed in front of a house, the chyron reading, *Local Prosecutor's Sister Killed in Bizarre Downstate Accident.*

How sweet that they used the headline I wrote, Jubilee thinks. The man is speaking into a microphone held by a woman. His face tells Jubilee that he's alternately furious, then crushed, fighting sobs, then furious again, his hands balled into white-knuckled fists. Jubilee closes her eyes and savors the deliciousness of his anger and pain.

Her father was correct. Jubilee had thought at the time that he might have been a bit insane, but now she knew otherwise. He was dead-on correct.

———

Edward Rathman was sitting in the recliner facing the huge flat-screen TV in the family room in Clarkston, his wife, Heather, wrapped in a Red Wings afghan on a sofa. They were watching the evening news.

Fourteen-year-old Jubilee sat at a rolltop desk across the room, her back to them, writing a paper on a short story by Flannery O'Connor. She had just reread, three times, a line she had highlighted in yellow about an old woman who might have been a better person if there had been someone to shoot her every day of her life. It had given Jubilee a chill—a thrilling chill that had caught her by surprise—the first time she'd read it, and now she couldn't stop reading it over and over.

"Of course there were no weapons of mass destruction," she overheard her father saying. "We knew it, they knew it, everybody knew it."

"Eddie," Jubilee's mother said. "Your blood pressure will spike."

"But they looked at their polls, they saw what was necessary to keep themselves in office, and they lied. They lied, and they sent all those kids to die in that horrible country. Not *their* kids, of course. Never their kids. Other people's kids."

"Put *Wheel of Fortune* on, Eddie, before you have a stroke."

Jubilee heard the TV volume rise and looked over her shoulder toward her parents. On the TV, soldiers were scrambling behind an overturned truck, bursts of light flashing over their heads. The view lunged left and zoomed in on the body of a soldier splayed in mud, missing an arm.

"That poor goddamn boy," her father said as he strained forward to pick his glass of bourbon, two cubes of ice, off the coffee table.

"There's nothing we can do," his wife said. "Put Vanna on."

Jubilee's father took a gulp of bourbon. "Dear, there's always something the unnamed 'we' can do," he said, using his free hand to signify a quotation mark. "'We' don't have the will."

Heather didn't respond. Maybe she had heard this rant before. Jubilee had not. She turned back to the desk while continuing to eavesdrop. Her father's calculated tirades could be entertaining, as long as they weren't about Jubilee or her friends.

"One option, of course," her father said, "is to simply put a bullet through the head of one or more of the soulless bastards who put us in Iraq in the first place. Maybe put it on TV, let everyone see it."

"And that would change exactly what?" Heather said.

Jubilee heard the confident rattle of her father's ice cubes. "You are correct, dear—it likely would change very little," he said. "The one soulless bastard dies, security improvements are made, and the rest of the soulless bastards resume telling the lies necessary to advance their careers and fill up their pockets. You're right. Death is too easy an out for this scum."

Heather got off the couch and took up the remote. Jubilee heard the voice of a woman calling for an "R, please?"

"Blessed are those who hunger for righteousness," her father said, "for they shall have their fill."

"The Bible now? Please, can't we just have a pleasant Thursday evening?"

"The best policy, dear, would be to make these bastards suffer like the parents of the kids they sent to die. A bullet to their head isn't going to make them suffer. But a bullet to one of their kids'—"

"Dear God," Jubilee's mother said.

"—heads. A bullet to the head of someone they love—"

"You know who you sound like, don't you?"

"—now that might have a salutary effect on how the world works." Jubilee heard the glass hit the coffee table and her father say, "Nothing will change, dear. Nothing will change until these people know they can't get away with it. Where are you going?"

Heather was off the couch, folding the afghan. "I'm going into the bedroom. I've had enough insanity for one night."

"OK, I'll stop."

"No, you won't." Jubilee heard her mother's voice directed her way. "Juju? Can you go work somewhere else?"

"I'm fine," Jubilee said. "I'm not listening."

"Now. Anywhere but here."

Jubilee gathered up her laptop and notes and the photocopy of the O'Connor story. She looked again at the line about the woman who might have been a better person if she'd been threatened daily with sudden death.

"Juju," her mother said.

Jubilee stood, looked across the room, saw her father's jawbone working as he ground his teeth. *Who isn't at least a little crazy?* she thought. She repeated his words in her head: *Death is too easy an out for this scum.* It made the same sort of inverted sense that the O'Connor line did.

She would never forget it.

———

"How can I help you?" Jubilee says.

The man at the gate has identified himself as Will Northwood, representing the Bleak Harbor police. He has no badge, though. He has explained that he is the department's tech assistant but is helping out with other chores, as the officers are busier than usual with the hockey tournament in town. He asked Frances about Ophelia Wright, so Jubilee decided to commandeer the intercom.

"Is this Ms. Rathman?" Northwood says.

"Yes, sir. Call me Jubilee, please."

"Thank you, Jubilee. We are investigating the possible disappearance of a woman named Ophelia Wright. You don't happen to know her, do you? Or maybe you've been in her shop downtown, Pheelin' Groovy?"

Except for the one time she dropped Caleb at the Dragonfly Festival, Jubilee has not been into Bleak Harbor since Mayor Fisher and the city council rebuffed her effort to rename her property Paradise Lake. They are about to learn what a grievous mistake that was.

"I don't know the woman or the shop," she says. "Why?"

She zooms in on the man's face. Silvery flecks of sleet speckle his ruddy cheeks. His eyes shift from right to left, scanning the fence and house as he thinks of how to respond.

"Any chance we could talk inside, ma'am? It's a little wet out here."

"I'm a single woman living alone, and I don't know you from Adam," Jubilee says. "So forgive my rudeness, but no."

Northwood frowns, takes the phone off his ear for a second, then gets back on and says, "Ma'am, we believe a vehicle that was transporting Ms. Wright last night may have turned up this road, and seeing as it doesn't get a lot of traffic, we wondered if maybe you saw something?"

Jubilee is refocused on yet another screen, this one with a view of the concrete benches on the roof. Three drones wait there like vultures on a utility wire. *Where the hell is Caleb anyway?* she thinks, dragging a keyboard closer and rapping out a nine-stroke code.

"What kind of car?" Jubilee says to Northwood.

"A Volvo, ma'am. Black with Ohio plates."

The words *Ohio plates* zap an electric thrill through her breastbone. *Kehoe,* she thinks and wonders if they've made the connection yet. Probably not. There's been no apparent move to evacuate the rink.

"Have you tracked the plates?" she says.

"We have."

"And?"

One of the drones floats off the landing pad. Thumbing a joystick, Jubilee guides it into the sky over the house. The sleet could make it difficult for the drone to maneuver, so she pushes the speed as high as she can and sends the thing zipping southward, skirting the oaks along the road from Bleak Harbor.

"Sorry," Northwood says, "I'm not at liberty to discuss that. Don't you have security cameras around?"

"I have cameras that would track anything that passed on this road from one end of the bay to the other. Those views might be helpful, yes?"

"Very possible."

"Whose Volvo is it, then?"

"As I said, I'm not able to—"

"But you want me to just open up my camera files. To someone who doesn't even have a badge."

Northwood looks down at his feet. He's wearing sneakers, so his feet must be soaked and freezing by now. Jubilee glances at the view of the car down the road. It has moved a shade closer while apparently trying to stay far enough away so as not to be noticed by Northwood.

She shifts her gaze to the drone she dispatched, lowers its trajectory to eighteen feet above the ground, keeping it close to the roadside so this Northwood person won't see it. She activates the drone's tiny camera. The drone dips down, then flattens out, swooping past the house and the security gate toward the second car. Jubilee aims the drone's miniature camera at the face behind the car's windshield, adjusts the focus.

A second later, a slightly blurred image of the face appears on an adjacent screen. Jubilee covers the intercom microphone and tells the screen, "Recognize." Five seconds later, an identity appears beneath the image.

"No disrespect, Ms. Rathman," Northwood is saying, "but I could get someone with a badge if you would prefer."

Christian, Jubilee thinks. She wants to whoop with joy. Instead she gets back on the microphone and says, "Mr. Northwood, can you excuse me for one moment?"

"Of course."

Xavier Christian, she thinks. *The unctuous uniformed prick from that night at the state police post.*

She has since followed his career, such as it is, as a paid slave for the Petruglias. She figures he was probably working for them even back then, one of their well-compensated plants inside Michigan law enforcement, from lowly deputies in rural counties harboring Petruglia marijuana farms and meth labs to state troopers who were given heads-ups on which Petruglia trucks were shipping what and when.

She's glad Christian is here, within easy reach. Yet she realizes she has, to a degree, misapprehended him. His presence here, as his grandson is fighting for his life a hundred miles away, suggests he's even emptier than Jubilee thought. Her father's astute calculation didn't account for people as amoral as Xavier Christian. The only way to make Christian suffer is to make Christian himself suffer.

Can do, Jubilee thinks.

She halts the drone in midair, lowers it ten feet. The slightly downward shot will puncture the windshield and slice through Christian's wattle before shattering his spine. Jubilee feels the urge to hum, but she's still on the phone with this annoying noncop.

"Mr. Northwood," she says. "I mean no discourtesy, but I would prefer that you leave my property immediately. I wish I could help, but this is not a one-way road, if you know what I mean."

"I see," he says. "Perhaps I'll send an officer up this way, then."

"Go ahead," Jubilee says. "Tell him to bring a warrant."

She imagined, for a while, that she could get away with her mission. But she knew deep down that sooner or later the Petruglias, if not the authorities, would figure her out. Accepting that was actually liberating. Knowing that she couldn't avoid facing consequences for her crimes, Jubilee felt freer to indulge her urges to taunt and torture fools, like Fisher and Michaela, who imagined they were in control of their futures, who thought they couldn't possibly lose every single thing they treasured in a black flash.

Besides, in the end she didn't want to be anonymous; she wanted them all to know that Jubilee Rathman was delivering justice, that these were not the random acts of a random sociopath but calculated retribution exacted upon the wholly deserving. As for Caleb, he'd merely been an accessory, manipulated and controlled by Jubilee. Those who determined how or whether he would be punished would take that into account.

She watches Northwood shuffle across the road to his car, trying to stay upright on the slippery road. She wonders if he might spy the drone bearing down on Christian. Probably not, and it doesn't matter anyway.

213

She loads the hovering drone's payload. *This your brother?* she remembers Christian saying, the rising squeak in his rasp amplifying his sick pleasure. *Joshua, right?*

The drone's aiming mechanism is trying to fasten the digital bullseye to a spot one inch below Christian's chin. The target shimmies left, then right, as the drone wobbles in the sleet. Jubilee sees Christian's eyebrows shoot upward, sees his mouth move.

The car begins to slide backward, away from the drone. The scope adjusts for distance and angle, the drone itself now fixed in the air.

"Goodbye," she says.

28

"Talk to me, Bridge," Mikey says.

Bridget doesn't answer. She's sitting with her mother on a bench in the middle of an otherwise empty locker room, having been ejected from the game against Boston. Mikey didn't see what happened because she was with Malone and Northwood in a different room.

"Your dad told me what happened," Mikey says. "But I want to hear it from you."

"Fuck it," Bridget says. She's still wearing all of her gear. Mikey figures she left her helmet on so she could more easily avoid her mother's glare.

"I don't care about your language," Mikey says. "But you will not just 'eff it.' Talk. Now. Or I will invoke The Rule."

The Rule is that Bridget must let her mother look at the contents of her cell phone no more than once a month, no questions asked. Mikey has never taken advantage of it. Bridget plants her gloves on either side of her helmet, shakes her head. She's not happy with herself, and according to what Craig related, she shouldn't be.

The Pride was up four to one when one of the Baked Beans poked the puck off Bridget's stick as she was stickhandling into the Boston zone. It was a clean play, but Bridget stopped short, leaped off her skates in the other direction, chased the poke-checking player down, and swung her stick with two hands across the girl's calf.

The girl went down, the referee's arm went up, and Bridget went to the penalty box with a double minor for slashing. As she was climbing into the box, she snapped the blade off her stick on the floor. The ref gave her a ten-minute misconduct. So with less than twelve minutes to go in the game, here she is, trying to shut her mother out.

"Bridge? You have a count of three."

"I'm sorry."

"Sorry for what? Look at me."

She lifts her head, peers at Mikey through the crosshatched bars of her face guard. "Sorry for losing my temper."

"OK. What's going on? And could you take your helmet off, please?"

Bridget pulls her helmet off, lets it drop to the floor. "Nothing. I just got mad."

"Mad at the girl on the other team or someone else?"

"It's nothing, Mom." She starts to pull her jersey over her head. "I'm going to take a shower."

"Give me the phone, Bridget," Mikey says, hating herself a little.

"Mom, no," she says from inside the jersey. Then it comes off, and Bridget's head pops out, her eyes pleading. The instant takes Mikey back to Bridget's first year of squirt hockey, Mikey kneeling to tie her skates for her, Bridget squirming because she couldn't wait to get out on the ice. Mikey doubts her daughter is as enthusiastic for the game anymore.

"I'm sorry. I need to know what's going on."

"Did you find Aunt Pheels?"

"Don't change the subject." Mikey moves around the bench Bridget's sitting on toward the lockers behind her. They all hold identical Washtenaw Pride sweats. She can't tell which is Bridget's. "Where's your phone?"

Bridget turns and looks at Mikey over her shoulder. "I left it in the car."

"Don't lie to me. Where is it?"

Bridget bends, ignoring Mikey, and begins to untie her skates. This isn't like her. Mikey sits down next to her daughter and lays her hand on the back of her neck, the drying sweat clammy to her touch.

"That girl is here, isn't she?" Mikey says, recalling the girl who harassed Bridget on the oil-change team she used to skate for. Bridget pulls her left skate off, starts on the laces on her right. "Is that what's upsetting you?"

"I saw her," Bridget says. "No."

There's a knock at the locker room door. It opens a crack. "Everyone OK in here?" Craig says. "I apologized to the ref for you, Bridge, but you'll need to say something to him too."

"I think we need to see her phone," Mikey tells him.

"What?" he shouts.

"Can you just let me take a shower?" Bridget says, her voice straining into a whine. "Then I'll talk to the ref."

"I need your phone, Bridget."

"Michaela," Craig says. "Let her take a shower."

Mikey steps to the door, pushes it closed, turns the dead bolt.

"Mikey," her husband says from the hallway.

"Mom," Bridget says, "what the hell?"

"Do I have to go through every locker in this room? Because I will. And then you will be done playing in this tournament. Do you understand?"

Craig is thumping the door. "Michaela, open up, please."

Mikey ignores him and tells her daughter, "Now."

With one skate on and one off, Bridget thuds across the rubber-mat floor to a corner locker. She fishes her phone out of a Pride jacket, opens it, taps in a password. "Here," she says, tossing it to her mother. "Knock yourself out."

Mikey takes the phone—"Thank you"—and makes a quick read of Bridget's face as she slumps onto the bench and pulls her other skate off. She doesn't see guilt or fear, which is a relief.

She sets her own phone down on the bench, then clicks on Bridget's email. Her daughter is one of those zero-inbox people Mikey can't fathom. Her own inbox is as long and unkempt as a Russian novel.

There isn't much to see in Bridget's inbox: two emails from her algebra teacher about an assignment, one from a Pride coach with an attachment containing the weekend schedule, a few from friends Mikey knows and trusts, including her boyfriend, Quinn. She leaves those alone for now.

Bridget ditched Facebook a while ago—"That's for old people," she told Mikey—in favor of Instagram and Snapchat. Mikey goes first to texts, which the oil-change bully used before to taunt Bridget.

She scrolls quickly through. The names are all familiar, but one text near the top of the queue carries no name, just a phone number with a 315 area code. Mikey taps on the thread and sees four texts, all sent in the last few hours, the most recent from about twenty minutes ago, shortly after Bridget was sent to the locker room.

That one reads:

u can't lose yr sxxx and expect to play for the bombers

Mikey glances over the phone at Bridget, saying, "The bombers? Who is this?" Bridget averts her eyes. Mikey reads the previous texts. The first one arrived around the time the Minnesota game would have ended:

kelly here, hope to see the old bridget deming in the next game

And then, two hours later:

what's wrong w u? is it the stick? or yr skates? Something not right

A coach? Mikey thinks as she reads the next text:

maybe you lost the fire. happens

218

Jerk, Mikey thinks. "Who is this?"

"Coach Kelly. Darwyn Tech."

"An assistant?"

"Yeah."

Mikey knows Darwyn's head coach, a woman named Turner, but can't recall Kelly from all the coaches and assistants and trainers she and Craig and Bridget have met in the past year. She grabs a tournament program out of her back pocket, unfolds it with one hand. Her phone buzzes with a text. She sees it's from Gary.

"Michaela," Craig shouts, "are you f—are you kidding me? Let me in."

She imagines the exaggerated pout on his face. Sometimes it makes her laugh, in a nice way. Her husband is the kind of guy who thinks a put-upon pout will win the day. Sometimes she lets him think it does. Not now.

"Your daughter is undressed, Craig," she calls to her husband. "I will be out in a minute."

She hears him whack the door again—"I'll be in the stands," he says—and picks up her phone, checks Gary's text:

you know a vance robillard when you were a journalist?

"Mom," Bridget says.

"One minute," Mikey replies, turning back to the tournament program even as the name Robo echoes in her head.

Somewhere in the program Craig has scribbled the names and cell numbers of all the college coaches coming to Bleak Harbor. She finds his list opposite a page of ads for the supposedly best restaurants in town. His list starts, of course, with the guy from Wisconsin, who may have lost interest in Bridget after today's episode. Fine with Mikey. She scans through the names, not seeing Turner or Kelly from Darwyn, meaning either they aren't here or her husband didn't write them down.

But Kelly must be here, she thinks, if he saw what Bridget did, unless someone is simply pretending he—or she—is the coach.

Bridget's phone beeps. Another text, from Quinn. "That's enough, Mom," she says. "Give me my phone."

Mikey hands it to Bridget. "So this coach upset you," she says. "And you did what you did. It's almost like this jerk wanted you off the ice. I want you to block this person, not just from your phone but from your head."

"I guess I won't be playing for Darwyn, huh?"

Mikey crouches in front of her daughter, lays a hand on one of Bridget's knees. "That person in your phone means nothing," she says. "You're a great hockey player. But more important, you're a beautiful young woman, inside and out. Don't ever forget that, Bridge."

Bridget is staring at her phone. Mikey knows that moments like this can make her uncomfortable. She pulls her sweaty hair back and looks at her mother. "OK," she says. "I'm gonna get my stuff off."

"I love you," Mikey says.

"I love you too. What about Aunt Pheels?"

"Everything's going to be fine. I'm going to use your bathroom; then Dad and I will meet you outside."

While Bridget starts pulling off her other skate, Mikey walks to the bathroom adjoining the locker room. The door is locked, which is odd, so instead she unbolts the locker room door and walks down the hallway to the locker room on the opposite side of the bathroom.

She enters the bathroom there and locks that door behind her. She stands at the twin sinks near the door and dials Gary. The floor sticks to the bottoms of her shoes. Water trickles from one of the faucets. Mikey tightens each of the faucet knobs. The leak persists.

Gary doesn't pick up. She looks at his text again, deciding how to answer it. When she heard about Robillard that morning, how he'd been found dead in his car, it resonated with something she thought she'd heard on one of the overhead TVs in the rink lobby.

She types a name into Google: *Petruglia*. She clicks on the first link, from a website called Deadline Detroit. The headline posted earlier this afternoon reads, Drone Suspected in Failed Mob Hit.

She scans the first few paragraphs, then taps in another name: *Rathman*. The first link is two and a half years old. Survivor of Brutal Family Murder Commits Suicide in Mountains.

Mikey swallows hard and presses the phone against her chest, looks into a mirror over one of the sinks. She pictures her younger self, her hair without the streaks of gray, wearing a Michigan State cap, standing behind Robillard as he typed and deleted, typed again and deleted, while a half-eaten mushroom pizza moldered atop the stack of file folders on his desk, the *Times* newsroom almost empty near midnight on a Wednesday, a police scanner squawking in the background, the tall windows to Mikey's right glinting with the streetlights on Lafayette.

29

Twelve years earlier

"It's a hell of a story, don't you think?" Ellen Addams said. She dropped her cigarette butt hissing into one of the seven empty Diet Coke cans on her desk, let the smoke filter out both sides of her grin, like a dragon without the spiked tail. "You want in?"

Mikey looked out the window at the WDIV-TV sign glowing across Lafayette. There was only one answer to Addams's question. "Of course," Mikey said. "Great story."

She wasn't sure why Addams had chosen her. She'd been at the paper three years, bouncing from beat to beat, trying to find a home that liked her as much as she liked it, trying to outrun the cutbacks and layoffs that were eating away at both the *Times* and the *Free Press*. She had the advantage of being young and therefore cheap.

Now she was being asked by the top editor at the *Times* to work with one of the best reporters at the *Times* on the biggest investigative project of the year, a takedown of Detroit's most notorious Mafia family. The newsroom had been abuzz for days about the multipart series Vance Robillard was writing about how the Petruglias laundered the cash they collected from their various illegal businesses, using intermediaries ranging from the usual Caribbean banks to little guys like a suburban Detroit copy-shop owner.

"Can I ask a question?" Mikey said.

"You just did," Addams said as she swung her legs up on the desk and lit another Camel. The *Times* building had been a no-smoking zone for years, but Addams said she spent so much time there that her office was, in effect, her home, and she ought to be allowed to smoke in her home.

"Right," Mikey said. "So here's another: Why me?"

"Ever work with Robo?" Addams said.

"No."

"Well, there you go. Everyone's gotta try it once, right?" She laughed and took a hard drag on her smoke.

"But it's really his story."

"Yeah, yeah, he's been on the Petruglias like Ahab since about the time Melville croaked. But that can be a problem." Addams keeled her legs off the desk and hitched forward. "You know how it goes—the story's only three-quarters reported, but you're already writing the front-page headline, thinking about the rounds you're gonna buy at the bar that night. That is one terrific way to wind up stepping in a bucket of shit."

"For sure."

In the newsroom Addams was known as Morticia because she had long black hair as shiny as a raven's back and—more to the point—a reputation for killing stories she had lost patience with. She had started at the paper one day before Robillard. The story went that they had screwed one night in his car inside the *Times* parking garage while midnight editors had filed past and James Brown had wailed from Robillard's radio.

"So you're the counterweight here," Addams said. "Robo's had a hard-on for these Petruglia shitheads forever, so you have to keep him honest, get the other perspectives, do whatever needs to be done to double- and triple-check every damn fact. Do what he says, in other words."

"And he knows about this?"

"He will now." She nodded toward Robillard's desk across the newsroom. Mikey looked and saw him returning from his seven p.m. cocktail break, sitting down with a white paper sack streaked with grease. "He'll be happy to have you."

"If you say so," Mikey said.

"First, though, you might wanna lose the Michigan State cap. Robo's a U of M guy."

She took off the cap and walked toward Robillard where he sat amid a sea of emptied-out desks and wall-mounted TVs gone blank. She was a little nervous to be approaching such a newsroom legend, but she told herself she was lucky to be working on such a big story, the kind of thing she'd gotten into journalism for.

Robillard was chewing and typing when Mikey appeared at his right elbow. Two framed photographs sat on his desk. She recognized one as Vincent Petruglia, patriarch of the mob family. She had no idea who was in the other. To the left of Robillard's swivel chair stood a tower of purple milk crates and one yellow one, bulging with file folders.

"Mr. Robillard," Mikey said.

Robillard swiveled to face her and stuck out a hand. Mikey shook it. "Call me Robo," he said. "I hear we're gonna be partners."

"If that's OK with you."

"Well, we will see if it's OK with you. I want to introduce you to our other partner." He plucked the photo Mikey didn't recognize off the desk. "This is my dear old great-grandfather, Jamison Mitzelfeld, city editor of this fine publication 1908 to 1934, presided over the '31 Pulitzer."

"Wow," Mikey said.

"He is our inspiration," Robillard said.

His silver hair was slicked back from a mottled forehead and rubber-banded at the back of his neck into a truncated ponytail. He wore an ashen soul patch under his lower lip that other reporters said he'd had long before a single hipster had even been born.

"OK," Mikey said. "Jamison."

"See these?" Robillard said, pointing to the milk crates. "Your first job is to read every damn word in every damn document in there. Except the yellow crate. That one's for my eyes only."

Holy shit, Mikey thought.

"After that, kid, you got the Rathman family."

"The who?"

"Exactly. Start reading."

———

Mikey swung the brass knocker three times, turned her back on the door. She had tried the doorbell but assumed it wasn't working. She dug a digital audio recorder out of her backpack, held it close to her mouth, pushed the record button.

"Home of Edward Rathman," she whispered into the mic. "Nine fifty-five a.m., Thursday, March ninth."

She left it on.

Nine hours earlier, Robillard and Addams had agreed that Mikey would show up on the Rathmans' doorstep that morning. The series was almost ready to publish, but it lacked any comment from Edward Rathman or his lawyer, probably because the Petruglias had told them to shut up.

Mikey had tried the family's lawyer, a man named Phillips, every day for two weeks, called each of the six KopyKwik shops looking for Edward Rathman, and once driven past the Rathman house but failed to work up the courage that time to stop and knock on the door.

That night in the *Times* newsroom, she had pleaded with Robillard and Addams that she had done what she could, and anyway, the Rathmans had kids she didn't want to upset.

"His kids aren't our problem," Addams had said. "They're gonna go to Ivy League schools because their daddy is a bitch for the mob. We need the readers to know we made every effort to get to this guy before we throw him to the wolves." She had already written the headline for the fifth and final installment in the blockbuster Petruglia series: No Place Like Home: How KopyKwik Became a Mob Money Go-To.

"I know it's shitty work," Robillard had told Mikey. "I'd do it myself, but I have a source who's tied pretty tightly to Rathman, and I can't afford to have Rathman look me in the eye and figure out who it is."

Mikey had doubted anyone could execute such a magic trick, but there'd been no point in saying so. Instead she'd said, "Can I ask who this source is?"

"Don't go there," Addams had said.

"Look," Robillard had said, "you'll get the top byline on this story, OK?"

"Really?" Mikey had said, knowing she was sounding too eager. So far, she'd had second bylines on two of the four stories in the series.

"Really," Addams had said.

"They live way the hell out in Clarkston," Robillard had said. "Don't you gain an hour driving there?"

The colonial on Ellis Street was red-and-gray brick along the lower level with a partial second story clad in aluminum siding the color of buttermilk. Four bedrooms, three baths, a deck overlooking an in-ground pool in the backyard. It reminded Mikey of her parents' house before they had moved to that cottage in Bleak Harbor.

She waited on the front porch, hoping nobody would answer. She knocked again. Still nothing. She peeked through the beveled windows alongside the door. A corridor led past a stairway into a dining area with an oval kitchen table dressed with a vase of white roses and ringed by six chairs. Through a pair of sliding glass doors behind the table, Mikey saw a woman moving around on the deck.

Heather Rathman was not implicated in anything Robillard had uncovered. Perhaps she had no idea that her husband's businesses were money funnels for the mob. She was wearing gray sweats and a long-sleeved flannel shirt beneath a down vest, her honey-colored hair secured in a clip atop her head. The tail of the hair flopped around as she carried empty planters from one side of the deck to the other, stacking them next to a gas grill and a pair of propane tanks.

Perhaps there was no point in speaking with Edward Rathman's wife. But Mikey couldn't tell that to Addams and Robillard. She walked around to the back of the house. The pool was covered with a black tarpaulin marred in one corner by pasty blots of bird shit. Heather Rathman was still busy on the deck.

"Mrs. Rathman?" Mikey said.

Heather fumbled the planter in her left hand, almost dropping it, and said, "Oh dear, you scared me there."

"I'm sorry; I tried the front door."

"Yes, and I didn't hear you." She set the planter down on the top of the grill. "Can I help you?"

"Yes, ma'am, I'm Michaela Wright. From the *Times?*"

"Are you asking me or telling me?"

Mikey managed a smile. "Sorry. I'm a reporter, ma'am—"

"Heather, please. And you don't mean the *New York Times*, do you? You mean the other *Times*."

Touché, Mikey thought. "Yes, Heather, the *Detroit Times*. I was wondering if your husband was around."

Heather folded her arms on the deck railing, saying nothing. She studied Mikey for what felt like ten minutes until Mikey, nervous, said, "I'm here because we've been—"

"I know why you're here. Don't they call you Mikey? Isn't that a boy's name?"

How would she know that? Mikey thinks. "Mikey is sort of my nickname. My dad—"

"I really don't care."

"Oh, OK. Is there any chance Mr. Rathman is available?"

Heather Rathman studied Mikey for a few more seconds, then came down a short stairway, leaving mucky imprints on each step, and walked across the matted brown lawn between them until she was barely a foot away. Up close, Mikey decided, Mrs. Rathman wasn't as beautiful a woman as she was substantial. She appeared to be about the same age that Mikey's mother had been when Zeke had died.

"We've heard all about what you and Mr. Robillard have been doing," she said. "Can you give me one reason why my husband should speak with you?"

In her mind Mikey scrounged in her journalist's bag of platitudes. It was a big bag. "Well," she said, "as you might know, this is a rather serious—"

"Not 'might.' We know. One reason, please."

"Mom," came a voice from over their heads. Mikey looked up and saw the face of an adolescent girl in a second-floor window. "Where's the Aleve?"

Heather Rathman turned and answered, "Where it always is, Jubilee. In the bathroom cabinet."

"No," the girl replied, petulant. Mikey wondered why she wasn't at school. Was she ill? Having her period? "Kara probably didn't put it back, like she always does."

"I'll be up in a minute," Heather said. The girl's face disappeared. "OK," Heather said to Mikey. "Got a reason for me, girl?"

Girl? Mikey thought, then let it go. "It's just, we want to get his side of the story."

"Please," Heather said. "If he gave you his side of the story, assuming he has one, and you believed it, you wouldn't have a story at all, would you? And you would just drop the whole thing? Is that right?" Mikey started to reply, but Heather went on. "All that work, all those leaks, down the drain, right? Give me a break. You're just covering your ass. You don't give a damn about his side of the story."

Mikey tried to imagine what Robillard might say to Heather. She had heard him on his phone telling sources they could eat shit and die. Mikey didn't think that would be helpful here. Instead she said, "That's not true. We want to hear Mr. Rathman's perspective."

"His 'perspective'? I'll tell you something, young lady. You may not have learned this yet, but you will. Sometimes you have a choice in the matter. Sometimes you don't. When you do have a choice, it's good to choose wisely. But again, sometimes—"

"Heather."

"—you don't have a choice."

Edward Rathman stepped onto the deck behind his wife. He was shirtless, a towel draped around his narrow shoulders, wearing dark slacks and black dress shoes. His appearance startled Mikey, though she would realize later that she actually felt relieved to see him.

"Mr. Rathman," she said.

"We are off the record," he said as he strode across the deck and down the stairs, stopping behind his wife and drawing her back from Mikey with a hand on her shoulder. "She is off the record."

"Mr. Rathman, could I ask you—"

"Did you hear me?" he said. A spot of shaving cream flecked one of his earlobes. "We are off the record."

"I heard you, sir."

"We're clear?"

"Yes, sir."

"I assume you have nothing better to do than investigate hardworking taxpayers who are trying to enjoy a nice simple life without having strangers invade their privacy. I don't know a single one of these people you're writing about. Not a soul. Do you hear me?"

"May I ask you a question, Mr.—?"

"You just asked me one, and it's your last. You are on private property. Please leave now."

"Sir, could I just—"

"Would you prefer that I call the police?"

As she was rounding the corner of the house, Mikey glanced up at the second-floor window. The girl was watching her.

Two miles from the Rathman house, Mikey parked behind a White Castle. She listened to the recording on her phone, jotting in a notebook, then dialed Robillard.

"Rathman and his wife were there," she told him. "But I didn't get much."

"Lemme patch in Morticia."

Mikey waited until she heard Addams on the line. "Way to go, youngster."

"You got him and his wife?"

"Not quite. He was clearly off the record. But I did talk with his wife briefly before that." Mikey looked at the page she'd bent back in the notebook propped on her knee. "I kind of surprised her while she was working in her backyard."

"And she said what?"

"Not a lot really, but one thing that's probably relevant: quote, 'Sometimes you have a choice in the matter. Sometimes you don't,' unquote."

The line went silent for a moment. Then Robillard said, "Scha-weet! No unquote there, baby. All quote."

"Nailed it," Addams said.

"I did? Seems kind of nebulous to me."

Mikey heard the rat-a-tat of Robillard's keyboard as he spoke. "She's saying her hubby had no choice; the Petruglias told him what's what, and he had to follow orders. It's a reasonable defense, and it gets his voice—or at least his wife's voice—into the story. We don't need his lawyer now."

"It's almost better that it's the wife saying this," Addams said. "She's a more sympathetic character."

"So we can use it?" Mikey said. "It doesn't matter that Rathman said they were off the record?"

"Wait," Addams said. "You said you talked to the wife first."

"Yes, in the backyard. Then Rathman came out, and he said they were off the record."

"Did you agree to that?" Robillard said.

Mikey hesitated a second, trying to recall exactly what she'd told Rathman. She remembered agreeing that she had heard him—*Yes, sir*—but not that his wife was off the record. "I agreed Rathman was off the record, not his wife."

"End of story. She's on."

"So," Mikey said, "we'll say Rathman declined to comment?"

"We can't," Robillard said. Mikey heard his keyboard going again. "He did comment, just not on the record."

"But—wait. If we don't say he declined to comment, wouldn't, I mean . . . the Petruglias and their lawyers are going to read these stories."

"Hell, I hope so," Robillard said.

"But if we don't give Rathman some cover—you know, he declined to comment—but his wife is quoted, aren't they going to at least suspect that he's somehow complicit, that maybe he's telling us stuff too?"

Addams loosed an exaggerated sigh that Mikey heard as, *Why the hell did I put this youngster on such a big story?* "So," Addams said, "you call us up all excited and give us this hellacious quote, and now you got cold feet? You wanna walk it back? You're wasting our time."

Mikey started to answer, but Robillard cut her off. "Look, it's OK. You're just overthinking things. The wife's on the record; Rathman's not. We're good."

"I'm sorry," Mikey said. "I'm just . . . I'm worried—"

"Hang on a second."

There was a pause on the line. Mikey imagined Robillard hitting the hold button while he conferred with Addams. She thought of the picture of Vincent Petruglia on Robillard's desk. Robillard had told her about the rumors he had tried for years to confirm that Vincent kept in his office a glass vase floating with tongues cut from the mouths of employees who had said more than they should have to someone they shouldn't have. And they were the luckier ones.

Mikey waited, thinking about that jar, what it might smell like, what color the liquid inside might be. The longer she waited, the more nervous she got about being left out of whatever discussion Robillard and Addams were having. She started to pull out of the White Castle lot as Addams came back on the line.

"Very glad you ventured out to bumfuck, Mikey," Addams said. "Take the rest of the day off."

No, Mikey thought, not liking this vibe, feeling like she was suddenly being shoved away from the story. "I still think we need to say something to, you know, give Rathman a little bit of cover."

"Not our concern, girl," Robillard said.

"Please don't call me *girl.*"

"OK, *woman.* Now I'm gonna shoehorn this sweet quote in and shoot you the latest draft. Go get yourself a beer."

The call ended. Mikey pulled up to a red light. A mother pushing a child in a stroller passed in front of her. The kid was screaming and bucking while the mother shoved on, sucking on a straw dipped into a 7-Eleven cup the size of a football. Mikey remembered what Addams had said about Rathman's children not being Mikey's problem.

The light turned green. She started to edge ahead, then slammed her brake pedal as a punk in spiky red hair, ripped jeans, and a black leather jacket strode across the street, flinging a middle finger at the waiting cars. The car behind her began to honk. *Go to hell,* she thought, picking up her phone again and hitting the speed dial for Robillard. The call rang out as she pulled through the light. *And you too, Robo,* she thought.

She slid onto I-75, stayed in the right lane. *Girl,* she thought. She noticed that she was still gripping her phone, tossed it on the passenger seat. She recalled Heather Rathman saying, "Don't they call you Mikey? Isn't that a boy's name?" Her byline was Michaela C. Wright, and she was no star, not well known outside the cop shop or the newsroom or the Anchor Bar.

But Rathman's wife somehow knew her nickname.

Girl, she thought yet again. Robillard had called her that; the Rathman woman had too. For some reason, as Mikey slow-drove at fifty-four miles an hour, semis rumbling by on her left, she imagined Robillard ordering a drink for Heather Rathman at the corner of the bar at the Anchor, across from the big framed photograph of Gordie Howe. At first it made her giggle, but then, out of nowhere, she felt a chill ripple through her forearms, and she thought, *No way.*

"Don't go there," Addams had said when Mikey had asked about Robillard's sources. And there was that yellow milk crate of documents that she wasn't allowed to see. "For my eyes only," Robillard had told her. Mikey placed a palm flat on her belly, feeling suddenly queasy. Something wasn't right, but she couldn't put a finger on what it was. How would Heather Rathman know she was called Mikey? She had to have heard it from her husband. And how would her husband have known, if not from Robillard? It wasn't like she and Robo were out advertising their project. On the contrary, they had tried to keep it quiet, lest the Petruglias start threatening sources and shut them down.

Could Edward Rathman have been whispering to Robillard? Or providing him with documents? But why? Why would he risk bringing the Petruglias' wrath down upon him?

No way, Mikey thought again, and then she thought of something else Robillard liked to say: "Anonymous sources are like Bigfoot; no such thing exists in this world." If Rathman was indeed a source, he couldn't possibly hope to keep himself anonymous. So no way was he a source. No way.

Mikey took a deep breath and thought about the bylines that would appear on the story: *Michaela C. Wright and Vance Robillard.* *OK,* she thought, shifting into the middle lane and pushing her speed toward seventy.

30

6:07 p.m.

What in God's good name is that? Christian thinks.

Something he can't quite make out through the crystalline sludge smearing his windshield, something like a bird or a giant insect, hovers above the road fifty feet from his car. He might not have noticed it if not for the tiny red light blinking on its underside.

"Holy balls," he says aloud, thinking of the news reports he heard on the radio, realizing what the thing is. He saw one like it in a video an old state cop buddy had posted on Facebook, like a goddamn hornet with a firing pin. He slams the car into reverse, hits the gas, and fishtails backward, Christian flipping his foot from the brake to the accelerator and working the steering wheel to stay out of the roadside ditch. His chest hurts with the pounding of his heart. "Fuck fuck fuck," he tells himself.

He glances back over his shoulder—*The little light is green now, holy shit*—before spinning the wheel hard right and gunning the car down the road and away from Jubilee Rathman's monstrosity of a house, listening for a hiss, trying to remember what the hornet in the Facebook video sounded like, or maybe he didn't have the sound on. *Jesus H. Christ.*

He catches a slick spot in the road, and the car skims sideways to the right, the rear end swinging around behind him as he glimpses the rearview mirror, now filled with the image of the drone swooping low.

"Shit!" Christian yells as he yanks the wheel to the right so hard that the car whirls into an uncontrolled spin, the road falling away, the seat belt biting into his collarbone. He glimpses the drone whiz past the passenger window, hears an explosion. *Missed?* he thinks.

The car bounces off a tree and catapults into the air, grazing another tree. The windshield caves in on him, ragged bits of glass cutting into his neck and cheeks, as the whole steaming crooked mess lurches to a halt.

Christian is dangling upside down from his seat belt, smelling piss and gasoline. He cranes his neck around to see what that missile thing did to whatever it hit, but the belt slips, and he smacks his forehead on the dashboard, drawing blood.

"Shit," he rasps, reaching back for the knife on his belt. He draws the blade through the shoulder harness and grabs the steering wheel to right himself as he slips downward, then unclicks the other belt and hitches himself past the steering wheel to the passenger door, praying it isn't so damaged that it won't open.

As he grasps the door handle, he hears the chuff and pebble spray of tires digging into the shoulder of the road above him. He pushes the door. It creaks open. He falls into the leaves and branches.

"Christian," comes the driver's voice from up the slope. "Stay where you are."

Langreth? Christian thinks. *What the hell?*

He doesn't bother to look back.

"Christian. Stop right there."

Or what? You'll shoot? You can't be shooting anymore. Christian tucks the knife away, ducks low, and scrabbles down the slippery hill, grabbing at poplars for balance.

"You're making a mistake, Christian."

Christian doesn't know where he's going or what he's going to do next except get the hell away from the flying gizmo that apparently fired at him and then vanished into the sky. Where the slope flattens out, he dares to stop and look back, and he sees the shape of a person crouched at the crest of the hill.

Langreth isn't giving chase. Which is good. But Christian's relief vanishes when he recalls one instant later that Gemma Petruglia sent him on a mission at which, so far, he has failed. Then there's his right eye, which feels as if it might explode out the back of his skull. Anger smothers his fear.

That Rathman bitch, he thinks, *is going to pay.*

The hill gives way to the muddy bank of a creek, the sleet disappearing on the water's surface. The creek must lead to somewhere that resembles civilization—or back to Purgatory Bay. He leans out over the water and peers in both directions. In one, he sees, maybe a hundred yards away, maybe two hundred, what looks to be an enormous fence spanning the creek. *She's going to pay,* he thinks again.

Christian digs his phone out, thanking God that he didn't lose it in the crash, and clicks on a mapping app. Just as he does, the phone lights up with a call: Gemma.

Christian stares at the phone for a second, trying to quell his rising panic, then glances back up the hill. Langreth is gone. Christian reaches inside his jacket for his handgun. The feel of the grip is reassuring. He leaves it there and returns to the mapping app, letting the call from Gemma go, and starts trudging down the bank of the creek.

31

A noise from the locker room rouses Mikey from her reverie. Probably Bridget on the phone with Quinn. Mikey unbolts the bathroom door she tried to use the first time and steps into the locker room.

Bridget's hockey bag sits opened on the floor, a jumble of pads, a toilet kit, and a threadbare UM skate towel. Her left skate is propped inside the black steel locker.

"Bridge?" Mikey says, looking around and seeing no one. "Bridget?"

She opens the door to the hallway, expecting to see Bridget standing out there with Craig. But there's no one. She looks both ways down the corridor. At one end is an emergency exit that probably leads out to the parking lot. An orange traffic cone stands next to the twin doors.

At the other end of the hall Mikey can see Boston Baked Beans parents clapping along the glass in a corner of the ice surface. She walks down to that end and looks around. She knows none of the Boston people and doesn't see any Pride moms or dads nearby. She looks over her shoulder at the snack bar. No Bridget.

"Dammit," she says. "Where are you?"

She scans the area down the side of the rink, looking for Craig. He's probably in the stands or the bar. She dials him as she starts walking back toward the locker room.

"Hey," he says, answering. "This game is amazing. We might pull this off even without Bridge."

"Is she with you?" Mikey says.

"That Cerruti girl for Boston is killing us, though—sorry. Bridget? Isn't she with you? You wouldn't let me talk to her."

"She's not with me. I went in the bathroom, and when I came out, she was gone."

"Gone where? Where's there to go?"

"I thought with you, but . . ." Mikey shoulders the locker room door open and goes to Bridget's locker, feeling the creep of panic.

"Craig," she says. "Where's her other skate?"

"What do you mean?"

"Her other skate. The only one here is her left. She always puts them on left, then right, and takes them off the same way."

Mikey squats and digs around in Bridget's bag. No skate. "Holy God," she says. "What's going on?"

"You want me to come down there?"

Mikey realizes what she has to do, what she doesn't want to do. "Wait," she says. "I'll call you right back."

She kills the call and goes to her "Favorites" queue, hits the one marked *B* for Bridget. She hears the ring inside her phone, waiting, hoping—then hears what she doesn't want to hear, the faint but insistent chimes of the old *Hockey Night in Canada* theme song: Bridget's ringtone.

Mikey picks up Bridget's hockey bag, dumps out the contents. Bridget's phone bounces off the floor, still chiming. Her phone is here. She is not. Mikey bursts out into the hallway and sprints toward the bleachers, yelling, "Craig! Craig!"

32

Sleet pelts the back of Langreth's neck as he watches Christian from the top of the hill, one hand on the pistol in his pocket. Christian's too far away to chase, and what would be the point anyway? Even if Langreth could arrest him, what would it be for? Reckless driving? He decides he'll let Malone know, call a tow truck for the wreck.

He left the courthouse and drove as fast as he could without risking a tailspin. Half a mile from the house on Purgatory Bay, a Bleak Harbor police vehicle passed him going in the opposite direction, back toward town. *Why would a cop be coming up here,* Langreth thought, *to this lonely house on this lonely body of water?*

Down the slope, a gnarled oak branch about ten feet long hisses in the slush, smoke rising from the charred end where it was severed from a tree, as if it had been struck by lightning. Though there was no lightning.

Langreth checks his phone. There's a voice mail from Cooper and a missed call from Mikey, who has yet to respond to his text about Robillard. He dials a number.

"Chief Malone, please," he asks the dispatcher. Then, "Gary Langreth. From the prosecutor's office."

Malone comes on. "Why is your boss calling me about you?"

"No idea."

"I don't mind having your help, but I can't afford to get in bad with your boss, OK? She puts the crooks we catch in jail."

"Got it. You sent someone out here, right?"

"Where?"

"Purgatory Bay."

"So that's why Cooper called. Why are you there?"

"She has no idea I'm here. Long story. Just saw a guy run his car off the road into the trees, then take off down the hill. Car's probably totaled. Got a plate number. But I think I actually know the guy."

"Call back and give the number to the dispatcher."

"Will do." Langreth squints through the sleet up the road. "Remind me what the deal is with the woman who lives out here?"

"How long have you been in Bleak Harbor?"

"Two years."

"And you've never heard of Jubilee Rathman?"

The name is familiar. "Don't tell me," Langreth says. "Is she the— oh shit. The family the Petruglias took out. Has to be, what, ten years ago?"

"Something like that. The Petruglias?"

"Detroit mobsters," Langreth says. "This woman's dad was a money cleaner who made the mistake of ratting them out."

"I have trouble keeping up with all the Detroit mob guys," Malone says. "Anyway, what does any of this have to do with Ophelia Wright?"

Good question, Langreth thinks. "Not sure," he says, "but this guy who crashed the car is an ex–state cop who's supposedly on the Petruglia payroll."

"That's quite a coincidence."

"Yeah. And there's a big damn tree branch lying here smoking like the Lord struck it down."

The phone goes silent. Langreth hears Malone murmuring to some-one else. While he waits, he tries to recall who handled the Rathman murder case. He remembers reading about it in the Detroit papers, hearing some of his fellow cops say maybe it would hurt the Petruglias. He never thought it would and unfortunately was correct.

He makes what connections he can: Christian works for the Petruglias. The Petruglias are connected in a bad way to this Jubilee woman. There was an attack on a Petruglia girl this morning—by a drone, of all things—on the other side of the state. The Volvo that was carrying Ophelia was headed up the road he's standing on. But why would the Petruglias care about a blind woman living alone in a little shit town across the state? And why would anybody be crazy enough to try to kill a Petruglia kid?

He stares at the gray wisps curling off the branch, then looks in the direction of the house he can't see from here. *Maybe it's not just Ophelia someone's after,* Langreth thinks. *Maybe it's someone other than the Petruglias.*

"Gary." It's Malone, back on the line. "Jesus, the shit is flying in heavy. Real quick: we have a match on the print on the motel key. One Joshua Rathman."

"Who is that?"

"Brother of Jubilee, the woman we were just talking about."

"What? No. Can we track him down?"

"He's dead. Offed himself a few years ago."

"So how the hell is his print on that key?"

"Don't know. But there's worse. Meet me at the hockey rink ASAP. Mikey's daughter is now missing."

33

"I knew it," Fisher says. "Dammit. I frigging knew it."

He's standing at a laptop on the second floor of his house on Blossom Hill. A five-year-old email is on the screen. The subject line: Corruption . . . The body of the email: . . . follows corruption.

A PDF is attached. Before Fisher opens it again for the first time in five years, he recalls sitting in an aluminum fishing boat with his father on Purgatory Bay. Out on the Bleak family's lonely water, the shoreline all pine stands and sand, father and son discussed what "inquiries," as Senior called them, would come next. Junior took to imagining them as "Fisher & Sons." He loved those mornings and came to love Purgatory Bay. "Perhaps our friends the Bleaks," Senior liked to say, "will let us buy this one day."

Fisher knows what the attachment says, knows how it will sting him yet again, but he opens it anyway. It's a grainy photocopy of two pages from the Bleak County Register of Deeds. The first page, dated December 31, 2001, shows that an entity called BLK LLC deeded Purgatory Bay to Fisher's father, Harland Fisher Sr., in exchange for $254,342.88. The second, dated April 6, 2011, shows that Harland Fisher Sr. deeded the property to JMR Inc. for $1.3 million. Fisher's father brokered the sale of Purgatory Bay. His greedy, selfish, lying father had owned the place for years. And instead of leaving it for his son, he sold it for a lousy $1.3 million, a mere tenth of the Fisher fortune.

The email and the attachment were sent by cwhite@yoyo.com, two weeks after Fisher had turned away Jubilee Rathman's request to rename her property from Purgatory to Paradise. He assumed that cwhite was some citizen who agreed with the council's decision and figured knowing the secret would ensure that Fisher didn't let the council change its mind.

Now he knows it was actually a sneering taunt. From Jubilee Rathman.

"The witch," Fisher says, staring into the computer screen. "JMR. Jubilee M. Rathman. Charlotte fucking White."

He slides to a different laptop in front of a different monitor. He taps some buttons, and a grid of images three deep and five across appears on the monitor. *I should have done this last night,* Fisher thinks. He was lazy. Not now.

He scans the images, focuses on one that might bear fruit, rewinds it to nine o'clock last night, stops it, starts it moving forward again. The camera is fixed to a utility pole next to a boat launch on the bay, with a view up Lily Street toward Blossom. At 9:16, a Volvo SUV emerges from Jeremiah Street, on the right, and turns up Lily. Then it makes an abrupt turn left—which Fisher couldn't have seen on the city camera he lazily relied upon last night—and disappears into an alley between the shops on Blossom and the bars and restaurants along the bay. Fisher had a camera installed in the alley last summer because he thought, correctly, that it would supply compromising pictures of bar patrons engaging in romantic and other acts—some illegal, some merely unsavory—that could be used against them if necessary.

The alley has just the one outlet, so Fisher waits, and sure enough, two minutes later, he sees the Volvo emerge and then stop, waiting at the alley's opening. Thirty-seven seconds later, a pair of headlights glares on the screen as another car turns onto Lily, moving toward the camera, blinker flashing for a turn onto Jeremiah. *Maybe Ophelia's sister,* Fisher thinks. The Volvo then bolts into the middle of Lily and stops, blocking the other car. The Volvo then creeps forward, angling toward the other vehicle as if the two drivers were communicating. If so, the conversation lasts only a matter of seconds before the Volvo speeds away.

Fisher stops the tape, rewinds it one minute, to an image of the Volvo stopped in the street. He zooms in on the passenger window, sees the blurry shape of something apparently leaned against the window. Probably a person. *Ophelia,* he thinks.

"OK," he says aloud. "Let's try this, then."

He moves to a different monitor displaying the city camera views he looked at last night. He zeroes in on the one near the edge of town that showed the Volvo proceeding toward Purgatory Bay. He sets it at midnight, hits fast-forward mode, folds his arms, and waits on a hunch he wishes he'd had earlier.

"Show me the Volvo," he says.

The image frames a two-lane asphalt road winding up and then left between two walls of trees. The dark morning unfolds in choppy jumps of the clock in the bottom right corner of the screen. At 5:27:13 a.m., Fisher sees a glimmer of light at the top of the screen. He unfolds his arms and steps closer. The glimmer separates into two cones. Headlights. A Volvo. A Volvo leaving Purgatory Bay after arriving there the night before.

"*The* Volvo," Fisher says. "Oh yes."

It didn't travel on past Purgatory Bay. It stopped there. Ophelia must be there.

Fisher swivels to another screen, types *www.freep.com* into an internet browser. He saw a headline on a TV that afternoon as he was waiting for coffee downtown, but he wasn't able to follow the story because some resident interrupted to grouch about her trash collection.

The *Detroit Free Press* website loads. A picture of a Red Wing hockey player extending his arms above his head fills most of the screen. Next to the photo is a queue of headlines. The second headline, below one about the arrest of a county commissioner's son, is the one Fisher is looking for:

Petruglia Girl Targeted in Failed Drone Hit

He shifts to an adjacent monitor and clicks on an app called FindEmFaster. The app wasn't cheap, as apps go, but it has proven its worth. A form pops up. He inserts *Charlotte White* in the narrow box for a name, *Michigan* in the state field.

Instantly, the mitten-shaped map appears, dotted with four pulsating green circles. Fisher clicks on one northwest of Detroit. The view swoops in and hovers over Brighton. A photograph of a girl, no older than seventeen, appears in a corner of the screen. Fisher tries another circle, at Swartz Creek, further north of Detroit. The girl is replaced by a white-haired woman. Beneath the photo, a list of her jobs unfolds. "Post commander, Lapeer," Fisher says, just as a brilliant light flashes through a window to his right, the one looking east toward I-94.

"What the hell," Fisher says. One of his backyard motion sensors has gone off. It blinks out as quickly as it came on. Fisher leaves the desk and squints through the window, seeing nothing except blackness, the shapes of trees. An animal may have tripped it, though he thought he'd programmed the sensitivity of the thing to ignore squirrels and small birds.

He goes back to the computer, calls up Google, types in the search window: *murder family northern Michigan petruglia*. He clicks on the link at the top of the results, a 2008 *Detroit Times* story, Vance Robillard byline, headline, One Year Later, No Justice in Brutal Family Murders. He scrolls slowly through, stopping briefly to read: E. Jonathan Phillips, attorney for Jubilee Rathman, declined to comment on behalf of his client. Fisher keeps scrolling down. And there, near the end, also declining to comment, is Michigan State Police commander, Lapeer post, Charlotte White.

"Damn," Fisher says.

The sensor lights blast on again, this time near the window looking north. "Son of a bitch," Fisher says. He doesn't want to have the technician out again, pay him another $350. He walks to the window. Nothing. Then, behind him, a different sensor flashes on through the window facing Lake Michigan. Frigging birds must be flying around. Gotta be crows, big enough to trip the sensors. That last one goes black again, and Fisher returns to his screens.

He grabs a mouse, watches the Volvo again. "Charlotte White," he says. Fisher doesn't know why the Witch of Purgatory Bay would give a damn about Ophelia Wright, but he knows enough. Certainly more than Malone and the Bleak Harbor police. "You're so smart," he says as the car exits the view on the screen. "Except I know who you are."

He picks up his phone and starts to dial Malone, then changes his mind. Sure, what he knows gives him an edge with the chief. But there might be greater opportunity elsewhere.

He steps two screens to his left and calls up his official mayoral email, clicks on the archive folder, types a name into the search box. A list of old emails appears. He opens one near the bottom of the list. He doesn't care what it says; he just wants the cell phone number on the tag at the bottom. He taps it into his phone, walking over to the window looking out on Bleak River. The call flips into voice mail. Fisher listens to the greeting, hears the beep.

"Mr. Phillips," he says, grinning into the dark, imagining the river snaking its way to Purgatory Bay in the distance, picturing the rich and reclusive Jubilee Rathman standing on the parapet, overseeing her weird little kingdom. Fisher isn't sure what she's up to, but he has some leverage now, and he wants her to know it.

"A voice from your past here, Mr. Phillips: Harland Fisher Jr., mayor of lovely Bleak Harbor, Michigan. I'm sorry we couldn't accommodate you and your client at our last meeting, but we should definitely have a discussion now, sir, and soon. I'm afraid Ms. Rathman is about to get into some very large trouble. I hope you'll call me at your—what the—?"

The phone clatters to the floor as Fisher falls back, shielding his eyes from the light filling the window in front of him. *Goddamn sensors,* he thinks, but he never finishes the thought. The last thing he feels before his knees buckle is a sear of pain inside his left cheek that tears through the back of his head.

34

"What is this room?" Ophelia says. "Where am I?"

Caleb, who brought her here, fingers pinching her left biceps, does not reply.

"Caleb."

He's waiting for Frances to speak. He has come to dislike the waiting for her voice. It was almost all he heard during the many weeks he lived alone in this room, becoming Caleb, preparing for the mission, sleeping, training, choking down his grains, taking his Ho Hos.

"Caleb," Ophelia says.

"P-p-please w-wait."

"Stop. You're not fooling me."

She's standing against a wall. The room is a rectangle, twelve feet by fourteen, empty of anything but a chair, a pull-up bar bolted to one wall, a video screen built into the wall facing Ophelia, some video equipment on a rolling cart set in a corner.

The room is dark, as it usually was when Caleb dwelled here. His eyes have adjusted. Ophelia stands with folded arms. She refused to sit in the chair against the wall where she stands. Her brown hair flows in ragged waves over her shoulders, her eyes awash in blue. Caleb is relieved to know she cannot see him.

On the other side of the wall she stands against, unbeknownst to Ophelia, is the girl. Caleb brought her from the rink, blacked out in the back seat of the Volvo, Minnesota plates now installed on the rear bumper.

Grabbing the girl was an unexpected and somewhat risky bonus. Jubilee didn't really expect to have both Bridget and her aunt Ophelia in her clutches. But she dispatched Caleb to the rink, having him wait outside while she watched what was happening inside. Her goading of the girl in the guise of the Darwyn Tech coach was primarily for Jubilee's amusement. But it presented an opportunity.

Caleb expected the girl would be strong—*She's an athlete,* Jubilee had said, *take no chances*—but she had no time to resist. He entered from the bathroom, where he'd been waiting, after her mother left the locker room. He moved without hesitation, as Jubilee had instructed.

A thin squeak issued from the girl's mouth as Caleb clapped the cloth to her face, her body going almost immediately limp. He wrapped her in a black blanket and hefted her in one arm out to the Volvo, parked in shadow between two dumpsters beneath a lamp Caleb had disabled four nights before, when he had slipped in through the Zamboni door and silently set the explosives and listening devices.

"Where am I?" Ophelia says. "What is this room? Why does it smell like disinfectant?"

Caleb sniffs at the odor he knows too well. He remembers waking here, on his back on a mat on the floor, not knowing if the darkness was morning or afternoon or night, not knowing when Jubilee would come with food or Ho Hos, less concerned about the former than the latter.

He would flip onto his stomach on the cold concrete and do push-ups. He started, as Jubilee stood over him, with ten at a time and increased it by five each week, until he could do two hundred and fifty at once. Then he started with the one-armed push-ups, gradually building that number up to one hundred. On each arm.

He asked Jubilee, begged her, to let him use the rock climbing wall where he had spent so many hours before he was becoming Caleb. "The rock climbing wall no longer exists, Caleb," she would say. "Just as Joshua no longer exists. You will have other pursuits when you are ready."

So he did: With the drones, on the roof at midnight, dressed all in black. The near sprints around the bay, also at night, always at night, always garbed in black. Until the past several weeks—the driving instruction from Jubilee, the raiding of the sculptures, the dry runs of the mission—Caleb left the compound only once, to see the Dragonfly Festival.

"Why did you ruin my sculptures?" Ophelia says. "Please don't stutter either. I know you're faking it."

In the rare instance that Caleb would have to speak to another human outside the mansion, the stuttering would make the other person sympathetic. The way he talked would distract from the way he looked. That's what Jubilee taught him. He wasn't sure she was right, but he had learned to follow her instructions. Most of the time.

"H-h-how do y-you know?"

She smirks, shaking her head. "Come on—what did you do, buy a *Stuttering for Dummies* tape online?"

He studies her. She's looking at him now as if she can actually see him. He says nothing.

"Why did you do those things to my sculptures?" Ophelia repeats. "Why the black paint on the faces? Because I'm blind, was that it?"

Caleb knows that Jubilee had something else in mind. She whispered it to him, a fevered chant, as he slumbered in his Ho Hos haze. *We will blot out their lives,* she said, *like ours were blotted out.*

"I don't know what you're talking about," he says.

"Wait—don't you mean, *I d-don't know w-w-what you're t-talking about?*"

Caleb feels an unaccustomed urge then—the urge to laugh. He hears the sound of a girl's laughter in the back of his mind, as if she were in the next room. *Kara,* he thinks. *Kara's laughter.* In the hallway.

Beyond the bolt-locked door to his room. As the staccato whir of crickets rose around his bed.

He touches his face, digs his nails into a cheek. *Kara, I'm sorry.* He wishes Jubilee would come on the intercom. She must be busy, perhaps with the girl.

"Caleb," Ophelia says. "I know you've been to the sculptures."

"N-no."

"Stop. You didn't stutter one bit when you were talking on the phone at my house. I was listening, you know."

"N-not the sculptures."

"Yes, you did. Otherwise, how did you know a leg was missing from the sculpture of my brother?"

"No."

"Yes, you did, and you do. You told me when I showed you pictures of the sculptures at my house. You said the vandals—that would be you—took a leg."

"The police—"

"No, the police never released that detail."

"I could have—I saw it on television."

"No. You're lying."

He doesn't know how she knows or what to say.

"I hear lies, Caleb. They scream at me. And I'm hearing you lie."

"Ophelia."

It's Frances. Caleb hears the voice coming from above and behind him. He wonders why she waited so long to interrupt.

"Sit, please," Frances says.

Ophelia cants her head as if to look past Caleb to Frances. "I prefer to stand," she says.

"Caleb can sit you down."

Now Ophelia adjusts her vacant gaze to Caleb. He averts his eyes. "She will sit down on her own," he tells Frances. He turns back to Ophelia, hears her breathing harder. "Please."

"Prepare the equipment, Caleb."

The door lock clicks. Jubilee enters the room. "Caleb," she says. "What are you doing in here?"

He lets his gaze linger on Ophelia for another second. He turns to Jubilee. "We are almost ready."

"Why isn't the video equipment set up?" Jubilee says.

"Who are you?" Ophelia says.

Jubilee ignores her. "We're behind schedule, Caleb."

"We will get back on schedule."

"You see?" Ophelia says. "You're not stuttering anymore."

Caleb realizes she's right, looks down at the floor, feeling Ophelia's gaze along with Jubilee's glare.

"Quiet," Jubilee tells Ophelia.

"Caleb," Ophelia says, "you are a sculpture, aren't you? Someone has carved you into something you're not."

"Sit down and shut up," Jubilee orders. If Ophelia hears her, it doesn't show. "The girl is ready. And we had another visitor. I wasn't able to eliminate him on the first pass, but a drone is following him on autopilot."

"What girl?" Ophelia says.

"Is she afraid?" Caleb says.

"Who's afraid, Caleb?" Ophelia raises her voice. "Caleb. What are you doing?"

Caleb hears Kara again beyond the bolt-locked door, but this time she is not laughing. She is screaming.

"I told you to shut up," Jubilee says. Caleb looks up, sees her produce a handheld device from a pocket and aim it at the blank video screen in the wall. The face of a teenage girl appears in black and white. Caleb looks at it. His stomach turns over, surprising him.

It's Bridget, the girl he brought from the rink. She looks like she's trying to burst out of the duct tape over her mouth. And she is afraid.

He looks at the floor again, willing his stomach to quiet. He feels an urge for a Ho Ho.

"What girl, dammit?" Ophelia says.

Jubilee slowly ratchets up the volume. The girl's muffled squawks slowly fill the room.

Caleb goes back. Twelve years. Hears again the explosions and the shrieking, feels the blast of heat on his face, his eyebrows, the tops of his ears. He opened his bedroom door and saw Kara down the corridor. She was curled against a kitchen wall in a flannel nightgown, pink with little blue giraffes, surrounded by flames, the double-barrel lowering to her face. Caleb turned and ran. Ran back into his room, through the flames and smoke, wrenched from the wall the barrier his father had built to protect him, the hinges searing his hands. Ran away.

Left Kara to die.

"Bridget?" Ophelia says, rushing at Caleb, finding him, clawing at his chest. Caleb lets her. "Is that my Bridget?"

"The tape, Caleb," Jubilee says. "Now."

He grabs one of Ophelia's wrists but can't secure the other one for her flailing. "No, no, Caleb, no," she says. "You don't want this."

"We'll start soon," Jubilee says. "Focus, Caleb."

The door clicks shut.

"Caleb," Ophelia screams. Now he has her other wrist, both of them in one of his hands. "This won't change anything, Caleb. This changes nothing. This, this violence changes nothing. Stop. Let us go."

He forces her backward, trying not to hurt her, and presses her down into the chair, plucks the roll of duct tape from under the chair, hearing Jubilee telling him, *Focus, Caleb,* hearing his sister Kara louder in his head, shrieking for her mommy and daddy, hearing what Ophelia told him, thinking, *Violence changed me.*

35

Gary Langreth pulls into the rink lot, phone to his ear. He almost slid off the road into Bleak Harbor googling Charlotte White again.

Now he's waiting for someone to answer the number he just dialed, hoping he has the one for White's home. He's parked at the far edge of the packed lot and can see a police cruiser's lights flashing near the entrance a hundred yards away.

"Hello?"

It's an older man. Good.

"Good evening," Langreth says. "Mr. White?"

"This is Horace White, yes." Good again. "Who's this?"

"This is Gary Langreth, sir. I'm an investigator for the prosecutor's office in Bleak Harbor, Michigan, across the state from you."

"I've heard of it. How can I help you?"

"I'd like to speak with your wife, Mr. White. It's a police matter. Is she available?"

"I'm afraid—I don't think she can be of any help to you."

"I'm sorry, sir; it's rather important. I'd appreciate it—"

"She's not well," Horace White says, speaking with the voice of someone who has said these words many times of late. "Charlotte suffers from dementia, rather advanced."

"Oh," Langreth says. "I'm sorry."

"So am I."

"Can I just ask—this is the Charlotte White who was post commander at Lapeer, is that right?"

"Twenty-three years, yes."

"And she hasn't been on email or the phone recently?"

"She does speak occasionally on the phone—my phone—to her
grandchildren, when she's feeling up to it. Why would you ask?"

"I'm sorry, Mr. White. It's part of this situation we're looking into,
something that was handled at the Lapeer post years ago. Might be a
case of mistaken identity."

"I see."

"You weren't in law enforcement, were you?"

"No. I'm a retired GM."

"Forgive me for bothering you. I wish you and your wife the best."

"Thank you."

———

"Katya, wait up."

The shout catches Malone off guard because Gary hasn't called her
anything but Chief or Malone since their sole tryst. She stops outside
the double doors to the rink, waits for him as she checks her phone,
sees she somehow missed a call from Northwood.

"Had to park out on the road," Langreth says.

"You need a police cruiser," Malone says.

"I'll tell Cooper. The Deming girl still missing?"

"Her mother is hysterical."

"She was playing in the tournament."

"Yes, until she"—Malone hesitates at the word *disappeared*, not
wanting to think she could lose another kid—"until Mikey called me.
Come on, inside."

Parents and coaches and girls are streaming up from the packed
lobby to the stairway leading to the second-story bar overlooking the

arena. Malone squeezes through, phone out in front of her, telling the crowd, "Police, please, let me through," as Gary wriggles along behind. Out on the ice surface, she can see hockey players and referees standing around, looking up toward the bar.

A text from Northwood buzzes in. Malone ignores it for now. As she hurries past the bleachers, nearing the bar, she sees through a window set into the door what everyone is gaping at: a split screen view of two female faces on the TVs above the bar.

The side-by-side black-and-white frames glow soundlessly on each of the five TVs. On the left half of the screen is a girl, eyes filled with tears, cheeks straining at a band of tape pinching her mouth. The other half shows a woman, also taped but not straining, her eyes closed, cheeks slack and relaxed, almost as if she might be meditating.

Beneath the screens, Mikey leans halfway against her husband and halfway against the bar. "Mikey," Malone calls out. Mikey spins around and, seeing Malone, starts shaking her head, her reddened cheeks slick with tears, and falls into Malone's arms. Malone lets her while looking up at the TVs.

The girl is Mikey's daughter, Bridget, whom Malone was sitting with earlier in this bar. The other, she presumes, is Mikey's sister, Ophelia. Someone obviously has hijacked the rink's in-house video network.

"Mikey," Malone says, gently pushing her back without letting go entirely. She nods upward. "How long has that been up there?"

Before Mikey can answer, her husband leans in. "What the hell kind of town is this?" he says. Malone recalls his name as Greg—no, Craig. "We came here for a damn hockey tournament, and half our family has gone missing."

"Mr. Deming," Gary says, placing a hand on Craig's biceps. "We're going to make it right. We just need everyone to calm down, and"—he looks around the room—"maybe clear this room? Ma'am?" He gestures at the bartender, a woman in her twenties wearing a Notre Dame hockey T-shirt. "You're closed."

"I'm sorry?" she says.

"Now," Malone says, swiveling to the crowd in the bar. "Time to leave, folks. Take your drinks and go." She points at the bartender. "You too. Get out of here."

Malone looks back at Mikey, who's staring up at the TVs. *Her daughter,* Malone thinks, wobbling herself on a tightwire between anger and despair. An image flashes unbidden in her head, her own daughter's face, the speckles and ribbons of blood, her vacant eyes, the pickup truck wrapped around the oak. She wills the image away, hears Gary whisper:

"You call the FBI?"

That didn't go well the last time someone was missing in Bleak Harbor.

"In a minute," Malone says, grabbing his sleeve, dragging him out of the bar.

Northwood is waiting. "Chief," he says. "I've been trying to contact you."

"What happened with the Rathman woman?"

"She wasn't helpful, but listen, I've—"

"And that fingerprint. Is there any doubt that it's the Rathman boy's? Her brother, yes?"

"No doubt. And yes, her brother, but Chief—"

"Michaela C. Wright."

Malone, Northwood, and Gary jerk their heads toward the female voice booming from inside the bar. Through the window in the door, Malone sees Craig catch his wife in his arms as her knees buckle. She and Gary rush back in, Malone propping an arm beneath Mikey's elbow.

"Mikey," Malone says. "Are you all right?"

Mikey is shaking her head, saying something Malone can't make out. Malone leans in closer to her face. "It's . . . ," Mikey gasps. Malone grasps Mikey's hand, feels it shaking. "It's me."

"Your old byline," her husband says. "Where's it coming from?"

"Your byline indeed," the voice says.

"The speakers," Gary says, pointing to ceiling grilles at opposite ends of the bar.

Malone whispers to Mikey, an arm around her shoulders, "What's going on? What does your byline have to do with it?"

"It's me," Mikey says, more to herself than Malone. "It's me. It's me and Robillard and"—she closes her eyes—"and the Petruglias."

Malone looks at Craig. "What is she talking about? Who is Robillard?"

"He's no longer with us," the voice says.

Craig looks from Malone to Mikey to Gary, then addresses Malone. "Mikey helped write some stories about the Petruglia family."

"What she did was much worse," the voice says. "Save your First Amendment blather. This is not about someone's 'right to know.'"

Mikey looks toward one of the speakers. "Jubilee?"

"Ah," comes the voice.

"Jubilee Rathman."

"Welcome to Bleak Harbor. I'm aware that most people refer to you as Mikey, but that seems too frivolous a name for someone with the gravitas required to precipitate the murder of a family."

"No," Mikey says. "I didn't . . . I was just trying to do my job."

"I'm sure that's what you told yourself then too, Michaela. Now I'm doing my job. It is time for the righteous to be satisfied."

Malone looks at Gary. He starts to say something, but she stops him with a finger to her lips, takes her phone out so he can see, then taps out a text.

"Jubilee," Mikey says, struggling to steady her voice. "Let them go. Take me."

"No," Craig says. "Just let them go. Chief."

Langreth looks at the text—pUrg bay now

"You lied, Michaela. You know you lied."

"I did not—" Mikey stops to collect herself. "I, I did not—"

"You lied. Now you will pay. Like the others."

Malone doesn't want to abandon a mother with a child in danger. But she knows she can't stay here negotiating with a voice. She can't believe this is the woman who led the press conference that morning with such grace and selfless courage. What did Malone miss?

It doesn't matter now. She whispers into Mikey's ear: "We're going to stop her. I promise. But I have to go."

The last time, there was an autistic boy and an odd ransom and a family that was in extreme disarray even without the kidnapping. Malone failed to take control of the situation. She deferred to the chief at the time, to the showboats from the FBI, to the family, to everybody but herself.

Not this time.

"Mikey," she says. "What does she think you lied about?"

Mikey is breathing so hard she can barely talk. "I didn't lie." She raises her voice toward the ceiling, suddenly shouting. "Robillard lied. I didn't lie."

"You made your choices then, Michaela," Jubilee says. "Now it's time for new ones."

"I did not lie."

"Which of these beautiful innocents should die, Michaela?"

"No. No. No."

Mikey is screaming now. Her husband gathers her into his arms as she struggles against his grip. The last thing Malone hears as she bolts out the bar door is Jubilee: "Do you remember that morning in my backyard?"

36

Christian crawls on hands and knees along the bay, far enough from the shoreline that he's not as visible to the mechanical bird humming around him overhead.

A drone? he thinks. *The one that almost killed Dora?* He fears it less when he can hear it than when it goes silent and he has no idea when it might swoop down on him.

He ducks his head beneath a low tree branch and digs forward a few feet. His fingernails are thick with mud, his knuckles stiff from the wet and the cold. He thinks he may have broken a foot, either in the car crash or when falling off the fence he had to scale.

But he has made it to Jubilee Rathman's house.

It stands atop the rise above him, a gigantic rectangular gray box shrouded in shadow, lit only at the four corners of its third story. Seeing it from fifty yards down the slope, Christian is reminded of the castles in the old black-and-white Dracula and Frankenstein movies.

He rears back on his knees to survey the scene, steadying himself with one hand on a tree trunk. He realizes that he has no plan, no idea how he's going to get to Jubilee Rathman or what he will do if he does, but he can't afford to have Gemma Petruglia think he gave up on his task.

Holy hell, he thinks. *What in God's name am I doing here?*

He doesn't get a chance to answer the question. A muffled click is the last sound Christian hears as the bullet tears through the back of his head and out his right cheek.

37

Northwood is waiting when Malone and Gary emerge from the bar, Malone saying she'll call Bleak County and the state police to get to Purgatory Bay.

"Chief," Northwood says. "We have a problem."

"I'm well aware—"

"Will you fucking listen to me?"

Malone stops, looks at Northwood, who is red faced, flustered. He's not prone to dramatics, and she doesn't think she's ever heard him use the f-word. "You have thirty seconds," she says.

"Like you told me to, I checked into Robert Kehoe, the guy in Bath, Ohio, with the license plate on that Volvo."

"OK?"

"He's been dead for two years."

"But he still has a license plate?"

"His widow says no, and as far as she's aware, he never had any plates stolen. Which means someone went to the trouble to fake them."

"The unspoken question being: Why that guy's plates?"

"Exactly. I talked to his widow and to their son, asked them about any connections to this area. Turns out Robert Kehoe is a distant relative of another Kehoe who also lived in Bath, but in Bath, Michigan, near Lansing, back in the twenties."

"That's quite a coincidence, but it doesn't sound like it has much to do with what's going on here."

"It does if you know that Bath, Michigan, is famous pretty much for one thing."

"Holy hell," Gary says. "We studied that case in criminology."

Northwood swallows hard and continues. "Andrew Kehoe was the perpetrator of what came to be known as—"

"The Bath School Massacre," Gary says. "Jesus."

"Cut to the chase, Will."

"He wired up a school with dynamite, killed a bunch of kids, killed his wife, killed the mayor, killed himself."

"Wait," Malone says, digesting Northwood's words while looking out at the rink where the girls were playing earlier, not wanting to believe the thought forming in her head. "You're saying that that license plate was chosen to send some sort of message about this massacre in the twenties."

Northwood nods. "Remember the message that came in that FedEx package with the bloody leg?"

"Criminals are made, not born," Malone says, thinking again, *Yeah, that's usually pretty close to the truth.*

Northwood holds his phone up for Malone to see. "This is from the *New York Times* story on the Bath massacre."

Her throat tightens as she reads:

Investigators found a wooden sign wired to the farm's fence with Kehoe's last message stenciled on it: "Criminals are made, not born."

She thinks, *This can't be happening.*

She flashes back to the press conference that morning, how noble and inspiring Jubilee Rathman appeared, how the young woman had transformed her personal tragedies into empathy and generosity, with no apparent trace of enmity or bitterness over what she had suffered. Watching Jubilee confront the journalists' questions, Malone couldn't help but remember her own tragedy, thinking that, even today, she couldn't speak about Louisa's death to a crowd of strangers with such poise and dignity.

Though there was one instant, Malone now recalls, where Jubilee seemed to falter, if only briefly—when the reporter asked about the murder attempt on the Petruglia girl. At the time, Malone put it off to Jubilee's recoiling at the mention of that name and the memories it inevitably evoked. But now . . .

Malone glances back at the bar, then at Langreth.

"Wait," she says. "I gotta—hold on." She digs in a jacket pocket, comes out with a crumpled business card. "This guy," she says, thinking, *Deeth like teeth*. She takes out her phone and dials the number he wrote on the card. "Come on," she says.

"Who?"

"Hang on."

The guy answers. "Brian Deeth."

"Mr. Deeth, this is Chief Malone."

"Chief. You were great at the puck drop. What's—"

"I need the name of your anonymous donor."

"I'm sorry?"

"Whoever gave you the pile of money that got Bleak Harbor the tournament. Who was it?"

"Chief, I would love to help you, but I'm not at—"

"Was it Jubilee Rathman?"

"I'm sorry, I can't—"

"Tell me now, Mr. Deeth, or I will make you regret it."

"I—OK—it's not the name you said."

"I didn't think so. So it's Charlotte White. Isn't it?"

Deeth doesn't respond. Malone repeats, "Charlotte White."

"I won't disagree with that, Chief."

Malone hangs up. "How could somebody get explosives in here?"

"She got listening devices in here," Langreth says. "She got Bridget and Ophelia. Who knows what else she did? We've got to clear this place now."

"She's frigging toying with us," Malone says. "Will, get county and have them get a bomb squad here and enough deputies to empty the place. Now. Jesus. These kids."

"Will do."

"And good work."

Malone moves then to the bar door and presses an ear against it. "Wait, Will. Did you say the girl left her phone?"

"Here," he says, handing Malone a phone encased in pink plastic. "Password?"

"Her mom wrote it down. Here."

Northwood hands Malone a scrap of paper. Malone taps it into the phone, then goes to the voice-memo app and switches it on. She tells Gary, "Wait here."

She goes back into the bar and hears Jubilee talking, Mikey choking on a sob. Malone feels her sorrow like the jagged blade of a dagger to her solar plexus. She could tell Mikey that she knows how she feels, but she cannot tell her without suggesting that Bridget, like Louisa, could wind up dead.

Malone walks up to the bar holding Bridget's phone hidden behind a leg, then swings her arm up and places the phone on the bar, looking to see that the app is recording sound. She steps away from the phone and says, "Ms. Rathman, this is Bleak Harbor police chief Katya Malone."

"Welcome back."

"Jubilee," Malone says, "don't do this. You cannot escape. Just let the girl and her aunt go."

"Oh, I will escape, Chief. Everyone—all of us, you included—will escape."

"What about Joshua?"

"Joshua escaped a long time ago, Chief."

"No, he didn't. You know he didn't. You couldn't have been holding your press conference this morning and making an attempt on the Petruglia girl. And there's no one else for you to call on."

Malone isn't quite bluffing—she knows about Joshua's fingerprint, after all—but she's only guessing that Jubilee's brother is her accomplice. When Jubilee doesn't respond immediately, she says, "We know, Jubilee. Let them all go. Let your brother go. We will take you quietly, no trouble."

Jubilee says, "Michaela, please take two steps to your right. Look at the back of the bar. You'll see a small silver cube mounted on the top of the Labatt Blue sign. Look into it. And don't forget to smile."

"Mikey," her husband says, "just stay where you—"

"Chief, you may remove Mr. Deming now. And you can leave with him. This is between Michaela and me."

Malone touches Craig's elbow. "Come on," she says.

"I'm not leaving." His left cheek is twitching with fear. "I can't leave her; I can't leave my daughter."

Malone steps into him until her face is only an inch from his quivering cheek, squeezes his left arm as hard as she can. "You have to," she whispers. Then she motions to Mikey. "Get in front of the camera."

"Thank you, Chief," Jubilee says.

Malone looks back toward the source of the voice. She wants to step up and tell it, *I know your pain, Jubilee. I have felt your rage, and I will feel it for the rest of my life. I hope it will never consume me as it has you.*

But she says nothing.

As the door closes behind Malone, she sees Northwood is on his phone, grabs his arm. "That county?"

He nods yes, and she says, "Tell them to be sure to clear the place quietly, one by one out a back door. I don't know where else she might have cameras."

He nods again.

"What's going on?" Craig says. "I'm not leaving."

"No, you're not. But tell me, and I need the truth. Your wife was a reporter at the *Detroit Times*, right?"

"Yes."

"Was she good at what she did?"

"What does that have to do with anything?"

"Answer me."

"She was a fairly promising young reporter. Better at writing than reporting, maybe a little gullible at times."

"Did she like being a reporter?"

He hesitates, then says, "Yes. To a point."

"What point? She's only, what? Forty?"

"Thirty-nine."

"And she stopped being a journalist when?"

"I see where you're going with this, Chief, and I don't—"

"I don't care, Craig. Did she leave journalism because of whatever she wrote about that Petruglia family?"

He looks at the tavern door. "She never told me everything. Said she had sources to protect. But you're close enough."

"Good."

"Are you going to save our daughter?"

"No, you and your wife are going to save your daughter. Here's what I need you to do."

38

Jubilee sits facing a bank of screens arranged atop a crescent-shaped desk in the lower depths of her fortress. She's wearing a wireless headset fitted with a microphone. She left the whimpering girl taped to a chair in a room one floor above. Caleb is with the blind woman in a separate room on the same floor. Frances is monitoring both. Soon Michaela C. Wright Deming will watch one or perhaps both of her loved ones die. And Jubilee will watch and listen and glory in every second.

The screen directly in front of her shows Michaela standing at the bar in the rink, itself not long for the world. Caleb will ignite the explosives on the schedule she has set, using the wireless detonator Jubilee constructed from instructions she found online. She made her anonymous donation to assure Bleak Harbor would host the tournament with the expectation that Michaela and her family would come. The leveling of the rink will punish not just Bleak Harbor but all the delusional parents thinking their special daughters have special futures.

So perhaps Michaela will die too. Jubilee is relishing her alive at this moment, seeing her lower lip tremble and her eyes well, imagining the sheer terror coursing through her muscles just as it seized Jubilee's parents, Kara, and Joshua on the night that their nameless killer descended on them.

Flanking the live feed of Michaela in the rink are screens replaying two television tapes. One, from 1994, shows Michaela speaking to a

TV station on a beach near Bleak Harbor. The other, from 2007, shows Michaela being interviewed on a Detroit PBS station.

Jubilee has watched each tape hundreds of times preparing for this day, sometimes separately, sometimes simultaneously, always noting how Michaela's face changed as she answered certain questions, as she lied about her brother's death and about her reporting on the Petruglias.

"So, Michaela," Jubilee says into her microphone, "where is your cap?"

———

The phone that Malone set on the bar to Mikey's left is vibrating. Bridget's phone, in the pink case.

Mikey looks into her daughter's tear-filled eyes on the video screen, wishing Bridget could see her. She reaches over to the phone without taking her eyes off the video screen, slides it nearer, glances down. There's a text on the screen:

> it's craig. gotta keep her talking. argue. hold yr ground. police on way to bridge love u.

"Where is your cap?" Jubilee is saying.

"What cap?"

"The cap you were wearing outside the funeral for my family. A Michigan State winter hat. You were standing outside the church with the other reporters. You told me you were sorry."

Mikey recalls being at the funeral, watching Jubilee walk past outside. But not much else. "If you say so," she says.

"Why did you say you were sorry?" Jubilee says. "What exactly were you sorry about, Michaela?"

"I was sorry for you and your family. What happened was terrible."

"You're lying again, Michaela. As a reporter you covered other tragedies, and you didn't go to the victims and tell them how sorry you were. You just did what you do and walked away and collected your paycheck and went to the bar with your friends and hoped you'd win prizes. Didn't you?"

Mikey takes a long, slow breath, tells herself to stay calm. "It's not—it's never—that simple," she says.

"You told me you were sorry because you felt responsible. Because you felt guilty. And you felt responsible and guilty because you were, weren't you, Michaela?"

———

Twelve years earlier

Mikey sat curled on a sofa in her and Craig's two-bedroom apartment with a cup of strong tea, watching herself on TV. It was a Sunday morning. An all-night rain streaked the window overlooking Atwater Street. Craig and their three-year-old daughter were visiting Craig's parents in Saginaw. Mikey had stayed home in case she was needed for any weekend follow-ups on the Petruglia stories.

Mikey had tried to get out of doing the TV interview, but Robillard wouldn't do it, and Addams had ordered Mikey to "put a face to our great stories." So instead of going to Friday-night drinks with *Times* pals at the Anchor, Mikey had gone to the Detroit PBS station for a taping about the Petruglia series.

"One of the more interesting characters in your project is this copy-shop guy turned money launderer, Rathman," said the host and interviewer, a retired *Free Press* newsman named Stamm. "Did you get a chance to actually speak with Edward Rathman? It's really not clear in what you wrote."

The camera shifted from Stamm to Mikey. She was biting her lower lip, and as Mikey watched herself bite her lower lip, she realized she was doing the same as she sat on the sofa. In her head she heard her father gently coaching her, *Why are you biting your lip, Mikey? Tell the truth now. It won't hurt.*

On the tube, Mikey crossed her legs and uncrossed them before answering Stamm. *Jesus,* Mikey thought as she watched herself, *I'm trying to look like I'm pondering when really I don't know what to say.* "I really . . . ," said Mikey on TV as Mikey on the sofa cringed, "I mean, I really shouldn't talk about sourcing."

"Well, I understand," Stamm said, "but reading through this excellent piece you wrote on Rathman—who's got to be under scrutiny by the feds by now, am I right, for tax evasion if nothing else?—I can't find where *Rathman himself* declined to comment."

"I'll have to let the story speak for itself," Mikey said on TV, while her counterpart on the sofa thought, *Jesus, shut up.*

"Yet," Stamm continued, "you quote his wife, Heather: 'Sometimes you have a choice in the matter. Sometimes you don't.'"

"We quoted Mrs. Rathman, yes," TV Mikey said.

"That's a killer quote, isn't it?"

A news bulletin began to scroll across the bottom of the TV screen. Mikey initially ignored it as she watched herself answer Stamm. "She said it," Mikey told him. "We reported it."

"You must've been pretty glad she said it."

"I wasn't glad about—I mean, let me clarify: I'm proud of the stories we wrote. But they didn't make me glad or sad or anything."

"It must have occurred to you and your cowriter that the Rathmans might face retribution from the Petruglia family."

The Mikey on TV hesitated. *Too long,* Mikey on the sofa thought. *Come on, answer.* "Of course we—we don't want any of our—I'm sorry; I shouldn't be talking about sources."

"So I assume that you never actually spoke with Edward—"

As Stamm kept speaking, Mikey clattered her teacup onto an end table and lurched forward on the sofa as she saw the first part of the bulletin, white letters encased in bloodred, disappearing off the left edge of the screen . . .

BREAKING NEWS: CLARKSTON FAMILY MURDE

. . . and the rest circling in from the right edge . . .

RED IN APPARENT MOB HIT.

"Oh no," she said. "Holy . . . shit, no."

She grabbed her phone off the weeks' worth stack of *Times* and *Free Press* copies next to the sofa and called Robillard, got his message: "You've almost reached Robo. Please leave—" She cut that off and started to call Addams but changed her mind and dialed the *Times* city desk.

"*Times*," the desk guy said.

"Hey, it's Mikey. Is that the Rathman family I'm seeing on TV?"

"I was just about to call you."

That was all Mikey needed to hear. She hung up on the editor and hit Robillard's number again, feeling herself begin to hyperventilate as it rang once, twice, three times. "Come on, Robo," she said. When it kicked to voice mail, Mikey almost hung up but decided to wait, then left a message:

"Robo, it's Mikey. We killed"—Mikey stopped to swallow a sob she didn't want him to hear—"We killed that family. The Rathmans. We killed them because you and Addams wouldn't protect him. You hung him out to dry. You hung me out to dry. Go fuck yourselves, you heartless bastards."

She snapped the call off and went to the kitchen, where she opened the narrow corner cupboard door by the sink and yanked out the bottle of Crown Royal she and Craig had half emptied the night the Petruglia series had been complete, after she'd taped the PBS interview.

She took the bottle down and twisted off the cap and closed her eyes while she swallowed a slug that made her gag a little, the whiskey slopping out a corner of her mouth as she heard Stamm's voice again from the living room.

". . . certain to win some big prizes."

Mikey leaned her elbows on the kitchen counter, dropped her head into her hands, and began to cry. The sobs heaved up from the well of her belly, convulsing her diaphragm as she confronted the irrevocable knowledge that she herself had done almost nothing to protect Rathman and his family, that she had let Robillard and Addams do what they wanted, that she was no less a heartless bastard than either of them.

———

"I was doing my job," Mikey tells Jubilee, trying to keep the emotion out of her voice, trying to keep Jubilee talking until the police can get to her. "I can't help it that your father—"

"Don't even," Jubilee says, her voice creeping upward a pitch, her anger seeping into the bar. "You people and your 'doing my job.' What about the assassin? Was he just doing his job?"

"If what you seek is revenge, why don't you go after him?" Mikey says.

"How do you know that I haven't?" Jubilee goes silent for a moment, then says, "You exposed my father, Michaela. You exposed my family. You exposed me. I was just a kid, like your precious daughter."

"Leave my daughter alone. Please. She has done nothing to you."

"No, she hasn't. Which is precisely the point."

"I was doing my job."

"As if your job was the most important thing in the world. When you collected your prizes—"

"I didn't collect any prizes. I quit."

"Oh, how righteous of you, Michaela."

Another text buzzes into Bridget's phone:

tell her baby xox hang in there xox tell her about the source you know what i mean

"The time to be righteous, Michaela, was *before* all the applause started. The time to be righteous was *before* you wrote your stories that got my family killed, *before* you lied about—"

"I didn't lie."

"Oh, you lied, Michaela. You know you lied. And you're lying now. Do you know how I know? I can see you lying."

Mikey undoes her lip from her teeth as she realizes what Jubilee is saying. "No," she says. "Just take me if you want to hurt me so badly. Let my daughter and my sister go."

Jubilee laughs. "Yes, see. You bite your lip. That's what you do. You bite your lip when you're lying. I've watched you, Michaela. I watched you do your little interview with that old PBS fart who thought you were so special. I watched it a thousand times. 'Killer quote'? Killer's the word, all right."

"I didn't—"

"And you bit your lip the day your brother died too. Because you lied about that too. You lied about your brother's horrible death. And I watched you lie then too."

"Zeke," Mikey says, barely able to get the words out for the catch in her throat. "My brother has nothing to do with this."

Mikey remembers standing on the beach, the microphone in her face. She told the TV person that she was the one who had dragged Ophelia out of the tunnel, that Mikey—not Ophelia—was the one who had panicked and cost Zeke his life. She lied then without thinking, acting on instinct as a big sister, to keep the police and the curious public and Bleak Harbor and anyone else from thinking it was younger Ophelia who had failed to save their brother, but mostly to protect Ophelia from their mother, who would forgive Mikey but never Ophelia.

"Oh, no," Jubilee says, "Zeke has everything to do with this. Because you, of all people, should have known better before you lied about my father and mother. You should have known better because you lost someone you loved."

"I lied then to help my sister."

"'Help my sister'?"

"I was fourteen, for God's sake."

"What you did was foist a lifetime of guilt on your sister. You're such a hero, you unctuous, pathetic, hypocritical slut."

The phone zizzing: tell her source now

———

Twelve years earlier

Mikey had waited until almost midnight that Sunday to go to the *Times* newsroom. She had begged off helping Robillard write the day's story about the Rathman murders. He'd seemed genuinely enthused about the task. "Talk about impact," he had told Mikey before she'd hung up on him without saying goodbye. If he had gotten Mikey's angry voice mail from that morning, he hadn't acknowledged it.

Now the newsroom was vacant but for a single editor monitoring wires around the corner from Robillard's desk. She assumed the editor already had made his nightly visit to the Anchor Bar for a liquid lunch and would soon be napping. Addams's office was empty.

Robillard had tucked the yellow milk crate beneath his desk, where he evidently trusted that no one, certainly none of his *Times* colleagues, would touch it. Mikey hauled it out and set it on the desk between Robillard's photographs of his great-grandfather, Jamison Mitzelfeld, and the late Petruglia don. She started going through it, front to back, page by page. Much of what she saw was financial records suggesting how the Petruglias had used Edward Rathman's copy shops to clean illicit cash. Mikey was somewhat familiar with those details because the juiciest ones had appeared in the *Times*.

But she had not seen or heard of the printouts of emails she found in a frayed manila envelope in the yellow crate. The envelope was marked on the outside in black felt pen: *EJP*. Robillard always printed out emails because, he said, he could then purge the electronic email from his computer and no hacker could find it. Mikey had told him he was probably mistaken about that, but Robillard had, of course, ignored her. She was grateful for that now.

Up till then, Mikey had idly wondered if Edward Rathman himself had supplied Robillard with the most revealing documents. She had even asked Robillard about it once, almost as a joke. "Now why would he do that?" Robillard had responded. "Ed Rathman is a lot of things, but I don't think insane is one of them." True enough, Mikey had thought, and she'd dropped the subject.

But that evening, after putting little Bridget to bed, she'd poured herself a glass of pinot noir and turned on CNN. Anderson Cooper had been interviewing a senator who had been accused of misusing campaign donations. The senator had spoken at length about the many ways he had properly and legally used his campaign funds. Craig, who'd been checking student papers at the kitchen table, had piped up, "Is that mope ever gonna deny the charges, or what?" And Mikey had realized that Robillard had never actually denied that Edward Rathman was one of his sources.

Now, reading the emails stuffed into the envelope marked *EJP*, she began to understand why Robillard had dodged her question. Her instinct to guess that Edward Rathman was a source had in fact been wrong—but not by much.

She returned the yellow crate to its place under Robillard's desk. She kept what she had discovered to herself, as she felt she had to. They were Robillard's papers, not hers, and he had his agreements with his sources that she was not at liberty to violate. Only after she'd been out of journalism for several years did she even tell her husband, and even then, she revealed only that she knew who Robillard's most important source was, and it wasn't who she'd thought it was.

———

"Hypocritical slut," Mikey hears. And thinks of Bridget's bully calling her *a little slut.*

Mikey tries to ignore the words, but the tone, the pitch of Jubilee's voice, makes Mikey's belly roil with fear that Jubilee is nearing some peak of delusional fury.

Mikey checks the view of Ophelia. The way she's holding her face suggests she's listening to something. Maybe someone other than Jubilee is with her. Mikey turns to Bridget. She seems to have calmed some, which makes Mikey worry that maybe her daughter has accepted her fate. *I'm coming for you, baby,* she thinks.

"How do you know," Mikey says, "that your father didn't help us?"

"My father?"

Again, Jubilee goes briefly silent. Then the image of Bridget's face fades from the screen, replaced by that of a knife the size of Mikey's forearm. She can see in the steel of the knife's serrated blade the blurry reflection of a woman's face. She tries to recall young Jubilee, annoyed, adolescent, calling down to her mother that morning at the Rathman home.

Mikey swallows. "That's what I said."

"My father is dead. Because of—"

"No," Mikey says, remembering Robillard telling her to keep trying for a comment from Rathman's attorney. What a head fake that was. "Not because of me, Jubilee. Because of his lawyer. One E. Jonathan Phillips. Your father's attorney."

39

Phillie? Jubilee thinks. *Impossible. The bitch is lying again.*

She gets up out of her chair, wanders away from the desk. "You are desperate, Michaela, and you have nothing to offer," she says. "So you lie."

Her father's most loyal friend. Jubilee's only momentary solace in these years of rage and loneliness.

"There was a large cache of documents at Vance Robillard's desk that I did not see before the stories ran," Mikey says. "He kept them in a yellow milk crate. Among other things, they contained big chunks of your father's income tax records for the five years before his death."

"You're lying. And it's not going to help you."

Frances interrupts: "We have intruders."

"Phillips got sloppy, apparently, because on one of the envelopes containing the records, there was a partially taped-over mailing label for an address in Charlevoix, Michigan. I did a little research and discovered Phillips had—maybe still has—a cottage on that lake. Nice place, probably worth two million now. Did you know that?"

Jubilee has been at that house, before the deaths. Phillie had her and five of her soccer teammates up for a long weekend of sun and wakeboarding and lunch at the Weathervane on the channel out to Lake Michigan.

"So what?"

"And there were emails," Mikey continues. "They were cryptic, or at least someone intended them to look cryptic. But I could read between the lines because I was involved in the story. They were between your father's attorney and one Jamison Mitzelfeld, Robillard's late great-grandfather."

"Who? You're lying. How could—?"

"Obviously Robillard used a fake email account."

"Jubilee." Frances again.

"Phillips didn't much like the media. I'll bet you know that too. In one of his emails, he referred to Robillard as a barking hyena. Which Robillard loved."

Jubilee stops pacing, closes her eyes, remembers the last time she spoke with Phillie, that afternoon after the press conference.

"Tamed those barking hyenas," he said. "Joshua would be proud."

"Why would Phillips betray my father?"

"I don't know for sure. I could guess—but it's only a guess—that Phillips was in trouble with the family. There was this weird gap in the emails. Robillard and Phillips were going back and forth pretty regularly, and then Phillips basically told Robillard to go to hell, and they apparently didn't correspond for several weeks. But then they started up again, and it was Phillips, not Robillard, who initiated it."

"How do you know that?"

"I don't a hundred percent, but it looked that way."

Jubilee keeps watching for Mikey to bite her lip, but she doesn't. "But you didn't tell your boss, did you?"

"Tell my boss I went digging through a colleague's desk? I would have gotten fired."

"Nor did you go to the authorities."

"I actually considered that, but the next time I looked, the yellow milk crate was gone. I asked Robillard about it, and he said, 'What yellow milk crate?'"

"You're lying."

"No, I'm not."

Jubilee wonders if Mikey can hear her aggravated breathing. "You were a coward, Michaela."

"Yes," Mikey says. "I was."

Jubilee snatches the headset off and throws it at the desk.

"Frances," she says. "What intruders where?"

———

Mikey sneaks a glance at the fresh text on Bridget's phone: holy shit yes baby

When she looks up, the screens over the bar are black, silent.

"Jubilee?" Mikey says, worrying she shouldn't have said what she had said. "Bridget? Ophelia? Jubilee? Where did you go? Please. Where are you? What am I supposed to do?"

Craig rushes in, taking Mikey by the shoulders. "We have to get out of here."

Mikey looks around the bar, as if Jubilee might appear there in person to hand over Bridget and Ophelia.

"I can't leave them," she says.

"You've done what you can. Come on—we have to go."

As Craig pulls her away, Mikey spins, agitated but calm, angry but certain, an image of her father, Bob Wright, suddenly ablaze in her head. He's sitting on the end of the dock with his arm around Ophelia. It is July 14, 1995, one year to the day after Zeke died, and Bob Wright is hugging Ophelia and telling her that Zeke is proud of his twin and everything is going to be OK.

Mikey makes a decision. She shouts back at the video screens, "You, Jubilee, are the coward. No better than your father. And you weren't worth it. You weren't worth it at all."

———

"The intruders are police," Frances says. "Thirteen. On the road at the front entrance. There is also someone moving along the bayfront slope. He appears to be looking for a way into the house."

"It's got to be Christian," Jubilee says.

"Facial recognition is negative for Xavier Christian."

"It must be a cop, then. He's not gonna get here in time."

"No. We have positive facial identification on Camera Twenty-Seven."

"For whom, Frances?"

"Facial recognition has a 96.5 percent chance of accuracy. But it is dark and—"

"Who is it?" Jubilee says. Then, recalling what Mikey just told her, she feels a tangible dread spread over her like a cold, wet blanket. She answers her own question at the same time Frances tells her: "Mr. Phillips."

"Phillie."

"Yes."

"You're certain?"

"Facial recognition has a 96.5 percent—"

"Enough, Frances."

Jubilee walks back to the desk, scans the screens. Michaela was not lying. "Frances," she says. "Where is the blind woman? And where is—where is Caleb, for God's sake?"

"He has removed the woman from the room."

"And you didn't alert me?"

"You were having your conversation with the hockey rink."

"Turn off all the lights in the house, except for where I am. And Caleb."

"Done."

Jubilee leans into another screen tracking Mikey's car. "And Michaela—or at least her car—appears to have left the rink, probably on her way here." She reaches for a mouse, clicks it, and all the screens go dark. "Foolishly," she says. "Frances, where is Mr. Phillips now?"

"He is moving along the bayside fence."

Jubilee pictures Phillie, tall and lean, a black number on his chest, that loping stride taking him over the bumps and ridges of the Lake Saint Clair shoreline in a triathlon the year before the murders. "He must have noticed the police lights by now," Jubilee says. "Which gate is he nearest?"

"Approaching North Four."

"Good. Unlock the gate. Guide him to the roof."

"You want me to let him in?"

"Yes, Frances," she says. "I want you to let him in."

40

Caleb waits with Ophelia. It seems as if she's trying to catch his gaze. He keeps looking away.

Now she begins to shake her head. Slowly. He turns to the video screen showing the frightened girl in the other room. But he can't look for long, turns back around, sees Ophelia still shaking her head. She should be afraid. She doesn't seem to be. But why? What is she trying to tell him?

He looks at the single door to the room. If Jubilee comes, he won't hear her until she's there. He takes a step toward Ophelia, stops. She stops shaking her head, and her cheeks widen slightly as if she's trying to smile beneath the tape around her mouth.

He takes another step. She begins to shake her head again. *No,* Caleb thinks, pushing away the creeping realization that he is afraid, though he isn't sure of what. He stops again, glances at the door again. Decides.

He takes three swift steps forward and, quickly as he can, swipes the tape off Ophelia's face.

———

Ophelia listens. She takes long, slow breaths, the kind she has learned in her yoga classes, to slow her heart and quell her fear.

She turns her face up to Caleb. "Do you read the Bible, Caleb?"

She hears him take a step back. After a moment, he responds, "The righteous. Blessed are the righteous."

"There is a blind man in the Bible, Caleb," she says. "He is a righteous man, but he is also sad and tired."

"I don't know about that man."

"An angel named Raphael makes him see again. It's my favorite story in the Bible, from the book of Tobit."

She imagines Caleb looking confused, as most people would. He says, "I have not . . . I do not know that."

"Now you do."

He goes quiet again. Ophelia thinks. When the woman was in the room—Caleb's mother? Keeper? Sister? Aunt?—she heard what she thought was Bridget's soft sobbing coming from nearby. Ophelia leaped from her chair, seeking the woman, and ran into Caleb, and within seconds, she was bound to the chair and silenced.

"Focus," she had heard the woman command.

Not long after the woman left the room, the Bridget sounds Ophelia was hearing went away. Ophelia wondered if Caleb had somehow made the sounds go away, either for her sake or for his. Then she began to shake her head.

No, Caleb, she thought. *You don't want this.*

Now she says, "Who was that woman, Caleb?"

He has moved away from her, but not far.

"Caleb," Ophelia says. "I heard my niece. You won't let that woman hurt my niece, will you? Do you know my niece's name?"

"Stop talking," he says, "or I will have to tape you again."

"It's Bridget. Her name is Bridget. She is beautiful and funny, and she loves to play ice hockey. And she loves her mother and her aunt, Caleb."

"Please."

"She loves her uncle, too, even though she never knew him."

She hears him step closer and bows her head to hide her sudden fright. He stops where she would reach out to touch him if her hands weren't taped behind her. "She has no uncle," Caleb says.

———

Bridget has no uncle, Caleb thinks. *There is only Ophelia and the sister who betrayed Jubilee and her family.*

"Yes, she does," Ophelia says, raising her head to face him again. "His name was Zeke. He died on the dunes here when he was thirteen years old."

Kara was fourteen when she died, Caleb thinks, then says, "There are no dunes on Purgatory Bay."

"On the lake, at Jeremiah Jump."

Caleb shakes his head, knowing nothing of those dunes or that jump. Ophelia says, "He was the boy in the sculpture you . . . the leg you took."

"I'm sorry," he says, surprising himself.

"It was my fault that my brother died," Ophelia says. "I killed him."

"No. Please."

"Caleb," Frances interrupts. "You removed the tape."

Another picture of Kara appears in Caleb's head. She's sitting across from him at the supper table up north, eating spaghetti with clam sauce. She likes the sauce but thinks the clams are gross, picks them off her plate and wraps each one in a separate wad of napkin. She has a hunk of garlic bread next to her plate that he wants. He knows she will give him half if he asks.

Her last meal.

He hears the crickets again, the sound of Kara's laughter.

"Tell me," Caleb says. "Your brother."

"We were digging a tunnel," Ophelia says. "It collapsed, and he was trapped in the sand. He suffocated. It was my fault."

"How? You couldn't see."

"Yes, I could then. At least some. I could have saved him. I panicked."

"Caleb," Frances says.

He looks over at the speaker projecting Frances into the room. It wouldn't take much to tear it out of the wall. He slides one hand into a pocket in his hoodie, fingers the small plastic switch inside, the tip of the collapsed antenna. Jubilee won't be giving that order for a while yet.

"Leave me, Frances."

"The mission. Jubilee is counting on you."

"I understand."

Caleb turns toward Ophelia, walks to her chair.

"Did you have a sister?" she says.

He hesitates, hovering over her, feeling himself breathing hard, wondering what he's going to do next.

How could she know? he thinks.

———

Purgatory Bay, Ophelia thinks. *He said we're on Purgatory Bay.*

She came to the bay when she was in her late teens, after her family had moved to Bleak Harbor for good. Her sight wasn't yet entirely gone.

She and a boyfriend rode bicycles to the bay, sneaked through the woods to a muddy outcropping of shore. He wanted to drink and make out. She wanted to watch the loons and read the large-print book her father had given her for a birthday.

A storm rose up, slicing over the bluffs across the bay. It came up so fast that Ophelia and her boyfriend bolted from the woods as hail like bullets tore at their skin. They left everything but their bikes behind: a thermos of Gatorade, two blankets, grape leaves wrapped in foil, and Ophelia's book, about some English boys trapped on an island.

She has heard of the woman who took up residence on the bay after losing most of her family to murder and a brother to suicide. *Charlotte White?* she thinks, feeling again a stab of guilt at her greed-induced naivete. But this man, this boy, in front of her, who is he?

She looks up, imagining she's staring into Caleb's eyes, and says, "Did you have a sister, Caleb?"

He moves closer. She can hear his breathing over her, feel the anxiety beneath it. Then comes the voice of Frances again:

"Plans are changing, Caleb. The outer world is here."

"All right," he says.

Ophelia feels his hands reach behind her. In an instant her hands are free. She rubs them together once, then reaches up for Caleb, expecting him to resist her or pull away. But he lets her touch him. She runs her palms along his cheekbones, the sides of his face, his forehead. He holds still, his breath quickening. She lowers one hand to his chest. His heart is pounding.

"Caleb," the voice commands.

"It's over now, Frances."

Caleb grasps Ophelia by the arms, pulls her gently up out of the chair. She smells his skin, whispers, "Raphael."

"Follow me."

41

"Just about everyone's out of the rink except for the bomb crew," Gary says. "But still a bunch of people in the parking lot."

He's on his phone as he and Malone trot up the slickened road to the house on Purgatory Bay. The sleet has turned to fat wet snowflakes like goose feathers, plummeting on a slant.

Half a dozen police cruisers from Bleak Harbor, Bleak County, and the Michigan State Police are parked haphazardly along the road shoulder, lights blazing scarlet and blue. More are on the way, along with a hostage negotiator, though Gary has no idea how the negotiator is going to reach the sociopath inside the house. Hell, he doesn't even know if Jubilee Rathman is actually inside. She could be anywhere.

"Mikey and her husband are out of the rink?" Malone says.

"Yeah. They're gone."

"Thank God."

Gary peers up at the concrete barrier fronting the house, a wall twice his height, topped by crisscrossed iron spikes. "That was a gamble," he says. "You figured she wouldn't blow the rink up so long as Mikey kept talking?"

"Something like that. Seemed like she wanted to watch Mikey suffer. I just told her husband to keep her talking."

———

Malone knows she was just guessing. Maybe she got lucky. Or maybe Jubilee by now has disposed of Bridget and Ophelia. She hopes to God not. "How the hell are we going to get in this place?"

They stop before a pair of enormous black iron doors set into the concrete wall. She pushes a palm into each; neither budges.

"Chief."

Malone turns and sees a state trooper approaching. He's wearing a blue slicker over his uniform and a navy wool cap dotted with snow. "Vellucci," he says. Other troopers and sheriff's deputies are beginning to fan out along the wall.

"Malone. You're in charge here?"

"For now. Do we know for sure that anyone's in there?"

Malone glances toward the house, then back at Vellucci. He's an older man who carries himself with authority. She decides he can run his own people, but he's not running her. "I honestly don't know," she says. "But I also don't know where else to look. Seems like we ought to get in there."

"We'll set up a perimeter first." Vellucci looks to his left, then his right, probably trying to see where the wall starts and ends, impossible in the dark. "Our SWAT guys can jump the wall, but it's gonna take time. Got a copter coming too."

"I don't know how it's gonna get near this place for all the trees," Malone says. "Plus the snow."

The woman's voice seems to emanate from above the doors. "You do not have much time," it says.

"What the hell?" Vellucci says. "Is that the kidnapper?"

"I don't think so," Malone says, recalling the intercom voice that herded the reporters that morning. "It's like her virtual assistant or something." As unnerving as the invisible voice is, it's reassuring because maybe it means Jubilee is here. Malone directs her next words upward at the doors. "We need to speak with Jubilee Rathman. We won't hurt her. Or you."

No reply comes.

Malone leans into Vellucci and whispers, "Get that perimeter going, OK? And get that negotiator here."

Vellucci glances up in the direction of the voice. "Will do," he says. "But don't be doing anything without my OK. We've got this now."

No, Malone thinks. *I'm not about to lose another kid.* She waits till Vellucci's out of earshot, then speaks to the voice again.

"May I ask who you are?"

"I am Frances."

"Frances, where is Jubilee? Can you put us in touch with her?"

Malone waits. Again, there's no reply. She steps closer to the doors, flattens a palm against each, presses an ear against the thin crack between them. Then feels the doors give, moving away from her hands and face on their own.

They're open.

She turns to Gary. He's on his phone again, his back to her. "Hey," she says. "You coming?"

"Chief," she hears Vellucci call out. He's across the road with some other troopers. He must see that the doors are open. He starts toward her. "Stop. Wait," he yells. "Don't go in there."

Believe me, Malone thinks, *the last thing I want to do is go into another big house to chase another kidnapper.* But she ignores Vellucci anyway, telling Gary, "I'm going in."

"Let's do it," he says, stuffing his phone in a pocket and tugging out his gun. "Hell, I'm not a cop anyway."

42

E. Jonathan Phillips shuffles sideways along the tower parapet, taking care not to slip in the scrim of wet snow beneath his feet. The roof below is an expanse of dull concrete, vacant but for half a dozen raised slabs of varying heights, washed by light from lamps on two of the towers. Tools appear to be scattered on one of the slabs; a drone waits on another. Phillie initially figures the slabs for workbenches of a sort, then thinks, *No. Launching pads.*

Among the photographs Phillie has seen of the house he never was invited to visit, he did not see the roof, which looks to him now like a crude miniature military base, Jubilee's personal staging ground. He listens again for the buzzing he heard earlier in the woods by the bay where he shot Christian through the back of his empty head. *Drone,* he thought then, like the one that targeted the Petruglia girl.

He doesn't want to be here, on this roof, in the dark, weapons at hand, stalking Jubilee. He never wanted things to come to this. Working for the Petruglias, unbeknownst to Jubilee's father, Phillie was able to protect Edward Rathman until he couldn't, and Jubilee herself until he couldn't.

Gemma Petruglia called him that afternoon and gave him his orders. She had little faith that Christian possessed the awareness or the competence to do what needed to be done, as subsequent events bore out. "We should have taken care of this years ago," she told Phillips, and in her words he heard both her fear of losing her position and, perhaps worse, reproach, for it was Phillie who had argued that Jubilee was too damaged to be a threat.

He was woefully mistaken about that.

Now, out of the corner of his left eye, Phillie detects movement in the window of the tower diagonally across from him. He doesn't look that way but halts his scuttling and holds still, listening. He fixes his gaze for now on the tops of the trees, the snowflakes coursing through the skeletal branches, the black shimmer of the bay beyond. He reaches behind him and unsnaps the scabbard holding the killing knife. Then he hears the buzzing again, suddenly close. He whips his head around and sees the drone hovering, swaying left to right and back, barely eight feet away, out of his reach, staring at him, daring him.

He finds it oddly amusing. And he's glad to be physically prepared for this moment, as physically prepared as a sixty-year-old can be. His predawn workouts, the quarterly triathlons recalling his college years as a cross-country runner, the running and swimming and bicycling against flat-bellied youngsters half his age. He's not going to let this silly flying machine—this glorified toy—intimidate him. He grips the parapet with one hand and vaults himself onto the roof.

———

Gary hears the sounds—weeping, someone speaking—as he creeps along a concrete wall one floor beneath the one where he and Malone entered. He stops, raises his pistol. Then the sounds are gone.

Malone sent him to find Bridget and Ophelia while she found a way to the roof. The room he's in—or maybe it's just a wide corridor—is as silent and dark as a tomb. He's reminded of the crack house he went into with his partner on what would be his last assignment. He remembers feeling his blood rippling hot through his chest, the anger building. He feels it again now, sucks in a breath, lets it out.

He holds his pistol behind him as he inches along the wall, stretching his other hand out against it.

He feels the flat edge of what might be a doorjamb.

Then he hears the sounds again, muffled words, a woman's voice—Ophelia: "I'm here, Bridget. I'm here, honey."

He reaches across the jamb, raps his knuckles on the door.

"Ophelia," he says. "It's Gary."

"Gary. Oh my God."

The door is steel and apparently thick, because Gary has trouble hearing Ophelia clearly. He looks back over his shoulder. If someone is watching him, they're well hidden. He reaches for the door handle, tries to twist it, but it won't give.

"Gary, get us out of here. Please."

"Bridget is with you?"

"Yes, she's here. She's fine."

"You can't open the door from the inside?"

"No. It's some kind of electronic lock."

Gary waits, collecting his thoughts, hearing sobs now from inside the room. Not Ophelia but Bridget. It strikes him that he isn't certain how he found his way to where he is and doesn't know how they'll all get out of there. They could all die here in the dark. He feels his blood again, the anger scalding his throat. He tries to imagine who would do this. He stops, takes another breath, tells himself, *Think, dammit.* He could leave Ophelia and Bridget and find his way back outside and bring in a squad of cops with a battering ram. But he's not sure he could find his way back here, and he can't be certain Ophelia and Bridget will still be here. Whoever stowed them might be back, might be watching him at this very moment, preparing to pounce.

"OK, listen," he says.

"Can you get us out?"

The answer is he doesn't know. He's never actually used his gun to shoot out a lock before, has never seen a cop do it except on TV. He's not even a cop anymore. But what else is he going to do?

"Listen," he says, "I want the both of you to squeeze yourselves into one of the corners along the wall away from the door."

"We'll do it. Just get us the hell out."

That's Bridget. Gary feels an unexpected swell of relief at hearing her voice. But still he knows if he finds the person who did this, if— *Calm the hell down,* he tells himself.

"Hey there, hockey goddess," he says, trying to sound cheerful, probably failing. He raises his pistol. "Ophelia? Get the both of you as far away from the door as you can."

43

Caleb checks the watch Jubilee gave him for this one piece of the mission. She texted him the command on the watch. It's nineteen minutes until he is supposed to push the button on the detonator that will ignite the explosives he placed inside the rink.

He's standing inside the northwest roof tower, peeking out through the slit of window in the door. Caleb's night vision is good because of the many hours he spent in sheer darkness, training.

His training is over now forever. Maybe everything is over.

He watches the crown of a head moving along the upper edge of the southeast tower. The intruder who distracted Jubilee from the mission is crouched in wait. Caleb removes a wireless controller from his pocket, taps a button, toggles a joystick. The drone Ralphie, waiting on the bay's southern edge, floats into the air. Ralphie is one of the drones that had technical problems, but he's the best Caleb has left.

What's happening now is not as Jubilee planned. Everything is different. Everything is about to end. Caleb isn't certain how anymore. He thinks of the feel of Ophelia's hands on his skin. "Raphael," she pleaded. Her angel.

He doesn't want everything to end. Not everything.

Ralphie, shrouded in the falling snow, wobbles into view above the intruder Caleb is watching. He zooms the drone's tiny video camera in on the man's face. It's hard to see him through the snow, but he appears to smile, and before Caleb can fire the drone's weapon, he springs from his crouch and hurdles the wall, landing on one foot and rolling to his right.

The man's face is shrouded in a black hood. Caleb can't see it clearly, but he doubts the man is here to help with Jubilee's mission. Caleb maneuvers Ralphie into position behind the man and fires a dart that, judging by how the man twists away, grimacing, catches him in the back of one of his legs. He writhes on the concrete for a second, then drags himself to one of the slabs and struggles halfway back to his feet.

Caleb sends the drone away, then reaches into another pocket for the detonator. It's about the size of one of the mice that occasionally skittered across the rooftop when he was practicing with the drones. He thinks of Simon then, how he swooped smooth and low over the water, flicking the orange plastic targets on the boat dock, the dive raft. So beautiful.

That, too, is over now.

Caleb sets the detonator on the narrow ledge of the window.

Fourteen minutes.

———

Jubilee emerges from the southwest roof tower to see Phillie collapsed behind one of the drone slabs. She watches his facial muscles corkscrew as he stretches to reach the dart in his leg.

She moves toward him, brandishing a Glock 17 pistol that she found in a false panel at the back of her parents' walk-in closet twelve years ago. She came to hate that place and all the suffocating memories that surrounded her there, reminders of a life she would never have again. She finally gave up on sorting and gathering her family's stuff and just sold the place as it was. With Phillie's help.

"Phillie," she says. "Barking hyena bite you in the ass?"

He groans, mumbles a curse under his breath.

Jubilee steps closer, eight feet away now, locking her gaze on his face, his eyes squeezed shut in pain. She thinks she should be relishing this moment, but she is not. The suffering of this man she trusted—her supposedly loyal friend and mentor—mocks her and her mission.

"You will never leave here, Phillie."

"And neither—God," he screams as he yanks the arrow from his hamstring. He flings it at Jubilee. It falls harmlessly at her feet.

Not because of me, Michaela told her. *Because of your father's attorney.* Because of Phillie.

"Why?" she says.

"It would have been better if you had been there."

"Been where?"

"At the cottage. That night."

"The night you murdered my family."

"You would have died quickly."

"My brother did not die quickly."

Phillie has to stop to catch his breath. "What did your mother tell the newspaper? 'Sometimes you have a choice; sometimes you don't'? I did not have a choice. But you did, Juju. And you blew it with your 'outer world' bullshit."

Jubilee resists the urge to blow off the top of Phillie's head. She raises the pistol until it's pointed at his face. "Explain yourself. Or take it back. You'll live longer if I hear the latter." *Though not much,* she thinks.

"The family wanted you and Joshua eliminated as quickly as possible. I held them off. You're lucky Vincent died when he did. Gemma took pity on you."

"I don't want her pity. Or yours. You killed my family."

"You had a choice," he gasps. He's holding the wound with one hand and trying to balance on the drone slab with the other. "You could have moved on, helped your brother, maybe helped the world."

The world, Jubilee thinks. Would she have made different choices if she had known the truth about Phillie? It doesn't matter, she tells herself. All that's left of the world is here before her now, in darkness and blood and death.

"Your father," Phillie says, "was just as hardheaded and, now I see, as cynical as you, Juju. He gave me no choice. He wanted out of the business. He was going to go to the feds. I could have been implicated."

"We couldn't have that."

"I persuaded him to go public instead."

"And how was that supposed to help him, Phillie?" She waits. He looks at her, saying nothing. "So," she says, "you told the Petruglias he did it on his own."

"I wasn't happy about it."

"And the Petruglias called your bluff."

"They gave me my orders. I had no choice."

"My father was a better man than you."

"And you, Jubilee."

Phillie almost topples sideways, then reaches behind him again; Jubilee wonders for a second if maybe the drone actually fired a second arrow, but he lunges upward, throwing something else, heavier, faster. It flashes silver in the lamplight, and Jubilee ducks left, but the knife blade lacerates the skin along her right cheekbone. She feels the blood spill down her neckline and raises the weapon she never expected to have to use on Phillie.

But Phillie has disappeared. Jubilee fires anyway, four rapid shots in the direction of where she last saw him. "You're brave, Juju. Was it hard?" he said to her that morning, just before asking about her reaction when the reporter inquired about the missed drone shot at young Dora. Her cheek stings, but she doesn't care. She steps forward, looking left, then right, and takes another step, wondering where Caleb is. She shouts then, "Time to die, Phillie. And then you will burn." Another step. "You will burn, and—"

She falls hard on her left hip, pain tearing down into her knee and shin, her pistol clattering away, something gripping her right ankle like a vise, pulling her along the wet concrete. "Caleb," she shouts as she rolls onto her back and stares up into Phillie's blood-smeared forehead.

———

The squawk box fixed to Malone's shoulder comes to life as she ascends the concrete stairway inside the tower one slow step at a time.

"Chief," comes the voice. Too loud. Malone isn't sure where she is or who's watching or listening or lying in wait. She assumes the voice is Vellucci. She leans into the mic and rasps, "Quiet."

Vellucci lowers his voice. "Help is on the way," he says. "Stay where you are."

She turns a corner, and a trapezoid of dull light appears on a wall at the top of the stairs.

"Ten four," she lies.

"Can you give us your approximate location?"

"I'm climbing some stairs. Is that copter here yet? Can you tell me what's going on up on the roof?"

"Almost there. Stay where you are. We will find you."

With the help of the light, Malone runs up to the stairway landing, turns left, and moves through a doorway into a small empty room with a door. Through a thin window set into the door, she looks out onto the roof. *God help me,* she thinks, yanking the door open and rushing out, service weapon out in front of her, shouting, "Police. Stop there. Stop. Now. Police."

A dim circle of light illuminates a man dressed in black who's straddling someone—maybe Jubilee Rathman, though Malone can't see a face—on the rooftop floor about fifteen feet away.

The woman is cursing a name Malone can't make out.

The man twists toward Malone, extending an arm. She squeezes her trigger. A microsecond later her left knee explodes, and her legs splay out from under her, her shoulder slamming into the concrete, gun skittering away. "Police," she gasps. Fire is blasting through her leg. She hears another shot and then another cracking the wall behind her.

Do not pass out, Malone tells herself. *Stay awake, find your gun, do not do not do not pass out.* There's more screaming, the unintelligible, wordless, furious howling of a dog in a fight. She forces her eyes open. The man straddling the woman keels forward, his face a blank stare, the back half of his head sheared away, blood spewing from his neck.

Gary, she thinks. *The screaming is Gary.* She's fighting to stay conscious. She thinks she sees Gary squatting over the man who shot her, swinging his arm upward and then bringing it down hard, again and again, blood spurting across the concrete, the woman squirming away, Gary shrieking at the slumped-over human heap as he pulverizes the skull and face and cheekbones.

Gary, she thinks, *you're not a cop anymore,* before everything goes away.

———

Gary finally feels the hot splatter on his cheeks. It wakes him, though he was not sleeping. He regards what he has done as if he hadn't known he was doing it.

The blood-clotted hammer drops from his hand.

Snapped again, he thinks, remembering Katya screaming in pain.

He sees the blood pouring from a bullet-size hole in the side of the dead man's neck. But Gary's other hand is empty. He feels in his pocket. The pistol is still there. He must have put it away before he started swinging the hammer. He looks around, sees Malone lying still across the rooftop. He's starting to move toward her when he hears a woman's voice and looks up. He wonders why she's pointing a pistol at him. In her bulky black coveralls, he would have taken her for one of the SWAT guys. But she's shaking her head and saying, "You can jump over the wall, or I can shoot you dead here."

Where the hell is *that SWAT team?* he thinks.

He takes a deep breath, straightens his arm, the pistol at its end a prosthesis he can't feel. A helicopter spotlight sweeps across the rooftop, illuminating the woman's face, all angry bones and empty translucence. Over the whopping of the blades, Gary shouts, "Jubilee Rathman, you are under arrest."

He hears her laugh—at least that's what he'll tell the real cops later—just as something from behind him chops his forearm so hard that he thinks his wrist might be broken. His gun falls away. Gary feels himself being lifted by the back of his jacket, his arms flailing and legs kicking as he is catapulted through the air into the brick side of the northeast tower, where he crumples, unconscious.

———

"The mission is nearly complete, Caleb." Jubilee points the barrel of her gun toward the mass of blood and slashed bone that was once Phillie. "We are so lucky."

Caleb stares at the dead man, feeling nothing.

"Is it time to complete your mission, Caleb?" he hears his sister say.

He thinks of Ophelia and Bridget. He assumes someone, maybe the police gathered near the front of the house, has found and collected them by now.

"Caleb?"

He looks up at Jubilee. She nods in the direction of Bleak Harbor, a smear of light beyond the snowfall and trees to the southwest.

"It must be time," she says, "yes?"

Caleb hears Jubilee's words and thinks, *Yes.*

But no.

It was time one and a half minutes ago for him to ignite the chain of explosions inside the hockey rink. He picked the device up off the windowsill where he'd set it. He held it gently in his hand as he watched the intruder straddling Jubilee shoot the police chief, the chief shoot back, hitting the intruder in his neck, and then the next intruder bash the first one's head in half. Caleb grabbed the second man by the back of his jacket and flung him into a wall. And he watched Jubilee approach the dead man.

A scene began then to unfold in his head. It was probably no more than a flash, but it took longer to play out, as if Caleb had somehow found a way to suspend time up here on this familiar rooftop. Maybe it was a memory from another life. Or maybe it was something he merely wanted to imagine.

He indulged it anyway.

Jubilee was a girl running toward him across a field of broad flat green. She was wearing a shiny blue short-sleeved shirt with a yellow number on the front. Her hair was in a ponytail tied with yellow and silver ribbons. She was carrying something shiny, something almost as big as him, with a shiny little statue of a girl at the top of it, balancing a soccer ball on one knee.

Jubilee ran to him and shifted the trophy to one of her arms and picked him up in the other and began to run again, laughing and shouting while other girls in shiny outfits ran alongside them, laughing and shouting too.

Now Caleb extends an arm to Jubilee, opens his palm. In it lies the detonator. He can hear the thudding of boots growing louder in the towers, the commands of voices from above, the whoosh of the hovering helicopter.

Everything is over now.

He gestures toward the dead man lying between Jubilee and him. "Nothing has changed, Jubilee. Nothing will ever change."

"It is time, Caleb. Now. Complete the mission."

Without taking his eyes off Jubilee, Caleb throws the detonator high into the air, off the rooftop, into the dark clusters of trees beyond.

The helicopter lights fan over Jubilee's face as she watches the detonator disappear into the black.

"I am Joshua," Caleb says.

She reaches into her clothing. Then she extends an arm to him, opens her palm. An identical device rests there.

"No," he says, moving toward her.

"Caleb," Jubilee says, "Joshua is dead. Leave him there. Allow him that mercy."

She turns and points the detonator in the direction of Bleak Harbor, but before she can push the button, Caleb is crushing her wrist in his hand, the device falling away. Then he takes his sister up in one arm and lunges toward the nearest edge of the roof. *No, Jubilee,* he thinks, *you are dead.*

He hears the cries of the officers streaming onto the roof, feels Jubilee struggling to free herself from his grip, her screaming, *Caleb no Caleb let me go put me down no,* as he catapults them off the roof into the dark.

44

Midnight

Mikey is staring into a vending machine filled with chips and peanuts and neglected bags of carrots, registering the sterile buzz of the fluorescent lamps overhead, when Bridget emerges from the double doors in the emergency department at Bleak County Community Hospital.

"Oh my," Mikey says, too overcome to finish the phrase as she springs from her waiting room chair and rushes to hug her daughter. Craig wraps his arms around both of them. "Oh my, oh my, Bridge," Mikey says, trying not to lose it.

The doctor waits a few feet away. Her nameplate reads *Nitsos*. Mikey and Craig and Bridget pull out of their embrace, and Dr. Nitsos steps closer, stethoscope dangling, clipboard cradled in her arms.

"Mr. and Mrs. Deming," she says. She has wide, striking eyes the color of chocolate milk. "Your daughter's going to be fine." She looks over at Bridget, offers a professional smile. "I've prescribed something to help her sleep." She hands a slip of paper to Mikey. "The hospital pharmacy is open."

"Thank you, Doctor," Mikey says. "Thank you for everything."

"Yes," Craig says, emotions swallowing his words.

"You all need sleep," Dr. Nitsos says. "But I'd like for one of you"— she means Mikey or Craig—"to call me first thing in the morning, please."

"What about Aunt Pheels?" Bridget says.

Dr. Nitsos looks around uncertainly before she finally realizes whom Bridget means. "Oh, of course, Ophelia. Pheels. Cute. She will be out shortly." Now the doctor's smile becomes something more than merely part of the job. "I love that name: Ophelia," she says. "I wanted to name our first daughter Ophelia—or at least make it her middle name—but my husband wasn't feeling it."

Mikey grasps Dr. Nitsos by the arm. "Trust me," she says. "You do not want to be dealing with an Ophelia."

Mikey and Craig laugh their laughs of thin and squeaky relief, their fright of a few hours ago trying to sneak away in the night, unnoticed.

Except for Bridget, who gazes over at the double doors before turning to her mother. "I think I need to sit down."

"Of course, honey," Mikey says. "Do you want something to drink or eat?"

Bridget lowers herself into a chair, her eyes downcast. "Not now. Can I have my cell phone?"

"Sorry," her father says. "The police have it."

"Well, that sucks."

Mikey sits down next to Bridget, puts an arm around her.

"Everything is going to be OK, Bridge. We're here now. We're here. We're going to G-Pa's tonight."

"They're going to mess up my phone."

"We will get you a new one."

Bridget leans out over her knees, goes quiet again. Then she says, "Can I sleep in your room with you?"

"Of course," Mikey says.

Again, Bridget doesn't say anything for a long minute. Mikey watches, not wanting to push her, not knowing exactly what to say or how to say it but knowing what she wants to say. And will say. In a minute.

Bridget breaks her silence without looking up. "Who won the tournament?"

"Nobody," Craig says. Bridget glances up at him and then Mikey, a look of mild surprise on her face. Her father continues, "There was—"

"Craig," Mikey says, cutting him off. Bridget doesn't need to hear about the bomb threat. "They just called it off, honey, after you were taken."

"OK."

Mikey sits next to her daughter. "Bridge," she says. "I need to tell you something."

"About the tournament?"

"No. Something else."

Mikey gives Craig a look. He nods and walks away, pulling his phone out.

"Now?" Bridget says.

———

"Really?" Bridget says. "Like, are there actually newspapers anymore?"

Mikey shrugs. "Not a lot in print, like something you can hold." She holds up her hands as if she were spreading an old-fashioned newspaper in front of her. "It's all on your phone now. And your earbuds."

"You're really going to be a reporter again?"

"Yes. At least I hope. Maybe nobody will want an old lady like me."

Mikey made the decision when she was leaving the rink bar after her back-and-forth with Jubilee Rathman. *You weren't worth it at all,* she shouted at the blank screens. Because Jubilee wasn't worth it. She wasn't worth the apology Mikey had innocently offered her at the funeral. She wasn't worth the guilt that had driven Mikey to walk away from what she had chosen to do with her life. It was her life, even if she'd made mistakes and trusted people she should not have trusted. Now she was going to take it back.

"What about the literacy thing?" Bridget says.

Mikey sighs. "You know," she says, "I don't really like that."

"I can tell."

"You can?"

"You almost never talk about it. You would talk about it if you loved it."

Mikey smiles. "Like I'm always talking about you."

"Whatever," Bridget says. "Wasn't I, like, in diapers when you were a reporter?"

"Close."

They sit in silence for a while, their hands still entwined. Bridget then slips her hands out of her mother's embrace. "I'm not sure about hockey," she says.

"Not sure how?"

"I'm just . . . I don't know. Not sure."

Mikey lets that hang on the air, trying to feel the shape and heft of those words. Bridget is not sure. Mikey would rather she be sure.

"It's OK, honey," Mikey says.

Again, a silence. Then, "What about Dad?"

"I'll handle Dad."

"I might not go to any of those colleges recruiting me."

"I don't care, honey." Mikey looks toward her daughter, puts a finger beneath her chin to lift it until she looks at her. "Whatever you do, I want you to be happy."

"You won't be mad at me? Or Dad?"

"No. If you don't get mad at me for going back to being a reporter."

Bridget laughs a little. It makes Mikey feel good, a sprinkling of peace washing over her. "I guess I won't," Bridget says.

"I'm going to need some luck," Mikey says. She reaches for Bridget's hands, squeezes them. "But you know, you can't get lucky if you don't try."

45

Six months later

"They wouldn't let you go to your sister's funeral?"

"Probably not."

"You didn't ask?"

"I didn't plan to go anyway."

"Why?"

"Ask me something else."

Joshua Rathman sits across a square gray table from Malone, her walking cane leaned against the table, her blue uniform jacket draped on the back of her chair. The room at the Ionia Correctional Facility is a cramped cube smelling of metal and disinfectant.

Through a window to her left, Malone can see the prison control center, momentarily unmanned. Her chair wobbles from one side to another. One leg must be shorter than the others. On the table before her rests a scrap of paper on which she has scribbled a few words she wants to ask about.

She is accustomed to Joshua's face by now, the hairless left eyebrow that obscures part of his eye, the flap of dead surplus skin bloating his chin. She saw him many times in the Bleak County courthouse, where he was sentenced to twenty-five to forty-five years in prison after pleading guilty to second-degree murder—of Vance Robillard and Portia Stone—and assault with intent to murder, with regard to Dora Petruglia and the Guilders boy. His lawyers urged him to go to trial, given his sister's influence over him, but Joshua refused. He said he wanted to take responsibility so as to restore some measure of honor to his family's name and to the memory of his parents and sister. The possibility of parole after twenty-five years gave him a glimmer of hope for a life in the outer world.

In the courtroom, Joshua frequently sought out Malone with his eyes. As if, she imagined, he wanted her approval or understanding or, perhaps, forgiveness. She knew he would never get that; she couldn't even forgive herself, let alone some stranger who had played at being an assassin.

Three weeks after Joshua Rathman entered prison, Malone received a handwritten note from him asking if she would pass a message to Ophelia Wright. He had written the message on a separate piece of paper. All it said was, *Thank you for restoring my sight. Joshua.*

Malone wrote him back. A correspondence began. She asked if she could visit.

Now he looks at her with a direct, unwavering gaze. In Malone's experience, this is a characteristic of both the sincerest truth tellers and the most heinous liars. She judges Joshua to be one of the former. Since he survived the fall from his sister's mansion roof and underwent the surgeries for his broken bones, he has told the truth, so far as Malone can tell. Not the whole truth but the truth. Because of his guilty plea, his courtroom testimony was minimal.

Joshua has yet to tell all of it. Or even most of it.

Which is why Malone is here on a September morning.

She sets her cell phone on the table.

"Selfie?" Joshua says.

Malone smiles. "Your sister," she says. "She had this song she hummed."

"She was a hummer, yes. She never told me why. But she hummed."

"She had a particular song she liked to hum," Malone says. "Or at least she liked to hum it when she was communicating with us."

"Probably when she was really worked up. Stressed. Which was a lot of the time."

"Do you know the song?"

"I probably heard it. But I don't know much about music. I never heard any in those years I was Caleb."

Malone picks up her phone, clicks on an audio app, and turns up the volume. The sound of Jubilee humming, captured on one of the recording devices planted in the fortress on Purgatory Bay, fills the tiny room.

Joshua stares at the phone, listening. He shrugs, says, "That's enough."

Malone shuts it off. "Have you ever heard of Justin Timberlake?"

Joshua leans back in his chair. Even now, months later, his shoulders and arms are thick with muscle. She recalls Gary Langreth marveling at how this young man—a boy, really—had flipped him through the air like a doll.

"The name actually sounds familiar," he says. "Was he a singer when I was young, like, before what happened up north?"

"Yes. In fact, this song was number one that year. It's called 'What Goes Around . . . Comes Around.'"

"Really?"

"Really. Your sister, she sort of paraphrased some of the lyrics and then sent them to people she wasn't happy with—"

"Pretty much everybody."

"—just to mess with them, to taunt them. She sent some to the mayor and to Gary, posing as Ophelia, telling them goodbye."

"How is Mr. Langreth?"

Malone considers this before answering. "He's doing better."

"And I see the police finally determined that a drone killed the mayor."

"A drone dispatched by your sister, yes. I'm thinking Mayor Fisher is in hell now."

"Or purgatory," Joshua says.

Jubilee died in the plunge off the rooftop, crushed beneath her brother. FBI profilers are still going through her voluminous video, audio, and written records trying to figure her out, to determine whether she was a natural-born sociopath or allowed circumstance to contort her into one—whether the criminal was made or born.

To Malone, it makes little difference. Jubilee was indeed grievously wronged. But her way of righting the wrong did nothing to make things right. Though Malone has to admit—and said it to Gary one morning as they sipped lattes at Bella's—that she would love to see every last Petruglia dumped into the cold, dark middle of Lake Michigan to drown.

"She was good at playing the media, huh?" Malone says. "They were all over your suicide in Colorado."

Joshua shakes his head. He's spent a lot of his time in prison reading. "I'll say. They believed our story—my sister's story—because I think they wanted to believe it. They kind of made it up themselves."

"And you didn't even know it was going on?"

"No, not really," he says. "I mean, I went to Colorado, and we took some pictures with some local paper before we were supposed to go up on the mountain. But I never went on the mountain. Jubilee kept me in one of the vans until the stunt had been pulled and we were on our way home."

"Why didn't you just get out?"

"I was . . ." He considers. "Out of it."

Malone thinks she knows what he means, makes a mental note to come back to it.

The world now knows that Joshua traveled to Colorado but never actually went mountain climbing. Jubilee smuggled him home on Amtrak trains that crawled across the country's middle but were filled with people who couldn't care less about who else was there. The media, so instantly obsessed with yet another wrinkle in the aftermath of the

Rathman murders, could have been more skeptical about whether Joshua had really died.

But a flurry of social media posts—all by Jubilee, under aliases—suggested that Joshua had committed suicide, so incapable was he of dealing with his bodily torture as well as recovering from the loss of his family. Jubilee's initial public denials, which she knew would stoke the media flames, led to a predictable rush to judgment. Soon Jubilee was tearfully admitting to the untrue truth, and Joshua was a suicide victim and namesake of a charity, the Joshua Project.

Now Malone recalls shaking Jubilee's hand at the press conference, telling her, "You're doing the Lord's work." She wishes Jubilee were here now with her brother. Maybe she would finally find some peace, even redemption. But those possibilities disappeared with her ashes in Purgatory Bay.

"You never made clear in court how she controlled you," Malone says.

"She was dead. It—she—didn't matter anymore." Joshua looks at the table, thinking. Malone lets him. "You have to understand," he continues, "how difficult her life was, dealing with me and the hospitals, the bills, the insurance companies, the cops and media hounding her, our family and friends shunning us. She felt guilty for not being at the cottage that night. She felt responsible."

"But she ultimately decided others were solely to blame. Not her."

"Apparently so."

"And you, Joshua? What did you decide on that rooftop that night?"

He pauses for a moment, then says, "I decided there was nothing beyond the mission."

Malone glances down at her list. "So how did she control you?"

Joshua sets his hands as flat on the table as he can. The left, which was burned the worst, is gnarled into a permanent claw. "Opioids," he says. "I got used to them during all my surgeries, of course. I started to wean myself, but then Jubilee turned them back on when she decided

Caleb had to be born. That's why I wasn't present for my suicide." He folds his right hand over the left. "She called them Ho Hos."

"Ho Hos? Like the Hostess cakes?"

"Like those, yes. When I finally came home from the hospital, I refused to take pills anymore. So she would crush up pills and jam them into Ho Hos and give them to me with milk. Later, when she decided to turn me into Caleb, the Ho Hos came back, though eventually I started using the standard syringe. I didn't care anymore; I just didn't want to feel as bad as I did without them."

"I'm sorry," Malone says. "And—don't tell anyone I said this—I'm sorry you're here."

"It's better than where I was before. That was the real prison."

"With your sister, in the house on the bay."

"Yes."

"You know the city's about to rename it Paradise Lake."

The interim mayor of Bleak Harbor, named to replace the late Harland Fisher Jr., has persuaded the city council to seize the property for failure to pay property taxes.

"I had heard that. Interesting."

Malone looks at her list, sees the word *UNLOCK*, recalls the giant doors on the front gate of the fortress, how they were locked until they weren't. "By the way," she says, "thanks for letting us into the house."

"Me?" Joshua says, leaning slightly forward as if he didn't hear correctly. "No. I didn't let you in. That had to be Frances."

"That voice?"

"Frances was smart and getting smarter. Whoever Jubilee hired built her that way. Maybe she figured out what was really going on, how many people might—you know—be affected."

Killed, Malone thinks.

Joshua looks up and away from Malone. "Maybe she learned something listening to me and Ophelia."

Ophelia Wright has been oddly reticent about her captivity on Purgatory Bay. The reporters who mobbed her house for weeks have finally given up on getting her to talk. Her sister, Mikey, moved to Bleak Harbor temporarily to help Ophelia recover. Malone, who has coffee with Mikey once a week, thinks her presence there is as therapeutic for Mikey as for Ophelia. One morning before dawn, as Malone was kneeling at Louisa's grave, she felt a hand gentle on her shoulder and looked up to see Mikey. She rose into Mikey's embrace, and they stood there together in silence until the sun's rays broke over the gravestone.

"Unlike Frances," Malone says, "Jubilee learned nothing. She would have blown up that entire rink if you hadn't gotten to her."

Joshua does not respond.

"How did you wire it, anyway?"

"I sneaked in late a couple of nights while the Zamboni driver was outside smoking."

"And drinking."

"That too. And the door on the bar was easy enough to pick. Speaking of hockey, how is the daughter, Bridget?"

"Not great," Malone says. "She's not back at school yet or playing. But she's getting better. Which reminds me." She looks at the word at the bottom of her list: *CHILD*. "I've decided to adopt."

Joshua smiles. "Wow. I'm happy for you. Girl or boy?"

"Not sure yet. The process is just getting started."

"That's good."

"Yes, it is," Malone says, thinking, *Finally*. "By the way, Gary Langreth said to tell you he wishes you the best."

"Ah. The man from the prosecutor's office?"

"Yes. Although now he works for me."

"Really?"

"He had to take some time off; then I brought him over as a detective. He spends a lot of time with Ophelia, which is good for both of them. And that reminds me."

Malone stands, reaches into the jacket on her chair back, and removes a manila envelope that she slides across the table to Joshua. Scrawled across the front in green felt pen is a name:

Raphael

Joshua picks the envelope up in both hands, smiles as broadly as his taut cheeks will allow. "From Ophelia?" he says.

"Yes. I'm going to go now."

"No, stay. I want you to see."

"Not necessary. That's between you and her."

"Chief Malone," he says, "we wouldn't be here today if you hadn't shot Phillips. We would be dead. Ophelia and Bridget would be dead. Please."

Malone isn't sure about that, but she sits.

Joshua opens the envelope slowly, taking care not to rip whatever is inside. He slides a folded sheet of construction paper out and sets it, still folded, before himself. Malone notices that his fingers are trembling. He closes his eyes and recites from memory: "I will walk all the days of my life on paths of fidelity and righteousness."

He opens his eyes, unfolds the paper, and flattens it on the table, then turns it around for Malone to see. At the top of the sheet in the same childlike lettering, it says, *My new sculpture.*

In pencil below it is a sketch of an angel.

ACKNOWLEDGMENTS

When I was nine years old, I read a story in the *Detroit News* that terrified me. Richard and Shirley Robison and their four children had been shot to death in their Northern Michigan cottage. A few years later, my parents bought a cottage up north not far from where the Robisons had died. I would lie awake at night, waiting for a stranger to sneak into our house and kill us all.

The Robison murders were part of the inspiration—if *inspiration* is the word—for this book. Jubilee Rathman came from somewhere else inside me that I will leave to your imagination.

Thanks to all my readers for giving my work a try.

I'm lucky to be published by the Thomas & Mercer imprint of Amazon Publishing, where everyone is smart and responsive and friendly, especially my editor and fellow Michigander Liz Pearsons (here's a secret, Liz: despite my Detroit upbringing, I'm a closet Packers fan). Heartfelt thanks to Gracie Doyle, Sarah Shaw, Dennelle Catlett, Ashley Vanicek, and everyone else at T&M who've put so much sweat and enthusiasm into connecting me with readers, as well as to Jeff Belle, the APub honcho who let me in the door. Thanks also to Shasti O'Leary Soudant for her amazing cover designs. If this were a journalistic enterprise, Caitlin Alexander, who line edited this book with grace, good humor, dexterity, and penetrating insight, might get a co-byline. The time I spend going back and forth with Caitlin about my words and sentences is invigorating.

My fireball agents, Meg Ruley and Amy Tannenbaum of the Jane Rotrosen Agency, are honest, enthusiastic counselors as well as good friends. I'm so happy to have them in my corner. I'd also like to say an overdue thanks to Trish Lande Grader, who got me started on this novel-publishing thing with the contract for what became the Starvation Lake trilogy.

I don't know much about much, so I frequently seek help. Jonathan Eig read some early chapters, and Marcus Sakey encouraged me to face the darkness and write it. Chicago ophthalmologist Rick Ahuja advised me about blindness. Barry Meier, the retired *New York Times* reporter who has written brilliantly about the nation's opioid epidemic, helped with Caleb's Ho Ho addiction, as did Dr. Edward Boyer of Harvard Medical School and Brigham and Women's Hospital. My fellow T&M scribe Joseph Reid and aerospace-engineering professor Todd Humphreys of the University of Texas offered counsel on drones. Matt Wood, senior science writer at the University of Chicago, shared his experience as a burn victim, and dermatologist Dhwani Mehta of the Dermatology Group of the Carolinas in Concord, North Carolina, patiently answered my questions about severe burn injuries. Help with cop and crime stuff came from my brother-in-law, retired Washtenaw County sheriff's deputy Joe Crova; old newspaper pal Allan Lengel; Terry Flanagan, criminal defense attorney and former Michigan Supreme Court commissioner; and my hockey buddy, Chicago detective John Campbell. *Chicago Tribune* reporter Dave Heinzmann edited a piece of the book that wound up on the cutting-room floor. He'll understand, but I still owe him a beer. Gary Greff, creator of astounding roadside sculptures in North Dakota, inspired me to imbue Ophelia with a similar passion.

Thanks, everyone. Anything I screwed up is my fault.

I wrote most of this book in some of Chicago's finest coffee shops—Heritage General Store, Osmium Coffee Bar, and Coffee Lab—in addition to emporiums offering stronger beverages, especially Beermiscuous and the Red Star Bar at Whole Foods (cheapest craft beer in Chicago). I was usually listening to the music of Bill Evans, Oscar Peterson, Brad Mehldau, Yundi Li, Joe Pass, Pablo Casals, Keith Jarrett, and the two Vladimirs, Horowitz and Ashkenazy. God bless you all.

It's cliché to say that writing is a lonely pursuit. It's not so lonely for me, because my wife, Pam, tolerates my babbling about characters and plot twists with patience, love, and only occasional gibes. Thanks, honey. And thanks for doing the driving when I needed to bang on my laptop.

Finally, I'd like to thank my late mom, JoAnne Margaret Polley Gruley, a voracious reader who bought me my first "real" book (*The Crisscross Shadow*, a Hardy Boys mystery), took me regularly to the public library, and encouraged me to write from the age of seven. Later in life, she was always asking me why I couldn't write a book like that Nicholas Sparks guy.

Sorry, Mom.

ABOUT THE AUTHOR

Bryan Gruley is the Amazon Charts bestselling author of *Bleak Harbor* and the award-winning Starvation Lake trilogy of novels. He is also a life-long journalist who is proud to have shared in the Pulitzer Prize awarded to the staff of the *Wall Street Journal* for their coverage of the September 11 terrorist attacks. Gruley lives in Chicago with his wife, Pam. You can learn more by visiting his website at www.bryangruley.com.